A NOTE FROM THE AUTHOR:

Like all the Darkover novels, this is an independent story and not an incomplete part of a series. But for those who actually like to trace the chronology of Darkover, the events in *Two To Conquer* take place toward the end of the Ages of Chaos, during what was later known as the Time of the Hundred Kingdoms; about two hundred years, more or less, after Allart Elhalyn reigned at Hali and Thendara, as told in *Stormqueen!* Wars and the devastation of matrix warfare had split the old kingdoms into many little independent kingdoms, city-states, baronies, shires and independent republics, none of them very large; it was said of some of the kingdoms that the king could stand on a hill and look out over all his kingdom and into the land of his neighbor kings.

Many men of that time had the dream of unifying the Hundred Kingdoms and bringing a reign of law into the anarchy of those days. And one of these men was Varzil, whom history was to subtitle The Good, *laranzu* of Neskaya; and another was Bard di Asturien, whom they called the Wolf of the Kilghard Hills. And this is their story.

—MARION ZIMMER BRADLEY

A Reader's Guide to
DARKOVER

THE FOUNDING

A "lost ship" of Terran origin, in the pre-empire colonizing days, lands on a planet with a dim red star, later to be called Darkover.
 DARKOVER LANDFALL

THE AGES OF CHAOS

1,000 years after the original landfall settlement, society has returned to the feudal level. The Darkovans, their Terran technology renounced or forgotten, have turned instead to freewheeling, out-of-control matrix technology, psi powers and terrible psi weapons. The populace lives under the domination of the Towers and a tyrannical breeding program to staff the Towers with unnaturally powerful, inbred gifts of *laran*.
 STORMQUEEN!
 HAWKMISTRESS!

THE HUNDRED KINGDOMS

An age of war and strife retaining many of the decimating and disastrous effects of the Ages of Chaos. The lands which are later to become the Seven Domains are divided by continuous border conflicts into a multitude of small, belligerent kingdoms, named for convenience "The Hundred Kingdoms." The close of this era is heralded by the adoption of the Compact, instituted by Varzil the Good. A landmark and turning point in the history of Darkover, the Compact bans all distance weapons, making it a matter of honor that one who seeks to kill must himself face equal risk of death.
 TWO TO CONQUER
 THE HEIRS OF HAMMERFELL

THE RENUNCIATES

During the Ages of Chaos and the time of the Hundred Kingdoms, there were two orders of women who set themselves apart from the patriarchal nature of Darkovan feudal society: the priestesses of Avarra, and the warriors of the Sisterhood of the Sword. Eventually these two independent groups merged to form the powerful and legally chartered Order of Renunciates or Free Amazons, a guild of women bound only by oath as a sisterhood of mutual responsibility. Their primary allegiance is to each other rather than to family, clan, caste or any man save a temporary employer. Alone among Darkovan women, they are exempt from the usual legal restrictions and protections. Their reason for existence is to provide the women of Darkover an alternative to their socially restrictive lives.

THE SHATTERED CHAIN
THENDARA HOUSE
CITY OF SORCERY

AGAINST THE TERRANS

—THE FIRST AGE (Recontact)

After the Hastur Wars, the Hundred Kingdoms are consolidated into the Seven Domains, and ruled by a hereditary aristocracy of seven families, called the Comyn, allegedly descended from the legendary Hastur, Lord of Light. It is during this era that the Terran Empire, really a form of confederacy, rediscovers Darkover, which they know as the fourth planet of the Cottman star system. The fact that Darkover is a lost colony of the Empire is not easily or readily acknowledged by Darkovans and their Comyn overlords.

REDISCOVERY (*with Mercedes Lackey*)
THE SPELL SWORD
THE FORBIDDEN TOWER
STAR OF DANGER
THE WINDS OF DARKOVER

AGAINST THE TERRANS

—THE SECOND AGE (After the Comyn)

With the initial shock of recontact beginning to wear off, and the Terran spaceport a permanent establishment on the outskirts of the city of Thendara, the younger and less traditional elements of Darkovan society begin the first real exchange of knowledge with the Terrans—learning Terran science and technology and teaching Darkovan matrix technology in turn. Eventually Regis Hastur, the young Comyn lord most active in these exchanges, becomes Regent in a provisional government allied to the Terrans. Darkover is once again reunited with its founding Empire.

THE BLOODY SUN
HERITAGE OF HASTUR
THE PLANET SAVERS
SHARRA'S EXILE
WORLD WRECKERS
EXILE'S SONG
THE SHADOW MATRIX*
THE CHILDREN OF KINGS*

THE DARKOVER ANTHOLOGIES

These volumes of stories edited by Marion Zimmer Bradley strive to "fill in the blanks" of Darkovan history, and elaborate on the eras, tales and characters which have captured readers' imaginations.

THE KEEPER'S PRICE
SWORD OF CHAOS
FREE AMAZONS OF DARKOVER
THE OTHER SIDE OF THE MIRROR
RED SUN OF DARKOVER
FOUR MOONS OF DARKOVER
DOMAINS OF DARKOVER
RENUNCIATES OF DARKOVER
LERONI OF DARKOVER
TOWERS OF DARKOVER
MARION ZIMMER BRADLEY'S DARKOVER
SNOWS OF DARKOVER

*forthcoming from DAW Books in hardcover.

TWO TO CONQUER

Marion Zimmer Bradley

D A W   B O O K S ,   I N C .
DONALD   A.   WOLLHEIM,   FOUNDER
375 Hudson Street, New York, NY 10014
ELIZABETH R. WOLLHEIM
SHEILA E. GILBERT
PUBLISHERS

ACKNOWLEDGMENTS

To "Cinhil MacAran" of the SCA for the first verse of "Four and Twenty *Leroni*"—to the tune of "The Ball of Kirriemuir" and

To Patricia Mathews for creating the Sisterhood of the Sword and dressing them in red.

FIRST PRINTING, JULY 1980

10   11   12   13   14

DAW TRADEMARK REGISTERED
U.S. PAT OFF AND FOREIGN COUNTRIES
—MARCA REGISTRADA,
HECHO EN U.S.A.

PRINTED IN THE U.S.A.

PROLOGUE: *The Alien*

Paul Harrell woke, blurred and semi-conscious, with a sense of having survived nightmares for a long time. Every muscle in his body ached like a separate toothache, and his head felt as if he had a truly monumental hangover. Blurred memories, vague, a man with his face, his own voice asking, *Who the hell are you, you're not the devil, by any chance?* Not that he believed in the devil, or hell, or any of those things invented to try to force men to do what other people thought they should do instead of what they wanted to do.

He moved his head, and the pain in it made him wince. *Whew! I really must have tied one on last night!*

He stretched, trying to turn over, and found that he was lying, his legs flung out at ease, comfortably stretched out. That brought him wide awake, in shock.

He could move, stretch; *he wasn't in the stasis box!*

Had it all been a nightmare, then? The flight from the Alpha police, the rebellion he had led in the colony, the final confrontation, with his men shot down around him, the capture and the trial, and finally the horror of the stasis box closing around him forever.

Forever. That had been his last thought. Forever.

Painless, of course, Even pleasant, like going to sleep when you were completely exhausted. But he had struggled and fought for that last instant of consciousness, knowing that it *would* be the last; he would never waken.

Humane governments had abolished the death penalty long ago. Too often, new evidence, a few years after the prisoner was executed, had proved him innocent. Death made the mistake irrevocable, and embarrassed the whole judicial system. The stasis box kept the prisoner safely removed from society . . . but he could always be reprieved and recalled to life. And no prisons, no traumatic memories of association with hardened criminals, no prison riots, no need for counseling, recreation, rehabilitation. Just stick them away in a stasis box and let them age there, naturally, and finally die, uncon-

7

scious, lifeless . . . unless they were proved innocent. Then you could take them out.

But, Paul Harrell thought, they couldn't prove him innocent. He was guilty as hell, and furthermore, he'd admitted it, and tried as hard as he could to be shot down before capture. What was more, he made sure he took about ten of the damn cops with him, so they couldn't legally grant him the option of Rehab.

The rest of his men, the ones they didn't shoot down, went meekly down to Rehabilitation like so many sheep, to be made over into the conformist nothings which are all they want in this stupid world. Pussycats. Gutless wonders. And right up to the end, he could see that the judge and all his legal advisers were hoping he'd break down and beg for executive clemency—a chance for Rehab, so they could tinker with his brain, with drugs and re-education and brainwashing, so they could make him over into a nobody, to march along in lockstep just like everybody else through what they call life. *But not me, thanks. I wouldn't play their damned game. When I finished my run, I was ready to go, and I went.*

And it had been a good life while it lasted, he thought. He'd made hash of their stupid laws because for years they couldn't even imagine that anyone would break laws except through accident or ignorance! He'd had all the women he wanted, and all the high living.

Especially women. He didn't play the stupid games women tried to make men play. He was a man, and if they wanted a man instead of a sheep, they learned right away that Paul Harrell didn't play by their conformist, ball-less rules.

That damned woman who led the police down on me.

Her mother had probably taught her that you had to make noises about rape, unless the man got down on his knees and pretended to be a capon, a gutless wonder who'd let a woman lead him around by the nose and never touch her unless she *said* she wanted it! Hell, he knew better than that. That was what women wanted and they loved it, when you gave it to them and didn't take no for an answer! Well, she found out; he didn't play their games, even with the stasis box hanging over him! She probably thought he'd go and whine for a chance at Rehab, and they'd make him over into a pussycat she could lead around by the balls!

Well, the hell with her, she'll wake up nights all the rest of her life, remembering that for once she had a real man. . . .

And when he had gotten this far in his memories Paul Harrell sat up and stared. He wasn't in the stasis box, but he wasn't anywhere else he could remember being, either. Had it all been a nightmare, then, the girl, the rebellion, the shootout with the police, the judge, trial, the stasis box. . . .

Had he ever been there at all, had any of it ever happened?

And if so, what had gotten him out?

He was lying on a soft mattress, covered with clean coarse linens, and over them, thick wool blankets and quilts and a fur cover. All around him was a very faint, dim, reddish light. He reached out and found that the light was coming through heavy bed-curtains; that he was in a high curtained bed such as he'd seen somewhere once in a museum, and that curtains around the bed were closing out the light. Red curtains.

He thrust them aside. He was in a room he had never seen before. Not only had he never seen the room before, he had never seen anything remotely like it before.

One thing was for damn sure. He wasn't in the stasis box, unless part of the punishment was a series of bizarre dreams. Nor was he anywhere in the Rehab center. In fact, he thought, glancing out the high arched window at a huge red sun beyond, he wasn't on Alpha at all, nor on Terra, nor on any of the planets of the Confederated Worlds that he had ever visited before.

Maybe this was Valhalla, or something. There were old legends about a perfect place for warriors who met a hero's end. And he had certainly gone down fighting; at his trial they said he had killed eight policemen and crippled another for life. He'd gone out like a man, not a brainwashed conformist; he hadn't cringed and whimpered and begged for a chance to crawl around on his knees a while longer in a world with no respect for anyone who'd rather die on his feet!

Anyway, he was out of the box, that was a good place to start. But he was naked, just the way he'd gone into the box. His hair was still clipped short, as when he'd gone into the box . . . no. They'd shaved it then, so he'd been in there a month or two, anyhow, because he could feel the thick soft nap of it. He looked at the room around him. The room had a stone floor with a few thick fur and skin rugs. There was no furniture except the bed and a heavy chest carved richly of some dark wood.

And now, through the pain that still pounded in his head, he remembered something else; flaring pain, blue lightnings around him, a circle of faces, falling as if from a great

9

height—pain, and then a man. A man with his own face, and his own voice asking, *Who are you? You're not the devil, by any chance?* Old legends. If you met a man with your own face, your double, your *doppelganger*, your fetch, it was either the devil or a warning of death. But he had died, for all practical purposes, when they put him into the stasis box, so what more could anyone do to him? Anyway, that had been a dream. Hadn't it? Or, when he went into the box, had they cloned him and brainwashed the clone into being the good respectable, conformist citizen they'd always wanted *him* to be?

Somehow, something had brought him here. But who, and when, and how? And above all, why?

And then the door opened, and the man with his face came in.

Not a close resemblance, as of brothers or twins. *Himself.* Like himself, the man had blond hair; only on the strange man, it was thick and long and twisted into a tight braid, wrapped with a red cord. Paul had never known a man who wore his hair that way.

He had never seen a man dressed as the man with his face was dressed, either, in garments of heavy wool and leather; a laced leather jerkin, a thick tunic under it of unbleached wool, leather breeches, high boots. Now that Paul was part way out from under the covers, he realized it was cold enough in the room for that kind of clothing to make sense; and now, through the windows, he saw that snow lay thickly on the ground. Well, he already knew he wasn't on Alpha; if he'd had any doubts, the faint purple shadows on the snow, and the great red sun, would have told him.

But beyond all that, the man with his face. Not just a close resemblance. Not a likeness which would fade at close range. Not even the image he would have seen in a mirror, reversed, but the face he had seen, watching taped video of himself, at his trial.

A clone, if anyone except rich eccentrics could have afforded such a thing. An absolute, identical replica of himself, down to the cleft chin and the small brown birthmark on his left thumb. *What the hell was going on here?*

He demanded, "Who the hell are you?"

The man in the leather jerkin said, "I was coming here to ask the same question of you."

Paul heard the strangeness of the syllables. They sounded a little like Old Spanish—a language of which Paul knew only a few words. But he could clearly understand the stranger's meaning, and that frightened him worse than anything else

10

that had happened yet. They were reading each other's thoughts.

"Hell," he blurted out. "You're *me!*"

"Not quite," said the other man, "but near enough. And that is why we brought you here."

"Here," Paul said, fastening on that. "Where is *here*? What world is this? What sun is that? And how did I get here? And who are you?"

The man shook his head, and again Paul had the eerie sense that he was watching himself.

"The sun is the sun," he said, "and we are in what they call the Hundred Kingdoms; this is the Kingdom of Asturias. As for what world this is, it is called Darkover, and it is the only world I know. When I was a boy they told me some fable about the other stars being suns like our own, with a million million other worlds circling them like ours, and perhaps men like ours on them, but I always thought that was a story to frighten babes and girl children! But I have seen stranger things, and heard stranger things than that, in the last night. My father's sorcery brought you here, and if you wish to know why, you must ask him. But we mean you no harm."

Paul hardly heard the explanation. He was staring at the man with his face, his body, his own hands, and trying to understand what he felt about the man.

His brother. Himself. He'd understand me. Those thoughts flickered through his mind. And at the same time, crowding them, a sudden raging anger: *How does he dare to go around wearing my face?* And then, in total confusion, *if he's me, who in hell am I?*

And the other man spoke his question aloud. "If you are me," he said, and his fists clenched, "then who am I?"

Paul said, with a harsh half-laugh, "Maybe you're the devil after all. What's your name?"

"Bard," said the man, "but they call me *Wolf*. Bard di Asturien, the Kilghard Wolf. And you?"

"My name is Paul Harrell," he said, and swayed. Was this all a bizarre dream of the stasis box? Had he died and wound up in Valhalla?

None of it made sense to him. None at all.

Seven Years Earlier...

BOOK ONE

The Foster Brothers

Chapter One

Light blazed from every window and embrasure of Castle
Asturias; on this night King Ardrin of Asturias held high festival, for he was handfasting his daughter Carlina to his foster son and nephew, Bard di Asturien, son of his brother,
Dom Rafael of High Fens. Most of the nobles of Asturias,
and a few from the neighboring kingdoms, had come to do
honor to the handfasting and to the king's daughter, and the
courtyard was ablaze with brilliance; strange horses and riding beasts to be stabled, nobles richly dressed, commoners
crowding in to spy what they could from outside the gates
and accept the dole of food and wine and sweets given out
from the kitchens to all comers, servants running here or
there on real or invented errands.

High in the secluded chambers of the women, Carlina di
Asturien looked with distaste on the embroidered veils and
the blue velvet over-gown, set with pearls from Temora, that
she would wear for the handfasting ceremony. She was fourteen years old; a slender, pale, young woman, with long dark
braids looped below her ears, and wide gray eyes which were
the only good feature in a face too thin and thoughtful for
beauty. Her face was reddened around the eyelids; she had
been crying for a long time.

"Come, now, come, now," her nurse, Ysabet, urged. "You
mustn't cry like this, *chiya*. Look at the pretty gown, you will
never have one so fine again. And Bard is so handsome and
brave; just think, your father made him banner bearer on the
field for bravery in the battle of Snow Glen. And, after all,
dear child, it is not as if you would be marrying a stranger;
Bard is your foster brother, reared here in the king's house
since he was ten years old. Why, when you were children,
you were always playing together, I thought you loved him
well!"

"And so I do—as a brother," Carlina said in a whisper.

15

"But to marry Bard—no, Nurse, I don't want to. I don't want to marry at all—"

"Now that is folly," said the older woman, clucking, and she held up the pearl-broidered overdress to help her nursling into it. Carlina submitted like a doll being dressed, knowing that resistance would do her no good.

"Why don't you want to marry Bard, then? He is handsome, and brave—how many young men have distinguished themselves before reaching their sixteenth year?" Ysabet demanded. "One day, I have no doubt, he will be general of all your father's armies! You are not holding it against him that he is *nedestro*, are you? The poor lad did not choose to be born to one of his father's fancy-women instead of to his lawful wife!"

Carlina smiled faintly at the thought of anyone calling Bard "poor lad."

Her nurse pinched her cheek. She said, "Now, that is the right way to go to your handfasting, with a smile! Let me do up these laces properly." She tugged at the lacings, then tucked in the ribbons. "Sit here, my pretty, while I do up your sandals. Look how dainty, your mother had them made to match the gown, blue leather with pearls! How pretty you are, Carlie, like a blue flower! Let me fasten the ribbons here in your hair. I do not think there is a prettier bride anywhere in nine kingdoms this night! And Bard handsome enough, surely, to be worthy of you, so fair where you are so dark. . . ."

"What a pity," Carlina said dryly, "that he cannot marry you, Nurse, since you like him so much."

"Oh, come now, he wouldn't want me, old and withered as I am," said Ysabet, bridling. "A handsome young warrior like Bard must have a young and beautiful bride, and so your father has ordained it . . . I cannot imagine why the wedding is not on this night as well, and the bedding too!"

"Because," Carlina said, "I begged my mother, and she spoke for me to my father and my lord; and he consented that I should not be married until I had completed my fifteenth year. The wedding will be a year from tonight, at Midsummer Festival."

"How can you bear to wait so long? Evanda bless you, child, if I had a handsome young lover like Bard, I could not wait so long. . . ." She saw Carlina flinch and spoke more gently. "Are you afraid of the marriage bed, child? No woman ever died of it, and I have no doubt you will find it

16

pleasurable; but it will be less frightening to you at first, since your husband is playfellow and foster brother as well."

Carlina shook her head. "No, it is not *that*, Nurse, though, as I told you, I have no mind to marriage; I would rather spend my life in chastity and good works among the priestesses of Avarra."

"Heavens protect us!" The woman made a shocked gesture. "Your father would never allow it!"

"I know that, Nurse. The Goddess knows, I besought him to spare me this marriage and let me go, but he reminded me that I was a princess and that it was my duty to marry, to bring strong powerful alliances to his throne. As my sister Amalie has already been sent to wed with King Lorill of Scathfell. Beyond the Kadarin, poor girl, alone in those northern mountains, and my sister Marilla married south to Dalereuth. . . ."

"Are you angry that they were wedded to princes and kings, and you, only, to your father's brother's bastard son?"

Carlina shook her head. "No, no," she said impatiently. "I know what is in father's mind; he wishes to bind Bard to him with a strong tie, so that one day Bard will be his strongest champion and protector. There was no thought for me, or for Bard; it is only one of my father's maneuvers to protect the throne and the kingdom!"

"Well," said the nurse, "most marriages are made for reasons less worthy than that."

"But it is not necessary," Carlina said, impatiently. "Bard would be content with any woman, and my father could have found some woman of noble rank who would satisfy Bard's ambition! Why should I be forced to spend my life with a man who does not care whether it is me, Carlina, or another, provided she is high-born enough to satisfy his ambition, and has a pretty face and a willing body! Avarra have mercy, do you think I do not know that every servant girl in the castle has shared his bed? They brag of it after!"

"As for that," said Ysabet, "he is no better and no worse than any of your brothers or foster brothers. You cannot blame a young man for wenching, and at least you know from their bragging that he is neither maimed nor a lover of men! When he is wedded to you, you must simply give him enough to do in your bed to keep him out of others!"

Carlina gestured displeasure at the vulgarity. "They are welcome to Bard and to his bed," she said, "and I will not dispute their place there. But I have heard worse, that he will not hear a refusal; that if a girl answers him *no*, or if he has

17

reason to think she might give him a *no*, his pride is so great that he will put a compulsion on her, a glamour, so that she cannot refuse, but will go to his bed will-less, without the power to help herself—"

"I have heard of men who have that *laran*," Ysabet grinned. "It is a useful thing, even if a young man is handsome and hearty; but I never put much stock in such tales of spellbinding. What young woman needs to be spelled to go to a young man's bed? No doubt they use that old tale to excuse themselves if they are found big-bellied out of season—"

"No, Nurse," Carlina said. "At least once, I know, it is true, for my own maid Lisarda, she is a good girl, and she told me that she could not help herself—"

Ysabet said with a coarse laugh, "Any slut says afterward that she could not help herself!"

"But no," Carlina interrupted angrily, "Lisarda is scarce twelve years old; she is motherless and hardly knew what he wanted of her, only that she could not choose but to do as he would. Poor child, she was hardly come into womanhood, and she cried, after, in my arms, and I was hard put to it to explain why a man could want a woman *that* way—"

Ysabet frowned. She said, "I wondered what had happened to Lisarda—"

"I find it hard to forgive Bard, that he could do that to a young girl who had never harmed him!" Carlina said, still angry.

"Well, well," said the nurse, sighing, "men do such things now and again, and women are expected to accept them."

"I don't see why!"

"It is the way of the world," Ysabet said, then started, and looked at the timepiece on the wall. "Come, Carlina, my pet, you must not be late to your own handfasting!"

Carlina rose, sighing with resignation, as her mother, Queen Ariel, came into her chamber,

"Are you ready, my daughter?" The queen surveyed the young woman from head to foot, from the braids looped under her ears to the delicate blue slippers embroidered with pearls. "There will be no prettier bride, at least, in the Hundred Kingdoms. You have done well, Ysabet."

The old woman bent in a curtsy, acknowledging the compliment.

"You need just a touch of powder on your face, Carlie, your eyes are red," said the lady. "Bring the puff, Ysabet. Carlina, have you been crying?"

Carlina lowered her head and did not answer.

18

Her mother said firmly, "It is unseemly for a bride to shed tears, and this is only your handfasting." With her own hands she dabbed with the powder puff at her daughter's eyelids. "There. Now a touch of the crayon there, at the brow—" she said, pointing for Ysabet to repair the makeup. "Lovely. Come, my dear, my women are waiting. . . ."

There was a small chorus of cooing noises and admiration as Carlina in her bridal finery joined the women. Ariel, Queen of Asturias, attended by her ladies, held out her hand to Carlina.

"Tonight you will sit among my ladies, and when your father calls for you, you will go forward and join Bard before the throne," she began.

Carlina looked at her mother's serene face and contemplated a final appeal. She knew that her mother did not like Bard—although for the wrong reasons: she simply objected to his bastard status. She had never liked it, that he should be foster brother to Carlina and Beltran. However, it was not her mother who had made this marriage, but her father. And she knew that King Ardrin was not accustomed to listening overmuch to what his womenfolk wanted. Her mother had won this one concession, that she should not be married until she was full fifteen years old.

When they call me forth to be handfasted I will scream and refuse to speak, I will cry out No when they ask me to consent, I will run out of the room. . . . But in her heart Carlina knew that she would not do any of these disgraceful things, but would go through the ceremony with the decorum befitting a princess of Asturias.

Bard is a soldier, she thought despairing, perhaps he will die in battle before the wedding; and then she felt guilty, for there had been a time when she had loved her playmate and foster brother. Quickly she amended her thoughts: perhaps he will find some other woman he wishes to wed, perhaps my father will change his mind. . . .

Avarra, merciful Goddess, Great Mother, pity me, spare me this marriage somehow. . . .

Angry, despairing, she blinked back the tears that threatened to flood her eyes again. Her mother would be angry if she disgraced them all this way.

In a lower room in the castle, Bard di Asturien, foster son to the king, and his banner bearer, was being dressed for his handfasting by his two comrades and foster brothers: Beltran, the king's son, and Geremy Hastur, who, like Bard, had been reared in the king's house, but was a younger son of the Lord of Carcosa.

The three youths were very different. Bard was tall and heavily built, already a man's height, with thick blond hair twisted into the warrior's braid at the back of his head, and the strong arms and heavy thews of a swordsman and rider; he towered like a young giant over the others. Prince Beltran was tall, too, although not quite as tall as Bard; but he was still thin and coltish, bony with a boy's roundness, and his cheeks still fuzzed with a boy's first traces of beard. His hair was cropped short and tightly curled, but as blond as Bard's own.

Geremy Hastur was smaller than either, red-haired and thin-faced, with sharp gray eyes and the quickness of a hawk or ferret. He wore dark, plain clothing, the dress of a scholar rather than a warrior, and his manner was quiet and unassuming.

Now he looked up at Bard, laughing, and said, "You will have to sit down, foster brother; neither Beltran nor I can reach your head to tie the red cord about your braid! And you cannot go to a ceremonial occasion without it!"

"No indeed," Beltran said, hauling Bard down into a seat. "Here, Geremy, you tie it, your hands are defter than mine, or Bard's. I remember last autumn when you stitched that guardsman's wound—"

Bard chuckled as he bent his head for his young friends to tie on the red cord which signified a warrior tried in battle and commended for bravery. He said, "I always thought you were cowardly, Geremy, that you did not fight in the field, and your hands as soft as Carlina's; yet when I saw that, I decided you had more courage than I, for I wouldn't have done it. I think it a pity there is no red cord for you!"

Geremy said, in his muted voice, "Why, then, we should have to give a red cord to every woman in childbirth, or every messenger who slips unseen through the enemy's lines. Courage takes many forms. I can do without warrior's braid or red cord, I think."

"Perhaps, one day," Beltran said, "when the day comes when I rule over this land—may my father's reign be long!—perhaps we may reward courage in some other form than that we see on the battlefield. What about it, Bard? You will be my champion then, if we all live so long." He frowned suddenly at Geremy and said, "What ails you, man?"

Geremy Hastur shook his red head. He said, "I do not

know—a sudden chill; perhaps, as they say in the hills, some wild animal pissed on the ground which will be my grave." He finished twisting the red cord around Bard's warrior braid, handed him sword and dagger and helped him to bind them on.

Bard said, "I am a soldier; I know very little of other kinds of courage." He shrugged his ceremonially embroidered cape into place, bright red to match the red cord twisted into the braid all along its length. "I tell you, it demands more courage to face this nonsense tonight; I prefer to face my enemies sword in hand!"

"What's this talk of enemies, foster brother?" Beltran asked, surveying his friend. "You surely have no enemies in my father's hall! Why, how many young men your age have been given a warrior's cord, and made the king's banner bearer on the field of war, before they were full sixteen years old? And when you killed Dom Ruyven of Serrais and his paxman, twice saving the king's life at Snow Glen—"

Bard shook his head. "The Lady Ariel does not love me. She would stop this marriage to Carlina if she could. And she is angry because it was I, and not you, who won renown on the battlefield, Beltran."

Beltran shook his head. "Perhaps it is simply the way of a mother," he hazarded. "It is not enough for her that I am prince, and heir to my father's throne, I must have renown as a warrior too. Or perhaps—" he tried to make a joke of it, but Bard could tell that there was bitterness, too— "she fears that your courage and renown will cause my father to think better of you than he does of his son."

Bard said, "Well, Beltran, you had the same teaching as I; you too could have won a warrior's decorations. It is the fortune of war, I suppose, or the luck of the battlefield."

"No," Beltran said. "I am not a warrior born, and I have not your gift for it. It is all I can do to acquit myself honorably and keep my skin in one piece by killing anyone who wants to have a swing at it."

Bard laughed and said, "Well, believe me, Beltran, that is all I do."

But Beltran shook his head gloomily. "Some men are warriors born, and others are warriors made; I am neither."

Geremy broke in, trying to lighten the tone, "But you need not be a great warrior, Beltran; you must prepare yourself to rule Asturias one day, and then you can have as many warriors as you like, and if they serve you well, it will not matter whether or not you know which end of a sword to take hold

21

by! You will be the one who rules all your warriors, and all your sorcerers, too. . . . Will you have me, on that day, to serve you as *laranzu*?" He used the old word for *sorcerer*, *wizard*, and Beltran grinned and clapped him on the shoulder.

"So I will have a wizard and a warrior for foster brothers, and we three will rule Asturias together against all its enemies, battle and sorcery both! But may that day, be the gods merciful to us, be long in coming. Geremy, send your page to the courtyard again to see if Bard's father has come to see the handfasting of his son."

Geremy started to signal to the youngster who waited to run their errands, but Bard shook his head.

"Save the child trouble." His jaw tightened. "He will not come, and there is no need to pretend that he will, Geremy."

"Not even to see you married to his king's own daughter?"

"Perhaps he will come for the wedding, if the king makes it clear that he will be offended if he does not," Bard said, "but not for a mere handfasting."

"But the handfasting is the true binding," Beltran said. "From the moment of the handfasting, you are Carlina's lawful husband and she cannot take another while you live! It is only that my mother thinks her too young for bedding, so that part of the ceremony is delayed for another year. But Carlina is your wife; and you, Bard, are my brother."

He said it with a shy smile, and Bard, for all his calm façade, was touched. He said, "That's probably the best part of it."

Geremy said, "But I am astonished that Dom Rafael should not come to see your handfasting! Surely he has been sent word that you were decorated on the field for bravery, made the king's banner bearer, killed Dom Ruyven and his paxman at a single blow—if my father heard such things of me, he would be beside himself with pride and pleasure!"

"Oh, I have no doubt Father is proud of me," Bard said, and his face twisted into a bitterness strange in one so young. "But he listens in all things to the Lady Jerana, his lawful wife; and she has never forgotten that he forsook her bed when she was childless for twelve years of their marriage; nor did she ever forgive my mother for giving him a son. And she was angry because my father brought me up in his own house, and had me schooled in arms and the ways of a court instead of having me nursed and fostered to follow the plow or scratch the fields farming mushrooms!"

Beltran said, "She should have been glad that someone had given her husband a son when she could not."

Bard shrugged. "That is not the Lady Jerana's way! Instead she surrounded herself with *leroni* and sorceresses—half her ladies-in-waiting have red hair and are trained witches—until sooner or later one of them could give her a spell to cure her barrenness. Then she bore my baby brother, Alaric. And then, when my father could deny her nothing because she had given him a legitimate son and heir, she set herself to get rid of me. Oh, Jerana could not show enough kindness to me, until she had her own son; she pretended she was a true mother to me, but I could see the blow held back behind every false kiss she gave me! I think, she feared I would stand in her own son's light, because Alaric was little and sickly and I was strong and well, and she hated me worse than ever because Alaric loved me."

"I would have thought," Beltran said again, "that she would welcome a strong brother and guardian for her son, one who could care for him. . . ."

"I love my brother," Bard said. "There are times when I think there is no one else in the world to whom it would matter whether I lived or died; but since Alaric was old enough to know one face from another, he smiled at me, and held up his little arms for me to carry him piggyback and begged for rides on my horse. But for Lady Jerana it was not seemly that a bastard half-brother should be *her* little princelet's chosen paxman and playmate; *she* would have princes' and noblemen's sons for her child's companions! And so a time came when I saw him only by guile; and once I angered her when he was sick, because I sneaked without permission into his precious nursery. A child of four, and she was angry because his brother could sing him to sleep and he would not sleep for *her* coaxing." His face was hard, bitter, closed away into memory.

"And after that, she gave my father no peace until he sent me away. And instead of bidding her be silent, and ruling his own house, as a man should do, he chose to have peace in his bed and at his fireside by sending me away from home and brother!"

Beltran and Geremy were, momentarily, silenced by his bitterness. Then Geremy patted his arm and said, with a half-embarrassed tenderness, "Well, you have two brothers to stand at your side tonight, Bard, and soon you will have kin here."

Bard's smile was bleak, unforgiving. "Queen Ariel loves me

23

no more than my stepmother. I am sure she will find some way to turn Carlina against me, and perhaps both of you. I do not blame my father, except for listening to a woman's words; Zandru twist my feet if I ever listen to what a woman says!"

Beltran laughed and said, "One would not think you a woman-hater, Bard. From what the maids say, quite the reverse—on the day you are bedded with Carlina, there will be weeping all over the kingdom of Asturias!"

"Oh, as for *that*," Bard said, making a deliberate effort to match the mood of merriment, "I listen to women only in one place, and you may guess what that place is. . . ."

"And yet," said Beltran, "when we were young lads and girls all together, I remember that you always listened to Carlina; you would climb a tree no one else would hazard to fetch down her kitten, and when she and I quarreled, I soon learned I must give way or you would pummel me, taking her part!"

"Oh—Carlina," Bard said, and his bitter face relaxed into a smile. "Carlina is not like other women; I would not speak of her in the same breath as most of the bitches and sluts in this place! When I am wedded to her, believe me, I shall have no leisure for the rest! I assure you, she will have no need to surround herself with spells as Lady Jerana did, to keep me faithful to her. Since first I came here, she has been kind to me—"

"We would all have been kind to you," Beltran protested, "but you would not speak to anyone and threatened to fight us—"

"Still, Carlina made me feel that perhaps, for once, someone cared whether I lived or died," Bard said, "and I would not fight *her*. Now your father has chosen to give her to me—which I never thought I could win, being bastard born. Lady Jerana may have driven me from my home, and from my father, and from my brother, but now, perhaps, I have a home here."

"Even if you must take Carlina with it?" Beltran mocked. "She is not what I would choose for a wife; skinny, dark, plain—I'd as soon bed the stick-poppet they mount in the fields to scare away the crows!"

Bard said genially, "I wouldn't expect her brother to be aware of her beauty, and it's not for her beauty I want her."

Geremy Hastur, who had the red hair and the *laran* gift of the Hastur kin of Carcosa, the gift to read thoughts even without the starstones which the *leroni* or sorceresses used, could sense Bard's thoughts as they went up toward the great hall for the handfasting ceremony.

There are plenty of women in this world for the bedding, Bard thought. But Carlina is different. She is the king's daughter; wedding her, I am no longer bastard and nobody, but the king's banner bearer and champion; I shall have home, family, brothers, children someday . . . for a woman who can bring me all this, I shall be grateful to her all my life; I swear she shall never have cause to reproach her father that he gave her to his brother's bastard. . . .

Surely, Geremy thought, this was enough reason for a marriage. Perhaps he does not want Carlina for herself, but as a symbol of all that she can bring him. Yet marriages are made in the kingdoms every day, with less reason than this. And if he is good to Carlina, surely she will be content.

But he felt disquiet, for he knew that Carlina was afraid of Bard. He had been present when King Ardrin mentioned the marriage to his daughter, and had heard Carlina's shocked cry and seen her weeping.

Well, there was no help for it, the king would have his way, and surely it was right that he should reward his banner bearer, who was also his nephew, though a bastard, with honors and a rich marriage into his household; this would cement Bard to King Ardrin's throne as champion. Perhaps it was a pity for Carlina, but all girls were given in marriage, soon or late, and she might have been married to some elderly lecher, or some grizzled old warrior, or even to some bandit barbarian from one of the little kingdoms across the Kadarin, if her father found it expedient to seal an alliance with another kingdom. Instead he was giving her to a close relative, one who had been her own playmate and foster brother and had championed her in childhood. Carlina would resign herself to it soon enough.

But his sharp eyes spotted the reddened eyelids, even behind the careful touch of powder and paint. He raised his eyes and looked compassionately at Carlina, wishing she knew Bard as well as he did. Perhaps, if she understood her handfasted husband, she could lessen his bitterness, make him feel less withdrawn, less outcaste among others. Geremy sighed, thinking of his own exile.

For Geremy Hastur had not come willingly to King Ardrin's court, either. He was the youngest son of King Istvan of Carcosa; and he had been sent, half hostage, half diplomat, to be fostered in King Ardrin's household as a token of friendly relations between the royal house of Asturias

25

and the house of the Hasturs of Carcosa. He would have wished to be his father's counselor, a sorcerer, a *laranzu*—he had known all his life that he had not the makings of a soldier—but his father had found him one son too many and had sent him away as a hostage, as he might have sent a daughter away to marry. At least, Geremy thought, Carlina would not be sent away from her home for this marriage!

The court rose for King Ardrin's entrance. Bard, standing beside Beltran, listening to the crying of the heralds, still found that he was glancing about the crowd to see if, perhaps, his father had come at the last moment, wishing to surprise him; desisted and angrily faced forward. Why should he care? King Ardrin thought more of him than his own father did, the king had decorated him in battle, given him lands and a rich estate, and a warrior's red cord, and the hand of his youngest daughter in marriage. With all this, why should he worry about his father, sitting home and listening to the poison that filthy hag Jerana poured into his ears?

But I wish my brother were here. I wish Alaric could know I am the king's champion and his son-in-law . . . he would be seven, now. . . .

At the appointed time he stepped forward, prompted by Beltran and Geremy. Carlina was standing at the right hand of her father's seat. Bard's ears were ringing, and he hardly heard the king's words.

"Bard mac Fianna, called di Asturien, whom I have made my banner bearer," Ardrin of Asturias said, "we have called you here tonight to handfast you to my youngest daughter, the lady Carlina. Say, Bard, is it your will to enter my household?"

Bard's voice sounded perfectly steady; he wondered at that, because inside he was shaking. He supposed it was like riding into battle, there was something that steadied you when you had to be steady. "My king and my lord, it is my will."

"Then," said Ardrin, taking Bard's hand in one of his, and Carlina's in the other, "I bid you join hands before all this company and exchange your pledge."

Bard felt Carlina's hand in his; very soft, the fingers so slender that they felt boneless. She was icy cold, and did not look at him.

"Carlina," said Ardrin, "do you consent to have this man for your husband?"

She whispered something Bard could not hear. He supposed it was a formal phrase of consent. At least she had not refused.

He bent forward, as ritual demanded, and kissed her trembling lips. She was shaking. Hellfire! Was the girl afraid of him? He smelled the flowery scent of her hair, of some cosmetic that had been dabbed on her face. As he drew back, a corner of her stiff embroidered collar scratched his cheek a little. Well, he thought, he had had enough women; soon enough she would lose her fear in his arms, they always did; even if now she was a dressed-up doll. The thought of Carlina in his bed made him feel dizzy, almost faint. Carlina. His, forever, his princess, his wife. And then no one could ever again call him bastard or outcast. Carlina, his home, his beloved . . . his own. He felt his throat thicken as he whispered the ritual words.

"Before our kin assembled I pledge to wed you, Carlina, and to cherish you forever."

He heard her voice, only a whisper.

"Before . . . kin assembled . . . pledge to wed . . ." but try as he might he could not hear her speak his name.

Damn Queen Ariel and her idiotic plans to rid herself of him! They should have had the wedding and the bedding tonight, so that Carlina could quickly lose her fear of him! He was trembling, thinking of that. He had never wanted any woman this much. He tightened his hand on her fingers trying to reassure her, but felt only her involuntary flinching of pain.

King Ardrin said, "May you be forever one," and he loosed Carlina's hand, reluctantly. Together, they drank from a wine cup held to their lips. It was done; Carlina was his bride. Now it was too late for King Ardrin to change his mind. Bard realized that until this moment he had felt that something would come between him and his good fortune even as they stood together for the handfasting, that his stepmother's malice, or Queen Ariel's, would come between him and Carlina, who meant to him a home, a place, honor . . . *damn all women! All women except Carlina, that is!*

Beltran drew him into a kinsman's embrace and said, "Now you are truly my brother!" and Bard sensed that somehow Beltran had always been jealous of his friendship with Geremy, too; now the tie with Beltran was so strong that Geremy had nothing to equal it. Beltran and Geremy had sworn brotherhood, exchanging daggers, before they were out of childhood. No one, Bard thought with a brief surge of resentment, had ever asked *him* to swear the oath of *bredin*; not him, bastard and outcaste. . . . well, that was over, over for his lifetime. Now he was the king's son-in-law, Carlina's

27

pledged husband. Brother-in-law, even if not sworn brother, to Prince Beltran. Somehow it seemed to him that he walked taller; catching a glimpse of himself in one of the long mirrors adorning the Great Hall, it seemed that he looked handsome for once, that he was a bigger and somehow a better man than had ever looked into that mirror before.

Later, when the minstrels struck up for dancing, he led Carlina out. The dance broke couples up and recombined them in elaborate twisting measures, brought them together again; as they passed and re-passed in the dance, joining and loosing hands, it seemed to him that Carlina was less reluctant to take his hand. Geremy was dancing with one of the queen's youngest ladies, a red-haired maiden named Ginevra—Bard did not know her other name; she had played with Carlina when they were little girls, then become a waiting-woman. Bard wondered briefly if Ginevra shared Geremy's bed. Probably; what man would spend so much time and trouble on a woman if she would not? Or perhaps Geremy was still trying to persuade her. Well, if so, Geremy was a fool. Bard himself never bothered about high-born maidens, they tended to want too much in the way of flattery and promises of devotion. Nor did he care for the prettier ones; they promised more, he had found, and yielded less. Ginevra was almost plain enough to be properly grateful for masculine attention. But what was he doing, thinking of such things when he had Carlina?

Or rather, he thought sullenly, as he led her toward the buffet for a glass of wine after the hearty dancing, he *didn't* have Carlina, not yet! A year to wait! Damn it, why had her mother done this?

Carlina shook her head as he would have refilled her glass. "No, thank you, I don't really like it, Bard—and I think you have had enough," she said soberly.

He blurted out, "I would rather have a kiss from you than any drink ever brewed!"

Carlina looked up at him in astonishment; then her red mouth crinkled in a small smile. "Why, Bard, I have never heard you make a pretty speech before! Can it be that you have been taking lessons in gallantry from our cousin Geremy?"

Bard said, abashed, "I don't know any pretty speeches. I'm sorry, Carlina, do you want me to learn the art of flattering you? I've never had time for such things." And the unspoken part of that, with resentment, *Geremy has nothing else to do*

28

but sit home and learn to say pretty things to women, was perfectly audible to Carlina.

Suddenly she thought of Bard as he had been when first he came to be fostered there, three years ago, and he had seemed to her a great countrified sullen lout, refusing to use the manners he had, sulking, refusing to join in their games and play. Even then, he had been taller than any of them, taller than most men, and more broadly built. He had little interest in anything but the arms-play of their lessons, and had spent his playtime listening to the guardsmen tell tales of campaigns and war. None of them had liked him much, but Geremy said he was lonely, and had gone to some trouble to try to coax him into joining their games.

She felt, suddenly, almost sorry for the boy to whom she had been pledged. She did not want to marry him; but he had not been consulted either, and no man could be expected to refuse marriage to a king's daughter. He had spent so much of his life in war and preparation for war; it was not his fault that he was not gallant and a courtier like Geremy. She would rather have married Geremy—although, as she had told her nurse, she would rather not marry at all. Not because she had any great fondness for Geremy; simply that he was a gentler boy and she felt she understood him better. But Bard looked so unhappy.

She said, drinking the last unwanted drops in her glass, "Shall we sit and talk a while? Or would you like to dance again?"

"I'd rather talk," he said. "I'm not very good at dancing, or any of those courtly arts!"

Again she smiled at him, showing her dimples. She said, "If you are light enough on your feet to be a swordsman— and Beltran tells me you are unequalled—then you should be a fine dancer too. And remember, we used to dance together at lessons when we were children; would you have me believe you have forgotten how to dance since you were twelve years old?"

"To tell you the truth, Carlina," Bard said hesitantly, "I got my man's growth so young, when the rest of you were all so little. And, big as my body was, I felt always that my feet were bigger still, and that I was a great hulking brute! When I came to ride to war, and to fight, then my size and weight gave me the advantage . . . but I find it hard to think of myself as a courtier."

Something in this confession touched her beyond endurance. She suspected he had never said anything like this to anyone before, or even thought it. She said, "You're not clumsy, Bard, I find you a fine dancer. But if it makes you uncomfortable, you need not dance again, at least not with me. We will sit here and talk awhile." She turned, smiling. "You will have to learn to offer me your arm, when we cross a room together. With the help of the Goddess, I may indeed civilize you one day!"

"You have a considerable task on your hands, *damisela*," Bard said, and let the tips of her fingers rest lightly on his arm.

They found a seat together at the edge of the room, out of the way of the dancers, near where some elderly folk were playing at cards and dice. One of the men of the king's household came toward them, evidently intending to claim a dance with Carlina, but Bard glowered at him and he discovered some urgent business elsewhere.

Bard reached out with the hand he thought was clumsy and touched the corner of her temple. "I thought, when we stood before your father, that you had been crying. Carlie, has someone ill-used you?"

She shook her head and said, "No." But Bard was just enough of a telepath—although when the household *leronis* had tested him, at twelve, he had been told he had not much *laran*—to sense that she would not speak the true reason for her tears aloud; and he managed to guess it.

"You are not happy about this marriage," he said, with his formidable scowl, and felt her flinch again as she had done when he squeezed her hand.

She lowered her head. She said at last, "I have no wish to marry; and I wept because no one asks a girl if she wishes to be given in marriage."

Bard frowned, hardly believing what he heard. "What would a woman do, in the name of Avarra, if she was *not* married? Surely you do not wish to stay at home all your days till you are old?"

"I would like to have the choice to do that, if I wished," Carlina said. "Or perhaps to choose for myself whom I would marry. But I would rather not marry at all. I would like to go to a Tower as a *leronis*, perhaps to keep my virginity for the Sight, as some of mother's maidens have done, or perhaps to live among the priestesses of Avarra, on the holy isle, belonging only to the Goddess. Does that seem so strange to you,"

"Yes," Bard said. "I have always heard that every woman's greatest desire is to marry as soon as possible."

"And so it is, for many women, but why should women be

30

any more alike than you and Geremy? You choose to be a soldier, and he to be a *laranzu*; would you say that everyone should choose to be a soldier?"

"It's different with men," Bard said. "Women don't understand these things, Carlie. You need a home and children and someone to love you." He picked up her hand and carried the small soft fingers to his lips.

Carlina felt sudden anger, mingled with a flood almost of pity.

She felt like giving him an angry reply, but he was looking at her so gently, with so much hopefulness, that she forbore to speak what she thought.

He could not be blamed; if there was blame, it was her father's, who had given her to Bard as if she were the red cord he wore about the warrior's braid, a reward for his bravery in battle. Why should she blame him for the customs of the land which made of a woman only a chattel, a pawn for her father's political ambitions?

He followed some of this, his brow knitted as he sat holding her hand. "Do you not want to wed with me at all, Carlie?"

"Oh, Bard—" she said, and he could hear the pain in her voice—"it is not *you*. Truly, truly, my foster brother and my promised husband, since I must marry, there is no other man I would rather have. Perhaps one day—when I am older, when we are both older—then, if the gods are kind to us, we may come to love one another as is seemly for married people." She clasped his big hand in her two small ones, and said, "The gods grant it may be so."

And then someone came up to claim Carlina for a dance; and though Bard glowered again, she said, "Bard, I must; one of the duties of a bride is to dance with all who ask her, as you very well know, and every maiden here who wishes to marry this year thinks it lucky to dance with the groom. Later we can speak together, my dear."

Bard yielded her, reluctantly, and, recalled to his duty, moved about the room, dancing with three or four of Queen Ariel's women, as was suitable for a man attached to the king's household, his banner bearer. But again and again, his eyes sought out Carlina, where her blue robe, pearl-embroidered, and her dark hair, drew his awareness back again.

Carlina. Carlina was *his*, and he realized that he hated, with a violent surge of loathing, every man who touched her. How dare they? What was she about, flirting, raising her eyes to any man who came to dance with her, as if she were

31

some shameless camp follower? Why did she encourage them? Why couldn't she be shy and modest, refusing dances except with her promised husband? He knew this was unreasonable, but it seemed to him that she was trying to win the approval and the flirtatious smile of every man who touched her. He restrained his wrath when she danced with Beltran, and her father, and the grizzled veteran of sixty whose granddaughter had been her foster sister, but every time she danced with some young soldier or guardsman of the king's household, he fancied that Queen Ariel was looking at him triumphantly.

Of course what she had said about not wanting to marry at all—that was girlish nonsense, he didn't believe a word of it. No doubt she was cherishing some girl's passion for some man, someone not really worthy of her, to whom her parents would not give her; and now that she was handfasted, and old enough to dance with men who were not her kinsmen, she could seek him out. Bard knew that if he found Carlina with another man, he would tear the man limb from limb, and Carlina herself he would—would he hurt her? No. He would simply demand of her what she had given the other man, make her so much his that she would never think of any other man alive. He scanned the ranks of guardsmen jealously, but Carlina seemed to pay no more attention to any one than another, dancing courteously with all comers but never accepting a second dance with any.

But no, she was dancing again with Geremy Hastur, a little closer to him than she had been to any other, she was laughing with him, his head was bent over her dark one. Was she sharing confidences, had she told *him* that she did not want to marry Bard? Was it Geremy, perhaps, she wished to marry? After all, Geremy was of the Hastur kin, descended from the legendary sons and daughters of Cassilda, Robardin's daughter . . . kin to the very gods, or so they said. Damn all the Hasturs, the di Asturiens were an ancient and noble lineage too, why should she prefer Geremy? Rage and jealousy surging in him, he crossed the floor toward them; he still had enough awareness of good manners to refrain from interrupting their dance, but as the music halted and they stepped apart, laughing, he moved toward them so purposefully that he shoved another couple, without apology.

"It is time again to dance with your promised husband, my lady," he said.

Geremy chuckled. "How impatient you are, Bard, considering that you will have the rest of your lives together," he said, resting an affectionate hand on Bard's elbow. "Well, Carlie, at least you know your promised husband is eager!"

Bard felt the twist of malice in the taunt and said angrily, "My *promised wife*—" he put heavy emphasis on the words, "is *Lady Carlina* to you, not *Carlie!*"

Geremy stared up at him, still not believing he was not making a joke. "It is for my foster sister to tell me when I am no longer welcome to call her by the name I called her when her hair was too short to braid," he said genially. "What has come over you, Bard?"

"The Lady Carlina is pledged as my wife," Bard said stiffly. "You will conduct yourself toward her as is seemly for a married woman."

Carlina opened her mouth in amazement, and shut it again. "Bard," she said with careful patience, "perhaps when we are truly man and wife and not merely a handfasted couple I shall allow you to tell me how I am to conduct myself toward my foster brothers; and perhaps not. At the moment, I shall continue to do exactly as I please in that respect! Apologize to Geremy, or don't presume to show your face again to me tonight!"

Bard stared at her in dismay and anger. Did he intend to make him crawl before this sandal wearer, this *laranzu* wizard? Was she willing to insult her promised husband in public over Geremy Hastur? Was it really Geremy she cared for then?

Geremy stared, too, hardly believing what he was hearing, but King Ardrin was looking in their direction, and there was enough trouble in this household tonight—he sensed it—so that a quarrel would not be wise. Besides, he didn't want to quarrel with his friend and foster brother. Bard was alone here, with no father to stand beside him, and no doubt he was feeling touchy because his closest kin could not be troubled to make half a day's ride to see him honored as the king's champion, and married to the king's daughter, So he tried to ease it over.

"I don't need any apologies from Bard, foster sister," he said. "If I offended him, I'll willingly beg his pardon instead. And there is Ginevra waiting for me. Bard, my good friend, be the first to wish us well; I have asked her for leave to write my father to make arrangements for a handfasting in *that* quarter, and she has not refused me, only said that she must ask leave of *her* father to accept my offer. So, if all the old folk are agreeable, I may stand, a year or so from now,

33

where you stand tonight! Or even, if the gods are kind, in the hills of my own country—"

Carlina touched Geremy's arm. "Are you homesick, Geremy?" she asked gently.

"Homesick? Not really, I suppose. I was sent from Carcosa before it could truly be my home," he said. "But sometimes—at sunset—my heart sickens for the lake, and for the towers of Carcosa, rising against the setting sun, and for the frogs that cry there after the sun goes down, the sound that was my first lullaby."

Carlina said gently, "I have never been far from home; but it must be sadness beyond all other sadness. I am a woman and I was brought up to know that whatever happened, I must leave my home someday. . . ."

"And now," said Geremy touching her hand, "the gods have been kind, for your father has given you to a member of his household and you need never leave your home."

She smiled up at him, forgetting Bard, and said, "If one thing could reconcile me to this marriage, I think it would be that."

The words were like salt in a raw wound to Bard, where he stood listening. He broke in sharply, "Go, then, and join Ginevra," and put his hand, not gently, on Carlina's, drawing her away. When they were out of earshot he spun her around roughly to face him.

"So—did you tell Geremy, then, that you did not want to marry me? Have you been babbling this tale to every man you dance with, making a game of me behind my back?"

"Why, no," she said, looking up at him in surprise. "Why should I? I spoke my heart to Geremy because he is my foster brother and Beltran's sworn brother, and I think of him as I would of my own blood kin, born of my father and my mother!"

"And are you sure it is so innocent with him? He comes from the mountain country," Bard said, "where a brother may lie with his sister; and the way he touched you—"

"Bard, that is too ridiculous for words," Carlina said, impatiently. "Even if we were wedded and bedded, such jealousy would be unseemly! Are you going to call challenge, when we are wedded, on every man to whom I speak civilly? Must I be afraid to say a pleasant word to my own foster brothers? Will you be jealous next of Beltran, or of Dom Cormel?" He was the veteran of fifty years service with her father and grandfather.

Before her wrathful gaze he lowered his eyes. "I can't help

34

it, Carlina. I am frantic with fear that I would lose you," he said. "It was cruel of your father not to give you to me now, since he had decided on the wedding. I cannot help but think he is making game of me, and that later, before we are bedded, he will give you to someone else he likes better, or who will pay a bigger bride-price, or whose station would make him a more powerful alliance! Why should he give you to his brother's bastard son?"

Before the dismay in his eyes Carlina was flooded with pity. Behind the arrogance of his words, was he so insecure? She reached out to take his hand. "No, Bard, you must not think that. My father loves you well, my promised husband, he has promoted you over the head of my own brother Beltran, he has made you his banner bearer and given you the red cord; how can you think he would play you false that way? But he would have cause to be angry if you made a silly quarrel with Geremy Hastur at our festival! Now promise me you will not be so silly and jealous again, Bard, or I will quarrel with you too!"

"If we were truly wedded and bedded," he said, "I should have no cause for jealousy, for I would know you were mine beyond recall. Carlina," he begged, suddenly, taking up both her hands and covering them with kisses, "the law recognizes that we are man and wife; the law allows us to consummate our marriage whenever we will. Let me have you tonight and I will *know* that you are mine, and be certain of you!"

She couldn't help herself; she shrank away in mortal terror. She had won a respite, and now he made this demand of her, as the price of ending his jealous scenes. She knew that her shrinking was hurting him, but she lowered her eyes and said, "No, Bard. I do not seek to—to pluck fruit from the blossoming tree, nor should you. All things come in their proper time." She felt stupid, prim, as she mouthed the old proverb. "It is unseemly to ask me this at our handfasting!"

"You said you hoped you might come to love me—"

"At the proper time," she said, and knew her voice was shrill.

He retorted, "This *is* the proper time, and you know it! Unless you know something I do not, that your father plans to play me false and give to another, meanwhile binding me to him!"

Carlina swallowed, knowing that he really believed this, and really sorry for him.

He saw her hesitation, sensing her pity, and put his arm around her, but she drew back with such distress that he let

35

her go. He said bitterly, "It's true, then. You do not love me."

"Bard," she begged, "give me time. I promise you, when the time has come, I will not shrink from you then. But I was not . . . not told of this, I was told I should have a year . . . perhaps when I am older—"

"Will it take a year to resign yourself to the horrible fate of sharing my bed?" he asked, with such bitterness that she wished she did not feel this dreadful reluctance.

"Perhaps," she said, faltering, "when I am older, I will not feel this way—my mother says I am too young for wedding or for bedding, so perhaps when I am old enough—"

"That is folly," he said scornfully. "Younger maidens than you are wedded every day, and bedded too. That is a ruse to reconcile me to waiting and then to losing you altogether; but if we have lain down together, my sweetheart, then no living person can separate us, not your father nor your mother. . . . I give you my word you are not too young, Carlina! Let me prove that to you!" He took her in his arms, kissing her, crushing her mouth under his; she struggled silently, in such dismay that he let her go.

She said bitterly, "And if I refuse you, will you put compulsion on me, as you did on Lisarda, who was also too young for such things? Will you put enchantment on me, so that I cannot refuse you whatever you want from me, so that I must do your will whether it is my own desire or no?"

Bard bent his head, his lips pressed bitterly together, a thin angry line. "So that is it," he said. "So that little whore went wailing to you and filled your mind with evil lies against me?"

"She did not lie, Bard, for I read her thoughts."

"Whatever she says to you, she was not unwilling," Bard said, and Carlina said in real anger now, "No; that is what is worse; that you forced her will so that she did not *want* to resist you!"

"You would find as much pleasure in it as she did," Bard said hotly, and she replied with equal anger, "And you could accept that—that I would not be Carlina, but only some wish of yours forced on my real self? No doubt I would do your will, and even do it willingly, if you put that compulsion on me—just as Lisarda did! And just as she does, I should hate you for every moment of the rest of my life!"

"I think not," Bard said. "I think, perhaps, when you were rid of your silly fears, you would come to love me and know that I had done what was best for us both!"

"No," she said, shaking. "No, Bard . . . I beg you . . . Bard, I am your wife." A guileful thought touched her; she was ashamed of herself for trying to manipulate him this way, but she was frightened and desperate. "Would you use me as if I were no better than one of my maids?"

He let her go, shocked. He said, "All gods forbid that I should show you dishonor, Carlie!"

"Then," she said, pressnig her advantage swiftly, "you will wait until the appointed time." She drew quickly out of reach. "I promise you," she said, "I will be faithful to you. There is no need for you to fear you will lose me; but all things come in their proper time." She touched his hand lightly and went away.

Bard, watching her as she went out of sight, thought to himself that she had made a fool of him. No, she was right; it was a matter of honor, that she, his wife, should come to him of her own free will and without compulsion. Yet he was excited, anger contributing to the uproar in his mind and body.

No woman had ever complained of his advances! How did that damned wench Lisarda have the presumption to complain of him? She hadn't minded, the little slut, he had only given her a chance to do what she wanted to do anyway! He remembered her; yes, she had been frightened at first, but before he was done he had made her moan with pleasure, what right had she to change her mind afterward and go and bewail her precious virginity to Carlina, as if it had any particular value? *She* wasn't an heiress who must keep it for honor and dowry!

And now Carlina had roused him, and left him in a state of need! Anger and resentment mingled in him; did the girl think he was going to await her convenience as patiently as a maiden?

Suddenly he knew what he should do to have proper revenge on them both, both damned women who had made a fool of him! Women were all alike, starting with the unknown mother who had been willing to give him up to his father's wealth and position. And Lady Jerana who had poisoned his father's mind and had him sent from his home. And that wretched little slut Lisarda with her whimpering and her tales to Carlina. And even Carlina herself was not free of the general damnableness of women!

In a rage he went out toward the galleries where the upper servants were watching the festivities. He saw Lisarda among them, a slender childish-looking girl with soft brown hair, her slight body just barely rounding into womanhood; Bard's own body tightened with excitement, remembering.

She had been untouched, even ignorant, and frightened, but she had soon enough lost her reluctance. And yet she had the presumption to go complaining to Carlina, as if she had minded! Damned girl, he would show her better this time!

He waited until she was looking in his direction, then caught her eye. He saw her shiver and try to look away, but he reached out, as he had learned how to do, into her mind, touching something deep down in her, below the conscious will, the response of body to body. What did it matter what she *thought* she wanted? This was there and it was real too, and all her arrogant notions about her pridefully held innocence meant nothing in the face of this reality. He held her until he felt her senses stirring, watched with a detached, malicious amusement as she made her way toward him. Staying out of sight, he drew her behind a pillar, kissed her expertly, felt her response flooding them both.

Far away, in a detached corner of her mind, he could sense, could see in her eyes, the panic of the conscious mind, now in abeyance, her dread and horror that this thing was happening to her again in spite of what she wanted, that her body was responding to him when her will did not. Bard laughed soundlessly and whispered to her; watched her go, like a sleepwalker, up the stairs to his room, where, he knew, she would be waiting for him, naked and eager, whenever he chose to come.

He'd keep her waiting awhile. That would prove to her what she really wanted, make her wait for him; her tears and cries would remind her that she had really wanted it all along. *That* would teach her to go complaining to Carlina as if he had mishandled her, or taken her unwilling!

And if Carlina did somehow come to hear of it, well, that was her fault too. She was his wife, in law and in fact, and if she did not recognize that as a responsibility, she had no right to complain if he went elsewhere.

Chapter Two

The year was well advanced, and early hay harvest had begun, when Bard di Asturien sought out King Ardrin in his presence-chamber.

"Uncle," he said, for he had this privilege, the king being his foster father, "will we ride to war before apple harvest?"

King Ardrin raised his eyebrows. He was a tall, imposing man, fair-haired like most of the di Asturiens, and had once been powerful, but he had taken a wound in the arm some years ago and it had left the arm paralyzed. He bore other scars too, the marks of a man who has had to keep his realm by force of arms for most of his life. He said, "Why, I had hoped not, foster son. But you know more than I of what is doing on the borders, since you have been there with the guardsmen these past forty days; what news?"

"No news of the border," Bard said, "for all is quiet; after Snow Glens there is no question of rebellion in *that* area again. But this gossip I heard as I rode homeward; did you know that Dom Eiric Ridenow, the younger, has married his sister to the Duke of Hammerfell?"

King Ardrin looked thoughtful, but all he said was, "Go on."

"One of my guardsmen has a brother-in-law who is a mercenary soldier to the Duke," Bard said. "He slew a man by misadventure, and went into exile for three years, so he took service in Hammerfell, and he has been released from his service oath. My guardsman said that when his brother-in-law took service at Hammerfell he made it a condition that he should not ride against Asturias; and I find it interesting that he should be released from his oath now, instead of at midwinter, which is customary."

"Then you think—"

"I think the Duke of Hammerfell is cementing his new kin tie to Ridenow of Serrais", Bard said, "by gathering his army against Asturias. We might have expected that in the spring.

39

If he strikes at us before the winter snow, he will hope to find us unprepared. Also, Beltran has a *laranzu* with his men, whose gift is for rapport with sentry bird; he said that although there were no armies on the road, men were gathering in the market town of Tarquil, which lies not all that far from Hammerfell. True, it is hiring fair there; but the *laranzu* said there were too few men with pitchforks and milking pails, and too many on horseback. It would seem that mercenaries are gathering there. And there was a train of pack beasts riding from Dalereuth Tower, and you know as well as I do what is made in Dalereuth. What does the Duke of Hammerfell want with clingfire, if not to ride against us with the Ridenow of Serrais?"

King Ardrin nodded, slowly. He said, "I am sure you are right. Well, Bard, you who have seen this campaign coming against us, what would you do if the command was yours?"

It was not the first time Bard had been asked this question. It had never meant anything, except that his foster father wished to see if he had a strong sense of military tactics; he would have asked Beltran and Geremy the same question, had they been present, and then would have gone to his ordinary advisers. Nevertheless, Bard gave his best thought to the problem.

"I would ride against them now, before they can gather their mercenaries, before ever they leave Hammerfell," he said. "I would lay siege to Hammerfell, long before he expects us to know what is happening. He does not expect the war to come to his country, he is merely gathering mercenaries to send to the aid of Dom Eiric, so when the Ridenow come against us this summer, as they are sure to do, we will find his forces unpleasantly swollen. But if we strike at Hammerfell *now*, and lay siege to the duke until he is willing to take oath and send hostages not to move against you, you will confound Dom Eiric and confuse his advisers. Also, if I were in command, I would send a few of the troops south to capture and destroy the clingfire before it can be used against us; perhaps to add to our own stockpiles. And since it will certainly be guarded by sorcerers, I would send a *laranzu* or two in that party."

"How soon could we be ready to move against Hammerfell?" King Ardrin asked.

"Within a tenday, sir. Roundup of the horse levies will be finished by then, and the men will be free to answer the war call," Bard said. "But I would send it out in secret, rather than summoning men with the beacon fires; they may have wizards spying to see the beacons from afar. Then we can strike Hammerfell within a tenday of the time he knows we have crossed the border—if we can move swiftly, with a few picked men, we can cut off the bridges over the Valeron, and hold anyone who rides against us, sending one detachment inside to lay siege to the castle."

King Ardrin's stern face broke into a smile. He said, "I could not have made a better plan myself; in fact, Bard, I doubt I could have made one so good. Now I have another question for you: if I lead the troops north to Hammerfell, can you go south to capture the clingfire? I can give you some *leroni*, and three dozen picked horsemen—you may choose them yourself—but no more; will it be enough?"

Bard did not answer for a moment. He said, "Can you not spare four dozen, sir?"

"No; I shall need those extra dozen horsemen to ride to Hammerfell," King Ardrin said.

"Then I shall have to make do with three dozen, sir. At least they can move swiftly when the need arises." His heart was pounding. He had never been given an independent command before.

"Prince Beltran will lead you—officially," King Ardrin said, "but the men will follow you. You understand me, Bard? I must give this command to Beltran. But I shall make it clear to him that you are the military adviser."

Bard nodded. That was simply the reality of the matter; a member of the royal house must be in nominal command. King Ardrin was a seasoned war leader; but he, Bard, was being given a tricky fast mission with a picked striking force. "I will go and choose my men, sir."

"A moment." King Ardrin gestured him back. "A time will come when you, as my son-in-law, will be empowered to command. Your bravery is welcome to me, Bard; but I forbid you to run into too much danger. I need your skill at strategy more than I need your strong arm or your courage. Don't get yourself killed, Bard. I have my eye on you; I am too old to be my own general for more than a few more years. You know what I am trying to say."

Bard bowed deeply and said, "I am at your command, my king and my lord."

"And a day will come when I will be at yours, kinsman. Go now and choose your men."

"May I bid farewell to the Lady Carlina, my lord?"

Ardrin smiled. "You may, certainly."

Bard thought, exultantly, about his good fortune. Now it

seemed that his career was assured, and it might be that if he brought this mission successfully to an end, King Ardrin would grant him a further favor, that he might have Carlina at Midwinter festival. Or he might prevail upon her, at least, to consummate their marriage on that night of traditional license! Surely, when he was the king's commander and champion, she would not continue to refuse him!

He admitted it to himself; he was tired of casual wenching. It was Carlina he wanted. At first he had cared for her only as a sign that the king regarded him highly, as a gateway to position and power in the realm, a power which a *nedestro* could not otherwise have within the realm of Asturias. But when she had spoken to him so gently at midsummer, he knew that she was the only woman he really wanted.

He was tired of casual wenching. He was tired of Lisarda, tired even of the game he played with her, making her unwilling body respond even while she wept and insisted she hated him. Wretched little spoilsport, when he had done his best to pleasure her! But now he no longer cared. He wanted no one but Carlina.

He found her in the sewing rooms, supervising the women who were making linen cushions, and beckoned her away from them. Again it struck him with wonder, why should he want this plain girl when there were so many pretty ones around her? Was it only that she was the king's daughter, that she had been his playmate when they were children? Her hair had been hastily braided and shoved back out of the way, but even so, lint was clinging to it, and her blue tartan dress was one he had seen her wear, it seemed, every day since she was ten years old; or did she simply have another one made for her when she had outgrown or outworn the old one?

He said, "There are feathers in your hair, Carlina."

She dabbed at it, preoccupied, laughed. "No doubt; some of the women are stuffing comforters for the winter to come, and making cushions and pillows; I rule over the feathers, while my mother's women are salting and pickling the bird's flesh for the winter." She looked at the bits of feather fluff clinging to her fingers. "Do you remember, foster brother, the year that you and I and Beltran got into the feather vats and feathers flew all over the sewing rooms? I felt so guilty, for you and Beltran were beaten, and I was only sent to my room without dinner!"

Bard laughed. "Then we had the best of it, for I would rather be beaten any day than go fasting, and I have no

42

doubt Beltran feels much the same! And for all these years I have felt you had the worst of it!"

"But the prank was mine; you and Beltran, and Geremy too, were always being beaten for mischief that I thought up," she said. "We had merry times, did we not, foster brother?"

"We did indeed," Bard said, and took her hands in his. "But I would not call you foster sister now, Carlina *mea*. And I came to bear you great news!"

She smiled up at him. "What is it, my promised husband?" she asked, using the words shyly.

"The king your father has given me command of troops," he burst out exultantly. "I am to go with three dozen picked men and capture a caravan of clingfire . . . . Beltran is nominally in command, but you know, and I too, that the command is truly mine . . . and I am to pick my own men, and to have *leroni* with us. . . ."

"Oh, Bard, how wonderful," she said, warming against her will as he poured out his good news. "I am so glad for you! Surely this means, as you have hoped, I know, that from banner bearer you will rise to one of his captains, and perhaps one day to lead all his armies!"

Bard said, trying not to show too much pride, "Surely that day will be many years from now. But it does show that your father continues to think well of me; and I have thought, Carlina *mea*, that if this mission comes off well, then perhaps he will put forward our wedding by half a year and we can be married at midsummer—"

Carlina tried to control her involuntary flinching. She and Bard must be married; it was her father's will, which was law in the land of Asturias. She genuinely wished Bard well; there was no reason they should be unfriends. There was not, after all, so much difference between midwinter and midsummer. Yet, however she tried to tell herself this, she was still, helplessly, reluctant.

But Bard's delight in the thought was so great that she could not bear to quench it. She temporized. "That must be as my father and my lord wills it, Bard."

Bard saw only a proper maidenly shyness in the words. He tightened his fingers on her hands and said, "Will you kiss me in farewell, my promised wife?"

How could she deny him so much? She let him draw her close, felt his lips, hard and insistent, over hers, stifling her breath. He had never kissed her before except for the brotherly and respectful kiss they had exchanged, before witnesses, at their handfasting. This was different, and somehow frightening, as she felt him trying to open her lips with his mouth; she did not struggle, submitting, scared and passive, to the touch, and somehow this was more exciting to Bard than the most violent passion could have been.

As they moved apart he said in a low voice, half afraid of his own emotion, "I love you, Carlina."

At the shaking of his voice she was moved, again, with reluctant tenderness. She touched his cheek with her fingertips and said gently, "I know, my promised husband."

When he had left her again, she stood staring after the closed door, her emotions in turmoil. Her whole heart yearned after the silence and peace of the Isle of Silence; yet it seemed that it was never to be, that she must go, will she nill she, to be the wife of her cousin, her foster brother, her promised husband, Bard di Asturien. Perhaps, she told herself, perhaps it will not be so bad, when we were little children we loved one another well.

"Ah, Carlina," called one of the women, "what am I to do with this bolt of material; the threads are all drawn at the edge and there is a big piece spoilt here—"

Carlina came and bent over the material. She said, "You will have to straighten it as best you can; and if it is not wide enough after for a sheet, then you must save this end for cushion covers, which can be worked over in wool, with colored designs embroidered here to hide the crooked weave. . . ."

"Why, lady," mocked one of the girls, "how can you give thought to such things, when you have had a visit here from your lover. . . ."

She had used the inflection that changed the word subtly from *promised husband* to *paramour*, and Carlina flushed, feeling the heat flooding into her cheeks. But all she said, schooling her voice to calm and uninvolvement, "Why, Catriona, I thought you had been sent here to learn weaving and embroidery and all manner of womanly arts among the queen's women, but I see you need schooling in *casta* too, to say *promised husband* with the proper courtesy; if you say it like that among the queen's other women, they will mock at you for being countrified."

Chapter Three

Bard rode forth before dawn the next morning. The hour was so early that the easternmost sky had not yet begun to flush with the red dawn; all four of the moons were in the sky, though only one near the full; three small crescents, and the pale disk of Mormallor, floating over the distant hills behind them. Bard's mind was filled with the memory of Carlina's shy kiss; perhaps a day would come when she would kiss him of her own free will, when she would be glad and proud of being married to the king's banner bearer, the king's champion, perhaps the general of all his armies. . . . His thoughts were pleasant enough as he rode at the head of his first command, small though it was.

On the other hand, Beltran, somberly dressed and wrapped in a great cape, was sullen and morose; Bard sensed that he was angered and wondered why.

Beltran growled, "You seem content enough, and perhaps for *you* this command is welcome, but I would rather ride north to Hammerfell at my father's side, where he could see whether I do well or ill; and here I am sent to capture a caravan, sent off like the leader of a bandit gang!"

Bard tried to tell his foster brother how important it might be, to make sure that the clingfire from Dalereuth never reached Serrais, to be used against the fields and villages and forests of Asturias; but Beltran could only see that he had not been given the privilege of riding at his father's right hand, in sight of his armies. "My only comfort is that you will not take my rightful place there," he grumbled. "*That* post he gave to Geremy . . . damn him, damn all the Hasturs!"

Here Bard shared Beltran's displeasure and thought it politic to let him know it.

"Right; he promised me I should have Geremy at the head of the sorcerers riding with us, and at the last moment he tells me he cannot spare Geremy to me, and has given me three strangers," he added his grumbling to Beltran's. He

45

looked ahead to where they rode, a little apart from the picked combat men he had chosen; a tall *laranzu*, graying, his red moustaches hiding half his lower face, and two women, one overplump for riding, ambling on a donkey, and one thin, childish girl, so deeply shrouded in her gray sorcerer's cloak that Bard could not make out whether she was fair or plain. He knew nothing of these three, nothing of their competence, and he wondered nervously if they would be willing to accept him as leader of this expedition. The *laranzu* in particular; although, like all of his kind, he rode unarmed except for a dagger at his side, a small knife such as a woman might wear, he looked as if he had been riding on campaigns such as this since long before Bard was born.

He wondered if this was Beltran's apprehension, too, but he soon found that the prince's displeasure was from quite another cause.

"Geremy and I pledged one another we would ride together to battle this year, and now he has chosen to remain at the king's side——"

"Foster brother," Bard said seriously, "a soldier hears only the voice of his commander, and his own wishes must be subordinate to that."

Prince Beltran's voice was petulant. "I am sure, if he had told my father of this, Father would have honored our promise and given Geremy to this expedition. After all, it is only a stupid matter of chasing down caravans, not much more important than riding out to capture bandit raiders on the border," he added; and Bard, frowning, knew suddenly why the king had said firmly to him that he, and not Prince Beltran, was really in command of this expedition; quite obviously, the prince had no notion of the strategic importance of the clingfire caravans!

If Prince Beltran has no military sense, no wonder my lord the king is eager to train me for command at last; so that if he cannot leave his armies in the hands of his son, he may leave them to his son-in-law. . . . If he has no son fit for a general of all his armies, he will marry his daughter to his own general instead of to a rival outside his borders. . . .

He tried to make Prince Beltran see something of the importance of his mission, but Beltran was sulking, and at last said, "I can see that you want it to be important, Bard, because it makes *you* feel more important." And Bard shrugged and let it go.

By midafternoon they were near to the southern border of Asturias; and during the midafternoon rest to breathe the horses, Bard rode toward the sorcerers, who had stopped a little apart from the rest. This was customary; most fighting men (and Bard was no exception) were wary of *leroni*.

He thought King Ardrin must have regarded this mission as important, else he would hardly have sent a man long seasoned in campaign, but would have given them the young and inexperienced Geremy, if only to please his son and his foster son. Still, Bard found himself echoing the wish of the prince, that Geremy, whom he knew so well, had been with them, rather than this stranger. He did not know how to talk to a *laranzu*. Geremy, from the time they were all twelve years old, had had lessons apart, not in swordplay and unarmed combat and dagger fighting like the rest of the king's fosterlings, but in the occult mastery of the starstones, the blue wizard's crystals which gave the *leroni* their powers. Geremy had shared their lessons in military tactics and strategy, in riding and hunting, and had gone with them on fire watch and ridden with them against bandits, but it was clear even then that he was not intended for a soldier, and when he had given up wearing a sword, exchanging it for the dagger of a sorcerer, and saying he needed no weapon but the starstone about his neck, a great gulf had opened between them.

And now, as he faced the *laranzu* the king had sent with them, he felt something of the same gulf. Yet the man looked hardened to campaigns, rode like a soldier, and even had a soldierly way of handling his horse. He had thin, hawk-like features and keen, colorless eyes, the gray hardness of tempered steel.

"I am Bard di Asturien," he said. "I do not know your name, sir."

"*Gareth MacAran, a ves ordras, vai dom . . .*" said the man, saluting briefly.

"What have you been told about this expedition, Master Gareth?"

"Only that I was at *your* orders, sir." Bard had just enough *laran* to catch the very faint, almost undetectable emphasis put on *your*. Inwardly he felt a definite satisfaction. So he was not the only one to believe Beltran was completely hopeless in military matters.

He said, "Have you a sentry bird?"

Master Gareth pointed. He said, gently, but in definite reproof, "I was riding on campaign before you were begotten, sir. If you will tell me what information is needed. . . ."

Bard felt the sting of the reproof. He said stiffly, "I am

47

young, sir, but not untried in campaign. I have spent most of my time with the sword, and am not accustomed to the proper courtesy in dealing with wizardry. I need to know where the clingfire caravan rides to the south, so that we can take them by surprise, and before they have a chance to destroy what they have."

Master Gareth set his mouth. He said, "Clingfire, is it? I'd be glad to see all that stuff dumped into the sea. At least it will not be used to set siege to Asturias this year, then. Melora!" he called, and the older *leronis* came toward him. He had thought her, from her thick body, to be an older woman; now he saw that she was young, but heavy-bodied, her face round and moon-shaped, with pale, vague eyes. Her hair, brilliantly fire red, was twisted into an untidy bun.

"Bring the bird to me. . . ."

Bard watched with amazement—an amazement not new to him, but one that never failed—as the woman deftly unhooded the great bird riding on a block on her saddle. He had had occasion to handle sentry birds; by comparison, even the fiercest of hunting hawks were gentle as a child's cage-bird. The long snakelike neck writhed around and the bird screamed at Bard, a high snarling cry, but when Melora stroked its feathers it quieted, giving a chirp which seemed almost plaintive, eager for caresses. Gareth took the bird, while Bard cringed inwardly at the proximity of those fierce, unclipped talons near his eyes; but Master Gareth handled it as Carlina would have held one of her tiny singing birds.

"There, my beauty . . ." he said, stroking the bird lovingly. "Go and see what they are doing. . . ."

He flung the bird into the air; it winged away on long, strong pinions, wheeling overhead and disappearing into the clouds. Melora slumped in her saddle, her vague eyes closed, and Gareth said in an undertone, "There is no need for you to stay here, sir. I'll stay in rapport with her and see all she sees through the eyes of the bird. I'll come and make my report to you when we ride on again."

"How long will it take?"

"How should I know, sir?"

Again, Bard felt the sense of a reproof from the old campaigner. Was this, he wondered, why King Ardrin had given him this command, to show him all the little things he should know, in addition to fighting . . . including the courtesy one should show to a skilled *laranzu*. Well, he would learn.

Master Gareth said, "When the bird has seen all it needs to see, and is on its way back to us, then we can ride on. It will find us wherever we are; but Melora cannot ride and stay in rapport with her bird. She would fall from her donkey, and she is no skilled rider at the best of times."

Bard frowned, wondering why they had sent a woman with the troops who could scarcely sit a donkey, let alone a horse!

Master Gareth said, "Because, sir, she is the most skilled at rapport with sentry bird of any *leronis* in Asturias; that is a woman's art, and I am not myself so skilled. I can share rapport with the birds enough to handle them without being pecked to death, but Melora can fly with them and see all they see, and interpret it to me. And now, sir, if you will forgive me, I must not talk any more, I must follow Melora." His face shut down, his eyes rolled up into his head, and Bard, looking at the whites of his eyes, felt a shudder of dismay. The man was not *there*; some essential part of himself was off with Melora and the sentry bird. . . .

Suddenly he was glad that Geremy had not come with them. It was bad enough to see this stranger go away into some eerie realm where he could not follow; if it had been his friend and foster brother, he would have found it unendurable.

The third of the *leroni* had removed her gray riding cloak, throwing back the hood; he could see now that it was a slender young girl, with a pretty, remote face, her flaming hair curling around her cheeks, beautiful and serious. As she saw Bard's eyes on her, she colored and turned away, and something in the shy gesture reminded him of Carlina, frail, almost wraithlike.

She was leading her horse toward the spring, with only the faintest glance at her two colleagues, entranced on their mounts. Bard dismounted and went to take her horse's bridle.

"*Damisela*, may I assist you?"

"Thank you." She surrendered the reins to him. She did not meet his eyes; he tried to catch her glance, but only saw the color rising in her face. How pretty she was! He led the horse to the water hole, standing with one hand on the reins.

He said, "When Master Gareth and Dame Melora come back to themselves, I will send two of my men to care for their horses."

"Thank you, sir; they will be grateful, for they are always weary after long rapport with the birds. I cannot do it at all," the girl said. She had a small, whispery voice.

"But you are a skilled *leronis*?"

"No, *vai dom*, only a beginner, an apprentice. Perhaps I shall be one day," she said. "My gift at the moment is to see

49

where they cannot send a bird." Again she lowered her eyes and colored.

"And what is your name, *damisela?*"

"Mirella Lindir, sir."

The horse had finished drinking. Bard said, "Have you a food bag for your horse?"

"By your leave, not now, sir. The horse of a *leronis* is trained to stand quietly for a long time without moving—" She gestured to the two motionless figures, Master Gareth and Melora. "But if I feed mine, it will disturb the others."

"I see. Well, as you will," Bard said, recalling that he should go among his men and see what they were doing. Prince Beltran should see to them, of course, but already he had begun to mistrust Beltran's skill, or even his interest in this campaign. Well, so much the better; if this went well, it would be all the more to Bard's credit.

Mirella said shyly, "Don't let me keep you from your duties, sir."

He bowed to her, and went; her eyes, he thought, were beautiful, and she had a shyness not unlike Carlina's. He wondered if she was still a virgin. She had looked at him with interest, certainly. He had promised himself that he would give up his wenching, remain faithful to Carlina, but on campaign a soldier should take what was offered. He was whistling when he rejoined his men.

He was pleased when, some time later, the pretty Mirella, shrouded in her gray cloak again, modestly, before the eyes of the soldiers, rode toward him and said timidly, "By your leave, sir, Master Gareth has reported that the bird is on its way back and we can ride on."

"I thank you, *damisela*," Bard said, and meticulously turned to Prince Beltran for orders.

"Give the order to ride," Beltran said indifferently, getting into his own saddle. When the men were all on the road again, Bard, who had watched them all ride past, his eyes alert for anything amiss in any one of them, a piece of equipment rusty, a horse that might be showing the first signs of having picked up a stone or throwing a shoe, rode on to join the three *leroni*.

"What word from your sentry bird, Master Gareth?"

The old *laranzu's* lined face looked taut and weary. He was chewing on a strip of dried meat as he rode. Melora, next to him, looked almost equally exhausted, her eyes reddened as if with crying, and she too was eating, cramming mouthfuls of dried fruit with honey between her smeared lips.

"The caravan lies about two days' ride yonder," Master Gareth said, pointing, "as the bird flies. There are four wagons; I counted two dozen men beside the wagon drovers, and I saw from their gear and horses, and the fashion of their swords, that they are Dry-town mercenaries."

Bard pursed his lips, for the Dry-town mercenaries were the fiercest fighters known, and he wondered how many of his men had ever fought against their curious curved swords and the daggers they used in lieu of shields to their other side.

"I will warn my men," he said. Among the picked men were several veterans of the wars against Ardcarran. It had been, he thought, a good instinct prompting him to choose men who had fought against the Dry towns. Perhaps they could give the others some advice on how to cope with that style of attack and defense.

And another thing. He glanced at Master Gareth and said with a faint frown, "You are an old campaigner, sir. I do not expect the women to know this, but I was taught it was unsoldierly to eat in the saddle except in the gravest emergencies."

He sensed the smile behind the old man's copper-colored moustaches. "It is clear you know little of *laran*, my lord; how it drains the body of strength. Ask your quartermasters; they will tell you they have been issued triple rations for us, and with good reason. I eat in my saddle so that I will have the strength not to fall out of it, sir, which would be far more disruptive than eating as I ride."

Much as Bard hated to be reproved, he tucked the lesson away, as he did all military matters, for when he would have need of it. But he scowled at Master Gareth and rode away with the briefest of courtesies.

Riding among the men, he dropped the word to each of them that they would be fighting, when it came time to capture the caravan, against Dry-town mercenaries; and he listened for some time to the reminiscences of an elderly campaign veteran who had ridden to war with his own father, Dom Rafael, years before Bard was born.

"There's a trick to fighting Dry-towners; you have to watch both hands, because they're as good with those damned little daggers they wear as any of us is with an honest sword, and when you have your sword engaged, they'll come at you with the other hand, and bury the dagger in your ribs; they're trained to fight with both hands."

51

"Be sure to warn the men against that, Larion," he said, and rode on, deep in thought. What an honor it would be to him, if he could capture the clingfire intact and take it back to King Ardrin! Like most soldiers, he hated clingfire, thinking it a coward's weapon, although he knew the strategic importance it could have in burning an enemy's objective. At least he could make sure it would not be hurled against the towers of Asturias! Or used to burn their woodlands!

They made camp that night over the borders of Asturias, in a small village which lay on the outskirts of the Plains of Valeron, a no-man's-land which owed allegiance to no king, and the villagers gathered sullenly around Bard's men as if they would have denied them leave to camp there. Then, looking at the three *leroni* in their gray robes, they scowled and withdrew.

"These lands," Bard said to Beltran, as they dismounted, "should be under allegiance to some lord; it is dangerous having them here, ready to shelter outlaws and bandits and perhaps open to some malcontent who could set himself up as king or baron here."

Beltran looked scornfully around, at the lean fields of scanty grain, the orchards of sparse trees of poor-quality nuts, some so scanty of leaves that the farmers had been reduced to growing mushrooms on them. "Who would bother? They can pay no tribute. It would be a poor lord indeed who would stoop to conquer such folk! What honor could an eagle have in battling an army of rabbithorns?"

"That's not the point," Bard said. "The point is, that some enemy to Asturias could come here and put them against us, so that we would have enemies on our very borders. I shall speak to my lord the king about it, and perhaps next spring he will send me here, to make certain that if they pay now no tribute to Asturias, at least they will pay none to Ridenow or Serrais! Will you speak with the men and make sure all is in good order, or shall I?"

"Oh, I'll do it," Beltran said with a yawn. "I suppose they must know that their prince cares for their welfare. I don't know much of soldiering, but there are enough veterans here who can tell me if there is anything amiss."

Bard smiled wryly as Beltran went off. Beltran knew little of military tactics, perhaps; but he knew enough of statecraft so that he wanted to win the men's liking and allegiance. A king ruled by the loyalty of his soldiers. Beltran was intelligent enough to know that Bard had the military command of this compaign; it could hardly be otherwise. But he was taking no chances that the men would think their prince indifferent to their personal welfare! Bard watched Prince Beltran go from man to man, making inquiries about their horses, their blankets and gear, their rations. The mess cooks were building fires and something was stewing in a cookpot. It smelled extremely good, after a long day of riding, with no more noon meal than a hunk of hard journey-bread and a handful of nuts!

Left for a moment without occupation, he found himself drifting in the direction of the place, somewhat apart, where the *leroni* had their camp. The memory of the eyes of the pretty Mirella was like a magnet; she could not have been much more than fifteen.

He found her making a fire. A tent had been pitched, and through the fabric he could see the hefty form of the *leronis* Melora moving around inside. He knelt beside her and said, "May I offer you fire, *damisela*?" He held out the oil-fed flint-striker which was simpler to use than an ordinary tinder-box.

She did not turn her eyes toward him. He could see the blush he found so adorable, flooding over her pale neck.

She said, "I thank you, my lord. But I do not need it." And indeed, as she gazed at the piled tinder, her hand laid on the silken bag at her throat where, he guessed, she kept the starstone, the tinder burst suddenly into flame.

He laid a light hand on her wrist and whispered, "If you would only look into my eyes, *damisela*, I too would burst into flame."

She turned a little toward him, and although she did not raise her eyes, he saw the curve of a faint smile at the corners of her mouth.

Suddenly a shadow fell across them.

"Mirella," said Master Gareth sternly, "get inside the tent and help Melora with your bedding."

Coloring, she rose quickly and hurried inside the tent. Bard rose too, angrily, facing the elderly sorcerer.

"With all respect, I warn you, *vai dom*," Master Gareth said, "do your wenching elsewhere. That one is not for you."

"What is it to you, old man? Is she your daughter? Or perhaps your light-o-love, or handfasted bride?" Bard demanded in a rage. "Or have you won her loyalty with your spells?"

Master Gareth shook his head, smiling. "None of those," he said, "but on campaign I am responsible for the women who ride with me, and they are not to be touched."

"Except, perhaps, by you?"

53

Again the silent headshake and the smile. "You know nothing of the world in which the *leroni* live, sir. Melora is my daughter; I will not have her touched by casual amours except at her own wish. As for Mirella, she is to be kept virgin for the Sight, and there is a curse on any who should take her, unless she resigns it of her free will. I warn you, avoid her."

Stung, red-faced, feeling like a scolded schoolboy before the level eyes of the old sorcerer, Bard bent his head and muttered, "I did not know."

"No, and that is why I am telling you," said the old man genially. "For Mirella was too shy to do so herself. She is not accustomed to men who cannot read her thoughts."

Bard cast a resentful look toward the tent. He thought it should have been the fat and ugly Melora, the old man's daughter, kept virgin for the Sight, for what man would want her unless he could first hide her face with a horse bag? Why the pretty Mirella? Master Gareth was still smiling amiably, but Bard had the uncanny sudden sense that the old man was actually reading his mind.

"Come, come, sir," said Master Gareth with a good-natured grin, "you are handfasted to the princess Carlina. It's not worthy of you to look to a simple *leronis*. Lie alone tonight, and perhaps you will dream of the high-born woman who waits at home for you. After all, you can't have *every* woman on whom you cast your roving eyes. Don't show such ugly temper!"

Bard ripped out a curse and turned away. He knew enough not to anger a *laranzu*, on whom the fate of the campaign might rest, but the old man's voice, as if he spoke to the greenest of boys, infuriated him. What business was it of Master Gareth's?

The servant who rode to attend on the officers had made a small third camp for them, apart from the others. Bard went to taste the food cooked for the men—he had learned never to eat his own meal until horses and men were safely settled for the night—and to inspect the picket lines of the horses, then came back to find Beltran awaiting him.

"You look ill-tempered, Bard. What ails you?"

"Damned old bird of prey," Bard growled. "Afraid I should touch his precious maiden *leroni*, when I did no more than offer the young one a bit of tinder!"

Beltran chuckled. "Well, it's a compliment, Bard. He knows you have a way with the women! Your reputation, after all, has simply preceded you, that is all, and he is afraid

54

no maiden could resist you, nor retain her maidenhood in your presence!"

Put like that, Bard began to recover a little of his self-esteem, to feel less like a reprimanded schoolboy.

"As for me," Beltran said, "I feel it's wrong to bring women on campaign—good women, that is. I suppose any army should have camp followers, though I've no taste for them myself. If I must have women about, I prefer the kind who look as if they washed more often than when they got caught out of doors during the fall rains! But good women with a campaign are a temptation to the unchaste, and an annoyance to the chaste whose mind is on their business of fighting!"

Bard nodded, admitting the justice of what Beltran said.

"And what's more, if they're available, the men will fight over 'em; and if they're not, they'll moon about over them," he said.

Beltran said, "Should the day come when I command my father's armies, I will forbid any *leronis* to ride with the army; there are *laranzu'in* enough, and myself I think men better at that kind of skill; women are too squeamish and have no place with an army, no more than Carlina or one of our baby brothers! How old is your little brother now?"

"He must be eight now," Bard said. "Nine at midwinter. I wonder if he has forgotten me? I have not been home since my father sent me here for fostering."

Beltran patted his shoulder in sympathy. He said, "Well, well, no doubt you can have leave to go home before midwinter."

"If the fighting in Hammerfell is over before the snow closes the roads," Bard said, "I will do so. My foster mother does not love me, but she cannot keep me from home. It would be good to see if Alaric still holds me in affection." To himself he thought that perhaps he would ask his father to come to his wedding. It was not every one of the king's fosterlings who would be joined in *catenas* marriage by King Ardrin himself!

They sat late talking, and when at last they slept, Bard was well content. He thought briefly and with regret of the pretty Mirella, but after all, what Master Gareth had said was true: he had Carlina, and soon enough they would be married. Beltran was right, after all. Virtuous women had no place with the king's armies.

The next morning, after a brief conference with Master

Gareth and Beltran, they turned their steps toward the ford of Moray's Mills. No one now alive knew who Moray might have been, though stories in the countryside made him everything from a giant to a dragon keeper: but there was still a ruined mill near the ford, and a little upstream from it another mill still in operation. A toll gate closed the road, and as Bard's men came toward it, the toll-keeper, a fat and graying man, came out to say, "By order of the Lord of Dalereuth, this road is closed, my lords. I have sworn not to open for anyone who does not pay him tribute, or have his safe-conduct within his borders."

"Now, by all of Zandru's hells—" Bard began, but Prince Beltran rode forward, looming over the little man in his miller's apron.

"I am very willing to pay a head tax to the Lord of Dalereuth." he said. "I am sure he would appreciate the head of an insolent fellow like you. Rannvil—" he gestured, and one of the horsemen drew his sword. "Open the gates, man; don't be a fool."

The toll-keeper, his teeth chattering, went to the mechanism that trundled the great toll gate aside. Beltran contemptuously flung the man a few coins. "Here's your tribute. But if this gate is barred against us when we come back, take my word for it, I'll have my men tear it out of the ground and set your head on top of it to scare away crows!"

As they passed through, Bard heard the man grumbling and leaned down from his horse to grab him by the shoulder.

"Whatever you said, say it aloud to our faces, you!"

The man looked up, his jaw set and wrathful. He said, "I have no part in the quarrels of my betters, *vai dom*. Why should I suffer because you noblemen can't keep your borders? All I care about is running my mill. But you won't come back this way, or at all. I have nothing to do with what waits for you at the ford yonder. Now, if you wish, win honor by killing an unarmed man!"

Bard let him go and straightened up. He said, "Kill you? Why? Thanks for your warning; you've been well paid." He watched the man go off toward his mill, and although he had been a soldier since his fourteenth year, he frowned and suddenly wondered why it should be this way. Why should every nobleman who chose demand that he be sovereign over his own land? That only made more work for mercenaries.

Perhaps, he thought, *all this land should be under one rule, with peace at the borders, from the Hellers to the sea . . . and little men like this could grow their crops and turn their mills in peace . . . and I could live on the estates the king has given me, with Carlina. . . .*

But there was no leisure to think of that now. He called urgently to Master Gareth, raising his hand to halt the men.

"I have had a warning," he said, "that something waits for us at that ford; but I see nothing. Does your bird give you warning, or has either of your women seen anything by their spells?"

Master Gareth beckoned to Mirella, shrouded in her cloak, and spoke to her, softly. She took her starstone from about her throat and gazed into it.

After a moment she said, in a low, neutral voice, "There is neither man nor beast at the ford to wait for us; but there is darkness there, and a barrier we may not be able to pass. We must go with great care, kinsman."

Master Gareth raised his eyes and met Bard's. He said, "She has the Sight; if there is a darkness that she cannot penetrate, we must indeed go with the greatest of care, sir."

But the ford lay calm and peaceful in the sunlight, shallow ripples swirling with glints of crimson. Bard frowned, trying to assess what lay before them. He could see nothing, no signs of ambush, no twig or branch stirring on the far side of the ford, where a path led up between overgrown trees. That would, indeed, be a good place for ambush.

"If you cannot see beyond the ford by sorcery or the Sight," he said, "can the sentry bird pass and see if there is any ambush hidden beyond?"

Master Gareth nodded. "To be sure; the bird is only a beast and has nothing to do with sorcery or the magic of the trained mind. The only magic about the bird is the skill Melora and I have to remain in rapport with the creature. Melora," he called, "child, let the sentry bird go."

Bard watched as the fierce bird rose high over the ford, circling. After a time, Master Gareth shook himself, waked, beckoned to Melora, who reached out her hand and took the bird as it came circling back, stroking its feathers and feeding it tidbits before slipping the hood over its head. Master Gareth said, "There is no one, man or beast, hidden beyond the ford; no living creature for many leagues except a girl herding a flock of rabbithorns. Whatever waits here at the ford, *vai dom*, it is not an ambush of armed men."

Bard and Beltran exchanged glances. Finally Beltran said, "We cannot wait here all day for a terror no one can see. I think we must ride to the ford; but Master Gareth, stay back, for we must keep you in reserve if you are needed. I have known sorcerers to set a forest or a field ablaze in the path of armies on the march; and I suppose there could be something like that beyond the ford. We must be wary of that. Bard, will you order the men to ride?"

Bard's skin prickled. He had had this reaction once or twice before in the presence of *laran*; he had little enough of it himself, but somehow he could scent it. There was, he knew, a talent which could sniff out the use of *laran*; perhaps if he had been trained in its use, he would have had that. It might have been useful after all. He had always thought that Geremy, training as *a laranzu,* was somehow less a man, less a soldier, than Beltran and himself. Now, watching Master Gareth, he began to realize that this work might have its own dangers and terrors, even though a *laranzu* rode unarmed into battle. *That, in itself, might be frightening enough,* Bard thought, laying his hand for reassurance on his sword.

He turned to the men and commanded, "Count off by fours!" He could not order any man to be first to ride into some unknown terror. When they had done so, he said, "Group two, ride forward," and took lead of them.

His skin prickled again as he rode forward, and his horse tossed her head in protest as she set a fastidious foot within the ford; but the water was quiet, and he gave the order.

"Ride, slowly, keep together!"

Above them, at the very edge of his vision, he saw a flicker of motion. He thought Master Gareth had recalled the sentry bird. . . . A quick glance showed him that Melora's bird sat hooded and quiet, on the woman's saddle. *So, they were being watched from afar. Was there any defense against that?*

They were in the center of the ford now, the water at its deepest swirling around the hocks of the horses; thigh-deep on a tall man. One of his soldiers said, "There's nothing here, sir. We can call the others to come."

Bard shook his head. Inwardly he felt that prickling that warned of danger, growing, so that he clamped his teeth, wondering if he would spew up his breakfast like a breeding woman. . . .

He heard Master Gareth shouting, wheeled his horse in midstream. "Back," he yelled. "Get back—"

The water swirled upward, rising around his horses' withers, and suddenly the peaceful ford was a raging, foaming torrent, a racing undertow sucking, pulling. He felt his horse stumble under him as if he had ridden into a mountain stream swollen by spring thaw into furious rapids. *Witch waters!* He tugged at the reins, trying to soothe his neighing

58

plunging horse, hold her steady, against the threat of being swept away downstream. Around him every one of the group was struggling with horses maddened with fear at the peaceful water suddenly gone wild. Cursing, fighting his terrified horse, Bard managed to get her under control, urge her back toward the water's edge. He saw one of his men slip from his saddle, go down into the torrent. Another horse stumbled, and Bard reached over and grabbed the rein, trying to hold his own horse with one hand.

"Hold them! In the name of all the gods, hold them! Back to the bank!" he shouted. "Keep together!"

The surprise was the worst; his horse was used to mountain streams and fords. Warned in advance, he could perhaps have held her against this. Gripping with his knees, urging her carefully against the water that now raced up to her neck, he managed to get her back to dry land, stood grabbing the bridles of the others as they came up. One horse was down and had broken a leg; it lay kicking, screaming like a woman in the torrent, until it drowned. Bard swore, his throat tight. The poor creature had never harmed any living thing, and it had died a terrible death. Of the rider there was no sign. Another horse had gone down, and its rider, leaping off into the water, had managed to get it up, limping, and drag it back to the shore; he went down himself and floundered, half-drowned, until one of the men, leaping down the bank, grabbed him and hauled him out.

Bard saw the last man out of the water; then cried out in awe and dismay. For once again the water lay calm and shallow before them, the peaceful, normal ford of Moray's Mill.

So that was what the little man had meant. . . .

Grimly, they took stock of their losses. The horse that had broken a leg lay motionless now, lifeless; and of his rider there was no sign whatever. Either he lay dead beneath the waters of the ford or had been swept away on the torrent and his body would surface far downstream. Another man had gotten free but his horse was lamed and useless; still a third horse had thrown its rider and gotten to shore, but the man lay senseless, his body washing up and down at the edge of the water. Bard motioned to one of his fellows to go and drag him to dry land, ran his fingers briefly across the gaping wound in the skull. It was likely he would never waken.

Bard blessed whatever precognitive warning had prompted him to send only a quarter of the men into the stream. At that rate they would have lost half a dozen men, instead of two men and horses, and perhaps had more horses lamed or

59

damaged. But he beckoned to Master Gareth and his voice was grim.

"So this is what lay in the darkness your girl could not read!"

The man shook his head, sighing. "I am sorry, *vai dom*. . . . We are psychics, not sorcerers, and our powers are not infinite. May I venture to say in our defense that without us your men would have ridden completely unwarned into the ford?"

"True," Bard admitted, "but now what do we do? If the ford is spelled against us—have we sprung the trap, or will it rise again the moment we set foot within it?"

"I cannot say, my lord. But perhaps Mirella's Sight will tell us," he said, beckoning her forward. He spoke in a low voice, and again the girl gazed into her starstone, finally saying in her wandering, neutral, drugged spell-voice, "I can see nothing . . . there is a darkness on the water. . . ."

Bard swore, morosely. The spell was still there against them, then. He said to Beltran, "Do you think we can take the ford now we are warned?"

Beltran said, "Perhaps; if the men know what they must face, they are picked men and good riders, all of them. But Master Gareth, and the *leroni*, probably cannot pass, and certainly the one who rides on a donkey cannot. . . ."

Master Gareth said, "We are trained *leroni*, sir; we take what risks the army takes, and my daughter and my foster daughter go where I go. They are not afraid."

"It is not their courage I am doubting," Bard said impatiently. "It is their skill as horsewomen. Besides, that little donkey would be drowned at the first wave. I don't want to see any woman killed out of hand, but we will need you when battle is joined, too. And before we do anything, can you keep us from being spied on?" He gestured up impatiently at the sentry bird wheeling above them.

"I would do what I can, sir, but I think our spells will be needed more against the witch-waters of the ford," Master Gareth said.

Bard nodded, thinking about that. As a commander made the best use of his fighting men, so, he was beginning to know, he must hoard the strength of his army's *leroni* and use them to best advantage.

Did King Ardrin give me this command so that I might have a chance to command not fighting men alone, but sorcerers? Even in the press of decisions, he thought with excitement that this meant well for his future. *If . . .* he thought quickly sobering, *he could carry off this apparently simple commission without losing all his men at the witched ford!*

"Master Gareth, this is the province of your special knowledge. What do you recommend to me?"

"We can try to set a counter-spell on the waters, sir. I cannot guarantee—I do not know who we are facing or what their powers may be—but we will do our best to quiet the waters. We have this in our favor; to meddle this way with nature takes tremendous power, and they cannot keep it up for very long. Nature takes always the way toward the normal again; the water seeks its proper flow, and so we have the force of natural water working for us, while they must fight *against* that natural force. So our counter-spell should not be too difficult."

"All the gods grant you are right," Bard said, "but still, I will warn the men to be prepared for rapids." He rode among them, speaking to first one and then the other, telling the man whose horse had been lamed to take the one whose rider had been killed. Then he moved close to Beltran, saying, "Ride by me, foster brother; I don't want to face my lord and king if I let you be killed in the rapids! If you die in battle, I suppose he could face it; but I will not be responsible otherwise!"

Beltran laughed. "Do you think you ride so much better than I do, Bard? I don't! I think you overstep your authority—I, not you, command this expedition!" But he said it laughing, and Bard shrugged.

"As you will, Beltran; but in God's name, mind what you are about. My horse is bigger and heavier than yours, because it takes a big horse to carry weight like mine, and I had all I could do to keep my seat!"

He wheeled and rode forward to Master Gareth. "There is no way mistress Melora can cross the ford on that little donkey; certainly not if your spells fail. Can she sit a horse?"

Master Gareth said, "I am her father, not her mentor or the master of her destiny; why not ask the lady herself?"

Bard set his jaw. "I am not given to asking women questions when there is a man to command them. But if you insist—well, *damisela*, can you ride? If you can, your father will take mistress Mirella before him on his horse, since she rides lighter than you, and you shall ride her horse, which looks steady enough."

"I would rather trust to my father's spells and my own," Melora said firmly. "Do you think I will abandon my poor little donkey to drown?"

"Oh, hell and damnation, woman," Bard burst out. "If you

61

can manage to sit on a horse, one of my men will lead your donkey. I suppose the beast can swim!"

"You must do your best to ride, Melora," Master Gareth said. "And Whitefur must make shift to swim for himself. I am sure he can fend for himself in the ford better than you can. Mirella, my child, let Melora have your horse and climb up behind me on my saddle."

She scrambled up nimbly enough, although the watching men had a glimpse of long shapely legs in striped red and blue stockings, as she clambered up behind the elderly *laranzu* and settled herself, smoothing down her skirts, and clinging to his waist. Bard went himself to help lift the plump and ungainly Melora into the saddle of the other girl's horse. She sat a horse, he told himself uncharitably, like a sack of meal dumped into a saddle.

"Sit a bit straighter, I implore you, *vai leronis*, and hold more carefully to the reins," he said, then sighed. "I think perhaps I had better ride at your side and lead your horse."

"That would be good of you," Master Gareth said, "for we will need to concentrate on setting the counter-spell; and I would take it as a kindness, too, if one of your men can lead Melora's donkey, for she will be afraid for him."

One of the veterans burst out, laughing, "Mistress Melora, if you can set a spell to quiet these waters, I will myself carry your little donkey across my saddle like a baby!"

She giggled. Fat and ungainly as she was, she had a sweet voice and a lovely laugh. "I am afraid that would frighten him worse than the rapids, sir. I think, if you will lead him, he can manage somehow to swim, after your horse's tail."

The veteran brought a tie-rope and secured the bridle of the donkey to his own bridle. Bard took Melora's rein, thinking what a pity it was that it was not the pretty Mirella; and heard again Melora's sweet giggle. He wondered, uneasily, if she could read his mind, and cut off the thought. This was no time for thinking about women, not with a spelled ford to cross and a battle coming up!

"For the love of all the gods, Master Gareth, set your counter-spell."

Melora's heavy figure was motionless on her horse. The look of strangeness, of concentration, settled down over Master Gareth's face. Mirella's hood slid down over her face so that nothing was visible but her small chin. Bard watched the three *leroni*, feeling the prickling in his spine that meant *laran* was powerful somewhere near. . . . How could he tell, what was it?

Silently, feeling a curious reluctance to shatter the scary silence by a word or a shout, Bard beckoned the men forward. Still weighted by that sense of prickling intensity in the air, he twitched at his horse's rein and urged the animal forward. The mare tossed her head and whickered uneasily, remembering what had happened when she had set foot in the ford before.

"Easy. Easy, girl," he urged in a low voice, thinking, *I don't blame her at all, I feel the same way. . . .* But he was a reasoning human, not a brute beast, and he would not give way to blind, unreasoning fear. Urged on by voice and hands, the mare set foot into the ford, and Bard beckoned to the men behind him.

Nothing happened . . . but then, nothing had happened, before, until they were in midstream. Bard urged the horse on, holding to Melora's rein, half-turned in his saddle. Behind him Master Gareth rode, Mirella clinging to his waist, and behind him, the men of the party, Prince Beltran bringing up the rear.

They were all in the water now, and Bard felt his skin tighten on his face. If the spell was working, it would strike them now, sweep down on them like a torrent. He braced himself in his saddle, feeling the prickle, prickle, prickle that was his personal awareness of *laran* at work, growing in strength as if he could almost see the flare and interplay between the spell set on the ford and the counter-spell; his horse seemed to step through a tangle of thick weed although there was nothing tangible there . . .

Then, suddenly, it was gone; just gone, vanished, the ford running silent and innocent, just water again. Bard let out his breath and dug his heels into his mare's side. The first riders were partway up the far bank by now, and he held his mount there in midstream, watching them ride past and up the other side of the stream.

For now, at least, their *leroni* had out-spelled the wizards set against them.

So far, on this campaign, the weather had held fine. But now, as the day waned, the sky grew dark with thickening clouds and toward evening snow began to fall, softly, but with persistence; first a few thick, clumped, wet flakes at a time, then thick and fine and hard, coming down and down and down with idiot persistence. Melora, back on her donkey, swaddled herself in her gray cloak and wrapped a blanket over her head. The soldiers, one by one, got out scarves and

63

mufflers and thick hoods, and rode, sullen and glowering. Bard knew what they were thinking. By tradition, war was a summer business, and in winter, all but the mad, or the desperate, kept to their own firesides. There was a certain amount of danger in a winter campaign. The men might say, and with some justice, that while they owed service to King Ardrin, this went beyond what was customary and right, and riding like this into a snowstorm which might easily turn into a blizzard in intensity was not customary and therefore the king had no right to ask it of them. How could he command their loyalty? For the first time he wished he were not in command here, but that he was riding north to Hammerfell at King Ardrin's right hand, his sovereign's banner bearer. The king could command loyalty from his troops, use his personal influence and power to demand loyalty beyond custom. He could make the men promises, and make those promises good. Bard was painfully aware that he was only seventeen years old; that he was only the king's bastard nephew and fosterling; that he had been promoted over the heads of many seasoned officers. There were probably men in the ranks, even among these picked men he had chosen for this campaign, who might be waiting to see him come to grief; to make some dreadful mistake that he could never recoup. Had the king given him this command only that he might overstep his powers, see himself as the green and unseasoned warrior that he was?

Despite his triumph and promotion on the field of Snow Glen, he was only a boy. Could he carry through this mission at all? Was the king hoping he would fail, so that he could deny him Carlina? What would lie ahead for him if he failed? Would he be demoted, sent home in disgrace?

He rode ahead to join Master Gareth, who had wrapped his lower face in a thick, red, knitted muffler under the gray sorcerer's cape. He said with asperity, "Can't you do anything about this weather? Is this a blizzard coming up, or only a snow flurry?"

"You ask too much of my powers, sir," said the older man. "I am a *laranzu*, not a god; the weather is not mine to command." A touch of humor wrinkled up one corner of his face in a wry smile. "Believe me, Master Bard, if I had command over the weather, I would use it to my own advantage. I am as cold as you, and as blinded by snow, and my bones are older and feel the cold more."

Bard said, hating to confess his own inadequacy, "The men are grumbling, and I am a little afraid of mutiny. A winter

64

campaign—while the weather held fine, they did not care. But now—"

Master Gareth nodded. "I can see that. Well, I will try to see how far this storm extends, and if we will ride out of it soon; although weather magic is not my special gift. Only one of his majesty's *laranzu'in* has that, and Master Robyl rode north to Hammerfell with the king; he felt he would be needed more, on the northern border of the Hellers where the snows are fiercer. But I will do my best."

And as Bard turned away, he added, "Cheer up, sir. The snow may make it hard for us to ride, but not nearly as hard as for the caravan with the clingfire; they have all those carts and wagons to push along through the snow, and if it gets too deep they won't be able to move at all."

Bard realized that he should have thought of that. Snow would immobilize the carts and wagons of the caravan, while the light horsemen of the picked group were still well able to ride and to fight. Furthermore, if it was true that Dry-town mercenaries had been hired to escort the caravan, they were accustomed to warmer weather, and the snow would confuse them. He rode among the men, listening to their grumblings and protests, and reminded them of this. Even though the snow continued to fall, and even grew heavier, that thought seemed to cheer them a little.

However, the clouds and falling snow grew ever thicker, and after a word with Beltran, they called a halt early. Nothing was to be gained by forcing grumbling men to press on through the same snow that would immobilize their prey. Riding through the snow, the men were weary and disheartened, and some of them would have eaten a few bites of cold food and rolled into their blankets at once, but Bard insisted that fires must be lighted and hot food cooked, knowing this would do more for the men's morale than anything else. With fires lighted on stone slabs and blazing away, fed by the fallen tree branches of an abandoned orchard—hit by the nut blight of a few seasons ago—the camp looked cheerful, and one of the men brought out a small drone-pipe and began to play, mournful old laments older than the world. The young women slept in their shared tent, but Master Gareth joined the men around the fire, and after a time, though he protested that he was neither minstrel nor bard, consented to tell them the tale of the last dragon. Bard sat beside Beltran in the shadows of the fire, chewing on dried fruit and listening to the story of how the last dragon had been slain by one of the Hastur kin, and how, sensing with

65

the *laran* of beasts that this last of his folk was dead, every beast and bird within the Hundred Kingdoms had set up a wail, a keen, even the banshees joining in the lament for the last of the wise serpents . . . and the son of Hastur himself, standing beside the corpse of the last dragon on Darkover, had vowed never again to hunt for any living thing for sport. When Master Gareth finished his tale, the men applauded and begged for more, but he shook his head, saying that he was an old man and had been riding all day, and that he was away to his blankets.

Soon the camp was dark and silent; only the small red eye of the fire, covered with green branches against the morning's need for hot porridge, sizzled and watched from its cover. All around the fire dark triangles marked where the men lay in their blankets, beneath the waterproof sheets, stretched up at an angle, to protect them from the still falling snow; miniature open half-tents pitched on a forked stick apiece, each with two or three or four men beneath, huddled together and sharing blankets and body warmth. Beltran lay at Bard's side, looking curiously small and boyish, but Bard lay awake, staring at the fire and the white-silver streaks of snow that made pale arrows across the light. Somewhere, not far from them, the enemy lay immobilized, heavy carts mired in snow, pack beasts floundering.

At his side Beltran said softly, "I wish Geremy were with us, foster brother."

Bard laughed almost noiselessly. "So did I, at first. Now I'm not so sure. Perhaps two green boys in command are enough, and we are well off to have Master Gareth's experience and wisdom; while Geremy as an untried *laranzu* rides with your father who is well skilled in command. . . . Perhaps he thought if we three went together it would seem too much like one of the hunting trips we used to ride on, the three of us, when we were only lads. . . ."

"I remember," Beltran said, "when we three were younger and we rode out like this. Lying together and looking into the fire and talking of the days when we would be men, and on campaign together, in command, in real war and not our mock battles against *chervine* herds. . . . Do you remember, Bard?"

Bard smiled in the dark. "I remember. What mighty campaigns and wars we planned, how we would subdue all this countryside from the Hellers to the shores of Carthon, and beyond the seas. . . . Well, this much has come true of what we planned, that we are all on campaign, and at war, just as we said when we were boys who hardly knew which end of a sword to take hold by. . . ."

"And now Geremy is *a laranzu* riding with the king, and he thinks only of Ginevra, and you are the king's banner bearer, promoted in battle, and handfasted to Carlina, and I—" Prince Beltran sighed in the darkness. "Well, no doubt, one day I will know what it is that I want from my life, or if I do not, my father and king will tell me what it is that I will have."

"Oh, you," Bard said, laughing, "some day the throne of Asturias will be yours."

"That is no laughing matter," Beltran said, and he sounded somber. "To know that I will come to power only over my father's grave and by his death. I love my father, Bard, and yet at times I think I shall go mad if I must stand at his footstool and wait for something real to do. . . . I cannot even go forth out of the kingdom and seek adventure, as any other subject is free to do." Bard felt the younger lad shiver. "I am so cold, foster brother."

For a moment Beltran seemed, to Bard, no older than the little brother who had clung to his neck and wept when he went away to the king's house. Awkwardly, he patted Beltran's shoulder in the dark. "Here, have some more of the blanket, I don't feel the cold as badly as you do, I never did. Try to sleep. Tomorrow, perhaps, we'll have a fight on our hands, a real fight, not one of the mock battles we used to take so much pleasure in, and we must be ready for it."

"I'm afraid, Bard. I'm always afraid. Why are you and Geremy never afraid?"

Bard snorted brief laughter. "What makes you think we're not afraid? I don't know about Geremy, but I was afraid enough to wet my breeches like a babe, and no doubt I'll be so again, Only I haven't time to talk about it when it's happening, and no wish to do so when it isn't. Don't worry, foster brother. You did well enough at Snow Glens, I remember."

"Then why did my father promote you on the field, and not me?"

Bard half sat up in the darkness and stared at him. He said, "Is that flea still biting you? Beltran, my friend, your father knows you have all you need already. You are his son and his legitimate heir, you ride at his side, you are already acknowledged just one breath away from the throne. He promoted me because I was his fosterling, and a bastard. Before he could set me over his men, to command them, he had to make me somebody he could legitimately promote, which he could not do without acknowledging me specially. Promoting me was only sharpening a tool he wished to use, no more, not a mark of his love or special regard! By the cold whirlwind of Zandru's third hell, I know it if you don't! Are you fool enough to be jealous of me, Beltran?"

"No," Beltran said slowly in the dark, "No, I suppose not, foster brother." And after a time, hearing Beltran's silent breathing in the dark, Bard slept.

Chapter Four

In the morning it was still snowing, and the sky was so dark that Bard's heart sank as he watched the men going glumly about the business of caring for their horses, cooking up a great pot of porridge, making ready and saddling up to ride. He heard muttering among the men to the effect that King Ardrin had no right to send them out in winter, that this campaign was the work of his fosterling, who didn't know what was proper and right; who ever heard of a campaign like this with winter coming on?

"Come on, lads," Bard urged. "If the Dry-towners can ride in weather like this, are we going to stand back and let them bring clingfire to hurl against our villages and our families?"

"Dry-towners are likely to do anything," one of the men grumbled. "Next thing, they'll be holding harvest in springtime! War is a business for the summertime!"

"And because they believe we will stay snug at home, they think it safe to strike at us," Bard argued. "Do you want to stay home and let them attack?"

"Yes, why not stay home and let them come to us? Defending our homes against attack's one thing," a burly veteran growled, "but going out looking for trouble, that's something else!"

But, though there was grumbling and muttering, there was no open mutiny or rebellious behavior. Beltran was pale and silent, and Bard, remembering their talk last night, realized that the youngster was terrified. It was easy to think of Beltran as younger than himself, although in solid fact there was less than half a year between them; Bard had always been so much the larger of the foster brothers, the strongest, always best at swordplay and wrestling and hunting, their unquestioned leader.

So he made occasion to speak to Beltran about his fears that the men would mutiny, and asked Beltran to go among them and try to sound out their mood as they rode.

"You are their prince, and you represent the will of their king. A time might come when they would not obey me, but they would not be willing, I think, to defy their king's own son," he suggested guilefully, and Beltran, looking at Bard with a sullen scowl—after all, should he take orders from Bard?—finally nodded and drew back to ride alongside first one, then another of the men, asking questions, talking to one after the other. Bard watched, thinking that perhaps in this task Beltran had put aside his fears—and perhaps that touch of personal concern from their prince had quieted the men's rebelliousness.

And still the snow continued to fall. It was up, now, to the fetlocks of the horses, and Bard began seriously to worry about whether the horses could get through. He asked Master Gareth to send out the sentry birds, but received the halfway expected answer that they would not fly in such weather.

"Sensible birds," Bard grumbled. "I wish I needn't! Well, is there any way to find out how far from us the caravan is traveling, and whether we will come up with them today?"

Master Gareth said, "I will ask Mirella; this is why she is with us, so that she can use the Sight."

Bard watched as Mirella, seated on her horse amid the falling snow, her hair showing bright copper through the thickly salted flakes on her braids, sat staring into her crystal. The light reflected, faintly blue, on her face; the only light, it seemed, anywhere in that dismal day, was the blue light and the flame of her coppery hair. She was muffled in cloak and shawls, but they could not hide the slender grace of her body, and Bard found himself, once again, letting his mind linger on her beauty. She was, doubtless, the most beautiful young girl he had even seen; next to her Carlina was a pale stick. Yet Mirella was completely beyond his reach, sacrosanct, a *leronis*, vowed virgin for the Sight, and there were uncanny warning tales about what could befall the manhood of any man who would assail the virginity of a *leronis* against her will. He told himself that he could, with his gift, assure himself that it would *not* be against her will, that he could force her to come to his bed willingly. . . .

But that would make an enemy of Master Gareth. Damn, there were enough willing women in this world, and he was handfasted to a princess, and anyway this was no time to be thinking of women at all!

Mirella sighed and opened her eyes, the blue light dimming from her face, and her glance rested on him, shy, serious, so direct that Bard wondered, a little abashed, if she could read what he had been thinking.

Instead she only said, in her still neutral voice, "They are not far from us, *vai dom*. Three hours' ride over that ridge yonder—" She pointed, but the ridge she spoke of was invisible in the falling snow. "They have encamped because the snow has fallen deeper there, and thicker, and their carts cannot move. They are up to the hubs of the wheels, and the draft animals cannot move. One broke a leg in the harness and the others tried to stampede and nearly kicked themselves to death. If we ride on as we are going now, we will come upon them soon after midday."

Bard rode to relay this news to his men, and found them grim, not at all pleased by the news.

"That means we have to fight in deep snow, and what do we do with the caravan when we have captured it, if their pack beasts are not working?" one old veteran inquired sourly. "I suggest we make camp here and wait for a thaw, when we can take it easier. If they're unable to move, they'll wait there for us!"

"We'd run out of food and fodder for the horses," Bard said, "and there's an advantage to doing battle when *we* choose. Come on, let's get there as soon as we can!"

They rode on, the snow continuing to fall. Bard watched the gray-cloaked *leroni*, frowning. Finally he rode forward and asked Master Gareth, "How shall we protect the women in battle, sir? We cannot spare a man to guard them."

"I said it before," Master Gareth said. "These women are skilled *leroni*; they are capable of looking after themselves. Melora has been in battle before this, and although Mirella has not, I have no fear for her."

"But these men we shall fight are accompanied by Dry-town mercenaries," Bard said. "And if your daughter and foster daughter are taken prisoner—*leroni* or no—they will be dragged in chains to be sold in a Daillon brothel."

Melora, riding near them on her ambling donkey, said quietly, "Have no fear for us, *vai dom*." She put her hand on the small dagger she wore at her waist, under the cloak. "My sister and I will not fall into Dry-town hands alive."

The calm, matter-of-fact way she spoke made a cold shudder run up Bard's spine. Curiously, the note was one of kinship. He, too, had known that he faced death or worse in battle, and had come early to that knowledge, and the note in Melora's voice made him think of his own early battles. He found himself grinning at her, a tight, spontaneous grin. He said, "The Goddess forbid that it should come to that, *damisela*. But I did not know there were women capable of such decisions, or courage in war."

"It is not courage," Melora said, in her sweet voice. "It is only that I fear the chains and brothels of the Dry towns more than I fear death. Death, I have been taught, is a gateway to another and better life; and life would have no sweetness for me as a chained whore in Daillon. And my dagger is very sharp, so I could end my life very swiftly and without much pain—I am, I think, rather afraid of pain, but not of death."

"Why," he said, reining in his horse so that he rode beside her donkey, "I should use you to hearten my men, mistress Melora. I did not know women were capable of such courage." He found himself wondering if Carlina would be able to talk this way when she rode into battle. He did not know. He had never thought to ask her.

It occurred to Bard that he had known many women intimately, since his fifteenth year. And yet it seemed to him, suddenly, that he really knew very little about what women were like. He had known their bodies, yes, but nothing of the rest of them; it had not occurred to him that any woman could be interesting to him, except for coupling with them.

And yet, he remembered, when they were all children, he had talked with Carlina as freely as he had talked with his foster brothers, had spent time with her; he had known her favorite foods, the colors of frocks and ribbons she liked best to wear, knew her fear of owls and of nightflyers, her dislike of nut porridge and seed cake, her dislike of pink frocks and shoes with over-high heels, how bored she became at sitting for long hours over her sewing; he had comforted her for the callouses on her fingers as she learned to play the *rryl* and the tall harp, and helped her with her lessons.

And yet, when he had become a man, and begun thinking of women in terms of lust, he had grown away from Carlina; he did not know what kind of woman the child had become. What now seemed worse to him, he had not really cared; he had thought of her mostly as his promised wife. He had, lately, thought a great deal of bedding her; but somehow it had never occurred to him to talk with her, just talk with her as he was doing with this odd, soft-spoken, unbeautiful *leronis*.

It was disquieting; he had no particular interest in bedding this woman. In fact, the thought rather repelled him, she was so fat and so ungainly and so plain; she was one of the few women he had met who did not stir his manhood even slightly. Yet he wanted to go on talking with her; he felt closer to her, in a strange way, than he had felt in many years to anyone else except his foster brothers. He looked ahead of them, to where Mirella rode, silent and distant, and bewitchingly pretty, and as before, he felt the sudden stir of desire, and then he looked back at the solidly built, ungainly Melora, slumped on her donkey like, again the uncharitable comparison, a sack of grain. Why, he wondered, could not the beautiful Mirella also be soft-voiced and warm and friendly like this, why could she not ride at his side and look into his eyes with such sympathetic interest? Melora's hair was almost the same flame color as Mirella's; and behind her moon-faced chubby cheeks there was some faint hint of the same delicate bone structure. He said, "Mistress Mirella—you and she are very similar; is Mirella your sister or half-sister?"

"No," she said, "but we are kinswomen; her mother is my eldest sister. But I have another sister who is a *leronis* as well—all of us are gifted with *laran*. Are you not the son of Dom Rafael di Asturien? Why, then, my youngest sister Melisendra is one of your foster mother's women; she went to serve Domna Jerana three seasons ago. Have you never seen her there?"

"I have not been home for many years," Bard said shortly.

"Ah, that is sad," she said with warm sympathy, but Bard did not want to pursue that topic.

He said, "Have you been in battle before this, that you are so calm and not afraid?"

"Why, yes, I was beside my father at the battle of Snow Glen, with the sentry birds. I saw you given the king's banner."

"I did not know there were women there," he said, "not even among the *leroni*."

"But I saw you," she said. "Nor was I the only woman there. There was a detachment of Renunciates, the sworn Sisterhood of the Sword, and they, too, fought valiantly; had they been men, they would have won honor and the king's praise, even as you did. When the men broke through with axes on the southern flank, they held their shield-line against them until horsemen under Captain Syrtis could come to their aid. Two of them were killed, and one lost a hand; but they held that flank where they were stationed."

Bard grimaced. "I have heard of the Renunciates; I did not know King Ardrin would stoop to use them in battle! It is

73

bad enough that they share fire-watch with men. I do not think a woman's place is on the field of war!"

"Nor do I," Melora said. "But then, I do not think a man's place is on the field of war either; nor does my father. He would rather abide at home, playing the lute and the *rryl*, and using our starstones to heal sickness and bring metals from under the earth. But while there is war, we must even fight as our lord and king wills it, Master Bard."

Bard smiled genially and said, "Women don't understand these things. War is a man's business, and men are never happier than when they are fighting, I think; but women should be able to stay at home and make songs and heal our wounds."

"Do you truly think a man's business is fighting?" Melora asked. "Well, I do not, and I hope that a day may come when men are as free from war as you would like to have all women."

"I am a soldier, *damisela*," Bard said. "In a world of womanly peace I would have no place and no occupation. But if you love peace so well, why do you not leave war to men, who enjoy it?"

"Because," she said with spirit, "I do not know many men who truly enjoy it!"

"I do, *damisela*."

"Do you truly? Or is it only that you have never had much opportunity for anything else?" Melora asked. "There was a day when all these lands were at peace, under the Hastur kings; but now we have a hundred petty kingdoms, all fighting year in and year out because they cannot agree! Do you really think that is the way the world should go?"

Bard smiled and said, "The world will go as it will, Mistress Melora, and not as you or I would have it."

"But," Melora said, "the world goes as men make it go; and men are free to make it go otherwise, if they have the courage!"

He smiled at her. She actually looked pretty to him now, her eyes animated, her round moon-face crinkled like fresh cream. It struck him that in her own way, she had a warm and sensuous presence, that her heavy body might be warm, welcoming; certainly she would not whimper like that stupid doll Lisarda, but would speak up to him spiritedly. He said, "It might be a better world if you had the making of it, Mistress Melora. Perhaps it is a pity that women have no part in the decisions which make our world."

Beltran came riding up to him. With a word of apology, Bard excused himself and rode forward with the prince.

"Master Gareth says they are encamped just beyond that wood," he said. "We should draw up here, and let the men rest their horses and eat well. Then, since one of the wenches has the Sight, we can be certain how best to attack them."

"Right," Bard said, and gave the orders which brought the men into a close circle, alert for possible attack—it was not impossible that the Dry-towners, knowing they were fixed in one spot for an attack, would ride out to take the initiative.

"Possible," Beltran said, "but not likely. If possible they like the snow less than we do. And they have the caravan to defend." He dismounted and rummaged in his saddlebags for a nosebag of feed for his horse. "I see you were sweetening one of our *leroni*. You must indeed be an incorrigible wencher, if you can find it in your heart to say a word to that fat cow! How stupid she looks!"

Bard shook his head. "Oh, she is attractive enough, in her own way and her voice is sweet," he said. "And whatever one may say of her, she is far from stupid."

Beltran said, with a sardonic laugh, "Watching you, I begin to think the old proverb is true, that all women are alike when the lamp is out, for certainly you will play at gallantry with anything that wears a skirt! Are you so desperate for female companionship, then, that you will hanker after a fat, ugy *leronis*?"

Bard said, exasperated, "I give you my word I don't *hanker after her*. I have nothing on my mind now but the battle we have to face over that hill, and whether we will have to face clingfire or sorcery! I show her courtesy because she is Master Gareth's daughter, no more than that! In heaven's name, foster brother, give your attention to our mission, not to my shortcomings as a wencher!"

His helmet hung at the horn of his saddle. He pulled it free, fastening it over his head with the leather strap, meticulously tucking the warrior's braid out of his way. Beltran slowly followed his example. His face was white, and Bard felt a moment's sympathy, remembering their talk last night; but he had no time for that now.

He rode back along the line, checking each man's equipment, saying a word to each of them. His stomach was tight, and he felt braced, as always, by danger.

"We will come as near the top of the hill as we can, without being sighted," he said, "and wait there until Master

75

Gareth signals. Then we will charge down at them as fast as we can and try to take them by surprise."

One of the men grumbled, "If their *laranzu'in* are all sleeping!"

Bard said, "If they have sentry birds or sorcery watching us, perhaps we cannot take them entirely by surprise. But they cannot know in advance quite how many we are, or how fiercely we will fight! Remember, men, they're Dry-town mercenaries, this war is nothing to them, and the snow is our best ally, for they're not used to it."

"We're not, either," one man muttered in the ranks. "Sane men don't fight in snow!"

"Would you rather let this clingfire go through? If they can move clingfire in winter, we can capture it," Bard said sharply. "All right, men, no more talking now, they may hear us, and I want to surprise them as much as we can."

He rode ahead to Master Gareth, saying, "Try to see how many men are guarding the wagons."

Master Gareth gestured at Mirella. "I have done so already, sir. I cannot count up more than fifty; that is not counting the drovers, who may be armed, but who may have their hands full with the beasts."

Bard nodded. He beckoned to two experienced men, the best riders in the group, and said, "You two, just before we charge, take your shields for cover and ride down toward the head of the train; cut the animals loose and try to stampede them back toward the train. That will create more confusion. Ride warily; they may pick you off with arrows."

They nodded. Skilled men, veterans of many campaigns, each wore the red cord twisted around his warrior braid. One settled his helmet on his head and grinned, loosening the dagger he wore belted at his waist. "This is better for such work than a sword."

"Master Gareth," Bard said, "your part is done, and well done. You may stay here with the women. In any case you need not ride down into the charge with us. If they throw spells against us, you will be needed for counter-spells against their sorcery, but you are worse than useless in battle."

"Sir," said the *laranzu*, "I know my part in battle. And so do my daughter and my foster daughter. With respect, sir, mind you your fighting men, and leave my part to me."

Bard shrugged. "On your own head, then, sir. We shall have no time for you once the fighting begins." He met Melora's eyes and was suddenly troubled at the thought that she would ride, unarmed except for a dagger, on her little don-

76

key, into the thick of the battle. But what could he do? She had made it amply clear that she needed none of his protection.

Still, he looked at her, troubled, feeling the fear grow. It pulsed through him like a living thing, stark, unreasoning terror. He saw the flesh sliced living from her bones, saw her dragged away in chains, Dry-town bandits squabbling for her maimed body, saw his foster brother Beltran stricken down. . . . He heard himself moan with terror. One of the men in the ranks cried out, a high, shrill sound of sheer panic.

"Ah, no—look where it flies, the demon. . . ."

Bard jerked his head up, seeing the darkness hovering over them, clawed and terrible, swooping down, down; heard Mirella scream aloud . . . flame spouted over them and he shrank away, feeling the withering breath of fire. . . .

Suddenly reality struck; nothing smelled burned or charred.

"Hold your line, men," he shouted. "It's illusion, a show to frighten babies . . . no worse than fireworks at midsummer day! Come on, men, is this the best they can do? They'd set a real forest blazing if they could, but this thing can't burn anybody; nothing will burn in the snow—come on!" he shouted, knowing that action was the best thing to shake off illusion. "Charge! Down the hill, you men there!" He kicked at his horse's ribs, felt her break into a gallop, crested the hill and looked down, at last, on the wagons. There were four of them, and he saw his men racing, swooping swiftly down to slash across the reins of the pack beasts, lash at them with their long whips. Bellowing, the animals broke into a lumbering gallop, and one of the carts swayed and overturned with a crash. Bard yelled, and rode on. A Dry-towner, a tall, pale man with blond hair flying loose, rose up with a long spear, aiming at his horse. Bard leaned down and cut him down. Out of the corner of his eye he saw Beltran riding down one of the Dry-towners, who stumbled, rolled, screamed under his horse's hoofs. Then he lost sight of his foster brother as three of the Dry-town mercenaries came at him at once.

He never remembered anything, afterward, of that battle; only noise, blood spattered on the snow, choking cold, and that through it all the snow continued to fall. Somewhere his horse stumbled and he fell and found himself fighting on foot. He had no idea how many he fought, or whether he killed them or just beat them off. At one point he saw Beltran down, facing two huge mercenaries, and ran through the snow, feeling his boots soaking wet, drawing his dagger and

77

striking down one of the men; then the battle swept them apart again. Then he was standing on the first of the wagons, shouting to his men to rally there, to hold the wagons. All around them were the noises of battle, clashing sword and dagger, the screams of wounded men and dying horses.

And then all was quiet and Bard saw his men clambering toward the wagons, through the snow, rallying around them. He saw with relief that Beltran, though his face was bleeding under the helmet, was still on his feet. He sent one of the men to count their dead and wounded, and went with Master Gareth to inspect the wagons. He was thinking what a damned fool he would feel if these barrels contained dried fruits for the army quartermasters, instead of the clingfire they had been promised.

He set his foot into the wagons, cautiously unstoppered one barrel. He sniffed the bitter-acrid smell, nodding grimly. Yes, it was clingfire, the vicious stuff which, once set alight, went on burning whatever it touched, burning through clothing and flesh and bone. . . . It did not occur normally in nature; it was made by sorcery. He and his men were fortunate that, in the snow, probably the Dry-towners had felt that it would not ignite. Or perhaps they had not been told what they guarded; sometimes arrows tipped with clingfire were used to strike horses out from under men in the field, a cruel and unsoldierly trick, for the horses, maddened by the burning, went wild and ran amok, doing more damage than the fires.

He told off half a dozen unwounded or slightly wounded men to guard the wagons, placing them under Master Gareth. He saw with relief that Melora was unhurt, though her face was smeared with blood.

She said quietly, "A man came at me, and I stabbed him. It's his blood, not mine."

He ordered another three men to round up the missing horses. Of the Dry-towners who had not fled, the worst wounded were given a swift death. Those who could ride, or even run, had gone.

He was turning to take final inventory of how many pack beasts could be found—for they could not move the wagons without them—when there was a sudden yell behind him and he found himself facing a tall Dry-towner, rushing at him with sword and dagger. The man had evidently been hidden behind the wagons. He was bleeding from a great wound in the leg, but he parried Bard's sword stroke, thrusting under his guard with a dagger. Bard managed to get him away, strike down the sword, snatch his own dagger from his belt. Then they were in a deadly clinch, struggling, swaying, daggers raised, scissoring to Bard's throat. With his free sword hand Bard knocked up the two daggers, grabbed his own as it fell free and drove it, hard, into the man's ribs. He yelled, still struggling, and died.

Shaking, still sick with the shock of the surprise attack, Bard picked up his sword and sheathed it; bent to wrench his dagger free. But it was stuck in one of the vertebrae and resisted all attempts to pull it out; and finally he laughed mirthlessly, said, "Bury it with him. Let him take it with him into Zandru's hells. I'll have his in exchange, then." He picked up the Dry-towner's dagger, a beautifully ornamented one with a blade of dark metal and a hilt set with worked copper and green gems. He looked at it appreciatively. "He was a brave man," he said, and slid the dagger into his own sheath.

It took the rest of the day to round up the wagons and pack beasts, to bury the three men they had lost. Seven more were hurt more or less badly; one of those, Bard knew, and grieved, would never survive the long trek in winter back to Asturias. Master Gareth had taken a thigh wound but said that he would probably be able to ride the next day.

And through it all, with merciless silence and justice, the snow continued to fall. The short autumn day darkened early into night. Bard's men raided the wagons for the best of their supplies and cooked a feast. One of the pack beasts had broken a leg, and one man who had experience as a butcher slaughtered it properly, and set its carcass for pit roasting. The Dry-towners had plenty of wine with them, too, the sweet heavy treacherous stuff from Ardcarran, and Bard gave his men license to drink whatever they would, since the sentry bird, and Mirella's Sight, confirmed that there were no enemy near them. They sat and sang rowdy songs and bragged of what they had done in the battle, and Bard sat and watched them.

Melora said, standing behind him in her gray cloak, "I wonder how they can sit so, and laugh and sing, after such a day of blood and slaughter, and so many of their friends, and even their enemies, lying dead."

Bard said, "Why, *damisela*, you are not afraid of the ghosts of the dead, are you? Do you think the dead come around, jealous because the living are enjoying themselves?"

She shook her head silently. Then she said, "No. But for me this would be a time of mourning."

"You are not a soldier, lady. For a soldier, each battle he survives is an occasion to rejoice that he continues to live. And so they feast, and sing, and drink, and if we were on the march with a regular army, not a foray alone like this, they would take their pleasure with the camp followers, too, or be off to the nearest town for women."

She shuddered and said, "At least there are no towns near for them to pillage and rape—"

"Why, *damisela*, if men go into danger of death, it is the fortunes of war; why should women be immune from that fortune? Most women accept it peacefully enough," he said, laughing, and noticed that she did not look away or simper or giggle as most of the women he knew would have done, shocked or pretending to be so.

She only said, quietly, "I suppose it is so; the excitement, the relief of being alive, instead of dead, the general shock of battle. . . . I had not thought. I would not have accepted it peacefully if the Dry-towners had won, though. I am very glad they did not; glad I am still alive." She was standing close enough to him so that he could smell some faint perfume from her hair and her cloak. "I was frightened, for fear, if the battle went against us, I should not have courage to kill myself, but would accept—ravage, bondage, rape— rather than death—death seemed very horrible to me as I stood and watched men die—"

He turned and took her hand in his; she did not protest. He said in a low voice, "I am glad you are still alive, Melora."

She said, just as low, "So am I."

He drew her against him and kissed her, feeling with amazement how very soft her heavy body and full breasts felt against him, how warm her lips were under his. He could feel her yielding herself wholly to the kiss; but she drew back afterward, a little, and said softly, "No, I beg you, Bard. Not here, not like this, not with all your men around us. . . . I would not refuse you, you have my word of that," she said, "but not like this; I have been told . . . it is not right. . . ."

Reluctantly, Bard let her go. *I could love her so easily*, he thought. *She is not beautiful, but she is so warm, so sweet* . . . and all the pent-up excitement of the day surged in him. And yet he knew that she was right, too. Where there were no accessible women for the other men, it went against all decency and custom for the commander to have his own; Bard was a soldier and he knew better than to take any privilege his men could not share. Her willingness made it all the worse. He had never before felt so close to any woman.

Yet—he drew a deep breath of resignation. He said, "The fortunes of war, Melora. Perhaps—one day—"

"Perhaps," she said gently, giving him her hand and looking into his eyes. It seemed to him that he had never wanted any woman so much. Next to her all the women he had known were like children, Lisarda no more than a child playing with her dolls, even Carlina childish and unripe. And yet, to his surprise, he had no desire to press the matter. He knew perfectly well that he could put a compulsion on her, so that she would come, unseen by any of his men, to his bed after the whole camp slept; and yet the very thought filled him with loathing. He wanted her just as she was, her whole self, of her free will, desiring him. He knew that if he had only her body, all that made her *Melora* would be gone. Her body, after all, was only that of a fat, ungainly woman, young but already sagging and slovenly. It was something more that made her so infinitely desirable to him, and for a moment he wondered, and raised his eyes, blurting out the question.

"Have you put a spell on me, Melora?"

She raised her hands, laying them on either side of his face, the fat fingers closing around his cheeks with great tenderness, and looked straight into his eyes. Beyond the fire the men were singing a rowdy song:

> Four-and-twenty *leroni* went to Ardcarran,
> When they came back again, they couldn't
>   use their *laran*—

"Ah, no, Bard," Melora said very gently. "It is only that we have touched, you and I; we have been honest with each other, and that is a rare thing between a man and a woman. I love you well; I wish things were different, that we were somewhere else than in this place tonight." She leaned forward and touched his lips, very gently, with her own, not with desire but with a tenderness which warmed him more than the wildest passion. "Good night, my dear friend."

He pressed her fingers and let her go, watching her walk away, with regret and a sadness that was new to him.

> All the trailmen came, the place
>   was bursting at the seams;
> We watched them a-doing it, a-swinging
>   from the beams.

81

Four-and-twenty farmers, bringing sacks of
nuts;
Couldn't get the strings untied. . . .

Beltran said behind him, "They seem to be enjoying themselves. They've got some new verses I hadn't heard." He
chuckled. "I remember when our tutors beat us for copying
the dirtier verses of that one in Carlina's copybook."

Bard said, glad to have something else to think about, "I
remember you telling him that it proved girls shouldn't learn
to read."

"But I would as soon leave reading to women who have
nothing more important to do," Beltran said, "though I suppose I will have to sign state papers and such matters." He
leaned over Bard; his breath was sweet and winy, and Bard
realized the boy had been drinking, perhaps a bit more than
he could handle. "It's a good night to get drunk."

"How is your wound?"

Beltran chuckled and said, "Wound, hell! My horse ran
away with me down the hill and I slipped in my saddle and
bashed my face into the saddle horn, and gave myself a nose-
bleed; so I fought all the battle with blood pouring down my
face! I think I must have looked very fearsome!" He edged
under Bard's tarpaulin, pitched with the open end toward
the fire, and sat down there. The tarpaulin over them kept
the snow off. "It seems to be clearing, at last."

"We'll have to find out if any of the men have any skill at
driving wagons and handling pack beasts."

Beltran yawned hugely. "Now that it's over, I feel I could
sleep for a tenday. Look, it's early still, but most of the men
are drunk as monks at midwinter."

"What else do you expect them to do, with no women
around?"

Beltran shrugged. "I don't grudge them their skinful. Between you and me, Bard, I'm as well pleased. . . . I remember after the battle of Snow Glens, a group of the younger
men dragged me with them to a whorehouse in the town—"
He made a fastidious grimace. "I've no taste for such games."

"I prefer willing companions, not paid ladies, myself,"
Bard agreed, "though, after a battle like this, I doubt I'd
know the difference." Yet inwardly he knew he was not telling the truth. Tonight he wanted Melora, and even if he had
had the pick of all the courtesans of Thendara or Carcosa, he
would still have chosen her. Would he have chosen her over

82

Carlina? He found he did not want to think about that. Carlina was his handfasted wife, and that was different.

"You haven't had enough to drink, foster brother," Beltran said, and handed him a bottle. Bard put it to his lips and drank, long and deep, glad to feel the strong wine blurring away the pain of knowing that Melora had wanted him, as much as he wanted her, and that he had, surprising himself, agreed to let her go. Had she scorned him, regarded him as easy, a soft touch, a green boy who was afraid to impose his will on a woman? Was she playing games with him? No, he would have staked his manhood on her honesty. . . .

One of the men was playing a *rryl*. They shouted for Master Gareth to come and sing for them, but Melora came quietly from their tent.

"My father begs that you will excuse him," she said. "He is in great pain from his wound and cannot sing."

"Will you come and share our wine, lady?" But their tone was very respectful, and Melora shook her head. "I will take my father a glass, if I may. It will help him to sleep, perhaps; but my kinswoman and I must care for him, and so we will not drink. But I thank you." Her eyes sought out Bard where he sat in the darkness across the fire, and he thought there was a new sadness in them.

"I thought he was not much wounded," Bard said.

"Why, so did I," Beltran said, "though I have heard that sometimes the Dry-towners put poisons of one sort or another on their blades. Never heard of anyone who died from it, though." Again he yawned, hugely.

The men around the fire sang ballad after ballad. At last the fire sank down and was covered, and the men, in groups of two or three or four against the cold, settled down into their blankets. Bard went quietly to the tent shared by the women and now by the wounded *laranzu*.

"How does Master Gareth?" he asked, stooping close to the entrance.

"The wound is greatly inflamed, but he is sleeping," Mirella whispered, kneeling at the doorway. "I thank you for inquiring."

"Is Melora within?"

Mirella looked up at him, her eyes wide and serious, and suddenly he knew that Melora had confided in her—or had the younger girl read Melora's mind and her thoughts?

"She is sleeping, sir." Mirella hesitated, then said in a rush, "She cried herself to sleep, Bard." Their eyes met, with sympathy and warmth. She touched his hand, lightly. He found that he spoke through a lump in his throat.

"Good night, Mirella."

"Good night, my friend," she said softly, and he knew that she did not lightly use the word. Filled with a strange mixture of bitterness and warmth, he strode away, back to the dying campfire and the darkened half-tent he shared with Beltran. In silence, he drew off boots, sword belt, unstrapped the dagger at his waist.

"You are *bredin* to a Dry-town bandit, Bard." Beltran laughed in the darkness. "For you have exchanged daggers, one for the other. . . ."

Bard hefted the dagger in his hand. "I doubt I shall ever fight with it, for it is too light for my hand," he said, "but it is marvelously ornamental, worked with copper and gems, and it is a legitimate prize of war; so I will wear it upon great occasions, and excite the envy of all." He slid the weapon under the flap of the tarpaulin. "Poor devil, he lies colder than we do tonight."

They stretched out, side by side. Bard's thoughts were with the woman who cried herself to sleep, across the camp. He had drunk enough to blur the worst of the pain, but not all.

Beltran said into the darkness, "I was not as much afraid as I thought I would be. Now it is over, it does not seem so frightening. . . ."

"It never does," Bard said. "Afterward it is simple—even exhilarating—and all you want is a drink, or a woman, or both. . . ."

"Not I," Beltran said. "I think a woman would sicken me at this point; I would rather drink with my comrades. What have women to do with war?"

"Ah, well, you're still young," Bard said affectionately, and his hand closed over his foster brother's. Not knowing whether it was his own thought or Beltran's, a vagrant thought floated across his mind, *I wish Geremy were with us.* . . . He remembered, at the edge of sleep, nights when all three of them had slept together like this, on hunting trips, fire watch; fumbled, childish experimentation in the dark; memories pleasant, kindly, soothing the raw edges of his pain over Melora; he had loyal friends and comrades, foster brothers who loved him well.

At the edge of sleep, half dreaming, he felt Beltran's body pressed tight against his, and the boy whispered, "I would—would pledge to you, too, foster brother; shall we exchange knives, too?"

Bard, shocked awake, stared and burst out laughing.

"By the Goddess!" he said coarsely, "you are younger than I thought, Beltran! Do you still think I am boy enough to take my pleasure with boys? Or do you think because you are Carlina's brother I will take you for her?" He could not stop laughing. "Well, well, who would have thought it—that Geremy Hastur is still young enough to take field-license with his playmates!" The word he used was a coarser one, army gutter slang, and he heard Beltran's choked cry of shame and shock in the darkness. "Well, whatever Geremy may choose to do, Beltran, I am not fond of such childish games. Can't you behave like a man?"

Even in the dark he could see that Beltran's face was flooded with angry color. The boy choked, half crying, and sat up. He said, through a sob of rage, "Damn you, you whoreson bastard! I swear, I will kill you for that, Bard—"

"What, from love to hatred so quickly?" mocked Bard. "You are still drunk, *bredillu*. Come, little brother, it's only a game, you'll outgrow it someday. Lie down and go back to sleep now, and don't be silly." He spoke kindly, now that his first shock was past. "It's all right."

But Beltran was sitting bolt upright in the darkness, his whole body stiff with rage. He said between his teeth, "You taunt me, you—! Bard mac Fianna, I swear to you, roses will grow in Zandru's ninth hell before you take Carlina to bed!" He got up and strode away, snatching up his boots and thrusting his feet into them; and Bard, shocked, sat staring after him.

He knew, sobered as if by a dash of the still-falling snow, that he had made a grave mistake. He should have remembered how young Beltran really was, and refused him more gently. What the boy wanted, no doubt, was only affection and closeness; as Bard himself had wanted. He need not have taunted the youngster's manhood. He felt a sudden impulse to scramble up and run after his foster brother, apologize for mocking him, make up the quarrel.

But the memory of the insult Beltran had flung held him motionless. He called me *whoreson, Bard mac Fianna, not di Asturien as is my right now*. Although down deep he knew that Beltran had simply spoken the first insult that came into his head, the truth of it hurt beyond enduring. Angrily, gritting his teeth, he lay down again. Let Prince Beltran sleep in the wagons, or among the horses, for all he cared!

Chapter Five

At midwinter-night, Ardrin of Asturias celebrated his victory over the Duke of Hammerfell.

The winter was unusually mild, and folk came from far and wide. The son of the duke was there; Lord Hammerfell had sent him to be fostered at the court of Asturias—so it was said. They all knew, as the boy himself knew, that he was a hostage for peace between Hammerfell and Asturias. Nevertheless, King Ardrin, who was a kindly man, introduced the boy as his fosterling, and it was obvious that he was being well treated and given the best of everything, from tutors and governesses to lessons in swordplay and languages, the proper education for a prince. The same education, Bard thought, looking at the child in his elaborate festival clothing, that he himself had had, at the side of Geremy Hastur and Prince Beltran.

"Still," Carlina said, "I feel sorry for the child, sent so young away from his home. You were older, Bard. You were turned twelve, and already as tall as a man. How old is young Garris—eight, or is it nine?"

"Eight, I think," Bard said, thinking that his own father could have come, or could, if he wished, have sent his young legitimate son Alaric. He could not count bad weather an excuse, and Alaric was old enough to be sent for fostering.

"Would you like to dance again, Carlina?"

"Not yet, I think," she said, fanning herself. She wore a green gown, just a little less elaborate than the one she had worn at midsummer to their handfasting; he felt that the color did not suit her, making her look pale and sallow.

Geremy came toward them and said, "Carlie, you have not yet danced with me. Come now, Bard, you've had your share, and Ginevra is not here. She has gone to stay with her mother for the holiday, and I am not sure she will come back. Her mother has quarreled with Queen Ariel—"

"For shame on you for gossiping, Geremy!" Carlina struck him playfully with her fan. "I am sure that my mother and the Lady Marguerida will soon make it up, and then we shall have Ginevra back with us. Bard, go and dance with one of my mother's ladies. You cannot stand here all night beside me! There are many ladies eager to dance with the king's own banner bearer!"

Bard said sullenly, "Most of them don't want to dance with me. I am too clumsy!"

"Still, we cannot spend all evening here! Go and dance with Lady Dara. She is so clumsy herself that you will be graceful as a *chieri* beside her, and she will never notice if you step on her feet, for she is so fat she has not been on speaking terms with her own feet for twenty years. . . ."

"And you reprove *me* for talking gossip, Carlie?" Geremy chuckled and took his foster sister's arm. "Come and dance, *breda*. So already you are giving Bard orders as if he were your husband?"

"Why, he is all but so," Carlina said, laughing. "I think we have the right to give orders to one another already!" She smiled gaily at Bard and moved away on Geremy's arm.

Left alone, Bard did not take her advice, or go and offer himself to the ungainly Lady Dara as a partner. He went toward the buffet and poured himself a glass of wine. King Ardrin and a group of his councillors were standing there, and amiably made room for Bard to join them.

"A good festival to you, foster son."

"And to you, kinsman," Bard said—he called the king foster father only in private.

"I have been telling Lord Edelweiss what you told me about the folk who live near Moray's Mill," the King said. "It is chaos and anarchy for so many folk to live with no proper overlord. Come spring thaw, I think we must ride out and set things in order there. If every little village claims to be independent and to make its own laws, there will be borders everywhere, and a man will not be able to ride half a day without needing to cope with some new set of laws."

"The lad has a head on his shoulders," said Lord Edelweiss, a gray-haired man dressed like an elaborate fop, and behind Bard's back, he heard the old man say, "Pity your own older son shows no such talent for strategy and war skills. Let's hope he has some skill at statesmanship, or that boy there will have the kingdom in his hands before he's twenty-five years old!"

King Ardrin said stiffly, "Bard is Beltran's devoted foster brother; they are *bredin*. I need fear nothing for Beltran in Bard's hands."

Bard bit his lip, troubled. He and Beltran had been hardly on speaking terms since that battle and its aftermath; Beltran, tonight, had given him no midwinter gift, though he had meticulously sent the prince an egg from his best hunting hawk, to be hatched under a palace hen; a thoughtful gift and one that would normally have brought delighted thanks from his foster brother. In fact, it seemed that Beltran was avoiding him.

Again Bard cursed himself for his own folly in quarreling with Beltran. Raw-edged over his own frustration, the enforced separation from Melora—for he knew that she had wanted him then, as much as he wanted her—he had lashed out at Beltran because the boy was the most convenient object on which to vent his own fury. He should, instead, have taken that chance to cement his own bond with the young prince. Damn it, he missed their old closeness! Well, at least Beltran had not yet poisoned Geremy's mind against him . . . he hoped. It was hard to tell what went on behind Geremy's somber face, and although it might only have been that Geremy was missing his Ginevra, Bard found that hard to believe. They were not handfasted, and Ginevra was not really of sufficiently noble birth to be a proper match for the heir to Hastur of Carcosa.

Perhaps tonight he should seek out Beltran, make his apologies and explain to his foster brother why he had been so sharp with him. . . . His outraged pride cringed at that thought. But a serious and unmended quarrel with the prince could damage his own career, and if some of the king's councillors were already wondering if Bard stood dangerously close to the throne—he was, after all, the eldest son of the king's own brother—then he had better make sure that Beltran did not perceive him as a threat!

But before he could put his resolve into action, a voice at his shoulder said genially, "A good festival to you, dom Bard."

Bard turned to face the elderly *laranzu*. "And to you, Master Gareth. Ladies" he acknowledged, bowing to Mirella, lovely in her pale-blue gauze draperies, and to Melora, who wore a low-necked gown of green with a high collar; the dress cut as loose as a pregnant woman's, and indeed, her heavy body made her look very much as if she were pregnant, but the color showed the high color of her clear skin, made her red hair glow.

"You are not dancing, Master Gareth?"

The old man shook his head with a rueful smile. He said,

"I cannot," and Bard saw that he leaned on a stout walking stick. "A memory, sir, of that fight with the Dry-towners."

"Why, such a wound should be long healed," Bard said, with concern, and he shrugged.

"I think perhaps there was poison on the dagger; had it not been diluted by many other fights, I should have lost the leg," Master Gareth said. "It has never healed completely, and now I begin to think it never will. Even *laran* has not sufficed. But it does not keep me from the festival," he said, courteously dismissing the subject.

The young son of Hammerfell's duke came up and said shyly, "Will the Lady Mirella dance with me?"

She glanced at her guardian for permission—Mirella was too young to dance at public balls except with kinsmen—but evidently Master Gareth considered the youngster far too young to represent any threat; they were obviously children together. He gestured approval and they moved away together. The boy was not nearly as tall as Mirella, so they made a somewhat incongruous partnership.

Bard said to Melora, "Will you honor me, Melora?"

Master Gareth raised his eyebrows slightly at the informal use of her name, but she said, "Certainly," and held out her hand. She was, Bard reflected, probably several years older than he was himself, and he was surprised that she was not yet married or pledged.

After a moment, as they danced, he put the question, and she said, "I am promised to Neskaya Tower. I dwelt at Dalereuth for a time; but they set us to making clingfire, and I feel it very strongly—that *leroni* should be neutral in wars. So I am bound to Neskaya, where the Keeper has pledged to neutrality in all wars among the Domains."

"That seems to me an ill choice," said Bard. "If we must fight, why should *leroni* be exempt from battle? Already they do not carry weapons, even in battle. Are they to live at peace when the rest of us must fight for our lives?"

"Someone must begin the fight for peace," Melora said. "I have spoken with Varzil and I think him a great man."

Bard shrugged. "A deluded idealist, no more," he said. "They will burn the Tower of Neskaya about your heads, and go on making war as always. I only hope, Lady, that you may not share in their fall."

"I hope so, too," she said, and they were silent, dancing. She was singularly light on her feet, moving like a breath of air.

He said, "Dancing, you are very beautiful, Melora. How

strange, when first I saw you, I did not think you beautiful at all."

"And now that I look at you, I see you are a handsome man," she said. "I do not know how much you have heard about *leroni*—I am a telepath and I do not look much at people, what their outward aspect may be. I had no idea even whether you were fair or dark, when I talked with you on campaign. And now, you are the King's banner bearer and a handsome man and all the ladies envy me because you do not dance often with them."

From any other woman, Bard thought, this would have sounded unendurably coy and flirtatious. Melora stated it simply, like any other fact.

They danced, silently, the old sympathy beginning to build up again between them. In an isolated corner of the room, he drew her to him and kissed her. She sighed and allowed the kiss, but then, regretfully, drew away.

"No, my dear," she said, very gently. "Let's not allow this to go so far that we cannot part as friends, and no more."

"But why not, Melora? I know that you feel as I do, and now we are not hindered as we were after the battle—"

She looked straight at him. She said, "What we might have done, had occasion offered, in hot blood and after the excitement and danger of battle, is a thing apart; now, in cold blood, you know and I know that it would not be suitable. You are here with your promised wife; and the Princess Carlina has been most gracious to me. I would not step on the hem of her robe before her very eyes. Bard, you know I am right."

He did, but in his outraged pride, he would not acknowledge it. He flung at her, wrathfully, "What man except some sandal-wearer wishes to be only friend to a woman?"

"Oh, Bard," she said, shaking her head, "I think you are two men! One of you is heartless and cruel, especially with women, and cares nothing how you hurt! The other is the man I have seen, the man I dearly love—even though I will not share your bed this night, nor any other," she added firmly. "But I hope with all my heart, for Carlina's sake that it is always this other man I know that you show to her. For *that* one, I shall cherish all my life." She pressed his hand gently, turned away from him, and quickly lost herself in the crowd of dancers.

Bard, left alone, his cheeks burning with outrage, tried to follow her green-clad form through the crowds; but she had hidden herself from him as completely as if she had vanished right out of the hall. He had the faint prickling sense of *laran* in use and wondered if she had thrown a mantle of invisibility over herself, as he knew some *leroni* could do. His rage and wounded pride knew no bounds.

Fat, stupid woman, probably she had cast a glamour over him so that he wanted her, because no man before had ever done so. . . . Well, Varzil of Neskaya was welcome to her, damn him, and he hoped the Tower was burned over their heads! He went back to the buffet and wrathfully drank another glass of wine, and another, knowing that he was getting drunk, knowing King Ardrin, himself an abstemious man, would not approve.

Nor did Carlina; when she met with him again, there was gentle reproof in her voice.

"Bard, you have been drinking more than is seemly."

"Are you going to make me a henpecked husband even before the wedding?" he snarled at her.

"Oh, my dear, don't talk that way," she said, flushing to the neck of her green gown. "But my father will be angry too. You know that he hates it when any of his young officers drink so much that they cannot behave in a seemly manner."

"Have I done anything unseemly?" he demanded of her.

"No," she admitted, smiling a little, "but promise me not to drink any more, Bard."

"*A ves ordras, domna,*" he conceded, "but only if you will dance with me."

It was a couple-dance again, and, with the license allowed to a handfasted pair, he could hold her tightly, not at the decorous distance required of most couples. Geremy, he noticed, had been given the privilege of dancing with Queen Ariel, at a most respectful distance indeed. Beltran had (probably at Carlina's request) chosen to dance with the ungainly Lady Dara. She too was graceful on her feet, as much as Melora, was it so common for ladies who were over-plump to dance so gracefully? Damn it, he would not think of Melora now! She might dance with the friends from Zandru's hells, for all he cared! He drew Carlina vengefully close to him, aware of her thin, bony slenderness in his arms. A man could be bruised on those bones!

"Not so tightly, Bard, you are hurting me . . ." she protested. "And it is not suitable. . . ."

He let her go, stung with compunction. He said, "I wouldn't hurt you for the world, Carlie. Anyone or everyone else, but never you."

The dance ended. The king and queen, with the more

elderly and dignified ladies and lords of the court, were withdrawing, so that their presence might not inhibit the younger people at their revels. He saw that the young son of Hammerfell was being taken away by his governess, and that the pretty Mirella was being folded into her cloak by Master Gareth. King Ardrin made a little speech, wishing the youngsters a merry festival and bidding them dance till dawn if they wished.

Carlina stood beside Bard, smiling as her parents departed. She said, "Last year I, too, was taken away at mid-night when the elders and children were sent to bed. This year, I suppose, they think that as a handfasted bride I am in no danger, with my promised husband to guard me." Her smile was merry.

And, in truth, Bard knew that midwinter revels sometimes grew a little rowdy. They were certainly noisier, after the old people and children departed; there was more drinking, many boisterous kissing games, and the dances grew wilder and less decorous. As the night moved on toward dawn, more and more couples slipped away into the gallery and side passages of the castle, and once Bard and Carlina, dancing past a long passage, saw a couple closely embraced, so intimately so that Carlina quickly turned away her eyes. But Bard steered her into the galleries.

He murmured, "Carlina, you are promised to me already. I think already most of the couples here who are pledged or handfasted have gone apart—" He drew her into his arms, straining her close to him. "You know what I want of you, my promised wife. It is midwinter, we are handfasted, why not make it complete now, since the laws permit?" His mouth fastened over hers; when she twisted away to breathe he murmured thickly, "Even your father could not protest!"

She said softly, "Bard, no, no." He could sense the rising panic in her, but she spoke in an undertone, trying desperately for calm.

"I have resigned myself to this marriage, Bard. I'll honor my father's wish, I promise you. But not—not now." He sensed, and it struck pain deep into him, that she was fighting hard not to show her dismay and revulsion. "Give me time. Not—not now, not tonight."

It seemed that he could hear again the threatening words Beltran had hurled at him: *roses will grow in Zandru's ninth hell before you take Carlina to bed!*

He snarled at her, "Has Beltran made good his threat, then?"

Melora had refused him, too, though a scant forty days before she wanted him. Melora was a telepath; she must have been aware of the quarrel with Beltran, knew Beltran could poison the king's mind against him; a liaison with an out-of-favor courtier could do Melora no good. . . . Beltran had turned Melora against him, too, and now Carlina. . . .

Carlina said, her voice shaking, "I don't know what you are talking about, Bard. Have you quarreled with my brother?"

"And if I had, would that change your mind about me?" he demanded, bitterly. "So, you too are like all women, you will tease me as if I had no manhood! You are my promised wife, why do you draw away from me as if I meant rape?"

"You just now said," she replied, staring up at him with bitterness as great as his own, "that you would never want to hurt me. Does that hold only when I agree to everything you want of me? Do you think it would not be rape because I am your promised wife? I love you as foster brother and friend, and if the Goddess is merciful to us both, a day will come when I will love you as the husband my father has given to me. But that time is not yet; I have been promised that I shall have till midsummer. Bard, I beg you, let me go!"

"So that your father may have enough time to change his mind about me? So that Beltran may poison his mind against me, have you given to his own minion?"

"How dare you say that of Geremy," she demanded furiously, and somehow the name ignited the last reserves of Bard's wrath.

"So, you are so careful of *his* honor, that *ombredin*, that half-man—"

"Don't speak that way of my foster brother," she said in a rage.

"I'll speak as I choose, and no woman shall prevent me," he flung at her.

"Bard, you are still drunk; the wine cup speaks, not you," she said, and his own fury blazed up, the last vestiges of his self-control flaring. He had let Melora go out of respect for Carlina! How dared she refuse him now, as if he were nothing to her? He would not be un-manned twice on mid-winter night by some damned woman's whims! He dragged her into the gallery, gripping her so hard that she cried out, and forced his lips down on hers, ignoring her struggles. Mingled wrath and desire flamed high in him; for the second time, a woman he wanted and felt he had a right to have had denied him, and this time he would not submit to her meekly, but he would impose his will on her! Damn it, she was his wife, and tonight he would have her, willingly if she chose, but in any case he would have her! She struggled in his arms, in growing panic, exciting him unendurably.

"Bard, no, no," she pleaded, sobbing. "Not like this, not like this . . . oh, please, please. . . ."

He held her, fiercely, knowing that he was hurting her with the violence of his grasp. "Come to my room, then! Don't make me force you, Carlina!" How could she possibly be indifferent to this raging torrent of desire in him? Somehow, he must *make* her feel it! What he wanted was for her to want him as fiercely as he wanted her, to match his own desire and need with her own, and here she was fighting and struggling against him as if she were an unkissed child who did not even know what he wanted of her!

A hand alighted on his shoulder; tore them apart.

"Bard, you are drunk, or completely out of your mind?" Geremy asked, staring at them in dismay. Carlina covered her face with her hands, weeping with relief and shame.

"Damn you, how dare you interfere, you half-man—"

"Carlina is my foster sister," Geremy said. "I won't have her raped at a party, even by her promised husband! Bard, in the name of all the gods, go and slosh your face with cold water and apologize to Carlina, and we'll say no more of this; and next time, stop drinking while you can still master yourself!"

"Damn you—" Bard advanced on Geremy with fury, his fists clenched; Beltran seized him from behind. He said, "No, you don't, Bard. Carlina, you didn't want this, did you?"

She sobbed, "No, I didn't," and Bard said angrily, "She is my promised wife! She had no right to refuse herself to me this way—you did not hear her crying out, certainly! By what right do you assume she wishes to be released from me? She liked it well enough, until you came along to interfere—"

"Now there you lie," Beltran said in a rage. "For everyone in this hall with a scrap of *laran* must have heard her cry out against you! I'll see that my father hears of this! Damnable bastard, trying to take by force what he could never have had willing—"

Bard whipped his dagger out of its sheath. The green gems glittered in the light. He said low, between his teeth, "You meddling catamite, don't presume to interfere in what you don't know the first thing about! Get out of my way—"

"No!" Geremy grabbed his wrist. "Bard, you are raving mad! To draw steel at midwinter, before your prince? Beltran, he's drunk, don't listen to what he says! Bard, go and sober up, and I'll give you my word of honor, the king will hear no more of this—"

"So you're in this against me too, you filthy boy-lover, you and your minion," Bard yelled, and sprang at him. Geremy stepped aside, trying to avoid the thrust of the dagger, but Bard, beside himself with rage, hurled himself at Geremy and they slammed to the floor, struggling. Geremy twisted his body, grabbing his own dagger. He was still begging, "Bard, no—foster brother, don't—" but Bard did not even hear, and Geremy knew that he must fight in real earnest now, or Bard would kill him. They had fought before this, as boys, but never, before this, with real weapons in their hands. Bard was stronger than he was. He thrust up, trying to knock the dagger aside, to shove his knee between himself and Bard's descending blade. He felt his knife go into Bard's arm, slit the leather and scrape flesh; and in the next moment Bard's dagger went deep into his thigh, high up near the groin. He cried out, harshly, in agony, feeling the leg go numb.

Then a dozen of the king's men were dragging them apart, and Bard, abruptly sobered by the flood of adrenalin, like a cold wash over him, stared at Geremy, rolling about in convulsive agony on the floor.

"Zandru's hells! *Bredu*—" he begged, dropping to his knees beside his foster brother; but he knew Geremy did not hear him. Carlina was sobbing in Beltran's arms.

Beltran said to one of the soldiers, "Escort my sister to her apartments, and find her maids; then go and awaken my father. I will be responsible."

He dropped to his knees beside Geremy, shoving Bard viciously aside.

"Don't touch him, you—! You've done enough! Geremy, *bredu*, my beloved brother—speak to me, I beg you, speak to me—" He sobbed, and Bard heard the anguish in his voice. But Geremy was beyond hearing.

One of the soldiers grabbed Bard, not gently, and took the dagger, "Poisoned," he said. "A Dry-town dagger." And Bard, in horror, recalled, for the first time that evening, that it was the dagger he had taken in the fight. The slightest wound from a Dry-town dagger, poisoned like this, had meant that Master Gareth had been lamed, probably for life. And he had struck Geremy, in his rage, deep into the hamstrings. Shocked, too horrified to speak, he let the soldiers take him away and place him under arrest.

He spent forty days under house arrest, and no one came

near him. He had plenty of time to regret his rashness, his drunken rage; but there were times, too, when he blamed Carlina for it all. Food was brought to his rooms by soldiers, who told him that for a week Geremy had raved in delirium and hung between life and death; but they had sent for a *laranzu* from Neskaya who had saved his life and even his leg. But the leg, they had heard, envenomed by the poison, had withered and shrunk, and he would probably never walk again without support.

In a cold wash of terror, Bard wondered what they would do with him. To draw steel at midwinter Festival was a crime enough; to wound a foster brother even in play was a serious offense. Beltran had broken Bard's nose once, at one of their games, and he had been severely beaten, prince or no, by their tutors, had been forced to apologize at dinner time before everyone in the king's household, and had been required by the king to give Bard, in fine, his best hawk, and his finest cloak. He still had the cloak.

He tried to bribe the soldier who guarded him to smuggle out a message to Carlina. If she would intercede for him— she was his only hope. The least he could expect would be a year's exile, and forfeiture of the king's favor. They could not void his marriage to Carlina, but they could put some trouble in his way. If Geremy had died, he would have faced three years exile, at least, and blood-money to Geremy's family; but Geremy was not dead. But the soldier curtly refused, saying the king had forbidden any messages to be carried.

Wholly alone, thrown on his own resources, Bard's bitterness washed away his remorse. It was Melora's doing; if she had not refused him, he would not have had to take out his rage and frustration on Carlina, he could have given Carlina the extra half-year she wanted, until their appointed time. Melora led him on, then refused him, damned tease!

And then Carlina! She said that she would love him as a husband, yet she put him off this way! And how dared Geremy and Beltran, damned *ombredin-y*, to come interfering? Beltran was jealous, damn him, because Bard had refused him, and he had called his minion to fight him. . . . It was their fault! He had done nothing wrong!

Rage hardened his remorse, until the day, with soft spring rain flooding the castle roofs and the spring thaw at hand, when two soldiers came into his room and said, "Best dress yourself, Dom Bard; the king has called you to audience."

Bard dressed carefully in his best, shaving himself closely and braiding his hair into the warrior's braid, twisting the red cord around it. When the king saw it, perhaps he would remember how well Bard had served him, and for how long. If he had killed or maimed the king's son, he knew, nothing could have saved him; he would count himself lucky to be allowed a quick death and not be torn on hooks. But Geremy was a hostage, son of the king's enemies—

Geremy was the king's foster son and his own foster brother. It would not save him.

He came into the king's presence-chamber with a defiant stride, standing tall, staring down everyone in the room. Carlina was there, among the queen's women, pale and drawn, her hair dragged back from her face into a thin knot, her eyes huge and frightened. Beltran looked angry, defiant and would not meet Bard's eyes. Bard looked for Geremy. He was there, leaning on crutches, and Bard noticed that the wounded leg still bore a slipper rather than a boot and that Geremy did not set it to the ground.

He felt his throat tighten. He would not have harmed Geremy. Damn it, why hadn't Geremy kept out of it, why had they insisted on interfering in what was between Bard and his promised wife?

King Ardrin said, "Well, Bard mac Fianna, what have you to say for yourself?" The name of a bastard—the name of his unknown mother, not the *di Asturien* he was called in courtesy, boded ill.

Bard bent the knee before his foster father. He said, "Only this, kinsman; the fight was not of my seeking, but they forced it upon me. And that I have served you for five years, and I think I have served you well. With your own hand you commended me at Snow Glens and gave me a red cord, and I captured clingfire for your armies. I love my foster brother well and I would never have harmed him willingly; I did not know the dagger was poisoned, I swear it."

"He lies," Beltran said passionlessly, "for we made jokes about his having become *bredin* to a Dry-towner, and he had heard mistress Melora, the *leronis*, say that her father's wound was poisoned."

"I had forgotten it was not my own dagger," Bard protested angrily. "I admit it, kinsman, I should not have drawn my steel at Festival. I am so far guilty; but Geremy forced the fight upon me! Did Prince Beltran tell you that he was only jealous?"

King Ardrin said, "Was it Geremy who drew his dagger first?"

"No, kinsman," Bard said, dropping his head, "but I swear

I did not know the dagger was poisoned; I had forgotten. And I was drunk; if they are just, they will tell you that, too, and that they forced the quarrel by laying rough hands on me. I drew my dagger in self-defense. I did not want to be beaten by them like a lackey, and there were two of them!"

"Geremy," asked the king, "did you and Beltran lay hands on Bard first? I will have the truth of this matter, all the truth."

"We did, Uncle," Geremy said, "but he had laid hands on Carlina in a way she did not like, and Beltran and I would not have her mauled, or even raped."

"Is this true, Bard?" The king looked at him with surprise and displeasure. He said, "They had spared to tell me this! Did you so far forget yourself as to mishandle Carlina when you were drunk?"

"As to that," Bard said, feeling caution desert him with the remembered rage, "Carlina is my pledged wife and they had no right to interfere! Beltran has made a great thing of this because he is jealous, he wants to give Carlina to his *bredu* there, to bind them closer still! He is jealous because I have showed myself his better at swordplay and in war, and with women too—not that he would know what to do with a woman when he is alone with her! Where was Beltran when I defended you at Snow Glens, Uncle?"

He knew that he had struck inside the king's guard there; for Ardrin of Asturias flinched, and looked angrily at his son, then from one to the other of his foster sons.

"Father," Beltran said, "is it not clear to you that he has plotted to seize the kingdom from your hands, to take Carlina whether she will or no, to win your armies' allegiance behind your back? If he were still your loyal and obedient subject, would he have drawn steel at midwinter Festival?"

King Ardrin said, "Whether or no, it is clear that I have reared a wolf cub to bite my hand. Was it not enough to you, Bard, that Carlina was pledged to you and should have been yours at the proper time?"

"By all the laws of this kingdom, Carlina is mine," Bard protested, but the king stopped him with an upraised hand.

"Enough. You presume too much. A handfasting is not a marriage, and not even the king's foster son can lay a hand undesired upon the king's daughter. You have broken too many of the laws of this court, Bard; you are a troublemaker. I will have no lawbreaker and kin-maimer within this household. Get you gone from here. I give you horse and sword and hunting bow and armor, and purse of four hundred silver royals; and thus do I reward your past services to me. But I name you outlaw within Asturias. I give you three days to leave this realm; and after that, if you are seen within the borders of Asturias for seven years from midwinter, no law shall protect you. Any man may slay you like an animal, without blood-guilt, or blood-feud begun, or blood-money paid to your kinsmen for wounding or death."

Bard stood blinking in outrage at the severity of the punishment. He had expected to lose his place at court—the king could have done no less. He could have accepted, with equanimity, the usual sentence of a year's outlawry; had even steeled himself, if the king was in a mood to be severe, to the knowledge that he might have to go into exile for three years. He had also been sure that when next King Ardrin had gone to war and had need of him, he would have been forgiven and recalled to court. But *seven years' exile*!

"This is hard, *vai dom*," he protested, kneeling before the king. "I have served you faithfully and well, and I am not yet even full grown. How do I deserve such hard treatment?"

King Ardrin's face was like stone. "If you are old enough to behave like a man, and a vicious one," he said, "you are old enough to suffer the penalty I would lay on such a man. Some of my councillors have thought me over-lenient that I do not order you killed. I have taken a pet dog to my heart and I find a wolf biting my heels! I name you wolf and outlaw, and I bid you begone from this court before sunset and from this realm within three days, before I take second thought and decide I want no such man living within my kingdom. I love your father well, and I would prefer not to have the blood of his son on my hands; but don't presume on this, Bard, because if I see your face within the borders of Asturias within seven years, I shall certainly strike you down like the wolf you are!"

"Not in seven years, not in seven times seven, tyrant," Bard cried, leaping to his feet, and flung down at the king's feet the red cord the king had given him in battle. "All the gods grant that we meet in battle when you are guarded only by your son there and his trustworthy catamite! You speak of lawbreaking? What law is stronger than that which binds a man to his wife, and you, sir, are flouting that!" He turned away from the king and strode toward where Carlina stood among the women.

"What do you say, my wife? Will you, at least, show justice within the law, and follow me into exile as a wife should do?"

She raised her eyes to him, cold and tearless.

"No, Bard, I will not. An outlaw has no claim, and no protection in law. I would have done my father's will and married you; but I begged him once to spare me this marriage, and now I rejoice that he has changed his mind; and you know why."

"There was a time when you said you could love—"

"No," she interrupted him. "I call Avarra to witness; I thought, perhaps, when I had grown older and you, perhaps, wiser, if the Goddess was merciful to us, we might one day come to love each other as it was suitable for married people. It would have been even more truthful to say that I hoped for it, not that I believed it would come to pass. There was a time when I loved you well as foster brother and friend. But you have forfeited that."

His face twisted in a gesture of contempt. "So you are like all the other women, bitch! And I thought you something different and above them!"

Carlina said, "No, Bard, I—" but King Ardrin gestured her to silence.

"No more, girl. You need hold no more parley with him. Henceforth he is nothing to you. Bard mac Fianna," he said, "I give you three days to quit my realm. After that time I lay on you the doom of an outlaw; no man, woman or child in this realm may give you roof or shelter, food or drink, fire or fuel, aid or counsel. And for the space of seven years, if you are found within the borders of this realm, you shall be slain like a wolf at any man's hand, and your body given to wild beasts without public mourning or burial. Now go."

Custom demanded that the outlaw should bend the knee to his king in token that he accepted his doom. Perhaps, if King Ardrin had given him the customary sentence, Bard would have done so; but he was young and proud, and raging with frustration.

"I will go, since you leave me no remedy," he snarled. "You have named me wolf; wolf I shall be from this day forth! I leave you to the mercy of those two you have chosen over me; and I shall return when you cannot forbid me. And as for you, Carlina—" his eyes sought her out, and the girl cringed. "I swear that I will have you, one day, whether you will or no; and that I vow to you, I, Bard mac Fianna, I, the wolf!"

He spun on his heel and went forth from the great hall, and the doors swung shut behind him.

Chapter Six

"But where will you go?" Dom Rafael of Asturias asked his son. "What are your plans, Bard? You are over-young to set forth outside the realms of your own kingdom, alone and outlawed!" Bard's father all but wrung his hands. "Lord of Light, what folly and what misfortune!"

Bard shook his head impatiently. "What's done is done, Father," he said, "and bewailing will not better it. I was ill-done-by; the king your brother showed me small justice and no mercy, for a quarrel I never wanted. All I can do is to set my back to the court of Asturias and seek better fortune elsewhere."

They were standing in the room that had been Bard's own since his father had brought him to his own house, to rear with his own legitimate son; out of kindness or sentiment, Dom Rafael had kept the room ready for Bard, though he had not set foot in it since he was twelve years old. It was a boy's room, not a man's, and there was not much in it that Bard cared to take with him into exile.

"Come, Father," he said, almost affectionately, laying his hand on the older man's shoulder, "it's not worth grieving. Even if the king had showed me leniency, and had only sent me from court for that damnable midwinter folly, I could hardly have stayed here; Lady Jerana loves me as little as ever. And now she can hardly conceal her rejoicing that I am well out of her way, for good and all." His grin was fierce. "I wonder if she thinks I would try to seize Alaric's heritage, as the king came to think I coveted Beltran's? After all, in days past, the elder son was often shown preference over the legitimate son. Come, Father, has it never crossed your mind, that perhaps I would not be content to see Alaric preferred before me, and try to take what is lawfully his?"

Dom Rafael di Asturien looked up at his tall son seriously. He was a man a little past the prime of age, broad-shouldered, with the look of a muscular and active man who has let himself go soft in retirement. He said, "Would you so, Bard?"

Bard said, "No," and turned over in his fingers a hawk hood he had made when he was eight years old. "No, Father, do you think me wholly without honor, because of this quarrel I have had with my foster brothers? That was folly, drunken folly and something akin to madness, and if I could mend it—but not even the Lord of Light can turn back time, or undo what has been done. And as for Alaric and his heritage—Father, there are many bastard sons who grow up as outcastes, with no name but the name of a dishonored mother, and no man's hand to guide them, and no more fortune than they can wrest from the world by the toil of their hands, or by banditry. But you reared me in your own house, and from childhood I had good companions, and was well taught, and was fostered in the king's house when it was time for me to learn the skills of manhood." With a shyness surprising in the arrogant young warrior, he reached out and embraced his father. "You could have had peace in your bed and at your fireside, had you been willing to send me away to be prentice to a smith or a farmer or some tradesman. Instead I had horses and hawks and was raised as a nobleman's son, and you endured strife with your lawfully wedded lady for this. Do you think I can forget that, or try to have more than this generous portion, from the brother who has always called me brother, and never *bastard*? Alaric is my brother, and I love him; I would be worse than ingrate, I would be wholly without honor, if I laid a hand on what is rightfully his. And if I have any regret for my quarrel with that damnable sandal wearer Beltran, it is that I might somehow have harmed you or Alaric."

"You have not harmed me, my son," Dom Rafael said, "though I shall find it hard to forgive Ardrin for what he has done to you. When he cast a slight upon your loyalty, he cast a slight upon mine, causing me to question what I have never questioned before, that he was rightfully king of this land. And as for harming Alaric—" he broke off, laughed and said, "You may ask him that for yourself. I think he is glad enough to see you home that he would welcome whatever sent you here."

As he spoke the door opened, and a very small boy, about eight years old, came into the room. Bard turned away from the saddlebags he was packing.

"Well, Alaric, you were only a little boy when I went away to the king's court, and now you are nearly old enough for your own spurs and honor!" He hugged the child and swung him up in his arms.

"Let me go with you into exile, my brother," the child said fiercely. "Father wants me to go and be fostered in the house of that old king! I don't want to serve a king who would exile my brother!" He saw Bard laugh and shake his head, and he insisted, "I can ride; I can serve as your page, even your squire, take care of your horse and carry your arms—"

"No, now, my lad," Bard said, setting the boy on his feet, "I shall have no need for page or squire on the roads I must ride now; you must stay and be a good son to our father while I am in outlawry, and that means learning to be a good man. As for the king, if you are quiet and reasonable and speak low, he will like that better than being brave and speaking your mind; he is a fool, but he is the king and he must be obeyed, were he as stupid as Durraman's donkey."

"But where will you go, Bard?" the child insisted. "I heard the men crying the doom of outlawry on you at the crossroads, and they said that no one could give you food or fire or help—"

Bard laughed. "I shall carry food for three days," he said, "and before that time is over I shall be well out of Asturias, into lands where no one gives heed to King Ardrin's dooms and justices. I have money with me and a good horse."

"Will you go and be a bandit, Bard?" the boy asked, his eyes wide in wonder, and Bard shook his head.

"No; only a soldier. There are many overlords who can used a skilled man."

"But *where*? Will we know?" the boy asked, and Bard chuckled, answering only with a snatch of an old ballad:

> I shall fare forth to the setting sun
> Where it sinks beyond the sea;
> An outlaw's doom shall be my fate
> And all men flee from me.

"I wish I were going with you," the boy said, but Bard shook his head.

"Each man rides with his own fate, brother, and your road is to the king's house. His own son is grown, but he has a new fosterling, Garris of Hammerfell, who is your own age, and no doubt you'll be foster brothers and *bredin*; which, no doubt, is why he sent for you."

"That," Dom Rafael said with a sardonic curl of his lip, "and to make it certain I understood that his quarrel was with you, and not with me. Well, if he wishes to think me so quickly forgetful, be it so. And as for you, Bard, you could ride to the border and take service with The MacAran. He holds El Haleine against strife on all sides, and there are bandits, and cat-things coming down out of the Venza hills; he will be glad enough of a good sword."

"I had thought of that," Bard said, "though it is over near Thendara and there are Hasturs there. Some of Geremy's kin might declare blood-feud on me, and I would need to guard my back night and day. I would rather be out of Hastur country for a few years." He bit his lip and stared at the floor. A picture of Geremy was before his eyes, white and wasted from illness, halting on the lame leg. Damn Beltran who had drawn Geremy into their quarrel! If he must have maimed a foster brother, why could it not have been the one with whom he truly had a quarrel? A foolish quarrel, but still a quarrel; he and Geremy had seldom exchanged a cross word; and by his hand Geremy had been lamed for life. He set his teeth and mentally turned his back on the memory. What was done was done. It was all too late for regrets. But he felt he would give the best ten years of his life to see Geremy whole again, and feel his foster brother's hand in his. He swallowed fiercely and clenched his jaw.

"I had thought of riding to the east and taking service with Edric of Serrais. It would feed my soul to make war on King Ardrin! It would teach him, perhaps, that I am better as friend than foe!"

Dom Rafael said, "I cannot advise you, my son. Far less can I lay a command on you. You are of age, and soon you will be far beyond the reach of my word; and you have your own way to make in the world for seven years. But I beg of you; spend the years of your exile far from Asturias, and make no war upon our kinsmen."

"I had not thought of that," Bard said. "If I join the ranks of King Ardrin's enemies, he will consider you his enemy as well; in a sense, Alaric is hostage for my good behavior. I cannot face him in battle while he is foster father to the brother I love."

"Not only that," Dom Rafael said. "Seven years, at your age, will but bring you well into manhood. When you return—and after seven years have come and gone you will be free to return—you can make your peace with Ardrin, and make for yourself an honorable career in the land of your birth."

Bard snorted amusement. "Ardrin of Asturias will make

his peace with me when the she-wolf of Alar leaves off gnawing at her victim's heart, and when the *kyorebni* in winter bring food to the starving rabbithorns! Father, while Beltran and Geremy live, I will never find peace here, even if Ardrin no longer lives."

"You cannot be sure of that," Dom Rafael said. "One day Geremy will return to his own country; and Prince Beltran may die in battle. And Ardrin has no other son. Should Beltran die sonless, Alaric is the king's next heir, and I think he knows it; and that is why Alaric is being fostered in his house, for the proper education of a possible prince."

"Queen Ariel is not yet past childbearing," Bard said. "She might yet give the king another son."

"Still, if it came to that, the new king could have no quarrel with you, and might well be glad of a kinsman, even *nedestro*, with your skill at war."

Bard shrugged. "Be it so," he said. "For your sake, and my brother's, and for the sake of that claim to the throne, I will make no war on King Ardrin; though it would do my heart good to ride against him in war, or to storm Asturias and take Carlina by force of arms."

Alaric asked, wide-eyed, "Is the Princess Carlina so beautiful?"

"Why, as to that," Bard said, "I suppose all women are much the same when the lamp is out. But Carlina was the king's daughter, and she was reared as my foster sister, and I loved her well; and she was promised to me, and by all the laws she is my handfasted wife. It goes against all the laws and against all justice that some other man shall take my promised wife to bed!" And again the bitterness surged in him, rage against Carlina who had refused to follow him into exile as a promised wife should do, rage against Beltran and Geremy who had come between them, rage against Melora who had driven him to Carlina in such frustration that he had lost his self-control and drunk too much and laid rough hands on her. . . .

"Perhaps," said little Alaric, "you will do some foreign king a great service, and he will give you his daughter—"

Bard laughed. "And half his kingdom, as the old tales have it? Stranger things have happened, I suppose, little brother."

"Have you everything you need?" his father asked.

"King Ardrin, damn him, paid me off well," Bard said. "I rode away in a fury, too angry to claim what he had given me, and here comes a flunkey after me, hot-foot, with all the things the king had promised me, a golden gelding from the plains of Valeron, and a sword and dagger which might well have been heirlooms among the Hastur kin, and the suit of leather armor I wore on the fields of Snow Glen, and a purse of four hundred silver royals, and when I came to count it I found he had added fifty copper *reis* too. So I cannot say I was ill-paid for my years of service to him; he could hardly have been more generous to one of his captains of twenty years going home to retirement! He bought me off, Zandru lash him with scorpion whips! I would like to send it all back to him, saying that since he had defrauded me of my lawful wife, I would be no better than a pimp to take money and goods for her; yet—" he shrugged, "I must be practical. Such a gesture would not get me Carlina, and I shall need horse and sword and armor when I ride out of Asturias—"

He broke off as the door opened and a young woman, full-bodied, her hair falling in two long copper braids over her shoulders, came into the room. In an instant of shock he thought he looked on Melora; but no, this woman was slenderer, and much younger. She had the same round face, the same big, vague gray eyes. She said shyly, "My lord, the Lady Jerana has sent to ask if she shall make anything ready before your son leaves us. She said that if Bard mac Fianna has any needs he should make them known at once, to me or to her, so that we may fetch them from the storerooms and have them ready."

Bard said, "I shall need three days' journey food; and I would be grateful for a bottle or two of wine. I will not trouble the lady further." His eyes lingered on the familiar, yet subtly strange, features and body. The red-haired girl was prettier than Melora, more slender, younger, but she roused in Bard the same subtle combination of resentment and desire he had felt for Melora.

"You see," Dom Rafael said, "my wife bears you no ill will, Bard; she is eager to make certain you do not suffer from want in your exile. Have you a good store of blankets, and would you like a cooking pot or two?"

Bard laughed. "Would you persuade me of Lady Jerana's love, Father? By no means! Like the king, she is eager to pay me off and hurry me on my way! But I shall take advantage of her generosity; a blanket or two would not be amiss, and perhaps a waterproof cover for my packs. Are you going to supply them. *damisela*? You are new among my lady mother's waiting-women?"

"Melisendra is not a waiting-woman, but a fosterling of my

wife," said Dom Rafael, "and your kinswoman, too; she is a MacAran, and your mother was of that kindred."

"Is it so? Why, *damisela,* I know your kinsman," Bard said, "for Master Gareth was *laranzu* when I rode to battle for King Ardrin, and so, too, was your sister Melora, and your kinswoman Mirella—"

Her face lighted with a quick smile. "Is it so? Melora is far more skilled than I as a *leronis*; she sent me word she was to go to Neskaya," she said. "How does my father, sir?"

"When I saw him last, at midwinter, he was well," Bard said, "although, I suppose, you know that he was lamed at the battle near Moray's mill, with a stroke from a Drytowner's poisoned dagger; and he was still walking with the aid of a stick."

"He sent me a letter," she said. "Melora wrote it; and she spoke well of your bravery—" and suddenly she dropped her eyes and blushed.

He said with calm courtesy, "I am glad Melora thinks well of me," but inwardly he was raging with conflict. Melora, who had refused him, despite all of her fine words of friendship!

He said, "If your kinsmen think well of me, *damisela,* I am glad; for it had entered my mind to ride to El Haleine and take service with The MacAran."

She said, "But The MacAran has no need of mercenary soldiers, sir; he has signed a truce with the Hasturs and with Neskaya, and they have pledged to keep peace only within their borders and wage no war outside them. You can save yourself the trouble of traveling there, sir, for they will hire no mercenaries from outside their borders."

Bard raised his eyebrows. So the Hasturs of Thendara and Hali were extending their influence, then, to El Haleine? "I thank you for the warning, *damisela,*" he said. "Peace may be welcome to the farmers, but it is always unwelcome news to a soldier."

"But," said Melisendra, with her ingenuous smile, "if there is peace long enough, a day may come when men may do more with their lives than soldiering, and men such as my father may do more with their talents than risk their lives, unweaponed, in battle!"

Dom Rafael broke in, and somehow he looked a little displeased. "Go to your lady, my girl, and make my son's wants known to her; and tell her he will be riding out at sunset."

"Why, Father, are you so eager to be rid of me?" Bard

asked. "I intend to lie this night in my father's house; I shall not see it again, nor you, for seven long years!"

"Eager to be rid of you? God forbid," said Dom Rafael, "but you have only three days to leave Asturias."

"It will take me only a day's ride to reach the border, if I ride north to the Kadarin," Bard said, "for if El Haleine is in Hastur hands, that is closed to me; I shall away into the Hellers, then, and see if the Lord Ardais has need for a hired sword who is also a leader of men. Or do you think your worthy kinsmen will send assassins to waylay me on my way out of the kingdom, sir?"

Dom Rafael stopped and considered it. He said, "I sincerely hope not. Still, if you have a blood-quarrel with Geremy, and with the prince—one of them might seek to assure that you do not seek to return and make peace with Ardrin after your seven years. I would go with great care, my son, and I would not delay until the last moment."

"I shall be careful, Father," Bard said, "but I shall not sneak forth into exile like a whipped dog, tail between my legs, either! And I shall lie this last night in my father's house." His eyes met Melisendra's in a long glance. The girl colored and tried to turn her glance away but Bard held her eyes, holding her in that close compulsion. Master Gareth had warned him away from Mirella as if he were an unruly schoolboy, and Melora had teased him, tormented him, finally refused him. He held Melisendra's eyes until she squirmed, her face flooding crimson, and finally managed to break eye contact and hurry out of the room, her head bent.

Then Bard laughed and bent to Alaric. He said, "Come, you shall take choice of all my bows and arrows and all my playthings. I am a man and will not need them, and who should have them, when I am gone, if not my own brother? Stay and look through these things and I will tell you what you will do in the king's house as his fosterling."

Later, when the child had gone away, his hands full of balls and shuttlecocks and hunting bows and such gear, Bard stood by the window, smiling in pleasant anticipation. The girl Melisendra would come. She would not be able to resist the compulsion he had put on her. Damn all women, who thought they could tease him and refuse him and make him less than a man with their whims! And so he smiled, not with surprise, but with a kind of fulfilled greed, when he heard the light step on the stairs.

She came slowly, with lagging step, into the room.

"Why, mistress Melisendra," he said, with a grin that showed his white teeth, "what are you doing here?"

She looked up at him, the big gray eyes wide and vague and somehow frightened. "Why—I don't know," she said shakily, "I thought—it seemed to me that I had to come—"

He reached for her, with a lazy smile, dragged her close and kissed her, pressing her roughly. Under his hand he felt her heart beating, and knew that she was terrified and confused.

He should have tried this with Carlina, then there would have been no trouble; he wouldn't have hurt her, she wouldn't have protested. He had been a fool. Somehow he had believed Carlina must somehow share the torment that raged in him, would want him as he wanted her. He still wanted her, like a ravenous itch in his blood, a thirst no other woman could slake; she was *his*, his wife, the king's daughter, sign and symbol of all he had done, of his honor, his achievement, and King Ardrin had dared to come between them!

His hands went to the laces of her undertunic, thrusting inside, and he let him do what he would, in terrified silence, like a rabbithorn in the grip of a banshee. She whimpered, a little, as his hand closed over her nipple. Her breasts were full, not like Carlina's meager bosom; this was a sow, a fat pig like Melora, like Melora who had teased him and played with his emotions! Well, this one would not do so! He dragged her toward the bed, keeping the relentless pressure on her mind and body. She did not struggle, even when he thrust her down on the bed, hauling at her skirts. She kept up the mindless whimpering, but he did not listen, flinging himself down on top of her. Once, she screamed. Then she lay silent, shaking, not even crying. Well, she knew better than that. Her very terror excited him, as Carlina's had done. *This* woman would not resist him, *this* one knew better!

He rolled away from her and lay spent, exhausted and triumphant. What was she sniveling about? She had wanted it as much as he did; and he had given her what all women wanted, once you got through the silly nonsense of pretty speeches and flattery. He supposed he would have owed some of that to a wedded wife. He remembered, with a sudden throb of pain, how he and Melora had sat beside the campfire, talking. He had not wanted to put compulsion on her; and so she had made a fool of him. Well, this woman would have no such opportunity to do that! Women were all whores anyway; he had had enough of them. They didn't make any fuss; why should a high-born girl be any different? They all

109

had the same thing under their skirts, didn't they? It was only that their price was different, the whores demanding money, the noblewomen demanding pretty talk and flattery and a sacrifice of his very manhood!

And then, suddenly, he was deathly sick and exhausted. Going into exile, leaving his home for years, and he was forced to waste time and thought on women, damn them all! Melisendra still lay with her back to him, shaking with sobs again. Damn her! It wouldn't have been like this with Carlina. She loved him, she would have learned to love him, they had been friends since childhood, all he should have done was to show her that he wouldn't hurt her. . . . It *should* have been Carlina. What was he doing with this damnable little whore in his bed? Had it been some confused notion of revenge on Melora? The red hair, limp on the pillow, somehow filled him with dismay. Master Gareth would have been angry, Master Gareth would know that Bard mac Fianna was no boy to be warned away from a woman he wanted. But her soft sobbing filled him with disquiet.

He put out a hesitant hand to her. "Melora," he said, don't cry."

She turned over and faced him. Her eyes, lashes damp and tangled, looked enormous in her white face. "I am not Melora." She said, "If you had served Melora so, she would have killed you with her *laran*."

No, he thought. Melora had wanted him, but for her own quixotic reasons had chosen to frustrate them both. This one—what was her name again—Mirella—Melisendra, that was it. She had been a virgin. He had not foreseen that; he knew that most *leroni* took the privilege of choosing lovers as they would. He wished it had been Melora. Melora would have responded to his own hunger. Melisendra had been only a limp, unwilling body in his arms. And yet—and yet, that was exciting too, knowing that he forced his will upon her and she could not make a fool of him as Melora had done.

"Never mind," he said. "It's done. Damn it, stop crying!"

She struggled to control her sobs. "Why are you angry with me, now that you have had your will?"

Why did she talk as if she had been so unwilling? He had seen her looking at him; he had simply given her the chance to do what she wanted to do, without need of silly scruples like those that had kept Melora from his arms!

"My lady will be angry," she said. "And what will I do, cousin, if you have gotten me with child?"

He thrust her clothing at her. "It's nothing to do with me," he said. "I am going into exile; unless you have grown so maddened with love for me that you wish to ride with me in male disguise, like a maiden in some old ballad, following her lover as a page, in men's dress—no? Well, then *damisela*, you will be neither the first nor the last to bear a bastard to di Asturien; do you think yourself better than my own mother? If it should be so, I am sure that my father would not let you or the babe starve in the fields."

She stared at him, her eyes wide, wiping away the tears that still flooded down her face.

"Why," she whispered, "you are not a man, but a fiend!"

"No," he said, with a bitter laugh. "Have you not heard? I am an outlaw, and wolf. The king has said so. Do you truly expect me to behave like a man?"

She caught up her clothes and fled, and he heard her sobbing fade away as her light footfall died out on the stairs.

He flung himself down on his bed. The sheets smelled of the scent of her hair. *Damn it,* he thought miserably, *it should have been Carlina. . . .*

Without Carlina I am an outlaw, a bastard . . . a wolf . . .
. . . and his rage and pride and longing overcame him.

It would have been so different with you . . . Carlina, Carlina!

He rode away at midmorning, taking leave of his father and Alaric with embraces and regrets; but he was young, and he knew that he was bound outward into the world to seek adventure. He could not remain cast down for long. They could call it exile, but for a young man with experience in war, there was adventure and the hope of gain, and he could return in seven years.

As he rode the mists cleared and the weather became fine. Perhaps he would ride into the Dry towns, and see if the Lord of Ardcarran had need of a hired sword, a bodyguard who spoke the languages of Asturias and the western country, to instruct his guardsmen in swordplay and defend him against his enemies. He must certainly have many. Somehow that made him think of his soldiers' rowdy song:

Four-and-twenty *leroni* went to Ardcarran,
When they came back, they couldn't use their *laran*

They must, he thought, have been like Mirella, *leroni* kept virgin for the Sight. Why, he wondered, should it be so, that only a maiden could exercise that particular form of *laran*? He knew so little about *laran*, except to fear it, and yet it could have been different, he could have been chosen, like Geremy, to become a *laranzu*, to carry a starstone rather than a sword in battle. . . . He whistled a few more verses of the improper ballad, but his voice died away alone in the vast spaces. He wished that he had some friend or kinsman, even a serving man, riding with him. Or a woman; Melora, riding at his side, on her little ambling donkey, to talk with him about war and ethics and ambitions as he had never talked with any living woman, or even a man . . . no. He wouldn't think of Melora. When he thought of Melora he thought of her shining red hair, and that made him think of Melisendra, limp, struggling in his arms. . . .

Carlina. If Carlina had agreed, as a wife should, to follow him into exile. She would have ridden at his side, laughing and talking as they had when they were children. And when they dismounted to make camp at night, he would hold her gently in his arms and fold his blankets around her, so tenderly . . . it made him faint to think of it. And then it made him dizzy with rage, to think that King Ardrin would lose no time in giving her to some other man, perhaps to Geremy Hastur. Savagely he wished Carlina joy of Geremy, crippled, with his withered leg . . . but the thought tormented him. Carlina, giving herself to Geremy as she would not to him! Damn them all, what did he want with women, anyway?

He stopped at midday to breathe his horse, tethering him to a featherpod tree, taking hard-baked journey bread and meat paste from his saddlebags, and munching while the horse cropped the new spring grass. He had food for several days—Domna Jerana had been generous with her stores—and he would not risk trying to buy food, or grain for his horse, until he was across the borders of Asturias. And he would fill his water bottles from springs, rather than at the wells in the towns; he was under a writ of outlawry, and they would have every right to refuse it to him. He was not really afraid he would be killed; King Ardrin had put no price on his head, and as long as he kept out of reach of Geremy's kindred, who might well declare blood-feud, he had little to fear.

But he felt very much alone, and he was not used to it. He would have enjoyed the company of someone, even a serving man. He remembered that once he and Beltran had ridden out this way, on a hunting trip. They had been thirteen or so, not yet declared men, and some trouble at home had made them talk of running away, of riding into the Dry towns together to seek employment as hired mercenaries. Even while

112

they knew it was half a game, it had been very real to them. They had been good friends then. A sudden snowstorm had made them seek shelter in one of the ruined barns, and they had shared blankets and talked very late, and before they slept they had turned to each other and given one another the pledge of *bredin*, as young boys do . . . why, in the name of all the gods, had he quarreled with Beltran about something like that? It had been that damned girl Melora, he had been raw-edged about her refusal, and it had caused him to fall out with his foster brother. Why should any woman come between the bonds between men? None of them was worth it! And because Melora had refused him, he had quarreled with Beltran, and spoken the unforgivable, and that had led to this . . . even if he had outgrown such boyish games, he should have remembered the long years of friendship with Beltran, his brother and his prince. Bard put his hands over his face, and for the first and the last time since his childhood, he wept, remembering the years of closeness among them, and that Beltran had become his enemy and that Geremy was lamed for life. The fire burned down, but he lay exhausted, his head in his arms, sick with grief, despairing. What had come over him, to fling away ambition, friendship, the life he had made for himself, for the sake of a woman? And now he had lost Carlina too. The sun set, but he could not make himself rise, wash his face, get on his horse again. He wished he had died at the battle at Moray's Mill, that Geremy's dagger had found him instead.

I am alone. I will always be alone. I am the wolf my foster father named me. Every man's hand is against me and my hand is against every man. Never before had he been fully aware of the meaning of the word *outlaw*, even when he stood before the king and heard his doom declared.

At last, exhausted, he slept.

When he woke, coming up out of sleep all at once like a wild animal, feeling his face stiff with the salt of the tears that had dried on his face, the tears of his last childhood, he knew suddenly that he had slept too long; someone was near him. He caught up his sword before his eyes were even fully open, and leaped to his feet.

It was gray with dawn; and Beltran, wrapped in a blue cape and hood, his hand on a naked sword, stood before him.

"So," Bard said, "you are not content with having me exiled; you felt that even seven years would not make you safe, Beltran?" He was sick with hate and weakness; had he wept

113

himself to sleep last night over the quarrel with his foster brother who would have killed him in his sleep?

"How brave you are, my Prince," he said, "to kill a sleeping man! Did you feel that even seven years could not make you safe from me?"

"I won't chop words with you, Wolf," Beltran said. "You chose to idle your way out of this kingdom instead of making all speed; now the doom is on you that any man may slay you unpunished. My father chose to show you mercy; but I do not want you in my kingdom. Your life is mine."

Bard snarled, "Come and take it," and ran at Beltran with his sword.

They were evenly matched. They had had lessons together, from the best arms masters in the kingdom, and they had always practiced together; they knew one another's weaknesses too well. Bard was taller, and his reach longer; yet never, before this, had they fought with real weapons, but only with blunted practice swords. And always before his eyes was the memory of that accursed midwinter night when he had fought Geremy, and maimed him for life. . . . He did not want to kill Beltran; he found it impossible that Beltran, despite their quarrel, would try to kill him. *Why, in Zandru's name, why?*

Only that he might give Carlina lawfully to Geremy, that Carlina would be widow before she was ever a wife? The thought enraged him; he beat down Beltran's defense, and, fighting like a berserker, managed to knock the sword from his hand. It fell some distance away.

He said, "I don't want to kill you, foster brother. Let me go peacefully out of this kingdom. If after seven years you are still ready to kill me, I will call challenge and fight you fair at that time."

"Dare to cut me down unarmed," Beltran said, "and your life will be worth nothing anywhere in the Hundred Kingdoms!"

Bard snarled, "Go, then, and pick up your sword, and I'll show you again that you are no match for me! Do you think, little boy, that you'll make yourself my equal by killing me?"

Beltran went slowly to pick up the sword. As he stooped to pick it up, there was a noise of racing hooves, and a horse dashed toward them at full gallop. As it jerked to a halt between them, Bard saw, stepping back in amazement, that the rider was Geremy Hastur, white as death. He flung himself from his saddle and stood, clinging to the saddle straps, unable to stand alone without support.

114

"I beg you—Bard, Beltran—" he said, breathlessly. "Will nothing amend this quarrel between you but death? Don't do this, *bredin-y*. I will never walk again; Bard must go outlaw into exile for half a lifetime. I beg you, Beltran—if you love me—let this be enough!"

"Don't interfere, Geremy," Beltran said, his lips drawn back in a snarl.

But Bard said, "This time, Geremy, I swear by my father's honor and my love for Carlina, the quarrel was none of my making; Beltran would have killed me as I slept, and when I disarmed him, I forbore to kill. If you can talk some sense into the damned little fool, in God's name, do it, and let me go in peace."

Geremy smiled at him. He said, "I don't hate you, foster brother. You were drunk, beside yourself, and I believe it, if the king does not, that you had forgotten you were not carrying that same old blunted dagger you had cut your meat with since we were boys. Beltran, you idiot, put away that sword. I came to say farewell, Bard, and make peace with you. Come and embrace me, kinsman."

He held out his arms, and Bard, his sight blurring with a mist of tears, went to embrace his foster brother, kissing him on either cheek. He felt that he would weep again. And then the world blurred in rage and hate as over his shoulder he saw Beltran rushing at him with a drawn sword.

"Traitor! Damned traitor," he shouted, tore himself from Geremy's arms and whirled, his sword flashing out. Two strokes beat down Beltran's sword, and even as he heard Geremy cry out in horror and dismay, he ran Beltran through the heart, felt the other man crumple on his sword and fall.

Geremy had fallen, striking his lame leg hard, and lay moaning on the ground. Bard stood looking down at him, bitterly.

"The *cristoforos* tell a tale of their Bearer of Burdens," he said, "that he too was betrayed by his foster brother while he stood in kinsman's embrace. I did not know you were a *cristoforo*, Geremy, or that you would play such a treacherous game on me. I believed you." He felt his mouth twist in a weeping grimace, but he bit his tongue hard and betrayed nothing.

Geremy set his teeth and struggled to rise. He said, "I did not betray you, Bard. I swear it. Help me up, foster brother."

Bard shook his head. "Not twice," he said bitterly. "Did you plot with Beltran to have your revenge?"

"No," said Geremy. Clutching at the stirrup, he managed to struggle to his feet. "Believe it or not, Bard, I came to try to make peace." He was crying. "Is Beltran dead?"

Bard said, "I don't know," and bent to feel his heart. There was no sign of life; and he looked at Beltran in despair, and at Geremy. "I had no choice."

"I know," said Geremy, and his voice broke. "He would have killed you. Merciful Avarra, how did we come to this?"

Bard set his teeth, nerving himself to wrench the sword out of Beltran's body. He wiped the blade on a handful of grass, and sheathed it. Geremy stood weeping, no longer making any attempt to conceal his tears. At last he said, "I know not what I shall say to King Ardrin. He was in my care. He was always so much the youngest of us—" He couldn't go on.

Bard said, "I know. Long after we were men, he was still a boy. I should have known—" and fell silent.

Geremy said at last, "Each man must ride the road of his own fate. Bard, I hate to ask this of you; but I cannot walk alone. Will you set Beltran's body on his horse, that I may lead it back to the castle? If I had paxman or serving man with me—"

"But," said Bard, "you wanted no witness to treachery."

"Do you still believe that?" Geremy shook his head. "No, to weakness, for I was ready to plead with Beltran to make his peace with you. I am not your enemy, Bard. There has been enough death. Do you want my life too?"

Bard knew he could have it easily enough. Geremy, as befitted a *laranzu*, was unarmed. He shook his head, and went to catch Beltran's horse and lead it to where he could lift the prince's lifeless form and tie it across the saddle.

"Do you need help to mount, Geremy?"

Geremy bent his head, unwilling to meet Bard's eyes. He accepted, reluctantly, Bard's hand to help him into his saddle, and sat there, swaying, shaking from head to foot. Their eyes met, and they both knew there was nothing more that they could say. Even a formal farewell would be too much. Geremy pulled at the reins, taking the reins of the horse which bore Beltran's lifeless body, and slowly turned on the trail and rode away toward Asturias. Bard watched him go, his face set and drawn, until he was out of sight; then he sighed, saddled his own horse, and rode away without looking back, out of the kingdom of Asturias and into exile.

BOOK TWO

The Kilghard Wolf

Chapter One

Half a year before the seven years of his outlawry had passed, Bard mac Fianna, called the Wolf, had news of the death of King Ardrin, and knew that he was free to return to Asturias.

He was far away in the Hellers then, in the little kingdom of Scaravel, helping to hold Sain Scarp against the assault of bandits from beyond Alardyn; a little time after the siege was lifted, Dom Rafael sent word to his son with news of the kingdom.

Three years after the death of Prince Beltran, Queen Ariel had borne the king another son. When Ardrin died, and the infant Prince Valentine succeeded to his father's throne, the queen had prudently fled to her kinsmen on the Plains of Valeron, leaving Asturias to whatever hands could take and hold it. The principal claim was being made by Geremy Hastur, whose mother was a cousin of King Ardrin, and who claimed that in times past all these lands had lain under the dominion of the old Hasturs and should still be under their wardship.

Dom Rafael had written: *I will never again bow the knee to the Hastur kindred, and my claim is better than Geremy's; Alaric is my rightful heir, and the heir to Ardrin, after Valentine. Come, my son, and help me take Alaric from Geremy's warding, and hold this kingdom for your brother.*

Bard pondered the message, standing half armored in the guard room of Scaravel, where it had reached him. In seven years he had served as mercenary, and later as captain of mercenaries, in as many little kingdoms; and he had no doubt at all that the fame of the Kilghard Wolf had spread beyond the Hellers and into the lowlands, even to Valeron. In those years he had seen plenty of fighting, and he read into the message the subtler news that there would be more fighting ahead; but at the end of *that* fighting there would be peace and honor, and a place near the throne of Asturias. He looked, frowning, at the messenger.

"And my father gave you no more message than this, no private intelligence for my ears alone?"

"No, *vai dom*."

No news, Bard wondered, of my wife? Has Geremy had the effrontery to marry Carlina? What else could give him the effrontery to claim Ardrin's throne, if not that he is wedded to Ardrin's daughter? All that talk of old Hastur kin is so much stable sweepings, and Geremy must know it as well as I do!

"But I bear you a message from the Lady Jerana," the messenger offered. "She bade me say to you that Domna Melisendra sends you greetings, and the greetings of your son Erlend."

Bard scowled, and the messenger flinched at the angry gesture.

He had all but forgotten Melisendra. There had been women enough in the time between, and it was likely that he had a son or two, scattered about the kingdoms. In fact, he gave one camp follower money, when he had it, because her son was so much like he had been as a child, and because she washed his clothes and trimmed his hair when it wanted cutting, and her cooking was better than he got in the guard room. He thought now with distaste of Melisendra. Whimpering, whining baggage! That encounter had left a bad taste in his mouth. It was the last time he had used his gift to lay compulsion on any woman to come to his bed. Well, she had been a maiden, right enough, and it was likely that the foolish girl had known no better than to tell her mistress all that had happened. Lady Jerana's knife had been sharp for him ever since he was a boy, and his brother Alaric had preferred him to any other companion. Now Jerana would have one more evil deed, or so she would certainly say, to hold over his head.

Melisendra's presence would be a good reason to avoid Asturias. And yet, it was not entirely unpleasant, to think he might have a son by a girl of good family, a son gently reared as a nobleman's *nedestro* son. The boy would be six or so. Old enough for some training in the manly arts; and no doubt Melisendra would try her best to make him into a milksop out of her grudge against his father. He wanted no son of *his* reared by that whimpering whey-faced wench, nor by her sour mistress. So if Lady Jerana thought she was warning him off, with the news that his mishandling of Me-

120

lisendra was common knowledge, well, she had better think again.

"Say to my father," he said to the messenger, "that I will ride for Asturias within three days' time. My work here is done."

Before he left, he went down among the camp followers to find the woman Lilla, and gave her most of the money he had earned at Scaravel.

"You should, perhaps, buy yourself a little farm somewhere in these hills," he said, "and perhaps a husband to help you to care for it, and to rear your son."

"By that," Lilla said, "I take it that you will not be coming back when your business in your homeland is done?"

Bard shook his head. "I don't think so," he said.

He saw her swallow hard, and flinched in anticipation of a scene; but Lilla was too sensible a woman for that. She stood on tiptoe and gave him a hearty kiss and hug.

"Then Godspeed you, Wolf, and may you fare well in the Kilghards."

He returned the kiss, grinning at her. "That's a soldier's woman! I'd like to say good-bye to the boy," he said, and she called the chubby boy, who came and stared up at Bard in his shining helmet, ready for the road southward. Bard picked him up and chucked him under the chin.

"I can't acknowledge him, Lilla," he said. "I don't know if I'll have a home to take him to; and in any case there were enough men before me and after me."

"I don't expect it, Wolf. Any husband I marry can rear my son as his own, or find some other woman."

"Just the same," Bard went on, smiling at the boy's bright eyes, "if he should show any talent for arms, in twelve years or so, and you have other children, so that you don't need his work on the farm to support you in your old age, send him to me at Asturias, and I'll put him in the way to earn his bread with the sword, or do better than that for him if I can."

"That's generous," Lilla said, and he laughed.

"It's easy to be generous with what may never come to pass; all this is supposing I'm still alive in twelve years or so, and that's the one thing no soldier can ever tell. If you hear that I'm dead—well, then, girl, your son must make his way in the world as his father did, with his wits and his strong arm, and may all the devils be kinder to him than they've been to me."

Lilla said, "That's a strange blessing you give to your son, Wolf."

"A wolf's blessing?" Bard laughed again and said, "It may be that he is not my son at all; and a kinsman's blessing would do him no good, just as my curse would do him no harm. I hold no faith in such things, Lilla. Curses and blessings are all one. I wish him well, and you too." He gave the boy a rough smack on the cheek and set him down, and gave Lilla another kiss. Then he got on his horse and rode away, and if Lilla wept, she had sense enough not to do it until Bard was well out of sight.

Bard, however, was elated as he rode southward. He had freed himself of the one tie he had made in all those years, and he had done it at no more cost than by lightening himself of money he did not need. Probably the boy was not his son, for all small fair-haired children looked very much alike anyhow, without need of kin ties, and would grow up with his feet firmly rooted in the dung of his mother's dairy, and he would never need to take any thought for either of them again.

He rode south alone, toward the Kadarin. He made his way through a countryside ravaged by small wars, for the Aldarans who had, in his father's time, kept peace through all this country had fallen out, and now there were four small kingdoms, and the forests lay waste where the four brothers, all greedy and land hungry, had fought through them with clingfire and sorcery. Bard had taken service one year with one of them; and when they fell out—Dom Anndra of Scathfell had taken for himself a girl Bard wanted, a wisp of a thing fourteen years old, with long dark hair and eyes that reminded Bard of Carlina—he had left and taken service with the man's brother and led Dom Lerrys right into the stronghold by a secret way he had learned when he served Scathfell. But then the two brothers had made up their quarrel, and banded together, swearing many oaths, against a third brother, and the girl had warned Bard that one price of their compact was Bard's head, for they both felt he would betray either or both of them; and so she let him out by the same secret door, and he fled to Scaravel, vowing he would never become involved again in kin strife!

And now he was riding homeward, to do just that. But at least these were his own kin!

He crossed the Kadarin and rode through the Kilghard Hills, seeing in the countryside the signs of war. When he crossed the borders of Asturias, he noted the tokens of fighting in the countryside, and wondered if he should hasten to the king's household? But no; Geremy claimed the throne, and sat in King Ardrin's stronghold, and if Dom Rafael had already laid seige to that place, his message would have sent for Bard to join him there; and so he rode toward his old family home.

He had not realized how much the countryside would change in seven years; nor, paradoxically, how much it would remain the same. It was early spring; a heavy snow had fallen during the night, and the featherpod trees had put on their snow pods. When he and Carlina were children they had played under a featherpod tree in the courtyard. He was already well beyond children's games, but he had climbed the tree to bring down pods for Carlina, so that she could make beds for her dolls with the feathery pods and the wool inside them. Once they found a really huge pod, and Carlina had put a kitten to bed inside the pod, cuddled in the feathery stuff, and sung it lullabyes; but the kitten had tired of the game and torn its way out of the pod. He remembered Carlina, her hair hanging in untidy ripples to her waist, standing with the torn pod in her hands, sucking on a finger where the kitten had scratched her, her eyes filling with tears. He had caught the kitten and threatened to wring its neck, but Carlina had grabbed it and sheltered it against her breast, warding him away with her small fingers.

Carlina. He was coming back to Carlina, who was his wife under the old law, and he would demand that his father enforce it. If they had given Carlina to another man, first he would kill the other man, and then he would marry Carlina. And if the other man was Geremy, he would cut off Geremy's *cuyones* and roast them before his face!

By the time he saw from afar the towers of Dom Rafael's Great Hall, he had worked himself into a fine frenzy against Geremy, and against Carlina; if she had stayed with him, even Ardrin could not have parted them lawfully!

The sun had set, but it was a clear night, and three moons were in the sky. He thought of that as a lucky omen, but when he rode up to the gates of the Great Hall the gates were barred against him, and when he dismounted and beat on them, the voice of his father's old *coridom*, Gwynn, came gruffly though: "Be off with you! Who rides here when honest folk be abed? If you ha' business with Dom Rafael, come back by daylight when the rogues run back to their dens!"

"Open this gate, Gwynn." Bard shouted, laughing, "for it is the Kilghard Wolf, and if you do not I shall leap the wall, and make you pay blood money if the rogues get my horse! What, would you bar me from my father's hearthside?"

"Young Master Bard! Is it really you? Brynat, Haldran, come here and unbar these gates! We heard you were on your way, young sir, but who'd think that you'd come at this hour?" The gate swung wide. Bard dismounted and led his horse in, and old Gwynn came and fumbled one-handed to embrace him. He was ancient, gray and stooped; he walked lamely, and one arm had been taken off at the elbow when he had held the towers of the Great Hall single-handed before Bard was born, and hidden the lady, Dom Rafael's first wife, in the lofts. For that service, Dom Rafael had sworn that none but old Gwynn should ever be *coridom* while he lived, and while the old man was long past his office, he jealously held on to it, refusing to let any younger man take over for him. He had shown Bard his first moves at swordplay when Bard was not seven years old. Now he hugged and kissed him, saying, "Foster father, why are the gates barred in this peaceful countryside?"

"There's no peace anywhere these days, Master Bard," the old man said soberly. "Not with the Hasturs swearing all this land round here is theirs from away back, land that's been held all these years by the di Asturiens—why, the very name *Asturias* means *land of di Asturiens*; how come all these damned Hasturs try to claim it? And now folk at Hali swearing to make all this one land under their tyrants, and trying to take weapons away from honest folk so we'll all be at the mercy of cutthroats and bandits! Oh, Master Bard, it's evil days in this land since you went away!"

"I heard King Ardrin was dead," Bard said.

"True, sir, and young Prince Beltran murdered by assassins, about that same time you left us, sir, though between you and me I've never been sure that Hastur who's trying to claim the throne now didn't have some hand in it. He and the young prince rode out together, so they said, and only one of them came back, and of course it was the Hastur, and him a dirty *laranzu* and sandal wearer. So with Beltran dead, and Queen Ariel fled out of the country—Dom Rafael said it, when the old king died, *'That land fares ill where the king's but a babe,'* and sure enough, they're fighting all up and down the land, and honest folk can't get their crops in for the bandits in the fields, if it's not the soldiers! And now, I hear, if the Hasturs win this war they'll take away all our weapons, even bows for hunting, leave us with no more than daggers and pitchforks, and if they have their way, I dare say a shepherd won't be allowed to carry a club to keep off the wolves!"

He added, taking the reigns of Bard's horse with his good arm, "But come away in, sir, Dom Rafael's going to be glad to hear you've come!" He shouted for a couple of grooms to come and unsaddle him, to carry his packs inside the Great Hall, and to bring lights and servants; in a little while, there were people running everywhere in the courtyard, dogs barking, noise and confusion.

Bard said, "I wonder, has my father gone to bed?"

"No, sir," said the childish voice almost under his feet, "for I told him you would come tonight; I saw it in my starstone. And so grandsire waited for you in the Hall."

Old Gwynn started back in dismay.

"Young Master Erlend!" he said crossly. "Ye've been forbidden the stables, ye uncanny wee man, you might have been trampled under all the horses! Yeur mammy will be angry with me!"

"The horses know me, and my voice," said the child, coming out into the light. "They won't step on me." He looked to be about six years old, small for his age, and with a great mop of curly red hair, like freshly minted copper in the torchlight. Bard knew who he must be, even before the boy bent his knee in an odd, old-fashioned bow, and said, "Welcome home to you, sir my father, I wanted to be the first to see you. Gwynn, you must not be afraid, I shall tell Grandsire not to be angry with you."

Bard scowled down at the boy. He said, "So you are Erlend." Strange that he had not thought of that; Melisendra had had the red hair of the old kindreds, bred into them generations ago, the blood of the Hastur kin, of Hastur and Cassilda; but he had not thought that the boy might be *laran* gifted. "And you know who I am, then?" How, he wondered, had Melisendra spoken of him?

"Yes," he said, "I have seen you in my mother's mind and memory, though more when I was smaller than now; now she is too busy, she says, bringing up a great boy like me, to have time for remembering the past days. And I have seen you in my starstone, and Grandsire has told me that you are a great warrior, and that you are called Wolf. I think perhaps I would like to be a great warrior too, though my lady mother said that more likely I will be a *laranzu*, a wielder of magic like *her* father. May I look at your sword, Father?"

"Yes, certainly." Bard smiled at the small, serious boy, and knelt beside him, drawing his sword from the sheath. Erlend

125

laid a small, respectful hand on the hilt. Bard started to warn him not to touch the blade, then realized that the boy already knew better. He sheathed the blade and swung the boy to his shoulder.

"So my son is the first to welcome me home after all these years of exile, and that is very fitting," he said. "Come with me when I greet my father."

The Great Hall seemed smaller than when he had last seen it, and shabbier. A long, low room, stone-floored, with the shields and banners of generations of di Asturien men hanging on the walls, and weapons too old for use displayed there too: pikes, and the old spears which were too clumsy for the close in fighting of the day, and tapestries woven hundreds of years ago, showing old gods and goddesses, the harvest goddess driving a banshee from the fields, Hastur sleeping on the shores of Hali, Cassilda at her loom. The stone floor was uneven under foot, and a fire was burning at each end of the long hall. At the far end, women were clustered together, and Bard heard the sound of a *rryl*; at the near fireside, Dom Rafael di Asturien rose from his armchair as Bard came near with his son in his arms.

He was wearing a long indoor gown of woven dark-green wool with embroideries at neck and sleeves. The di Asturien men were blond, all of them, and Dom Rafael's hair was so light it was impossible to see whether it was graying, or not; but his beard was white. He looked very much as he had looked when Bard had last seen him, only thinner, his eyes somewhat sunken as if with worry.

He held out his arms, but Bard set Erlend down on his feet, and knelt to his father. He had never done this to any of the overlords he had served in his seven years of exile.

"I have come back, my father," he said, sensing somewhere in his mind the surprise of his son, that his father, the renowned warrior and the outlaw, should kneel to his grandfather just as the vassals did. He felt his father's hand touch his hair.

"Take my blessing, son. And whatever gods there are, if any, be praised that they have brought you safely back to me. But then, I never doubted that. Get up, dear son, and embrace me," Dom Rafael said, and Bard, obeying, saw the lines in his father's face and felt the sharp thinness of his bones. He thought, with shock and dismay, *Why, he is already old. The giant of my youth is already an old man!* It troubled him, that he was taller than his father, and so much broader that he could have lifted him in his arms as he had done with Erlend!

So swiftly had the years passed, while he fought in strange wars in foreign lands! *Time has left its hand heavy on me too,* he thought, and sighed.

"I see that Erlend came to greet you," Dom Rafael said, as Bard joined him on the seat before the fire. "But now you must away to your bed, grandson; what was your nurse thinking of, to let you out into the night so late?"

"I suppose she was thinking I was already in bed, for that is where she left me," Erlend said, "but I felt it most seemly to go and greet my father. Good night, Grandsire, good night, sir," he added, with his funny, precocious little bow, and Dom Rafael laughed as he went out of the hall.

"What a little wizard he is! Half the serving folk are afraid of him already," he said, "but he is clever and well grown for his years, and I am proud of him. I wish, though, that you had told me that you had gotten Melisendra with child. It would have saved her, and me too, some angry words from my Lady; I did not know that Melisendra was being kept virgin for the Sight. And so we all suffered, for Jerana was wonderfully cross, to lose her *leronis* so young."

"I did not tell you because I did not know," Bard said, "and Melisendra's foresight could not have been so wonderful after all, if it did not keep her out of my chamber when I was alone and wanting a woman." After he said it he was a little ashamed, remembering that he had given her, after all, no choice in the matter. But, he told himself, if Melisendra had half as much *laran* as that red hair promised, she would never have fallen victim to that compulsion anyhow! He could not, for instance, have done it to Melora.

"Well, at least her son is handsome and clever, and I see you had him brought up in this house instead of fostering him out to some nobody!"

His father said, staring into the fire, "You were going into outlawry and exile. I feared he should be all I had left of you. And in any case," he added, defensively, as if he were ashamed of this weakness, "Jerana had not the heart to separate Melisendra from her baby."

Bard reflected that he had never suspected Lady Jerana of having any heart at all, so that was no surprise to him. He did not want to say that to his father, so he said, "I see that his mother has taught her son some of her craft too; already he bears a starstone, young as he is. And now enough of women and children, Father. I thought you would already have moved against that damned upstart of a Hastur who has tried to make himself master of this land."

"I cannot move against Geremy at once," said Dom Rafael, "for he still has Alaric in his keeping. I sent for you to try to devise some way to get your brother back, so that I can move freely against these Hasturs."

Bard said, enraged, "Geremy is a snake whose coils lie everywhere! I had him in my hand once, and forebore to kill him. Would I had been as foresighted as you say Melisendra was!"

"Oh, I bear the boy no ill will," Dom Rafael said. "In his boots I should have taken the same step, no doubt. He was hostage at Ardrin's court for the good will of King Carolin of Thendara! I have no doubt Geremy grew to manhood knowing that if ill will came between Ardrin and Carolin, his own head would be the first to fall, be he ever so much the foster-brother of Ardrin's son! And speaking of Ardrin's sons—you knew, did you not, that Beltran was dead?"

Bard set his teeth and nodded. Some day he would tell his father how Beltran had come to die; but not now. "Father," he asked what he had never thought to ask before. "Was I hostage at Ardrin's court for your good behavior?"

"I thought you had known that all your life," Dom Rafael said. "Ardrin never trusted me overmuch. Yet, no doubt, Ardrin valued you at your true worth, or he would never have promoted you to his own banner bearer, nor set you above his own son. You flung that away by your own folly, my boy, but you seem to have prospered in these years of exile, so we will say no more of that. But while you, and then Alaric, were at his court, Ardrin knew I would make no trouble, nor strive with him for the throne, though my claim to sit there was as good as his own, and better than that of his younger son. Now, however, with both Ardrin and Beltran dead, it would be catastrophe, in times like these, for a baby king to reign—rats make havoc in the kitchen when the cat's a kitten! If you are with me—"

"Can you doubt that, Father?" Bard asked, but before he could speak further, a woman came from the woman's fire, slender, with graying hair, clad in a richly embroidered and braided robe.

"So you are back again, foster son? Seven years outlawry seem to have done you no very great harm, after all. Indeed," she added, looking at his fur-trimmed garb, the jeweled dagger and sword hanging at his side, the warrior's braid banded with jewels, "you must have prospered in the foreign wars! This is no wolf's pelt!"

Bard bowed to the Lady Jerana. He thought, *still the same sour-faced, ill-spoken bitch, it would take three times seven years to make any improvement in her, and the best improvement would be a shroud*, but in seven years he had learned not to say everything that came into his head.

"Seven years indeed have made small change in you, foster mother," he said, and her smile was sour.

"Your manners, at least, are much improved."

"Why, *domna*, I have lived seven years by my wits and my sword; in such lands and circumstances, lady, one improves quickly or one dies, and as you see, I still walk among the living."

"But your father is remiss in hospitality," Lady Jerana said. "He has offered you no refreshment. How came you to ride so late in such times?" she added when she had signaled to her servants to bring food and wine.

"Is it so unsafe, *Domna*? Old Gwynn said something of this, but I thought, at his age, his wits might well have gone roving."

"His wits are clear enough," Dom Rafael said. "It is I who have given orders for the gates to be barred every night at sunset, and that every beast and man and woman and child shall be within the walls. And I have set rangers to ride the borders, with beacon fires to warn us if more than three riders are sighted in a party—which is why we did not welcome you properly. It never occurred to us that you would ride alone, without bodyguard or paxman or even serving manor squire!"

"I am not called Wolf for nothing," Bard said. *"Lone wolf,* and *rogue,* are the kindest of the names they give me."

"Yet, despite all these precautions," Dom Rafael said, "raiders, bandits they said, but I think myself they may be Geremy's men, have broken into the villages and driven off some horses. We built stockades here in the castle, where they may keep their beasts if they will, but they have begun to keep them at home again. The raiders also took sacks of grains and nuts, and half the harvest of apples. There will be no great hunger, but the markets will go short, and people will have little coined money, and some of the village folk have armed themselves. There was even talk of hiring a *leronis*, to frighten away the raiders with sorcery, but nothing came of it, and I was not displeased; I like not that kind of warfare."

129

"Nor I," Bard said, "but little Erlend said something of being trained as *laranzu*."

Lady Jerana nodded. "The boy has *donas*," she said, "and his tutors think he has probably not the muscles for a swordsman." Servants had brought wine, and were handing around savory tidbits. Bard froze suddenly, looking down into the eyes of a small, round-bodied woman whose hair was like a living flame around her face, escaping in small fiery tendrils despite the modest braids coiled low on her neck.

"Melisendra?"

"My lord," she said, lowering her head in a bow. "Erlend said, when he came to me to be put back to bed, that he had seen you."

"He is a fine, likely-looking boy. Word came to me, just before I came here, of his existence; I had not thought of it before. Any man would be proud of such a son."

A faint smile touched her face. "And for such compliments, no doubt, a woman is rewarded for whatever price she paid. I think now, perhaps, he was a fair price for what I lost; but it took me many years to come to think so."

Bard studied the mother of his son in silence. Her face was still round, snub-chinned; she wore a sober gown of gray, over an under-tunic of blue, embroidered with a pattern of butterflies at neck and sleeves. She had a poise and dignity which reminded him, suddenly, of his young son's solemn way of speaking. He had not remembered her this way.

She said, "Lady Jerana has been kind to us both; and so has your father."

"I should hope so," said Bard. "I was brought up in my father's house, and there is no reason my son should not be treated as well."

Her eyes glinted with an ironic smile. "Why, yes, my lord, that was the last thing you said to me, that you were certain your father would not allow me and the babe to starve in the fields."

"A grandson is a grandson," Bard said. "Even if his birth was blessed with no ceremonious rubbish!"

Melisendra said quietly, "No birth is unblessed, Bard. Ceremonies are to comfort the heart of the ignorant; the wise know that it is the Goddess who gives a blessing. But how can anything which gives comfort be rubbish?"

"I take it, then, you are not among the ignorant who had need of such ceremonies?"

"When I had need of them, my lord, I was more ignorant than you can guess, being very young. Now I know that the

Goddess alone can give more comfort than any ceremony devised by mankind or woman."

Bard chuckled. "Which goddess is she, among the dozens who comfort the ignorant in this countryside?"

"The Goddess is one, by whatever name she may call herself, or whichever name the ignorant may give her."

"Well, I suppose I must find some name by which to thank her," Bard said, "for giving me such a fine son. But I would rather think that I owe thanks to *you*, Melisendra."

She shook her head. "You owe me nothing, Bard," she said, and turned away. He would have followed her, but the minstrels began to play near the fire. Bard went and sat beside his father again. At the other end of the hall some of the women were dancing, but he noticed briefly that Melisendra was not among them.

He asked, "How is it that Geremy is trying to claim the throne? The very name *Asturias* means *land of Asturiens*, what has a Hastur to do with it?"

"He claims," said Dom Rafael, "that once all this land was held by the Hastur kin, and that Asturias was given to the di Asturiens only to hold at Hastur's will; that *Asturias* means, in the old tongue, *land of Hasturs*."

"He is mad."

"If so, it is a self-serving madness, for he claims this land for King Carolin of Carcosa."

"What shadow of a claim—" Bard began, then amended himself. "Leaving aside the claim of Prince Valentine, and I would as soon leave *that*, for that land fares ill where the king's a child, what shadow of claim does he have, save the old myth of the sons of Hastur and Cassilda? I will not be ruled by a king whose claim comes from legend and myth!"

"Nor I," said Dom Rafael. "I would as soon believe that the Hasturs were once gods, as myth has it, and that the Hasturs were true sons of the Lord of Light! But even if the first Hastur were son to Aldones himself, I would not so peacefully give up my claim to the land the di Asturiens have held for all these years! I cannot move against him while he holds Alaric; but I think he knows that the people will cry out against a Hastur on the throne. Perhaps he holds Alaric to set him there as his puppet, but he must be shaking in his sandals, the wretch!"

"When he knows I have come back, he will have cause to tremble," Bard said. "But I thought, perhaps, he had chosen to marry the daughter of King Ardrin and hold the throne for his children."

"Carlina?" Dom Rafael inquired, and shook his head. "I know nothing of her, and certainly she is not married to Geremy; *that*, I would have heard."

Soon after that, the minstrels were dismissed, Lady Jerana sent her women away, and Dom Rafael bade his son an affectionate good night. Lady Jerana had sent a body servant to his old rooms, to take his boots and clothing, and see him to his bath; but when he came back to bed the servant omitted the customary courtesy of asking if he wanted a woman for his bed. Bard started to call him back, then shrugged; he had ridden far that day, and had seen no woman among Lady Jerana's maids who interested him. He put out the light and got into his bed.

And sat up in astonishment, for it was already occupied.

"Zandru's hells!"

"It is I, Bard." Melisendra sat up beside him. She was wearing a long thin bedgown in some pale color, her hair a luminous cloud. Bard laughed.

"So you have come back, though you whimpered and wailed when I had my will of you before!"

"Not my will, but Lady Jerana's will," Melisendra said. "Perhaps she does not wish to lose another of her virgin *leroni*; as for me, what I had to lose can be lost only once." She gave a cynical shrug. "She has allowed me to use these rooms, saying I had a right to them, and little Erlend and his nurse sleep yonder. You are no worse than any other; and the Goddess knows, I have had to protest often enough, to be left in peace here. Lady Jerana wishes to think of me as *barragana* to her foster son and I have borne you a child. But if you do not want me here I shall be more than happy to sleep elsewhere, even if I must share my child's cot."

Bard was infuriated by her quiet, indifferent acceptance, yet he realized he would have been equally angry if she had protested her distaste or dislike. He was ready to fling her out of his bed with a curse and a blow and bid her be gone from here. But he sensed that whatever he did she would accept with the same shrug of indifference, in order to infuriate him further. Damn the woman, one would think he had done her harm, instead of giving her a son of noble blood and a regular place as *barragana* in this great household!

And, since he could not have Carlina in his bed, one woman was very much like any other when the lamp was out.

"Come here, then," he said brutally, "and be quiet. I don't

132

like women who make a lot of noise, and I don't want to hear any more of your impudent chatter."

She looked up at him, smiling, as he seized her. "Why, just as you like, my lord. All the gods forbid you must endure anything to displease you."

She said nothing more. If she had, Bard thought in dull rage, he would have hit her and tried to see whether that drove the damned smile from her face.

Chapter Two

He wakened to a great clamor, and sat up, instantly awake. He had slept at too many battle posts not to know what that noise was. Melisendra sat up beside him.

"Are we under attack?"

"It sounds like it. How in hell's name should I know?" Bard was already out of bed, flinging on his clothes. She slid a long robe over her bedgown and said, "I must go to my lady and see the women and children safe. Let me help you with your boots," she added, and Bard wondered how she knew that he grudged the time to summon his body servant. "And here are your sword and cloak."

He hastened toward the stairs, flinging back over his shoulder, "See that the boy is safe!" He was vaguely surprised at himself; with a castle under attack it was no time to worry about women and children.

He found his father in the Great Hall, hastily dressed.

"Are we under attack?"

"No; a swift strike, they have come and gone in the villages, taking horses we could ill spare, and some sacks of grain. The noise was the villagers, riding in to tell us, and my guardsmen arming to chase them, perhaps to get the horses back. . . ."

"Geremy's men?"

"No, they would have struck at Great House, not villages. The men of Serrais, I think, swarming over our borders, taking advantage of anarchy to lead Dryland scum against us. . . . The land is overrun with them. I wish they would go and harry Geremy in Castle Asturias!"

Gwynn entered and Dom Rafael turned irritably toward the old *coridom*. "What now?"

"A king's messenger, my lord."

Dom Rafael scowled and demanded testily, "Where is there a king in this land to send a messenger?"

"Your pardon, my lord. I should have said a messenger

from Dom Geremy Hastur. He arrived in the midst of all this confusion, while your men were saddling to ride after the bandits—"

"I should have ridden with them," Bard said, and his father shook his head.

"No doubt that is what they wished, that you waste your strength on bandits and random strikes!" He turned to Gwynn and said, "I will receive Geremy's man. Tell Lady Jerana to send a *leronis* to set truthspell in the hall. I will hear no Hastur lackey without that. Bard, will you attend me?"

By the time Geremy's envoy came into the Great Hall, bearing truce flag and the banner of the Hasturs of Carcosa, the silver fir tree on blue, differenced with the blazing candles, Bard had breakfasted hastily on a bowl of nut porridge from the kitchens, washed down with a cup of sour beer, washed the sleep from his eyes, and dressed himself in his father's colors, blue and silver for di Asturien. Dom Rafael was seated in a carven chair on the dais, two steps behind him, in the paxman's place. Bard stood with his hand just resting on the hilt of his sword. Melisendra, also in the di Asturien silver and blue—and how, Bard wondered, had the Hasturs and di Asturiens come to have the same household colors?—was seated on a low stool, bending over her starstone that spread the blue haze of truthspell over the chamber. The envoy paused in the doorway, displeased.

"My Lord, that is not necessary."

"In my hall," said Dom Rafael, "I judge what is necessary unless I greet my own overlord; and I do not recognize any son of Hastur as my overlord, or his messenger as the voice of my lawful king. State your business under truthspell, or forbear to speak it at all and take yourself out of my hall again."

The envoy was too well trained to his work to shrug, but somehow he gave the impression of having done so.

"Be it so, *vai dom*. Since I speak no falsehood, truthspell says more of the customs of your hall than the message of my master. Hear, then, the word of the high lord Geremy Hastur, Warden of di Asturien and Regent of Asturias, holding this land for the rightful lord, King Carolin of Carcosa. . . ."

Dom Rafael interrupted, softly but audibly, "What is the *leronis* about? I thought truthspell was set in this room so that no falsehood could be spoken here, yet I hear a claim—"

Bard knew Dom Rafael had said this only to annoy; truth-

135

spell dealt with facts and intentions, not with disputed claims, and of course the messenger knew it too, and disregarded the interruption. His stance altered, and Bard knew he looked upon a Voice, or professional messenger-mimic, whose business was to speak a message in the very words and inflection exactly as it had been given. Any messenger could repeat his message verbatim; but the art of repeating them in the very voice of the speaker, and taking back any message in the very same tone, so that the recipient could judge for himself every subtlety, irony or innuendo, was a rare and special skill.

"To my kinsman and the old friend of my father, Dom Rafael of Asturias," the Voice began, and Bard shivered; it was uncanny. The Voice was a smallish fat man with gingery whiskers and nondescript livery, but through a trick of voice or glamour, it seemed that Geremy Hastur himself stood before them, a bent man, one shoulder higher than the other, one leg posed to take less weight, leaning on some kind of support. And Bard felt a cold grue running over him as he saw what the boyish quarrel had made of the embittered man before him. . . .

No. This was a trick, a trained Voice, a mimic, a special kind of servant; the real Geremy was far away.

"Kinsman, your claim and mine to the throne of Asturias may be disputed later; at the moment all of Asturias is under siege from the people of Serrais, who see the throne of Asturias under dispute and think this land a game bird flying free for any hawk to seize. Whatever the merits of your claim or mine, I ask truce, to drive these outsiders of Serrais from our borders; and after that, you and I may sit down as kinsmen and discuss who shall rule this land and how. I ask you to make common cause with me for the moment, as the greatest of the generals who served under my cousin Ardrin in the years past. I pledge the word of a Hastur that while the truce endures, your son Alaric, who dwells as a kinsman in my house, shall be safeguarded against the war; and when the invaders are driven forth, I pledge to meet with you myself, each of us unarmed and with no more than four paxmen, to discuss the fate of this land and the return of Alaric to his father's care."

And after a few seconds, the Voice added, now in his own voice, "And this is all of the message which the lord Geremy Hastur has sent to you at this time; except that he asks that you come as quickly as you can."

Dom Rafael sat scowling at the floor. It was Bard who

asked, "How many of the invaders have crossed the borders of Asturias?"

"Sir, they are an army."

Dom Rafael said, "It seems we have no choice; otherwise these Serrais will fall upon us one by one, and pick us off at leisure. Say to my kinsman that I will join him, with all the able-bodied men I can raise, and as many *leroni* as I can bring, as soon as I have made certain of the defense of my own house and of my lady and my grandson; and you may tell him that I have said this under truthspell."

The Voice bowed and there were a few more formal speeches. Then the Voice withdrew, and Dom Rafael turned to Bard.

"Well, my son? I have heard of your renown in war, and look, here is one waiting for you as soon as you come home to Asturias!"

"I would rather fight against Geremy himself," Bard said, "but the throne ofAsturias must be made secure before anyone can sit upon it! If Geremy thinks that our help will strengthen his claim to the throne, it will be for us to show him he is deluded when that time comes. When do we ride forth?"

All that day the beacon fires burned, summoning all men who owed service to Asturias, which meant every able-bodied man who could ride against invasion. As they rode out, more and more men joined them, noblemen in armor of metal-rein-forced leather, bearing sword and shield and ahorse; bowmen afoot with arrows and fire arrows and long pikes, farmers and peasants riding donkeys and horned pack beasts, carrying ancient spears, maces studded with deadly spikes, even cudgels and pitchforks.

Bard rode with his father's paxmen, and near them rode a small group of men and women, unarmed, wearing long gray cloaks and hoods which hid their faces; the *leroni* who would fight alongside the warriors. Bard realized that all during his absence his father must have been recruiting and training these men, and suddenly he shivered a little. How long had his father been hatching this rebellion, like some monstrous egg sheltered in his mind? Had he wanted the crown for Alaric, so long ago?

Well, he, Bard, was better suited for war than governing; he would rather be the king's man than the king, and if the king was one day to be his well-loved brother, there was a good life before him. He began to whistle, and rode on, cheerful.

But an hour or so later he had a shock, for among the *leroni* he had recognized, even under the hood, the form and face of Melisendra.

"Father," he demanded, "why does the mother of my son ride with the armies? She is no camp follower!"

"No, she is the most skilled *leronis* in our service."

"Somehow, from what you said, I thought Lady Jerana blamed me for spoiling her for that service—"

"Oh, she is useless for the Sight," Dom Rafael said. "We have a maiden youth for that, not twelve years old. But for all else, Melisendra is highly skilled. I had thought of taking her for my own *barragana*, at one time, because Jerana is fond of her, and as you will know when you are wedded, it is useless to take a concubine who is detestable to your lawful wife. But—" he shrugged, "Jerana wished to keep her virgin for the Sight, and so I let her be; and you know what happened. I would rather have a grandson anyway. And since Melisendra has proved herself fertile to you, perhaps you should take her to wife."

Bard frowned with revulsion. He said, "I remind you, sir, that I have already a wife; I shall take no other woman while Carlina lives."

"You may certainly take Carlina for wife if you can find her," Dom Rafael said, "but she has not been at court since her father's death. She fled the court even before Queen Ariel took Valentine to her kinsfolk at Valeron."

Bard wondered if she had left court to avoid marriage to Geremy. He would certainly have seen this marriage as the best road to claim Ardrin's throne. Was she waiting for him, somewhere, to come and claim her?

"Where is Carlina, then?"

"I know no more than you, my son. For all I know, she is within a Tower somewhere, learning the ways of a *leronis*, or even—" Dom Rafael raised his eyes to the newest group of fighters who had joined their army on the road, "she may have cropped her hair and taken the vows of the Sisterhood of the Sword."

"Never!" said Bard, with a shudder of dismay, looking at the women in their scarlet cloaks. Women with their hair cropped shorter than a monk's, women without grace or beauty, women who wore the Renunciate's dagger, not in their boots as men did, but strapped across their breasts, in token that a man who laid a hand upon them would die, and that the woman herself would die before surrendering herself as a prize of war. Under their cloaks they wore the odd garb of their sworn sisterhood, breeches and long laced jerkins to their knees, low boots tied around their ankles; their ears were pierced like those of bandits, long hoops dangling from the left earlobe.

"I wonder, my Father, that you will have these—these bitches with us."

"But," said Dom Rafael, "they are fighters of great skill, pledged to die rather than fall to an enemy; not one has ever been taken prisoner, or betrayed her oath of service."

"And you mean to tell me that they live without men? I do not believe it," Bard jeered. "And what do the men think, riding with women who are not camp followers?"

"They treat them with the same respect as the *leroni*," said Dom Rafael.

"Respect? For women in breeches, with their ears holed? I would treat them as all such women deserve who give up the decencies of their sex!"

"I would not advise it," Dom Rafael said, "for I have heard that if one of them is raped, and does not kill herself or her ravisher, her sisters hunt her down and kill them both. As far as any man can say, they are as chaste as the priestesses of Avarra; but no one knows for certain what goes on among them. It may simply be that they are very adept at the art of secret whoring. And they are, as I say, skilled fighters."

Bard could not imagine Carlina among them. He rode on, silent and moody, until they called him, in midafternoon, to examine the weapons of a band of young farmers who had joined them. One bore an heirloom sword, but the others had axes, pikes which looked as if they had been handed down for generations, pitchforks and cudgels.

"Can you ride?" he asked the man with the sword. "If so, you may join my horsemen."

The young peasant shook his head. "Nay, *vai dom*, not even a plowing beast," he confessed in his rude dialect. "The sword belonged to my great-grandsire, who bore it a hundred years gone at Firetop. I can fight wi' it, a wee bit, but e'en so, I better stay wi' my brethren."

Bard nodded in agreement. Weapons did not make a soldier.

"As you wish, man, and good fortune to you. You and your brothers may join those men there. They speak your tongue."

"Aye, they my neighbors, *vai dom*," he said, then asked

139

shyly, "Are ye no' the high lord's son, the one they call the Wolf, *dom?*"

Bard said, "I have been called so."

"What be ye doin' here, *dom?* I heard ye were outlawed, in foreign parts—"

Bard chuckled. "He who made me outlaw has gone to explain it in hell. Are you going to try to kill me for the head-prize, man?"

"Nay, no such thing," said the young peasant, his eyes round in dismay. "Not to the high lord's son. Only, with you to lead us, we canna' do other than win, *dom* Wolf."

Bard said, "May all the Serrais foxes and wild men think so, man," and watched as the peasants joined their own group. His eyes were thoughtful as he rode forward to join his father. Here and there he heard a snatch of conversation: *the Wolf, the Kilghard Wolf has come to lead us.* Well, perhaps it would serve them well.

When he joined his father, Dom Rafael gestured at the youngest of the *leroni*, a fresh-faced freckled boy, his hair blazing under the gray hood; he was only twelve or so. "Rory has seen something, Bard. Tell my son what you have seen, lad."

"Beyond the wood, Dom Wolf—Dom Bard," he amended quickly, "a party of men coming to ambush us."

Bard's eyes narrowed. "You saw this. With the Sight?"

The *laranzu* said, "I could not see so well, riding, as in the crystal, or in a pool of clear water. But they are there."

"How many? Where? How are they drawn up?" He fired questions at the boy. Rory got down from his pony, and taking up a twig, began to draw a pattern in the dust.

"Four, maybe five dozen men. About ten mounted, like this—" He sketched a line at an angle to the rest. "Some of the rest have bows. . . ."

Melisendra bent over the boy and said, "Are there *leroni* with them?"

"I think not, *domna.* It is hard to see. . . ."

Bard looked quickly around at the great body of men straggling along behind them. Damn! He had not thought it necessary, yet, to form them up; but if they were taken on the flank this way, even a few men could do dreadful damage! Even before he thought seriously about the ambush, he snapped, "Rory, see this! Are there men following us?"

The boy squinted his eyes and said, "No Dom Wolf, the road is clear behind us all the way to Dom Rafael's stronghold and as far as the borders of Marenji."

That meant that the invading army from Serrais was somewhere between them and Castle Asturias. Would they have to fight their way through it, and find the castle under siege? Perhaps the invaders could wear out Geremy Hastur before they ever got there. No, that was no way to talk about an ally under truce. And meanwhile there was an ambush waiting for his army. A laughably small one, intended—he was sure—only to delay them awhile, so they would halt to tend their wounded, not arrive at the Castle till after nightfall, or perhaps the next day. Which would mean an attack was planned for that night. An army of this size could not escape observation; if they had sentry birds or *leroni* with the Sight, the army of Serrais must surely know that they were on the way, and have some special interest in keeping them away for another day.

He said something of this to his father, and Dom Rafael nodded in agreement. "But what shall we do?"

"A pity we cannot get around them somewhere," Bard said, "and leave the men of this ambush to watch here like a cat at an empty mousehole. But we cannot take an army this size past this wood unseen. Rory says there is no *leronis* with them, but that does not mean there is no *leronis* in rapport with one of their leaders, seeing through his eyes. So we cannot attack them without also alerting the main army of Serrais." He considered for a time. "And if we do so, even though we annihilate them quickly—four dozen men cannot stand against all our army—it would give time for *leronis* or sentry bird to spy out our numbers and how we are positioned and weaponed. But what a *leronis* does not witness she cannot report. I think the main army must go past the wood where the ambushers will not see them. Father, give some man your cloak and let him ride your horse, and send him with me, with your banner, while you take the main army around the wood. Meanwhile, give me—" he paused to consider, "ten or twelve picked horsemen, and a dozen swordsmen with tall shields; and a couple of dozen bowmen. We will go the main path; and if we are fortunate, the watchers in rapport with the ambush will think that is all we have to lift the siege of Castle Asturias. Take all the *leroni* with you, and when you are past this wood, sit down with them and their sentry birds, and let them tell us what manner of army Serrais has sent against us this time."

This was quickly agreed to.

"Take the bowmen of the Guild," he was told, "and Lord Lanzell's horsemen—there are fifteen of them and they work well together and follow one man. Pick your foot soldiers yourself."

"Father, I do not know the men well enough, now, to find picked men so quickly."

"Jerrall does," Dom Rafael said, gesturing to his banner bearer. "He has been with me twenty years. Jerrall, go with my son and obey him as you would myself!"

Drawing up his picked men, watching the main army form up tightly to go the other way, Bard felt a queer tightening in his throat. He had been fighting since he was thirteen years old, but this was the first time he had fought under his father's banner; and the first time since he had been sent into outlawry that he fought for a land about whose welfare he cared a *sekal*.

They swept down on the ambush from behind, taking the mounted men unawares and killing half their horses before the foot soldiers could rally to them. Bard's men formed a shield wall and shot blazing arrows toward them. The battle lasted less than half an hour, after which Bard's men had the Serrais banner and the wounded remnant fled in all directions. Bard had lost two or three men, but they had captured or killed all of the enemy's horses. He gave orders to cut the throats of the most gravely wounded—they would not survive being moved, in any case, and this was more merciful than leaving them for *kyorebni* and wolves and—to take up the gear and armor.

Rejoining the main army, they had their prisoners interrogated by a *laranzu* who could mind-probe. From this they learned that they would, indeed, have to fight their way through the whole Serrais army before they came to Castle Asturias. The army, outside the walls of the castle, was preparing to attack, but was ready to hold it under siege if they could not capture it by surprise attack.

Bard nodded, grim-faced. "We must press on through the night. We cannot bring up all the supply wagons so quickly, but our best men must arrive in time to spoil the surprise those men of Serrais are planning!"

The nightly rain of this season was already beginning, but they went on at what haste they could, even after the rain had changed to light snow, and there was some grumbling in the ranks about this.

"Are you trying to tell us they'd attack Castle Asturias in *this*? They couldn't see the walls to shoot at them!"

It reminded Bard of the long-ago campaign, his first independent command. Melisendra, her bright hair covered by

142

the gray hood of a *leronis*, reminded him, suddenly and with a stab of poignant regret, of Melora. Where was she now? Even Melisendra's voice was like hers, as she said softly, "The weather will clear before dawn, you may be sure of that. And you may be sure that their sorcerers are well aware of it, too. Inside the castle they may think themselves secure because of the storm. But when the skies clear, there will be moonlight."

The man looked at her with respectful awe, and said, "Do you know that with your wizardry, *domna*?"

"I know it because I know the cycles of the moons," Melisendra laughed. "Any farmer could tell you as much. There are four moons in the sky tonight, and Liriel and Kyrrdis are at the full. It will be bright enough to fly hawks! So we must be there in time for battle; but," she added thoughtfully, "there will be light enough for their sorcerers to work wizardry too, and we must be ready for *that*."

Bard was glad of the intelligence; but he had no liking for wizardry in battle. He preferred honest swords and spears!

The storm grew to wild heights, so that the *leroni* were riding ahead, carrying lighted torches, and young Rory was spying out the trails with the Sight. Men and horses struggled along behind them, following the torches, fighting the snow and the drifts, cursing. Bard wondered if the enemy's *leroni* had brought the storm. It seemed too heavy to be natural. He had no way of knowing, and resolved, resentfully, that he would *not* ask Melisendra!

And then, suddenly, all was quiet; they moved out of the storm into clear night, the wind died, and overhead the great serene faces of the larger moons floated at full, pale Liriel, Kyrrdis glimmering bluish in the night. Bard heard the men's gasps of amazement. Atop a hill, they looked into the valley surrounding the castle.

It was eerie and quiet. He knew, from what the sorcerers had told him, that the whole army of Serrais lay there, encamped outside the castle, prepared to attack at dawn; but not a watch-fire glimmered, not a step rustled below them.

"Yet they are there," Melisendra said at his side, and through her mind he picked up the image of the valley below, not dark as he saw it, but lighted with strange flickers which, he knew, were men, and horses, and engines of war.

"How is it that you can see that, Melisendra?"

"I do not know. Perhaps my starstone feels the heat of their bodies, and translates it into a picture my mind can see . . everyone sees it differently. Rory told me that he could *hear* them; perhaps he feels the movement of their breath, or feels the crying of the grass as their feet crush it."

Bard shivered, wishing he had not asked. He had possessed this woman, she had borne him a son, yet he knew nothing of her, and he was afraid of her. He had heard of a *laran* gift which could kill with a thought. Did she possess it? No, or she would surely have struck him down in defense of her chastity. . . .

"Do their *leroni* know we are coming?"

"I am sure they know we are somewhere about. The presence of all these men and beasts cannot be hidden from anyone with *laran*. But Rory and I have closed down our Gifts as much as we can, and hopefully, they think us much farther away than we are. We left old Master Ricot, and Dame Arbella, with the supply wagons, and instructed them to send out false pictures, as if the army were still there with them. . . . All we can do is wait and see."

They waited. Kyrrdis was lowering toward the horizon and the eastern sky was just beginning to flush red when Melisendra touched Bard's arm and said, "The word has been passed for attack, down there."

Bard said grimly, "Then we will attack them first." He beckoned to his page and gave the word. He was not weary, though he had slept but little for three nights. He gnawed at a hard bread roll with meat baked inside. It tasted like leather, but he knew from experience that if he went into battle with his stomach empty he would get dizzy or squeamish. Other men, he knew, were the other way round, Beltran always said that if he touched a bite of food he would spew it up like a breeding woman—why was he thinking of Beltran now? Why must that ghost come to sit on his shoulder?

So they would cut through the invading Serrais army to save Castle Asturias, and Geremy Hastur's worthless life. And then would they attack again? With Dom Rafael's army there, did Geremy really think he could make good his claim to the throne? Did Geremy think the truce would last any longer than Dom Rafael found it convenient? Yet he had asked Dom Rafael to bring his army here.

How many of the army would stand for Dom Rafael? Probably most of them were as unwilling to see a Hastur on the throne, as was their leader

Below him a glimmer flashed, and he gave a quick command.

"Lights!"

From everywhere, torches were brought from behind their shielding. A fire arrow blazed a long, screaming comet tail into the midst of the Serrais army.

"Attack!" Bard shouted.

Screaming the ancient battle cries of di Asturien, the army charged down the hill toward the army of Serrais, taking them from behind as they charged upon the walls of Asturias.

By the time the red sun came dripping up over the eastern hills, the Serrais army lay cut to pieces, the remnant fleeing in confusion; the heart had gone out of them with Bard's first charge, which had killed and wounded half of their rearguard. They had never managed to bring up a single catapult or war engine, nor to get their clingfire alight; Bard had captured it all. Then some clingfire shells had been set to burn among them, fragile, exploding everywhere and bursting among their remaining horses, stampeding them in frenzy; and then it was all over but the slaughter, and the final surrender. The armed men inside the castle had covered them with bowmen from the walls, and at the end the *leroni* had massed to spread terror among the Serrais army, so that the rest of them fled shrieking as if all the demons in all of Zandru's nine hells were after them. Bard thought, having fought against *laran* terror himself, that the devils probably *were*—or at least the Serrais men *thought* they were, which amounted to the same thing.

Dom Eiric Ridenow of Serrais had been captured, and by the time Bard rode with his banner bearers into the castle, they were already debating whether to hold him as hostage for the good behavior of the other Serrais lords, ransom him and send him home after accepting an oath of neutrality or hang him from the castle walls as an example to others who might try to cross the borders of Asturias under arms.

"Do your worst," said the old man, setting his teeth so fiercely that his blond beard wagged. "Do you think my sons will not march on Asturias with all their might, now that they know what happened to their advance guard?

"He is lying," said a young *laranzu*. "This army was no advance guard; it was made up of every man he could put into the field. His sons are not of an age to fight. They risked all on one throw of the dice."

"And they would have succeeded, had it not been for your efforts, kinsman," said Geremy Hastur to Dom Rafael. He was wearing a long robe, a scholar's robe of purple so deep that it was almost black. He was unweaponed save for a

145

small dagger. The long robe hid the ungainly lameness, but could not conceal the uneven stance or his halting step, supported on a crutch like a man four times his age. His red hair was already graying at the temples, and he had begun, like an old man, to wear a fringe of beard at his jaws. Bard thought, with contempt, that his foster-brother looked less like a warrior than one of those Renunciates who had fought in his army!

Dom Rafael and Geremy embraced as kinsmen, but then they broke apart; Geremy's eyes fell on Bard where he stood two paces behind his father.

"You!"

"Are you surprised to see me, kinsman?"

"You were outlawed in this realm for seven years, Bard; and there is the blood of the royal house on your hands now. Your life is doubly forfeit here. Give me a single good reason I should not tell my men to take you out and hang you from the walls!"

Bard said hotly, "You know by what betrayal that blood came on my hands—" but Dom Rafael silenced him with a gesture.

"Is this gratitude, cousin Geremy? Bard led the assault which saved Castle Asturias from falling into Serrais hands. Had he not come, your head would now be hanging for a popinjay, for Dom Eiric's men to use at target practice!"

Geremy's mouth tightened.

"I have never doubted that my cousin was brave," he said, "and so, I suppose, I must grant him amnesty, life for life. Be it so, Bard; come and go in this realm as your lawful duties warrant. But not in my presence. When the army goes, go you with them, and do not come into my court for your life's span, for on the day I set eyes on you again, I will certainly have you killed."

"As for that," Bard began, but Dom Rafael cut in.

"Enough. Before you go to passing sentences of death or banishment, Hastur, you had better have a throne to speak from. On what grounds do you claim to reign here?"

"As regent for Valentine, son of Ardrin, at Queen Ariel's request; and as warden for these lands, which have been, since time out of mind, a part of the Hastur Domains, and shall be again, when these years of anarchy are past. The Hasturs of Carcosa are a peaceful folk, and will let the di Asturiens reign here, as long as they swear allegiance to the Domain of Hastur, and Valentine has already done so."

"Oh, brave!" retorted Dom Rafael, "Great glory and gallant deeds are yours, Geremy Hastur, to extort an oath from a babe not five years old! Did you promise the child a toy sword and a new pony, or did you get it cheaply from him for a sugared cake and a handful of candies?"

Geremy flinched at the sarcasm. "He listened to the persuasion of his mother, Queen Ariel," he said. "She knew well that I would guard the boy's rights till he was grown; at which time, he said to me, he would take oath as a man, to reign here as warden for the Hasturs."

Dom Rafael said fiercely, "We want no Hasturs in this land which the di Asturiens have held since they won it from the cat-folk ages ago!"

"The men of this land will follow Valentine, their rightful lord, in allegiance to the lawful Hastur King," Geremy said.

"Will they? If you believe it, you had better ask them, my lord."

"I had believed," Geremy said, holding his temper with obvious effort, "that we were under truce, Dom Rafael."

"Truce while the Serrais armies held you here; but behold, that army lies in ruins, and I doubt if Dom Eiric will muster enough men to put an army in the field for ten years or more! Even if we let him live! And as for that," he added, signaling to one of his bodyguards, "take Dom Eiric away and keep him secure."

"In a dungeon, my lord?"

Dom Rafael looked Eiric Ridenow up and down. "No," he said. "That would be over hard on his old bones. If he will give oath under truthspell not to attempt escape until we have determined his fate, we will house him in comfort befitting his rank and his gray hairs."

"For every gray hair on my head," Dom Eiric said truthfully, "there are ten on yours, Rafael di Asturien!"

"Even so, I shall house you in comfort till your sons can ransom you, for they will need you at home till they are grown. Little boys are impetuous, and they might try something too dangerous for them."

Dom Eiric glared, but at last he said, "Bring our *leronis*. I will swear by the walls of Serrais that I will not leave this place till you yourself dismiss me, dead or alive."

Bard laughed harshly. He said, "Take from him some oath stronger than the walls of Serrais, Father, for I can go and break those whenever I will."

Dom Eiric glowered, but he did not speak, for what Bard said was true, and he knew it. Dom Rafael said to his guard, "Take him to some comfortable chamber, and keep him there secure until I can take his oath. Your life for it if he escapes before a *leronis* has his oath."

Geremy Hastur scowled as the old lord was led away. "Don't presume too far on my gratitude, cousin. You are over free, it seems to me, in disposing of my prisoners."

"Your prisoners? When will you face the truth, cousin?" Dom Rafael asked. "Your rule here is ended, and I shall prove it to you." He gestured to Bard, who stepped out on the balcony.

In the courtyard below, where the army was quartered, he heard a wild outburst of cheering.

"The Wolf! The Kilghard Wolf!"

"Our general! He led us to victory!"

"Dom Rafael's son! Long live the house of di Asturien!"

Dom Rafael stepped out on the balcony, calling, "Listen to me, men! You have won freedom from Serrais. Will you turn Asturias over to the Hasturs? I claim that throne for the house of di Asturien; not for myself, but in ward for my son Alaric!"

Wild cheering drowned out his words. When there was quiet, he said, "Your turn, my lord Geremy. Ask if there are any men down there who wish to live for twelve years or so under the rule of Hastur while Ardrin's son Valentine grows to manhood."

Bard felt that he could taste Geremy's hate and wrath, it was so thick around them; but the young man did not speak, only stepped out on the balcony. There were one or two cries of "No Hasturs!" "Down with the Hastur tyrants!" but after a moment they quieted.

"Men of di Asturien," he called out. His voice was a strong, resonant bass which gave the lie to the frail body containing it. "In days past, Hastur, son of Light, won this realm and set the di Asturiens over it, in wardship! I stand here for King Valentine, son of Ardrin. Are you traitors, men, to rebel against your rightful king?"

"Where's that king, then?" shouted one man in the crowd. "If he's our rightful king, why isn't he here, being brought up among his lawful subjects?"

"No Hastur puppet kings here," another one shouted. "Get back to Hali where you belong, Hastur!"

"We'll have a real di Asturien on the throne, not a Hastur flunkey!"

"We'll kiss no Hastur arses in Asturias!"

Bard listened, with growing satisfaction, as the cries grew louder. Someone threw a stone. Geremy did not flinch; he flung up a hand and the stone exploded in a flare of blue light. There was a gasp and a yell of rage.

"No wizard kings in Asturias!"

"We'll have a soldier, not a damned *laranzu!*"

"Dom Rafael! Dom Rafael! Who stands for King Alaric?" they yelled, and there were even a few cries of "Bard! Bard di Asturien! We'll have the Kilghard Wolf!"

Someone threw another stone, which did not pass within a hand-span of Geremy. He did not bother to deflect this one. Then someone threw a handful of courtyard horse dung which splattered on the pruple robe. Geremy's paxman caught him by the elbow and dragged him away from the balcony.

Dom Rafael said, "Do you still think you can claim the throne of Asturias, Dom Geremy? Perhaps I should send your head back to Queen Ariel and the folk at Carcosa, as warning to the lady to choose her servants more carefully."

Geremy's smile was as grim as the old man's. "I would not advise it. King Valentine loves his playmate Alaric; but I doubt not that Queen Ariel could persuade him to send you back gift for gift."

Bard stepped forward, fists clenched, but Dom Rafael shook his head. "No, my son. No bloodshed here. We mean no harm to the Hasturs while they rule their own lands and meddle not with ours. But you will remain my guest until my son Alaric dwells again beneath this roof."

"Do you think Carolin of Carcosa will deal with an usurper?"

"Then," said Dom Rafael, "I shall be happy to entertain you as long as you desire, my lord. Should I not live long enough to see your return to Carcosa, I have a grandson who will reign as Warden of Asturias for my son Alaric." He said to Bard, "Conduct our royal guest to his chambers—he is royal in Carcosa, though he shall never be so in Asturias. And station servants to see that he lacks for nothing, and that he does not go exploring in the woods and perhaps fall and damage his lame leg. We must care for the son of King Carolin with great kindness."

"I shall see that he stays within his chamber in study and meditation, and takes no risk of injuring himself with exercise," Bard said, and laid a hand on Geremy's shoulder.

"Come, cousin."

Geremy shook off the touch as if it burned him. "You damned bastard, don't presume to put your hands on me!"

"I find no pleasure in the touch," Bard said. "I am no

149

lover of men. You will not come at my courteous request? Why, then—" He signaled to two of the soldiers, "My lord Hastur is experiencing some difficulty in walking; he is lame, as you see. Kindly assist him to his chamber."

Geremy yelled and shouted as the husky men-at-arms picked him up bodily and carried him; then, recalling his dignity, subsided and allowed them to take him. But the look he gave Bard told him that if he ever again met Bard armed and ready, he could expect to fight him to the death.

I should have killed him when I had the chance, Bard thought bitterly. *But I had lamed him by mischance. I could not kill him unarmed.*

I would rather have Geremy as foster brother and friend, not enemy. What god hates me, that this has come to pass?

The change of power in Castle Asturias was accomplished within a few days, without much trouble. They had to hang a few of Geremy's loyal men, who organized a palace rebellion, but one of the *laranzu* smelled out the plot before it had gone far. Soon all was quiet. Bard heard from Melisendra that one of the exiled Queen's ladies was bearing Geremy Hastur's child, and had begged to join him in his imprisonment."

"I did not know Geremy had a sweetheart. Do you know her name?"

"Ginevra," Melisendra said, and Bard raised his eyebrows. He remembered Ginevra Harryl.

"You are a *leronis*," he said. "Can't you force her to miscarry, or something of that sort? It is bad enough to keep one Hastur prisoner, without starting a dynasty."

Melisendra's eyes were pale with lambent wrath. "No *leronis* would so abuse her powers!"

"Do you think me a fool, woman? Don't tell me fairy tales of virtue! Every camp follower who finds herself breeding against her will knows a sorceress who will lighten her of that inconvenient burden!"

At white heat, Melisendra retorted, "If the woman does not wish to bear a child into squalor, or on campaign, or fatherless, or when she knows she will have no milk for it—then, no doubt, some *leronis* would take pity on her! But to kill a much-longed-for babe, simply because some man finds it inconvenient to his throne?" Her eyes flamed at him. "Do you think I wanted *your* child, Bard di Asturien? But it was done, and irrevocable, and whatever came of it, I had lost the Sight. . . . so I kept from damaging an innocent life, even though I had not desired it. And if I could keep from laying hands on *that*, do you think I would harm Ginevra's child even in thought? Ginevra loves her babe and its father! If you want your dirty work done, send a man with a sword to cut her throat, and be done with it!"

Bard found nothing to say. It was an unwelcome thought—that Melisendra might have rid herself, so easily, of that child who had become Erlend. Why had she held her hand?

And there was the problem of Ginevra. Damn women and their idiotic scruples! Melisendra had killed in battle, he knew that. Yet here was a potential enemy of the Asturiens, more dangerous than one who bore sword or pike, and that enemy was to live! He would not demean himself by arguing with her, but let her beware how she crossed him again! He told her so, and slammed out of the room.

Being forced to think of the woman he had and did not want reminded him, perforce, of the woman he wanted and could not have. And after a time he thought of a way to use Ginevra and her coming child.

When the countryside was quiet, and the armies had returned home, except for the standing army Bard was training for defense and perhaps conquest (for he knew perfectly well that the Hasturs would someday descend on them, hostages or no) Lady Jerana had lost no time in coming to court. Bard sought her out in the apartments that had been Queen Ariel's.

"The lady Ginevra Harryl, who is with child by Hastur—is she healthy and well? When will she be brought to bed?"

"Perhaps three moons," Lady Jerana said.

"Do me a kindness, foster mother? See to it that she is housed in comfort, with suitable ladies to care for her, and a good and trustworthy midwife in attendance.

The lady frowned. She said, "Why, so she is, she has three waiting-women known to have Hastur sympathies, and the midwife who delivered your own son waits on her; but I know you too well to think you do this out of any kindness to the Lady Ginevra."

"No?" Bard said. "Have you forgotten that Geremy is my own foster brother?"

Jerana looked skeptical, but Bard said no more. However, later that day, when he had verified for himself that all Dom Rafael's wife said was true, he went to Geremy's apartments.

Geremy was playing at a game called Castles with one of the pages who had been sent to wait on him. When Bard came in he put aside the dice and got awkwardly to his feet.

"You needn't stand on courtesy, Geremy. In fact, you need not stand at all."

"It is customary for a prisoner to stand in the presence of his jailer," Geremy said.

"Please yourself," Bard said. "I came to bring you news of the Lady Ginevra Harryl. I am sure you are too proud to ask news of her on your own, so I came to assure you that she is lodged in a suite next to that of my father's wife, and that her own women, Camilla and Rafaella Delleray and Felizia MacAnndra have been sent to wait upon her; and that a midwife trained in our own household is in attendance upon her."

Geremy's fists clenched. "Knowing you," he said, "I am sure this is your way of telling me that you have taken revenge for some fancied insult by casting her and her women into some dirty dungeon with an accursed and filthy slut to mishandle her in childbirth."

"You misjudge me, cousin. She is housed in comfort considerably greater than your own, and I will say so under truthspell, if you like."

"Why would you do that?" Geremy asked suspiciously.

"Because, knowing how a man is troubled for the thought of his womenfolk," Bard said, "I thought you might be as eager for news of your lady as I for mine. If you wish, it can be arranged for Ginevra to join you here. . . ."

Geremy dropped on his seat and covered his face with his hands. He said, "Do you take pleasure in tormenting me, Bard? You have no shadow of a quarrel with Ginevra, but if it gives you enjoyment to see me humiliated, I will crawl to you on my knees, if I must; do not harm Ginevra or her child."

Bard opened the door to admit a *leronis* of the household—not Melisendra. When the blue light of truthspell was in the chamber, he said, "Hear me now, Geremy. Lady Ginevra is housed in luxurious apartments, not a stone's throw from those of Queen Ariel when we were boys. She has ample food for a breeding woman, and such things as she best likes, by my orders. She has her own women with her, sleeping in her chamber so that no one will trouble her, and my own mother's midwife is within call."

Geremy watched the steady light of truthspell and it did not flicker. He was still suspicious, but he knew enough of *laran*, himself trained in that art, to know there had been no deceit in the setting of the spell. He demanded, "Why do you say all this to me?"

"Because," Bard said, "I too have a wife, whom I have not seen for seven long years of outlawry and exile. If you will tell me, under truthspell, where I can find Carlina, I am ready to allow Ginevra to join you here, or to move you, under guard, into her suite, until the birth of your child."

Geremy threw back his head and laughed, a long laugh of despair.

"Would that I could tell you!" he said. "I had forgotten how seriously you took that handfasting . . . we all took it seriously then, before your quarrel with Ardrin."

"Carlina is my wife," Bard said. "And since there is truthspell here, tell me this truthfully, too: did not Ardrin repent of his promise and try to give her to you, Hastur-spawn?"

"He repented it early and late," Geremy said, "and with Beltran dead, and you fled into outlawry, he held the bond between you forfeit. And, indeed, he offered her to me. But don't clench your teeth and scowl like that, Wolf; Carlina would have nothing to do with me, and she told him so, though the old king threw a mighty tantrum about it, and swore he would not be so defied by any woman living!"

The light of the truthspell on his face did not waver; Bard knew he spoke the truth. He felt an upsurge of joy. Carlina remembered their bond, she had refused to set it aside even for Geremy!

"And where is she, Geremy? Speak, and Ginevra is free to join you here."

Geremy's laugh held the bitterness of despair. "Where is she now? Willingly, willingly I will tell you, cousin! She has sworn the vows of a priestess of Avarra, which even her father dared not gainsay," he said, "and she has fled the court and the kingdom, and made her way to the Isle of Silence, where she is sworn to live out the rest of her life in chastity and prayer. And if you want her, cousin, you will have to go there and take her."

Chapter Three

After the conquest of Asturias, Bard's father had placed him in command of the armies. But Serrais had been subdued, for the moment, and he was not yet ready to take the field against the Hasturs, so he went to Dom Rafael and begged a few days' leave.

"To be sure, you have well earned it, my son. Where do you wish to go?"

"I induced Geremy to tell me where Carlina has gone," he said, "and I wish to take an honor guard and bring her back to me."

"But not if she has been married to any other man," his father said anxiously. "I know your feelings, but I cannot in good conscience give you leave to take the wife of any of my subjects! I rule this land under law!"

"What law is stronger than that which binds a man to the woman he has handfasted? But ease your mind, Father, Carlina is the wife of no man; she has taken refuge where she cannot be forced into marriage with any other."

"In that case," his father said, "take what men you will, and when you return with her, we will hold the marriage here in all splendor." He hesitated. "The lady Melisendra will be ill content to take her place as *barragana* when your wife is here. Shall I send her back to our estates? She can care for her son there and live honorably in retirement."

"No," he said savagely. "I will give her to Carlina for a handmaiden!"

Something in him rejoiced at the thought of Melisendra humbled, waiting on Carlina, combing her hair and fetching her shoes and ribbons.

"You must do as it seems good to you," Dom Rafael said, "but she is the mother of your eldest son, and in humiliating the mother, you belittle the son. Nor would Carlina, I suppose, find much pleasure in beholding, night and day, the

154

face of her rival. I do not think you understand women very well."

"Perhaps not," said Bard, "and you may be sure that if Carlina wishes me to send Melisendra away, I will lose no time in doing so. As my lawful wife, it will be Carlina's duty to foster all my sons, and I will put Erlend in her care." That, he thought, would be better than letting Melisendra poison the child's mind against him. He liked little Erlend, and had no intention of being parted from him.

He chose an honor guard of a dozen men; that would be enough to show the women of the Island of Silence that he intended to have his wife, and that they should lose no time in handing her over to him. No very great force would be needed against a handful of unworldly female recluses!

In addition to the honor guard, he brought with him two sorcerers; the young *laranzu* Rory, and Melisendra herself. From childhood he had heard tales of the sorcery of the priestesses of Avarra, and he wished to have sorcery of his own to contend with them. And it would do Melisendra no harm to know that he did, indeed, have a lawful wife, and that she could expect nothing more from him!

The Island of Silence lay outside the kingdom of Asturias, in the independent shire of Marenji. Bard knew little of Marenji, except that their ruler was chosen every few years by acclamation from among the rabble; they had no standing army, and kept themselves free of any alliances with kings or rulers nearby. Once Bard's father had entertained the Sheriff of Marenji in his Great Hall, dealing with him for some casks of their fruit wine, and making an arrangement to guard his borders.

He rode across the peaceful countryside of Marenji, with its groves of apples and pears, plums and greenberries, its orchards of nut trees and featherpod bushes. In a hilly ravine he saw a stream dammed up to give power to a felting mill where featherpod fibers were made into batting for quilts. There was a village of weavers; he recalled that they made beautifully woven tartan cloth for skirts and shawls. There was no sign anywhere of defenses.

If this place were armed, Bard thought, and soldiers quartered in the villages, it would make a splendid buffer state to hold off the armies of Serrais when they came down again toward Asturias, and in return the men of Asturias could protect them. The Sheriff of Marenji could surely be made to see reason. And if he did not, well, there was no army to show resistence. He would advise his father as soon as he returned to lose no time in quartering armies in Marenji.

As they rode, the land grew darker. They rode in the shadow of the high mountains, past lakes and misty tarns. There were fewer and fewer farms, just an isolated steading here and there. Melisendra and the boy rode close together and looked ill at ease.

Bard reviewed in his mind everything that he knew of the priestesses of Avarra. They had dwelt, as long as any living man could remember, on the island at the center of the Lake of Silence; and always the law had been that any man who set foot on that island must die. It was said that the priestesses swore lifelong vows of chasity and prayer; but in addition to the priestesses, many women, wives or maidens or widows, went to the island in grief or piety or penitence to dwell for a time under the mantle of Avarra, the Dark Mother; and whoever they were, so that they worshipped Avarra and wore the garb of the sisterhood during their sojourn there and spoke to no man and observed chastity, they might dwell as long as they wished. No man really knew what went on among them, and the women who went there were pledged never to tell.

But women in grief and despair from the loss of a child or husband, women who were barren and longed for children, women worn from childbearing who wished to petition the Goddess for health or for barrenness, women suffering from any sorrow, these went there to the shrine of Avarra to pray for the help of the priestesses, or for that of the Mother.

Once an old woman who served Lady Jerana—Bard had been so young then that he was not even chased away when women talked among themselves—had said in his hearing, "Secret of the Island of Silence? The secret is that there is no secret! I spent a season there once. The women live in their houses, in silence, chaste and alone, and speaking only when necessary, or to pray, or for healing and charity. They pray at dawn and sunset, or when the moons rise. They are pledged to give help to any woman who asks it in the name of the Goddess, whatever her griefs or burdens. They know a great deal of healing herbs and simples, and while I dwelt with them they taught me. They are good and holy women."

Bard wondered how any women could be good, being pledged to murder any man who set foot on the island? Although, he conceded, (making a joke of it to himself, to allay his anxiety) they must at least be unlike other women if they were silent! That was always a virtue in women!

It seemed, though, wrong for women to dwell alone, unprotected; if he were Sheriff of Marenji he would send soldiers to protect the women.

They stood now on the lip of a valley, looking down at the wide waters of the Lake of Silence.

It was a quiet place and an eerie one. There was no sound, as they moved down toward the shores of the lake, except the sound of their horses' hooves; and the cry of a water bird, her nest disturbed, flying up with a sudden squawk into the air. Dark trees bent flexible branches over the dark waters, black against the low sunset light in the sky; and as they came nearer they heard the complaining of frogs. They picked their way through the soggy swamplands along the shore, and Bard heard sucking sounds as his horse's feet sloshed in the marsh.

Ugh, what a dismal place! Carlina should be grateful that he had come to take her away from it! Perhaps she had shown good sense in taking refuge here, so that no other marriage could be forced on her for political reasons, but surely seven years was long enough to spend in piety and prayer, apart from all men! Her life as the Princess Carlina, wife to the Commander of the King's Armies, would be very different!

And now there was fog, rising in swirls from the surface of the lake, thick wisps of it, swirling and streaming toward them until Bard could hardly see the path before him. The men were grumbling; the very air seemed thick and oppressive! Small Rory, on his pony at Bard's side, raised a pale, frightened face.

"Please, *vai dom*, we should go back. We will be lost in the fog. And they do not want us here, I can feel it!"

"Use the Sight," Bard commanded. "What do you see?"

The child took out the seeing-stone and obediently looked into it, but his face was contorted, as if he were trying not to cry.

"Nothing. I see nothing, only the fog. They are trying to hide from me, they say it is impious for a man to be here."

Bard jeered, "Do you call yourself a man?"

"No," said the child, "but *they* call me one and say I must not come here. Please, my Lord Wolf, let's go back! The Dark Mother has turned her face to me, but she is veiled, she is angry—oh, please, my lord, we are forbidden to come here, we must turn and go away again or something terrible will happen!"

Furious, frustrated, Bard wondered if those witches on the island thought they could frighten him by playing their witch

157

tricks on a harmless little boy with a seeing-stone? "Hold your tongue and try to act like a man," he told the boy severely, and the child, sniffling, wiped his face and rode in silence, shaking.

The fog thickened and grew darker still. Was it an oncoming storm? Strange; for on the hill above the lake, the weather had been fine and bright. Probably it was the dampness from that unhealthy marsh.

What a superstitious lot his men were, grumbling that way about a little fog!

Suddenly the fog swirled and flowed and began to shape itself into a pattern; he felt his horse nervously step aside, as directly before him, it flowed, moved within itself and became the form of a woman. Not a fog ghost, but a woman, solid and real as he was himself. He could see every strand of the white hair, braided in two braids down the side of her face, covered, all but a few inches, by a thick, woven black veil. She wore a black skirt and the thickly knitted black shawl of a country woman, simple and unadorned over some form of chemise of coarse linen. Around her waist was a long belt, woven in colored patterns, from which hung a sickle-shaped knife with a black handle.

She held up her hand in a stern gesture.

"Go back," she said. "You know that no man may set foot here; this is holy ground, sacred to the Dark Mother. Turn your horses and go back the way you came. There is quicksand here, and other dangers about which you know nothing. Go back."

Bard opened his mouth and had a little trouble finding his voice. At last he said, "I mean no harm or disrespect, Mother, not to you or to any of the devout servants of Avarra. I am here to escort home my handfasted wife, Carlina di Asturien, daughter of the late King Ardrin."

"There are no handfasted brides here," said the old priestess. "Only the sworn sisters of Avarra, who live here in prayer and piety; and a few penitents and pilgrims who have come to dwell among us for a season for the healing of their hurts and burdens."

"You are evading me, old Mother. Is the Lady Carlina among them?"

"No one here bears the name Carlina," said the old priestess. "We do not inquire what name our sisters bore when they dwelt in the world; when a woman comes here to take vows among us, the name she bore is lost forever, known only to the Goddess. There is no woman here you may claim as your wife, whoever you are. I admonish you most sincerely: do not commit this blasphemy, or bring on yourself the wrath of the Dark Mother."

Bard leaned forward over his saddle. "Don't you threaten me, old lady! I know that my wife is here, and if you do not deliver her up to me, I will come and take her, and I will not be responsible for what my men may do."

"But," said the old woman, "you will certainly be held responsible, whether you take responsibility for it or not."

"Don't chop words with me! You would do better to go and tell her that her husband has come to take her away; and if you will do that, I will commit no blasphemy, but await her here outside your holy precincts."

"But I do not fear your threats," the ancient priestess said. "Nor does the Great Mother." And the fog swirled up around her face, and suddenly there was no one where she had been standing, only empty swirls of mist rising from the reeds at the water's edge.

Bard gasped. How had she vanished? Had she ever been there at all, or only an illusion? Perversely, he was more sure than ever that Carlina was there, and that they were hiding her from him. Why had the old lady not seen the sense of doing as he bade her, going to Carlina and telling her that he had come in peace, willing no harm or blasphemy, to take her home to his fireside and his bed? She was, after all, his lawful wife. Must he be forced, then, to commit a blasphemy?

He turned and drew up his horse beside Melisendra.

"Now is the time to use your sorcery," he said, "unless we are all to be caught in quicksand. Is there quicksand here?"

She drew out her starstone and gazed into it, her face taking on that same distant, abstracted look he had seen so often on Melora's face.

"There is quicksand near, though not dangerously near, I think. Bard, are you resolved on this folly? Truly, it is unwise to brave the wrath of Avarra. If Carlina wished to come to you, she would come; she is not held prisoner there."

"I have no way of knowing," Bard said. "These are madwomen, who try to live alone, putting chastity and prayer into the place of those things which are proper for women—"

"Do you think chastity and prayer improper for women?" she inquired, sarcastically.

"By no means; but surely a woman can pray as much as she wishes by her own fireside, and no wedded wife has the right to commit herself to chastity against the will of her lawful husband! What good are these priestesses to anyone if they flout the laws of nature and of man this way?"

He had meant the question rhetorically, but Melisendra took it literally. "I am told that they do many good works," she said. "They know much of herbs and medicines, and they can make the barren fertile; and prayer is always a good thing."

Bard ignored her. They had come through the fog and out on to a small sandy beach, free of the reeds that lined the lakeshore elsewhere; and there was a small hut there, and a tethered boat.

Bard got down from his horse and shouted.

"Hi! Ferryman!"

A small slouched figure, wrapped in shawls, came out of the hut. Bard was outraged to discover that it was no ferryman but a little old woman, crippled and gray and bent.

"Where is the ferryman?"

"I keep this ferry, *vai dom*, for the good ladies."

"Take me across this lake here to the island, quickly!"

"I can't do that, sir. It's forbidden. Now the lady there, if *she* wants to go over, I'll take her. But no man, it's not allowed, the Goddess forbids it."

"Rubbish," Bard said. "How dare you pretend to know what the immortals want, even assuming that there are any gods, or any goddesses either? And if the priestesses don't like it, well, there's nothing they can do about it."

"I won't be responsible for your death, *vai dom*."

"Don't be foolish, old dame. Get into that boat and take me over, at once!"

"Don't call names like fool, sir; you don't know what you're talking about. That boat won't take you over to the other shore. Me, yes; the lady, yes; but it won't take you, not at all."

Bard decided the woman was a halfwit. Probably the priestesses had given her the task of ferrying, out of charity, but her main task was to scare people away. Well, he didn't scare. He drew his dagger.

"See this? Get into the boat! Now!"

"Can't do it," she wailed. "Indeed I can't! The water's not safe except when the priestesses want it to be! I never come over unless they call me from the other side!"

Frowning, Bard remembered the spelled ford near Moray's mill, where a quiet, shallow stream had suddenly become a torrent. But he gestured, menacing, with his dagger.

"The boat!"

She took a step and then another, shaking, then collapsed, sobbing, a sodden bundle of rags. "Can't," she wailed. "Can't!"

Bard felt like kicking her. Instead, his jaw set, he stepped over her cowering body and got into the boat, picking up the paddle and driving it, with a few long, strong strokes, out into the water.

The lake water was rough, with a savage undertow unlike anything Bard had ever felt before, tossing the little boat around like a cork; but Bard was very strong, and had learned to handle small boats on the troubled waters of Lake Mirion. He drove the boat through the water with firm strokes. . . .

. . . and discovered, to his dismay, that somehow he had gotten turned around, and instead of heading for the shore of the Island of Silence, the boat was heading right up on the sandy beach where the ferrywoman's hut was located.

Bard swore, impotently, as he felt the boat being rushed by the savage current, right back on the shore he had left. He thrust with the paddle, fending the boat out into the stream again. It took every scrap of his strength to keep the boat in the channel, but try as he might, he could make no headway toward the island. Slowly, inexorably, the boat turned in circles, drifting, no matter how he paddled it. The ferrywoman had hauled herself to her knees and was watching him, cackling with laughter. The boat moved on shore, no matter how hard he paddled, scooted up, scraping on the sand, and his last paddle stroke actually drove it hard aground.

The little ferrywoman cackled, "I told ye, sir. Not if you was to try all day and all night. That boat there won't go to the island unless the priestesses *call* it there."

Bard fancied he saw grins on the faces of some of his men. He glared around with such rage that they quickly assumed total impassivity. He took a threatening step toward the old ferrywoman. He felt ready and willing to wring her neck. But she was only an old simpleton, after all.

He considered, standing over her. The ford at Moray's Mill had been spelled. Evidently the boat, here, had been put under sorcery as well. In any case, if the priestesses really meant to keep Carlina from him, and it was fairly obvious that they did, one man alone would meet only more bewitchment and sorcery.

Perhaps a *leronis* could calm the waters, as Melora had

161

done at Moray's Mill; and his men could swim their horses across.

"Melisendra!"

She came quietly. He wondered if she had been laughing behind his back at his struggle with the boat.

"If the priestesses have put a spell on the water, you can calm it and reverse it!"

She looked straight at him and shook her head.

"No, my lord. I dare not risk the anger of Avarra."

"Is she the Goddess of whom you prate?" he demanded.

"She is the Goddess of all women, and I will not anger her."

"Melisendra, I warn you——" He raised his hand, ready to strike her.

She looked at him with deadly indifference. "You cannot do anything to me worse than you have done. After what has already befallen me, do you think that a few blows will make me obedient to your will?"

"If you dislike me as much as all that, I would think you would be glad to help me recover my wife! Then you will be free of me, if I am so hateful to you!"

"At the cost of betraying some other woman into your hands?"

"You are jealous," he accused, "and want no other woman in my arms!"

She kept her eyes on him, straight and level. She said, "If your wife were held captive on that island and wished to rejoin you, I would risk the anger of Avarra to help her to your arms. But she seems not very eager to leave her place of refuge and come over to you. And if you are wise, Bard, you will leave this place at once before something worse happens."

"Is that the Sight?" Frustration made his words sarcastic.

She bowed her head. She said, and he saw that she was weeping silently, "No, my lord. That is—gone from me forever. But I know the Goddess cannot be defied with impunity. You had better come, Bard."

"Would you grieve if some dreadful fate befell me?" he asked, savagely, but she did not answer, only turned her horse about and rode slowly away from the lake.

Damn the woman! Damn all women, and their Goddess with them!

"Come on, men," he shouted. "Swim the horses; the spell is only on the boat!" He urged his horse right up to the water's edge, although it fought, shying nervously and backing, from

162

the water under its feet. He swiveled his horse and saw that they were not following him.

"Come on! What's the matter with you? After me, men! There are women on that island, and they have defied me, so I make you free of them all! Come on, men, plunder and women—not afraid of some old witch's jabberings, are you? Come on!"

About half of the men hung back, muttering fearfully.

"Nay, Dom Wolf, it's uncanny, it's forbidden!"

"The Goddess forbids it, Lord! No, don't do this!"

"Blasphemy!"

But one or two of the others urged their horses forward, eagerly, hauling at the reins, forcing the unwilling beasts into the water.

The fog was rising again, thicker and thicker; and this time it had a strange, eerie greenish color. It seemed that there were faces within it, faces that grimaced and leered and menaced him, and slowly, slowly, the faces were drifting ashore. One of the men hanging back, unwilling to go near the water, suddenly howled like a madman, and cried, "No, no! Mother Avarra, have mercy! Pity us!" He jerked the reins savagely and Bard heard his horse's hoofs suck and splash as he turned about and galloped back the way they had come. One after another, although Bard rose in his stirrups and yelled and cursed them, his men turned and bolted their animals back up the trail, until Bard was alone at the water's edge. Damn them all! Frightened of a little fog! Cowards, he'd break them all and reduce them to the ranks, if he didn't hang them one and all for cowardice!

He sat defying the fog. "Come on," he said aloud, and clucked to the horse, but she did not move, quivering beneath him as if she stood in the chill of a blizzard. He wondered if she could see the horrid faces, drifting nearer and nearer the shore.

And suddenly a blind terror chilled Bard, too, to the bone. He *knew*, with every fiber in him, that if one of the faces touched him through the fog, all the courage and life in him would drain out, cold, and he would die, the fog would bite through to the bone and he would fall from his saddle, strengthless and screaming, and never rise again. He jerked at the reins of his horse and tried to gallop after Melisendra and his fleeing men, but he was frozen, and the mare sat trembling under him and did not stir. He had once heard that the Great Mother could take the form of a mare. . . . Had she bewitched his horse?

The faces drifted closer and closer, horrible and formless, the faces of dead men, ravished women, corpses with the flesh hanging from their bones, and somehow Bard knew they were all the men *he* had led into battle and death, all the men *he* had killed, all the women *he* had ravaged or raped or burned and driven from their houses, the screaming face of a woman in the pillage of Scaravel, when he had taken her child from her and flung it over the wall to be shattered on the stones below . . . a woman he had taken in the sack of Scathfell, her husband lying dead beside her . . . a child, bruised and bleeding from a dozen men who had used her . . . Lisarda, weeping in his arms . . . Beltran, all the flesh melted from his bones . . . the faces were so close now that they were formless, lapping at his feet, his knees, swirling higher and higher. They wrapped about his loins, sucking, biting, and under his clothing he felt his genitals shrink and wither, unmanning him, felt the cold rise in his belly; when they rose to bite at his throat his breath would fail and he would fall, screaming, choking, dying. . . .

Bard screamed, and somehow the sound gave him life enough to grab at the reins, to kick frantically at his horse's flanks. She bucked and bolted. He clung for his life, letting her run, letting her take him anywhere, anywhere away from that place. He lost the stirrups, he lost the reins as she bolted, but panic somehow gave him strength to cling to her back; at last he felt her slowing under him to a walk, and came to consciousness dazed, finding that he was riding at the rear of his men, next to Melisendra.

If she said a single word, he resolved, if she spoke a syllable indicating that she had warned him, or that he should have taken her advice, he would hit her! Somehow that damned woman always seemed to come off best in their encounters! He was sick to death of having her there to sneer at him! If she said one word about what a ludicrous figure he had cut, fleeing, clinging to his horse. . . .

"If you're so damned well suited by piety and chastity," he snarled at her, "and so glad of my defeat, why don't you go back to them yourself and stay there?"

But she was not jeering at him. She was not looking at him at all. She had her veil pulled over her face and she was weeping quietly behind its shelter.

"I would go," she said in a whisper. "I would go, so gladly! But they would not have me." And she lowered her head and would not look at him again.

Bard rode on, sick with rage. Once again, Carlina had escaped him! She had made a fool of him again, when he had been so sure of her! And he was tied still to Melisendra, whom he was beginning to hate! He turned as they rode up the steep path, and shook an angry fist at the lake which lay silent, pale in the falling dusk, behind them.

He would come back. The women there had defeated him once, but he would devise some way to come back, and this time he would not be driven away by their witchcraft! Let them beware!

And if Carlina was hiding there, let her beware too!

Chapter Four

Summer had come to the Kilghard Hills, bringing fire season, when the resin trees burst into flame and every available man was called out on fire watch. On a day late in summer Bard di Asturien rode slowly southward, with a small group of picked men and bodyguards, and at last crossed the border from Marenji into Asturias.

No longer, he thought, *truly a border.* The Shire of Marenji, despite the protests of the sheriff, lay under arms, protected by soldiers quartered in every house and village in Marenji. A system of beacon fires and telepathic relays had been established to warn the people of Asturias of any attack from north or east, from bandits from over the Kadarin, or riders from Serrais.

The people of Marenji had protested. When had the people, he wondered, ever known what was good for them? Did they *want* to stand unarmed between Serrais and Asturias, being ridden over by armies every few years? If they did not want soldiers there from Asturias, they should have had their own armies to keep them out.

He spent one night in his old home, but no one was there except the old *coridom*; Erlend had been sent to join his mother at court. Soon, Bard thought, he would have to take thought about suitable fosterage for his son in some nobleman's house. Even if Erlend was destined to be a *laranzu,* he should know something of war and arms. Bard remembered that Geremy, who knew he would never carry arms in battle, had been nothing behind his foster brothers in swordplay. . . . he cut that thought off, clean, setting his jaw, refusing to think about it.

Erlend should be a *laranzu,* if his gifts lay that way; he was only a *nedestro* son. When he had found the right way to reclaim Carlina, she could give him lawful sons enough. But Erlend must be fostered as befitted his rank, and he supposed Melisendra would make some sort of scene over that. Damn the woman, all the disadvantages of having a wife, and none of the advantages! If she were not his father's most valued *leronis* he would send her away at once. Perhaps one of Dom Rafael's men would be willing to marry her, surely his father would give her some kind of dowry.

He rode in to Castle Asturias at dusk, finding the courtyard filled with strange horses, Hastur banners, embassies from all over the Hundred Kingdoms. What had happened? Had King Carolin sent at last to ransom Geremy?

That, he learned, was only a part of it. Forty days before, the Lady Ginevra Harryl had borne a son to Geremy Hastur; Geremy had chosen, first, to legitimatize the boy, and at the same time had chosen to marry the woman *di catenas*. As a way of proving that Geremy Hastur was no prisoner but an honored guest (the legal fiction, Bard thought wryly, about all hostages), Dom Rafael had chosen to perform the marriage himself, and to hold the wedding with great ceremony, with Hasturs coming from far and wide to attend the wedding. And while Dom Carolin would not venture, himself, into Asturias, he had sent one of his ministers, the *laranzu* Varzil of Neskaya, to solemnize the ceremony.

Bard cared little for this kind of merry-making, and the preparations reminded him, painfully, of the fact that he had hoped to hold this kind of wedding for himself some time this summer, before his defeat at the Lake of Silence. Nevertheless, the commander of the king's armies must be present; brooding, he got into his embroidered tunic and ceremonial cloak of blue, richly trimmed with copper threads and fine embroidery. Melisendra, too, looked noble and proud, her hair done high in looped braids, in a gown of green and a cape of marl-fur. Before they left the suite little Erlend came in, stopping wide-eyed to admire his parents.

"Oh, Mother, you are beautiful! And you too, Father, you are beautiful too!"

Bard chuckled and bent to lift up his son. Erlend said wistfully, "I wish I might go down and see the wedding and all the fine clothes and noblemen and ladies. . . ."

"There is no place for children—" Bard began, but Melisendra said, "Your nurse may take you into the gallery for a peep at them, Erlend, and if you are a good boy she will fetch you some cakes from the kitchen for your supper." Bard put him down, and Melisendra knelt to kiss him.

Bard, jealous of the way the boy clung to his mother, said, "And you shall ride with me tomorrow." Erlend trotted away with his nurse, quite dazzled at the thought of the promised treats.

But Bard frowned as he went, at Melisendra's side, down the great stairway.

"Why in the name of all the gods did Father choose to hold Geremy's wedding in such state?"

"I think he has a plan, but I do not know what it is; I am sure it was not because of any good will he holds toward Geremy. Nor, I suppose, toward Ginevra; although Dom Regis Harryl is one of the oldest nobility of Asturias, and of the Hastur kin a few generations back."

Bard thought about this. Of course, Dom Rafael sought to hold the throne for Alaric, and must do it in part by keeping the goodwill of all the nobles who owed allegiance to the di Asturiens. A court wedding for the daughter of a valued supporter was a simple diplomatic move, well worth what it cost. Although personally Bard would have hesitated at showing such favor at one of his own allies marrying into the Hasturs when the Hasturs could, all too soon, be enemies.

"Do you really think we shall have to go to war with the Hasturs, Bard?"

Bard scowled, annoyed at Melisendra's habit of reading his mind, but said, "I see no way that it can be avoided."

Melisendra shivered a little. "Why, you are *pleased*...."

"I am a soldier, Melisendra. War is my business, and the business of every loyal man of Asturias, so that we have to keep this realm by force of arms."

"I should think it would be easy to make peace with the Hasturs. They don't want war any more than we do."

Bard shrugged. "Well, let them surrender to us, then." He wished Melisendra would stop talking about things that did not really concern her.

"But it does concern me, Bard. I am a *leronis*, and no stranger to battle. And even if I were not, if I were such a woman as had nothing better to do than bide at home and keep my house, I should still have to deal with wounds and pillage and bearing of sons to ride into war . . . war is a concern of women, not only of men!"

Her face was flushed with indignation, but Bard only said roughly, "Nonsense. And if you read my thought again, Melisendra, without leave, you will be sorry for it!"

She shrugged and said with composure, "I am sorry for *anything* I have to do with you, my Lord. And if you wish me not to read your thoughts, you should refrain from send ing them forth so that no one can help but hear them; I am seldom sure whether you have spoken aloud, or no."

Bard wondered about that. He had never thought he had any measurable *laran*. Why did Melisendra find him so easy to read?

The Great Hall was crowded with men and women. There was also the howling of two or three young infants; there had recently been a silly fad among noblewomen for suckling their babes themselves, instead of giving them properly to wet nurses, and Ginevra was recently a mother so that many other young matrons had seen fit to bring their unweaned babes into the hall. He hoped they would be carried out before the ceremonies began! He decided that when Carlina came to court he would insist that she should behave in a more dignified fashion; with all these squalling weanlings about, the place was like the pasture of mares in foal!

But Lady Jerana had evidently insisted that all the babies be taken away before the ceremony. The marriage bracelets were locked, with great solemnity, on the wrists of Geremy and Ginevra, as the Regent of Asturias said, "May you be forever one." Well, Geremy had a wife, and at least she was of proven fertility. He shrugged and went to congratulate his kinsman.

Ginevra and Melisendra were hugging one another and squealing inanities as young women always did at weddings. Bard bowed.

"I congratulate you, cousin," he said courteously. If Geremy were halfway intelligent, he thought, he would chalk their differences up to the fortunes of war, and have done with it. He bore Geremy no special ill will; he supposed that in Geremy's shoes he would have done much the same.

"I see your kinsmen have come far and wide to do honor to you, foster brother."

"Mostly, I think, to my lady," Geremy returned, and presented Ginevra to Bard. She was a small, swarthy woman, who looked almost as if she might have been born to the mountain forge-folk; even though Geremy did not stand straight, she came only up to his shoulder. She was flat-chested too, and had followed the stupid fashion of having her gown made with lacings so that she could nurse her infant in public; how undignified!

But he spoke politely, bowing.

"I hope your son is strong and hearty as a man-child should be."

She said a courteous word or two; and Geremy evidently

169

shared Bard's feeling that it was prudent for them to be seen in civil chit-chat for a moment or two.

"Oh, yes, the women say he is a fine boy. I am no judge of such things. To me he looks like any other newborn babe, soggy at both ends, and howling early and late; but Ginevra thinks he is pretty, even after all the trouble he gave her."

"I was fortunate," Bard said, "for I made the acquaintance of my son only after he could walk and talk like a reasonable person, not an untrained puppy."

"I have seen young Erlend," Geremy said, "and he is handsome and clever. And his mother, I have heard, is a *leronis;* is the boy *laran*-gifted as well?"

"His mother tells me so."

"I should expect it, with the red hair of the Hastur kin," Geremy said. "Have you given thought to having the boy fostered at one of the Towers, Hali or Neskaya? I am sure they would be glad to have him. My kinsman Varzil of Neskaya is here, and he could arrange for it."

"I doubt it not. But it seems to me that Erlend is over young to be sent out of this realm in time of war, and I have no wish to see him held hostage."

Geremy looked shocked. "You misunderstand me, kinsman. The Towers are sworn to neutrality, which is how a Ridenow came to be Keeper at Hali. And after the burning of Neskaya, when the Tower was rebuilt, Varzil came there with a circle, and swore they would observe the Compact of the Hasturs, and fight no more wars with *laran* weapons."

"Except in the cause of the Hasturs, you mean," Bard said with a cynical grin. "Clever of Carolin, to insure their loyalty like that!"

"No, cousin, not even that. They are sworn not to fight even for the Hasturs, but to use their starstones only in the cause of peace."

"And Carolin lets their Tower stand unburned within his realm?"

"My father wishes it so," said Geremy. "This land is torn yearly with foolish and fratricidal wars, so that the peasants cannot even get in their crops. Clingfire is bad enough, but worse weapons are made now by sorcery. The Lady of Valeron used air-cars to spread bonewater dust north of Thendara, and I think perhaps no crops will ever grow there again, and any man who travels through that country dies, afterward, with blood turned to water and bones gone brittle . . . and worse things, such things as I would not speak of at a festival. And so we have all sworn that we will use no *laran*

170

against any foe from these Towers, and all the lands near the Hastur realms have pledged themselves to observe the Compact."

"I know not of this Compact," Bard said. "What means it?"

"Why, where the Compact is in force no man may attack another with any weapon save one that brings the wielder within arm's reach of death. . . ."

"I had not heard of it," Bard said, "and I too would rather fight with honest sword and pike than with sorcery. I have no love for using *leroni* in battle, nor, I think, has any soldier. But I would not have *leroni* within my realm at all, unless they were sworn to fight with me, and protect my armies against the attack of wizardry. Tell me more."

"Why, I have not been within my father's realm since I was a boy, and I do not know much of it, except what my kinsman Varzil has told me."

"You own a Ridenow of Serrais as *kin*?"

"We are all Hastur kin," said Geremy, "and bear alike the blood of Hastur and Cassilda. Why should we be at strife?"

This sobered Bard and shocked him. If the Hastur and the Serrais were to make common cause, what would then become of the realm of Asturias? He wanted to rush off to his father with this new intelligence, but the minstrels had begun to play for dancing, and dancers were crowding onto the floor.

"Would you like to dance, Ginevra? You need not stay at my side because I am crippled; I am sure one of my kinsmen would lead you out."

She smiled, briefly pressing his hand. "At my wedding, I shall dance with no man, since my husband cannot join me. I will wait for a woman's ring dance and dance with my ladies."

"You have a loyal wife," Bard said, and Geremy shrugged. "Oh, Ginevra has always known that I should never win acclaim in the field of war, nor on the dancing floor."

One of the Hastur kinsmen in his blue and silver came up to request a dance with the bride. Watching Ginevra's gracious refusal, Bard began to realize why his kinsman had chosen this scrawny, dark, plain little thing. She had the charm and graciousness of a queen; she would, in spite of her unremarkable features, grace any court.

"But you must not do that," protested the man. "Why, dancing with a bride is a powerful charm for any man who

171

wishes to marry within the year! How can you have the heart to deprive us so, *domna?*"

Ginevra bantered gaily, "Why, I shall dance only with my unmarried ladies; that will help *them* to husbands, and since they must find some men to share the weddings, and so it will help the bachelors to find brides, too!" She signaled to the musicians, who began to play a ring dance. Taking Melisendra's hands, Ginevra drew her away on to the dancing floor, and many women and young girls, too young for dancing with strangers, or women whose husbands or brothers were committed elsewhere, came crowding out behind them. Bard watched Melisendra's green-clad form, weaving in and out of the patterns of the ring dance. Where, he wondered, was Melora now? Why did that memory haunt him so? The thought crossed his mind, and he knew it was insanity, that if he were tied to Melora like this, they would talk together, they could be friendly, close, in the way Geremy and Ginevra were. He remembered how Ginevra had pressed Geremy's hand against her cheek. No woman had ever behaved so with him, and yet he could imagine Melora doing such a thing.

Nonsense; he could not marry Melora, she was not wellborn, and in any case she was committed to a Tower. That was not the way marriages were made. He had criticized Geremy in his mind for marrying Ginevra, who was, despite the old family and her gracious manners, considerably below him in rank. Only a fool would marry a woman who could not bring him some powerful alliance or rich dowry. He could not, for instance, resign himself to marrying Melisendra; she was the daughter of a humble *laranzu* . . . though what was it Geremy had said about Hastur kin and red hair? Melisendra could not be so low-born after all. . . .

"I had believed," said Geremy, "that we were soon to have the honor of dancing at *your* wedding, Bard. Could you not persuade Carlina to leave the hospitality of the Sisterhood of Avarra?"

"I had no opportunity to speak with her. The shores of the Island of Silence are guarded with sorcery. It will take a regiment of *leroni* to break those spells! But mark my words, it shall be done!"

Geremy made a gesture which mimicked pious horror.

"And you do not fear the wrath of Avarra?"

"I do not fear any group of foolish women who pretend that their will is the will of some goddess or other!" Bard growled.

"But can it be that your bride prefers chastity and good

works to the pleasures that await her when she is wedded to you? Why, how can she be so foolish!" Geremy's gray eyes flickered with malicious amusement, and Bard turned on his heel and walked away. He did not want to embarrass his father by quarreling at a great entertainment like this. Not even to himself did he admit that he had no wish to quarrel further with Geremy.

Later, while all the young people were dancing, he talked a little to his father about what he had done on the northern borders.

"It is not likely we shall be attacked from Serrais while we have Dom Eiric hostage," he said, "but seeing us beset by the Hasturs, they may come down on us too. I have heard of a truce between Aldaran and Scathfell; if they come at us together we would be hard put to it to hold them off, with so many of our armies holding off any threat from Serrais. And there are some who would be glad to ally with the Hasturs. If Varzil of Serrais has made an alliance with Hastur, I think we must try to win over the MacAran, at El Haleine, to guard our southern borders, as Marenji stands between us on the north."

"I do not think either the MacAran, or the people at Syrtis, would be willing to anger the Hasturs," Dom Rafael said. "They say of Lord Colryn of Syrtis that he can stand atop his keep and look out over all of his small country, and while the mouse in the walls may look from afar at a cat, he does well not to go squeaking about it; and Dom Colryn has no wish to be mouse to King Carolin's meowing! Carolin could gobble him up without blooding his whiskers!" He scowled. "And unless we return Dom Eiric to Serrais, all those who are allied with Serrais will come down on us before winter. Perhaps we must swear Dom Eiric to a truce and gain time. It is time we need!" He struck his knee with his open hand. "We may be forced to swear truce with the Hastur too!"

Bard said scornfully, "I will take the field against the Hasturs. I am not afraid of them! I held Scaravel with a handful of men, and I can do as much for Asturias!"

"But you are only one man," Dom Rafael said, "and can lead only one army. With Serrais to the east, and the Hasturs to the west, and perhaps all those across the Kadarin ready to come down on us from the north, Asturias cannot stand!"

"We have some protection in Marenji," Bard said, "for anyone who comes at us that way must fight, now, across their land; and I think perhaps we could raise mercenaries in the north, and in the Dry towns—they know my reputation and will fight under my command. And perhaps we can bind Dom Eiric to a truce; his sons are young and must keep from war for a time. If we bind him to truce for half a year—and a released hostage must expect that, at least—he cannot put an army against us in the field until spring thaw. And by spring perhaps we could have mercenaries, and even allies, enough that we could move against Serrais and reduce them to vassalage. Think of it, Father! To have all those lands to the east peaceful, without continual fighting! It seems we have been at war against Serrais since I was a babe in arms!"

"We have," Dom Rafael said, "and longer. But even if we conquer Serrais we will still have to face the Hasturs, for King Carolin claims that all these lands were once Hastur lands—"

"Geremy said something to that effect. I paid him little heed. But if Carolin is claiming that, we will simply have to teach him better."

"But I will have to take oaths and make truces," said Dom Rafael soberly. "It is still a matter of time; for time has run out for holding Geremy as hostage. Carolin has called our bluff and Varzil of Neskaya was sent to escort Geremy home. He brought your brother Alaric home to us."

"I shall not be sorry to see Geremy go forth from this court," said Bard, but he was aware that this represented a diplomatic loss for Dom Rafael. With a Hastur hostage, he had some leverage for diplomatic compromise with the Hasturs. Still, the return of Alaric was a gain to offset that loss.

"How is it with my brother?" Bard asked eagerly. "Is he well and happy; has Carolin used him well? For when Queen Ariel fled there, I have no doubt he was in Carolin's hands and not hers."

"I have not seen him as yet," Dom Rafael said soberly. "He is still in the care of Varzil. The formal exchange will come later, for Varzil, I understand, is empowered with a message from Carolin, and has asked for formal audience in which to state his mission."

Bard raised his eyebrows. So the Keeper of Neskaya had sunk to the level of a Hastur flunkey? Perhaps it was worse than he thought, perhaps all the lands from the Kilghard Hills to Thendara lay under the Hasturs! Would the next few years see Asturias among them? *Over my dead body!*

And then he felt a small premonitory shudder. If it should indeed come about that way, well, it would certainly be over

174

his dead body. But that was a soldier's fate in any case! And whatever happened, he was not likely to escape it.

If Alaric were returned, that would at least give Dom Rafael excuse to hold a coronation; for Rafael still insisted he was not king, but regent for Alaric. Bard wondered what was the difference between one child king and another. But in any case, Alaric was here, not, like Valentine, fled to the protection of another kingdom. Then Bard realized that he had been thinking of Alaric as he had been almost seven years ago; a child, pleased at the thought of his brother's outgrown toys. Now Alaric must be fourteen or fifteen, close to legal manhood. His own son Erlend was not so much younger than Alaric had been when they last parted!

Time. Time was the enemy of every man. He himself had lived longer than most men who earned their bread as mercenary soldiers. At least he should lose no time in marrying and getting himself some legitimate sons. He must make the kingdom secure for his brother, and then he must discover some way to attack the Island of Silence, even if it took a whole army of wizards, and regain Carlina.

While she lives, I shall marry no other woman! It occurred to him, for the first time, that perhaps he had made a great mistake. If Carlina truly did not want him, perhaps there were other women who would. Again he thought of Melora . . . but no. Carlina was King Ardrin's daughter, she was his handfasted wife, and if she did not want him, well, he would soon teach her where her duty lay. No woman ever wanted to refuse him a second time!

Rafael of Asturias released Dom Eiric of Serrais the next morning.

"But why *now*, Father?" Bard asked. "Certainly you could delay him a few tendays more!"

"A matter of protocol," Dom Rafael said grimly. "Varzil of Neskaya, who is a Ridenow, wishes to interview him, but he cannot in courtesy do so until he has transacted his main business here, the exchange of hostages; and he cannot speak with my prisoner without my leave. So I will take oath from Dom Eiric and set him on his way, *before* Varzil is free to speak with him. I want no more Ridenow lords making allies of Hastur!"

Bard nodded, absorbing this. Once Dom Eiric had taken his oath not to work against Rafael of Asturias for half a year, he could not lawfully ally with any enemy of Asturias, either. Bard had all manner of knowledge of military tactics and strategies, but diplomacy was still new to him. But with his father's knowledge of statecraft, and his own skill at war, perhaps they could hold all this countryside one day.

He found that he was curious to see this Varzil, who had allied with the Hasturs. Neskaya had been in Ridenow hands—though it lay far outside the Serrais lands proper—for more than two hundred years. In those days the Hasturs and the Ridenow had fought a prolonged war, and peace had been made in the reign of Allart of Thendara. Did the Hasturs still entertain dreams of reclaiming all the Serrais lands?

Bard was summoned to the council, as his father's high commander; and Melisendra, too, for the setting of truthspell. As Bard watched her come into the presence chamber, in her thin unadorned gray dress and cape, the mark of a *leronis* present upon official duties, he realized that Melisendra, as his father's chosen court sorceress, now had status and power in her own right, power that had nothing to do with her official position as the mother of the regent's grandson. The thought made him vaguely angry; there were *laranzu'in* enough, why did his father not, in decency, choose one of them? Was his father trying to put Melisendra in a position where she could flout her lawful lord and the father of her son?

He hoped Alaric had some skill at arms. As Ardrin's fosterling, he should have learned *something*. Bard himself was only one man; but if he had a knowledgeable military leader backing him up from the throne—and certainly a king should be able, like Ardrin, to lead his fighting men into battle—it augured well for Asturias in the years that would come.

Varzil of Neskaya was a small and slender man. In the gorgeous ceremonial dress he had worn at the wedding he had looked impressive, but now, in the green and gold of his House, he seemed small, narrow-shouldered; his features were lean, scholarly, and his hands, Bard noted with contempt, were as small and well-kept as a woman's, with no callouses from sword or dagger, and no hair worn away at his temples from the facepiece of the helmet. Not a man of war, then, but a sandal wearer, a dandy. And this was Hastur's chosen embassy? Bard thought, with contempt, *I could break him with my two hands!*

Even Geremy, stooped though he was, dragging his lame leg, was taller than Varzil. Geremy wore his customary sober dress, unweaponed save for a small ornamental dagger, the hilt set with firestones. Bard watched, standing in the paxman's place behind his father's throne, as the formalities and the setting of truthspell took place.

"Geremy Hastur," said Dom Rafael, "since my son is to be safely returned to me, I declare you free to return to your father's kingdom, or wherever you choose to go, with your wife, who is my subject, and your son, and your vassals, and all that is yours. Furthermore, as a mark of the esteem in which my lady wife holds your lady, if your wife's waiting-women wish to accompany the lady Ginevra to her new home, they are free to do so, if they have leave from their own fathers."

Geremy bowed and made a short and courteous speech thanking Dom Rafael and reassuring him of his gratitude for his kind hospitality. The irony was heavy-handed enough so that the truthspell light faltered on his face, but it was not worth taking issue. Courtesy, Bard thought wryly, was mostly lies anyhow.

"Geremy, you are free, if you will, to leave your son to be fostered in my house. His mother's father is my loyal man, and I give you my personal assurance that he will be brought up in all respects as my own son, and as a companion to my grandson."

Geremy thanked him courteously and declined that his son was too young to be parted from his mother, being as yet unweaned, and that Ginevra had a fancy to nurse him herself.

Varzil stepped forward. "And I have come," he said, "in the name of Carolin, High King at Thendara, guardian of Valentine di Asturien, rightful king of Asturias and overlord of all these lands, to return Alaric di Asturien, son of the Regent and Warden of Asturias, to his father. Alaric—?"

Bard drew in his breath, in audible shock. From behind Varzil, a slightly built boy limped forward; his uneven step and twisted shoulders were like a ghastly parody of Geremy's own; and Bard could not contain himself.

"Father!" he cried out, stepping forward, "Will you let them mock us thus in our own halls? Look what they have done to my brother, in revenge for Geremy's hurts? I will swear before truthspell that Geremy was hurt by mischance, not by design, and Alaric has not deserved this of Carolin!" He drew his dagger. "Now, by all the gods, Hastur spawn, defend yourself, for *this* time your life is forefeit and it will be no accident! I'll make good what I should have done to you seven years ago—"

He grabbed Geremy's shoulder and spun him around.

177

"Draw your dagger, or I strike you down where you stand!"

"Cease! I command it!"

Varzil's voice was not loud, but it made Bard loosen his grip and fall back from Geremy, pale and sweating. He had not heard command voice for many years from the lips of a trained *laranzu*. Varzil's slender figure seemed to loom over him, menacing, as Bard's dagger fell from nerveless fingers.

"Bard di Asturien," Varzil said, "I do not war on children, nor does Carolin; your accusation is monstrous, and I stand here in the light of truthspell to give you the lie to your face. We told you nothing of Alaric's ills for fear you would come to exactly this conclusion. We had no hand in Alaric's laming. Five years ago he fell ill with the muscle fever which ravages so many children in the lake district, and although all of Ardin's healers did their best for him, and sent him to Neskaya for healing as soon as he was able to travel—which is why he was not left here to rejoin you when Queen Ariel fled the country, since he was in my care at Neskaya—despite all our best efforts, his leg withered, and his back is weakened. He can walk now with only a leg brace to help him, and he has recovered his powers of speech; so you may ask Alaric himself if he has anything to complain of from our treatment."

Bard stared in dismay. So this poor cripple was the fine, strong, manly brother who would help him to lead his armies! He had the feeling that the gods were mocking him.

Dom Rafael held out his arms and Alaric limped forward, into his father's embrace.

"My dear son!" he said in dismay and consternation, and the boy looked from his father to Varzil in distress.

"Dear Father," he said. "Truly, what has happened is not the fault of my kinsman Ardrin, and certainly not of the Lord Varzil. When I fell ill, and for many years after, he, and his *leroni*, cared for me night and day. They have been so kind and good to me, neither you nor my mother could have done more."

"Gods above!" groaned Dom Rafael. "And Ardrin sent me no word? Nor Ariel, when she fled into exile?"

"I had been sent to Neskaya years before," Alaric retorted, "and since you never came to court, I did not think that you cared much what befell me! Certainly," he added, in a detached, ironical way which convinced Bard that, if his brother's body was crippled, there was certainly nothing wrong with his mind, "you were not so eager to have me

178

back that you would contend very long with Carolin for me. I knew that you would hold your throne for me, at least until you saw me. After that, I was not sure whether you would care to ransom me at all."

Dom Rafael said loyally, "You are my own dear son, and I welcome you back to the throne I have claimed for you," but Bard heard the unspoken part of this, *if you can possibly hold it,* and was sure Alaric could hear it too.

Varzil's face was composed and compassionate; his eyes lingered on Alaric and Dom Rafael as if he had no thought except for the child and his stricken father. But Bard knew that Varzil, in spite of a very genuine concern for young Alaric, had nevertheless held him back to produce at the moment when it would cause the most confusion and consternation. He had intended to show them all, and as publicly as possible, that the young claimant to the throne of Asturias was no more than a pitiful little cripple!

Bard felt despair and rage—was *this* the strong young warrior who would ride to battle at his side? Yet his heart ached for the little brother he had loved. Whatever his father's disappointment and his own, Alaric must be feeling it more than either of them! It was inexcusable, to use the boy like this, to show forth the weakness of the Asturian throne! At this moment, had it not been for his knowledge of diplomatic immunity, he would willingly have strangled Varzil where he stood—yes, and Geremy too!

Yet—he thought, slowly coming to terms with this new knowledge—it could have been worse. Alaric was lamed, but otherwise he looked healthy and strong, and there was certainly nothing wrong with his mind! Geremy had a healthy son; there was no reason Alaric could not have a dozen. He would not, after all, be the first crippled king to hold a throne; and, after all, he had a loyal brother to command his armies.

I am not ambitious toward his throne, Bard thought. *I have no wit, nor yet skill, to govern; I would rather be the king's commander than the king!* He met Alaric's eyes and smiled.

Dom Rafael too had recovered his equilibrium. He rose from his presence seat and said, "In token that I reigned here only as regent, my son, I yield this place to you as rightful King of Asturias. My son and my lord, I beg you to take this place."

The boy's cheeks stained with color, but he had been well trained in protocol. When his father knelt at his feet, proffering his sword, he said, "I beg you to rise, Father, and take

179

back your sword, as regent and warden of this realm, until I have reached years of manhood."

Dom Rafael rose, taking his place three steps behind the throne.

"My brother," Alaric said, looking at Bard, "I have been told that you are commander of the armies of Asturias."

Bard bent the knee before the boy and said, "I am here to serve you, my brother and my lord."

Alaric smiled, for the first time since he had stepped out from behind Varzil, and the smile was like a sun coming out and warming Bard's heart.

"I do not ask you for your sword, dear brother. I beg you to keep it in defense of this realm; may it be drawn only against my enemies. I name you first man in this realm after our father the Lord Regent, and I will think soon of some way to reward you."

Bard said briefly that his brother's favor was reward enough. He had hated this kind of ceremony, ever since he had been a boy in the king's house; he stepped back, grateful that at least he had not made a fool out of himself by tripping over something.

Alaric said, "And now, kinsman Varzil, I know you were entrusted with a diplomatic mission which, quite rightly, you did not confide to a child. Will you now reveal it to the throne of Asturias, and to my father and Regent?"

Dom Rafael seconded the request. "I welcome Carolin's embassy," he said, "but would it be possible to hold it in a room more suited to this conference than this throne room where we must all stand about in ceremonial attitudes, waiting upon formalities?"

"I should be honored," Varzil said, "and I am willing to dispense with truthspell if you are; the matters to be discussed are not facts, but attitudes, claims, opinions and ethical considerations. Truthspell has no validity over honest differences of opinion where each side believes itself in the right."

Dom Rafael said ceremoniously, "This is true. By your leave, then, cousin, we will dismiss the *leronis* and her work, and meet again within the hour in my private drawing room, if that is not too informal for you, cousin. I offer more comfort, not any intended slight of the importance of your mission."

"I shall welcome informality and privacy," Varzil said. When the Hastur embassage had temporarily withdrawn,

Dom Rafael and his sons delayed for a moment before leaving the presence chamber.

"Alaric, my son, you need not sit through the conference if it would weary you!"

"Father, by your leave, I will stay," Alaric said. "You are my regent and guardian, and I will defer to your judgment till I am declared a man, and after, too, no doubt, for many years. But I am old enough to understand these matters, and if I am to govern one day, I had better know what statecraft you intend."

Bard and Dom Rafael exchanged glances of approval.

"Stay by all means, your highness." Dom Rafael used the very formal phrase *va' Altezu*, used only to a superior and one very near the throne. Bard knew that his father was acknowledging the boy as an adult, though he had not—quite—arrived at the age for legal manhood. Alaric might look like a sick child, but there was little question in either mind that he had the maturity to take his place as a man.

In Dom Rafael's private study they gathered again, around a table, and Dom Rafael sent for a servant to pour wine for them all. When the servant had withdrawn again Varzil said, "By your leave, Dom Rafael, and you, Highness," he added formally to Alaric, his tone quite in contrast to the affectionate informality he had shown Alaric before, "I am entrusted by Carolin of Thendara with a mission. I had intended to bring a Voice, that you might hear Carolin's very words. But, by your leave, I will dispense with this. I am Carolin's ally and his friend; I am Keeper of Neskaya Tower. And I have signed with him, for Neskaya, the Compact we now ask you to keep. As you know, Neskaya was destroyed by fire-bombing, a generation ago; and when Carolin Hastur had it rebuilt, we agreed upon the Compact. He did not require it of me as a sovereign lord, but requested it of me as a man of reason, and I was glad to do so."

"What is this Compact of which you speak?" asked Dom Rafael.

Varzil did not answer directly. Instead he said, "The Hundred Kingdoms are torn apart, every year, by foolish and fratricidal wars; your strife with Queen Ariel for the throne of Asturias is only one. Carolin of Thendara is willing to recognize the house of Rafael di Asturien as rightfully warden of this realm, and Queen Ariel stands ready to withdraw, for herself and her son, any claim to this throne, if you sign the Compact."

"I grant the generosity of the concession," Dom Rafael

said, "but I have no wish for Durraman's bargain, when he bought the donkey. I must know the precise nature of this Compact, cousin, before I agree to it."

"The Compact states that we will use no weapons of sorcery in war," Varzil said. "Perhaps war is inevitable among men; I confess that I do not know. Carolin and I are working for a day when all these lands will be united in peace. Meanwhile, we ask you to unite with us in a sacred pledge that fighting shall be done honorably by soldiers who go into battle and risk their own lives, not by coward's weapons to fling sorcery and chaos upon women and children, to burn forests and ravage towns and farmlands. We ask that you outlaw, within your realm, all weapons which go beyond the arm's reach of the man who wields them, so that fighting may be honorable and equal, and not endanger the innocent with evil weapons which strike from afar."

Dom Rafael said, "You cannot possibly be serious!" He stared at Varzil in disbelief. "What insanity is this? Are we to march to war with swordsmen alone, while our enemies fall upon us with arrows and clingfire, bombs and sorcery? Dom Varzil, I am reluctant to think you a madman, but do you truly think war is a game of *castles,* played by women and children with dice for cakes or pennies? Do you truly think that any sane man would listen for a moment to such an idea?"

Varzil's calm, handsome face was wholly serious. "I give you my word, in all honesty. I mean what I say, and there are many small kingdoms that have already signed the Compact with King Carolin and the Hasturs. Coward's weapons, and *laran* warfare, are to be completely outlawed. We cannot prevent war, not in the present state of our world. But we can keep it within bounds, keep war from destroying croplands and forests, prevent such weapons as the evil that ravaged Hali nine years ago, where children swelled and sickened of the disease that turns their blood to water, because they had played in forests where the leaves had been destroyed with bonewater dust. . . . The lands there are still unlivable, Dom Rafael, and may be so in the times of young Alaric's grandchildren! War *is* a contest, Dom Rafael. It could, indeed, be settled by a throw of the dice, or a game of castles. The rules of warfare are not decreed by the gods, that we must go on to greater and greater weapons which will destroy all of us one day, victor and vanquished alike. Before that day comes, why not limit it to such weapons as can be used with honor for all?"

"As to that," said Dom Rafael, "my people would never agree. I am no tyrant, to take away their weapons, and leave them defenseless against those unscrupulous people who would always refuse to give up *their* weapons. Perhaps, when I am sure that all our enemies have already done this . . . but I do not think so."

"Bard di Asturien," Varzil said, surprisingly turned to him, "you are a soldier; most soldiers are men of reason. You are commander of your father's armies. Would you not willingly see these atrocious weapons outlawed? Have you not seen a village burned with clingfire, or little children dying of the bonewater sickness?"

Bard felt an inward wrench, remembering just such a village near Scaravel; the endless screaming and crying of children burned by clingfire. It seemed to go on for days, until one by one they had died, all of them, and then the silence seemed even more terrible, as if he could still hear their screams somewhere in his mind. . . . He would not, himself, use clingfire; but why was Varzil asking *him*? He was only a soldier, his father's loyal man who must follow orders.

He said, "Dom Varzil, I would gladly fight with swords and shields alone, if others could be brought to do likewise. But I am a soldier, and my business is to win battles. I cannot win battles when I lead men armed with swords against an army who bear clingfire, or set demons of sorcery and fear against my men, to raise wind and water and storms and earthquakes against me."

"It would not be asked of you," Varzil said. "But would you agree that if *laran* is not used against you, you will not be the first to use it, and especially not to use it against non-combatants?"

Bard began to say that it sounded reasonable, but Dom Rafael broke in angrily, "No! War is not a game!"

Varzil said in contempt, "If it is not a game, what is it? Surely it is for those who make war to set the rules as they wish!"

Dom Rafael said with a scornful twist of his mouth, "Why, then, why not carry your policy all the way? Suggest that in future all our wars shall be settled by a game of football—or even leapfrog? Send our old gaffers to settle the war by a game of king's-man on a squared board, or our little girls for a game of jump rope, to settle our disputes?"

Varzil said, "The subject of most wars is a matter which would be better settled by reasonable debate among reasonable men. When reason cannot bring about a settlement, it

183

could be as well settled by a game of catch-ball among the children, as by these endless campaigns which prove only that the gods seem to love those who have the better trained soldiers!" He sounded immeasurably bitter.

"You speak like a coward," Dom Rafael said. "War may be disturbing to the squeamish, but you can't argue with facts, and since men aren't reasonable—and why should they settle for reason instead of what they want?—all arguments are, in the long run, going to be settled in favor of the one who can enforce settlement with the strongest hand. You cannot change the nature of mankind, and that's simply the knowledge we have from all the years of man. If a man isn't satisfied by the answer he gets, no matter how reasonable and right it may seem to others, he is going to go out and fight for what he wants. Otherwise we would all be born without hands or arms or the brains to use weapons. None but a coward would say otherwise; though I would expect it of a sandal wearer, a *laranzu*."

Varzil said, "Hard words break no bones, sir. I am not so much afraid of being called coward that I would fight a war to avoid it, like schoolboys blacking each other's eyes over the cry of *whoreson* or *sixfathered*! Are you telling me that if soldiers come against you armed only with swords, you will burn them with clingfire?"

"Yes, of course, if I have the clingfire. I do not make the evil stuff, but if it is used against me, I must have it, and I must use it before it can be used against me. Do you really think anyone will keep this Compact, unless he is assured of victory already?"

"And you will fight this way, even when you know it means your own lands will be poisoned with bonewater dust, or the new poison which brings out black sores on every man, woman and child who breathes it, so that they now call it the masking sickness? I had thought you a merciful and reasonable man!"

"Why, so I am," Dom Rafael said, "but not so reasonable that I will lay down my arms and resign myself to surrendering my country, and my people, to live in slavery to some other country! In my mind, anything which gives a quick and decisive victory is a merciful and reasonable weapon. A war fought with swords, like a tournament, may drag on for years—we have been fighting the Serrais for most of my lifetime—while sensible men will think twice before carrying on a war against such weapons as I can bring against them. No Dom Varzil, your words sound reasonable on the surface, but

184

under them lurks insanity; men would enjoy your kind of war too much, and prolong it like a game, knowing they could play at warfare without being seriously hurt. You may go back to Carolin and tell him that I despise his Compact and I will never honor it. If he comes against me, he will find me prepared with every weapon my *leroni* can devise, and on his own head be it if he chooses to arm his men with swords and shields alone; for all I care he may arm them with tennis balls, and make my work easier; or tell them to surrender at once. Is this nonsense of Compact all you were sent to tell me, Dom Varzil?"

"No," said Varzil.

"What more is there? I do not want war with the Hasturs. I would prefer a truce."

"And so would I," Varzil said, "and so would King Carolin. I was sent and empowered to take your oath to abstain from war against us. You are a reasonable man, you say; why, then, should this land be torn apart with fighting?"

"I have no wish to fight," said Dom Rafael, "but I will not surrender to the Hasturs where di Asturiens have reigned since time out of mind."

"That is not true," said Varzil. "Written records in Nevarsin and Hali—which are perhaps more reliable than the patriotic legends and folk tales you use to rally your men—would reassure you that less than two hundred years ago this land was all ruled by Hasturs; but after an invasion of catmen, Lord Hastur gave the di Asturiens the task of guarding it, no more. And now all these lands have split up into little kingdoms, each one claiming an immemorial right to be independent and sovereign over its own people. This is chaos. Why not have peace again?"

"Peace? Tyranny, you mean," Dom Rafael said. "Why should the free people of Asturias bow their heads to the Hasturs?"

"Why, then, should they bow it to the di Asturiens, for that matter? Peace is bought at the cost of giving up some local autonomy. Suppose each of your farmsteaders insisted that he was a free man, and had a right to absolute individual self-rule, refusing any other man the right to cross his borders without paying tribute, and owing loyalty to nothing but his own whim?"

"That," said Dom Rafael, "would be foolish."

"Then why is it not foolish to say that El Haleine and Asturias and Marenji are all kingdoms, each with separate king and government and each cut off from others? Why not make peace under the sons of Hastur, and have freedom to move about, and trade, without armed men everywhere? You will be free in your own realm, you simply pledge not to meddle with any other free and independent realm, but to cooperate with your fellow lords as friends and equals—"

Rafael di Asturien shook his head. "My ancestors won this land. Ardrin's son Valentine forfeited his right to it when he fled to King Carolin with his traitor mother. But I shall keep it for my sons, and if Hasturs want it, they will have to come and take it if they can." He spoke bravely, but Bard knew that his father was remembering their conversation the night of Geremy's wedding.

Serrais to the east. Aldaran and Scathfell to the north. Hasturs to the west and all their allies, and no doubt, someday people from the Plains of Valeron to the south.

"Then," said Varzil, "you will not swear allegiance to Hastur, even though all he asks is a pledge that you will not take up arms against Hali or Carcosa or Castle Hastur or Neskaya which is under his protection?"

"The throne of Asturias," Rafael said, "is not subject to Hastur. And that's my last word on the subject. I have no intention of attacking Hasturs, but they cannot seek to rule here."

"Alaric," Varzil said, "you are lord of Asturias. You are not of an age to make compacts, but I ask you nevertheless, out of kindness to kin, to ask your father to see reason in this matter."

"My son is not your prisoner now, Dom Varzil," Rafael said, his chin jutting hard. "I do not know how much treason you may have taught him against his own people, but now—"

"Father, that is unjust," Alaric protested. "I ask you not to quarrel with my kinsman Varzil!"

"For your sake, my son, I hold my peace. Yet I beg of you, Dom Varzil, set aside this foolish talk of surrendering the throne of Asturias to the Hasturs!"

Varzil said, "Even now you are contemplating war against peaceful neighbors—not invaders! I know what you have done in Marenji. I am informed that in the spring you intend war against Serrais; and you intend to fortify the lands along the Kadarin—"

"And what is that to you?" Bard asked with cold hostility. "The lands along the Kadarin are not Hastur lands!"

"Neither are they the lands belonging to Asturias," said Varzil, "and Carolin is sworn to make them safe against attack from land-greedy little kingdoms! Do what you will within your own realm; but I warn you, unless you are prepared to fight against all of those who give allegiance to Hastur and to the Compact, do not move outside them!"

"Are you threatening me?"

"I am," Varzil said, "though I would rather not. I ask as envoy of Hastur, that you and your two sons take oath not to move against the Compact lands who have sworn to one another as equals, or we will have an army in the field within forty days, and we will take the Kingdom of Asturias and put it into the wardenship of someone who will hold it in peace among the *com'ii* under Hastur."

Bard heard this with a dreadful sinking. They were not, in fact, prepared to make war against the Hasturs; not with the men rising past the Kadarin, not with Serrais on the east! And if the Hasturs came against them *now*, Asturias could not stand.

Dom Rafael clenched his fists with rage.

"What oath do you require of us?"

"I ask you to swear," Varzil said, "not to me, but to Geremy Hastur for his kinsman Carolin, an oath of kinsmen, not to be broken without warning of half a year on either side; which pledges you not to move against any land under Hastur protection; and in return you will be a part of this peace which reigns under the Alliance." He used the word *comyn* in a new way. "Will you swear?"

There was a long silence; but the di Asturiens were at the disadvantage and knew it. They had no choice but to swear. They were grateful when Alaric spoke, so that neither of them must lose face.

"Dom Varzil, I will swear the oath of kinsmen, although no oath to your Alliance. Will this suffice? I vow that I will not go to war against Carolin of Thendara unless half a year's warning is given. But," he added, and Bard saw the childish jaw clench, "this oath will endure only while my kinsman Carolin of Thendara leaves me in possession of the throne of Asturias; and on the day when he moves against the throne, on that same day I withdraw my oath and consider him my enemy!"

Geremy said, "I accept your oath, cousin. I swear to see it honored by Carolin. But how will you hold your father and your brother to this oath? For you are not yet of legal age, and they are the powers which hold your throne."

Alaric said, "By the gods and by the honor of my family; Bard, my brother, will you abide my oath?"

Bard said, "In the form the oath was given, my brother, I

will." He gripped his sword. "Zandru seize this sword and this heart if I prove false to your honor."

"And I," said Dom Rafael, tight-lipped, closing his fingers on his dagger, "by the honor of Asturien, which no man can gainsay."

No, Bard thought, as Geremy and Varzil, with endless formalities, took their leave, they had no choice, not with a crippled child on the throne, instead of the strong young warrior they had foreseen. They needed time, and this oath was only a way to give them time. His father maintained the façade of calm until the Hastur embassage had ridden away and Alaric, dreadfully pale from the strain of long ceremonial, was taken away to his rooms, then Dom Rafael broke down.

"My son! He is my son, I love him, I honor him, but in hell's name, Bard, is he fit to reign in times like these? Would to all the gods that *your* mother had been my lawful wife!"

"Father," Bard entreated, "it is only his legs that are crippled; his mind and wit are sound. I am a soldier, not a statesman; Alaric will make a better king than I!"

"But they look up to you, they call you Wolf and Commander, will they ever look up to my poor little lame lad that way?"

"If I stand behind his throne," Bard said, "they will."

"Alaric is blessed, then, in his brother! True is the old saying, *bare is back without brother.* . . . But you are only one man, and you are sworn to Hastur, which cripples you. If we had time, or if Alaric had been strong and fit——"

"If Queen Lorimel had worn trousers instead of skirts, she'd have been king and Thendara would never have fallen," said Bard, curtly. "There is no point in talking about *if,* and *would to all the gods,* and such rubbish. We must cut our coat as we find the cloth laid! The gods know I love my brother, and I could have bawled like Geremy's baby son to see him stand before us so bent and twisted, but what has come, has come; the world will go as it will. I am only one brother."

"It is the good fortune of the Hasturs that you were not born twins," said Dom Rafael with a despairing laugh, "for with two like you, dear son, I could conquer all the Hundred Kingdoms."

And then he stopped. His laugh broke off in mid-gasp, and he stared at Bard with such intensity that Bard wondered if the shock of Alaric's illness had turned the old man's brain.

"Two of you," he said, "with two such as you, Wolf, I

could conquer all this land from Dalereuth to the Hellers. Bard, suppose that there were two of you," he said in a whisper, "that I had another son, just like you, with your skill at warfare and your genius for strategy and your fierce loyalty—two of you! And I know how to find another. Not another *just like you*—another *you!*"

Chapter Five

Bard stared at his father in dismay. *The gods grant,* he thought, *that Alaric is mature enough to rule, for our father has suddenly lost his wits!*

But Dom Rafael did not look mad, and his voice and manner were so matter-of-fact that another, more rational explanation occurred to Bard.

"You had not confided in me, sir; but do you mean that you have another bastard son, enough like to impersonate me when it should be necessary?"

Dom Rafael shook his head. "No. And I am aware that what I have just said sounds like a madman's raving, dear son, so you need not bother to humor me; I shall not begin to rave like a breeding woman in the Ghost Wind, nor chase butterflies in the snow. But what I must now suggest to you is very strange, and—" he glanced around the empty throne room—"in any case we cannot talk here."

In his father's private apartments, Bard waited while his father sent the servants away, poured them both some wine.

"Not too much," he said dryly. "I do not want you to think me drunk, as you thought I was mad. I said, Bard, that with two like you, two generals with your sense of war and strategy—and this must have been born with you, since those who fostered you show no sign of it, and it is certainly not due to my teaching—with two of you, Bard, I could conquer all this realm. If the Hundred Kingdoms are to be united into a single realm—and I admit it is a sound idea, for why should all these lands be torn with war spring and fall—why should the Hasturs be overlords? There were men bearing the di Asturien name in these hills long before the Lord of Carthon gave his daughter to the Hastur kin. There is *laran* in our line, too, but it is the *laran* of humankind, of true men, not of the *chieri*-folk; the Hasturs are *chieri*, or of *chieri*-kind, as you may see if you care to count their fingers, and too many of them are still born *emmasca*, neither man nor woman; Felix of Thendara was born so, a few hundred years ago, and so *that* dynasty came to an end."

"There are no people in these hills who have not some *chieri* blood, father."

"But only the Hastur kin sought to preserve that blood in their line with their breeding program," Dom Rafael said, "and so many of the old families—Hastur, Aillard, Ardais, even the Aldarans and the Serrais, bear in their blood and heritage so many strange things that true men are wary of them! A child may be born who can kill with a thought, or see into the future as if time ran both ways, or cause fire to strike or the rivers to rise. . . . There are two kinds of *laran;* the kind which all men have and may use, aided with a starstone, and the evil kind borne by the Hastur kin. Our line is not altogether free of it, and when you got that redheaded son upon your mother's *leronis,* you brought the Hastur kin *laran* back into our folk. But what's done is done, and Erlend may be useful to us one day. Have you gotten the girl with child again yet? Why not?" But he did not wait for Bard's answer.

"Still, I am sure you can see why I have no will to be ruled by the Hasturs; they are riddled through and through with the *chieri* blood, and their Gifts are not diluted by the normal humankind, but fixed into their line by that breeding program. I feel that humankind should rule, not wizard-folk!"

"But," said Bard, "why tell me all this now? Or are you saying that when Erlend is grown he will be near enough to their kin that he can claim their line?" He spoke sarcastically, and his father did not bother to reply.

"What you do not know," he said, "is that I studied *laran* craft when I was a young boy. I was not, as you know, reared to king-craft, for Ardrin was the eldest, but I did not have the stronghold of di Asturien either, for there were three brothers between us, and I had leisure for study and learning. I was a *laranzu,* and dwelt for a time in Dalereuth Tower, and learned something of their craft."

Bard had known that his father bore a starstone, but that was in no way uncommon, and not everyone who bore a starstone knew *laran* lore. He had not known that he had dwelt within a Tower.

"Now there is a law in the use of the starstone," Dom Rafael said. "I do not know who formulated it, or why it should be so, but it is so; that everything which exists, except for a starstone, exists in one, and only one, *exact* duplicate. Nothing is unique, except for a starstone, which has no duplicate. However, everything else—*everything*, every rabbithorn in the woods, every tree and flower, every rock in the fields—has its precise duplicate, and also every human being has *one* exact double somewhere, more like him than his own twin. And that tells me that somewhere, Bard, you have an exact double. He may dwell in the Dry towns, or in the unknown lands beyond the Wall Around the World, he may be the son of a peasant, or live beyond the uncrossable gulf of the Sea of Dalereuth which leads into the Unknown Sea. And he would be more like you than your own twin, even though he dwelt far beyond the Hundred Kingdoms. I hope it is not so, I hope he dwells in the Kilghard Hills; otherwise it would be hard to teach him our language and the manners of our people. But whatever he may be, he will have *laran,* even if he has never been taught to use it; and he will have your military genius, once again, though he may not know yet how to use it; and he will look so much like you that your own mother, if she were still alive, would not be able to tell you apart by looks alone. Do you see now, dear son, why this would be good to have?"

Bard frowned. "I am beginning to see—"

"And another thing. Your double would *not* be sworn to Hastur, nor bound to him by any oath. Understand me?"

Bard saw. He saw indeed. "But where do we find this duplicate of myself?"

"I told you that I had studied *laran*-craft," Dom Rafael said, "and I know the whereabouts of a screen, a set of relay starstones constructed to bring these duplicates together. When I was a youth, we could, though it was difficult, bring men and women, other *leroni*, from one set of starstones to another. If we have one set of duplicates on the screen, we can bring your duplicate from wherever he may be living."

"But," Bard asked, "when we have him, how do we know he will be willing to help us?"

"He cannot help being what he is," said Dom Rafael. "If he were already a great general, we would know about him. He may indeed be one of my own bastard sons, or of Ardrin's, living in poverty without knowledge of war. But once we give him the chance of power and greatness—not to mention a chance to exercise the military genius which, if he is your duplicate, he will possess, if only as potential—then he will be grateful to us and willing to serve as our ally. Because, Bard, if he is your double—then he will be ambitious too!"

Three days later, Alaric-Rafael, heir to Asturias, was solemnly crowned in the regency of his father. Bard repeated in public the oath he had sworn to his brother, and Alaric presented him with a beautifully worked heirloom sword—Bard knew it was one his father had kept for many years, hoping that his one legitimate son would bear it into battle one day. But it was abundantly clear that King Alaric, whatever kind of ruler he might be, would not be a great warrior; so Bard accepted the sword from his brother's hands, and with it the command of all the armies of Asturias and all her subject kingdoms.

At the moment, I am general of Asturias and Marenji, and no more. But that is only a beginning.

A day will come when I will be general of all the Hundred Kingdoms, and they will all know and fear the Wolf of Asturias!

And as general of Marenji, he thought, he was legally entitled to go into that country and deal with those damned women on the Island of Silence!

I could declare them a treasonable assembly, and give them notice to quit the island! He was sure the people of Marenji would consider this a blasphemy, at present. But he asked Alaric to issue a proclamation that the people of Marenji were believed to be hiding the handfasted wife of Bard di Asturien; and that any person concealing the whereabouts of Carlina di Asturien would be considered a traitor and subjected to the extreme penalties of the law.

Alaric issued the proclamation, but in private he expressed dismay to Bard.

"Why do you want a woman who doesn't want you? I think you ought to marry Melisendra. She's very nice, and she's the mother of your son, and Erlend ought to be legitimate, he's a fine boy, and *laran*-gifted. Marry her, and I'll give you a fine wedding."

Bard said firmly that his brother and his lord ought not to talk about things he would not understand until he was older.

"Well, if I were ten years older, I'd marry Melisendra myself, so there," Alaric said. "I like her. She's good to me, she never makes me feel like a cripple."

"She had better not," Bard growled. "If she dared to be rude to you, I'd break her neck, and she knows it!"

"Well, I *am* a cripple, and I must learn to live with it," said Alaric, "and Lady Hastur, the *leronis* who cared for me at Neskaya, who helped me to talk again, taught me that it does not matter if my body is lamed. And Geremy—he is

193

crippled, and yet he is a fine man, strong and honorable—it will be very hard for me to learn to think of the Hasturs as enemies," he added with a sigh. "I find it hard to understand politics, Bard. I wish there could be peace among all people, and then we could be friends with the Lord Varzil, who has been like a foster father to me. But I am used to being treated like a cripple, because I *am,* and I must have help to dress myself, and walk—but someone like Melisendra, she helps me not to mind so much, because she helps me to feel, even when she is helping to tie me into my leg brace, that I am no worse off than anyone else."

"You are the king," Bard said, but Alaric sighed, a resigned sigh.

"You don't know what I mean *at all,* do you, Bard? You're so strong, and you've never been really sick, or frightened, so how could you know? Do you know what it's like to be really *scared,* Bard? When I first had the fever, and I couldn't even *breathe* . . . Geremy, and three of Ardrin's healer-women, sat up with me all night with their starstones, for seven nights, just helping me to breathe when I couldn't."

Bard thought against his will of the terror that had gripped him on the shores of the Lake of Silence when the eerie faces in the fog had drifted around him, turning his bowels to water . . . but even to his brother he would not confess that. "I was afraid when I rode first into battle," he said. That he did not mind saying.

Alaric sighed enviously.

"You were no older than I am now, and you were made King Ardrin's banner bearer! But it's different, Bard; you had a sword, you could *do* something against your fear, and I could—could only lie there and wonder if I was going to die, and know I had no way to help it, one way or the other, I was wholly helpless. And after that you—you always know that it can happen again, that you can die, or be destroyed. No matter how brave I am, I know, now, that there will always be something I can't fight," Alaric said. "And with some people, I feel like that all the time, that poor, sick, paralyzed coward. And some, like Varzil, and Melisendra, remind me that I don't have to be that way, that life is really not so terrible—do you know what I mean, Bard? Even a little?"

Bard looked at the boy and sighed, knowing that his brother was pleading for understanding, and not knowing how to give it to him. He had seen soldiers like this, wounded almost to death, and when they lived, after all, something had happened within them that he did not understand. That had

194

happened to Alaric, but it had happened to him before he was old enough to face it.

"I think you are alone too much," he said, "and it makes you fanciful. But I am glad Melisendra is kind to you."

Alaric sighed and held out his hand, small and white, to Bard, who engulfed it in his huge browned one. Bard, he thought, didn't understand him at all, but he loved him, and that was just as good.

"I hope you get your wife back, Bard. It's very wicked of people to keep her from you."

Bard said, "Alaric, Father and I must be away from court for a few days. Father and I and some of his *leroni*. Dom Jerral will be here to advise you, if you need him."

"Where are you going?"

"Father knows of someone who would be a great help in commanding the armies, and we are going to find him."

"Why not simply order him to come to court? The regent can command anyone to come."

"We do not know where he lives," Bard said. "We must find him by *laran*." That, he thought, was quite explanation enough.

"Well, if you must go, you must. But please, can Melisendra stay with me?" he asked, and Bard, though he knew Melisendra was one of the most skilled *leroni*, decided not to refuse his brother.

"If you want Melisendra," he said, "she shall certainly stay with you."

He had braced himself for an argument with his father, but to his surprise, Dom Rafael nodded.

"I had not intended to bring Melisendra in any case; she is the mother of your son."

Bard wondered what difference that made, but he did not bother to ask. It was enough for him that his brother wanted Melisendra's company.

They left the castle that night and rode toward Bard's old home. Three *leroni*, two woman and a man, had accompanied them, and Dom Rafael led them to a room Bard had never seen before, in an old tower room at the end of a broken staircase.

"I have not used any of these things in decades," he said, "but *laran*-craft, once learned, is not forgotten." He turned to the wizards and asked, "Do you know what this is?"

The man looked at the apparatus, and then at his two comrades, and Dom Rafael, in dismay. "I know, my lord. But I thought the use of such things was outlawed outside the safety of a Tower."

"In Asturias, there is no law but mine! Can you use it?"

The *laranzu* glanced again, uneasily, at the women. He said, "A duplicate under Cherillys' Law? I suppose so. But of what or whom?"

"Of my son here; the commander of King Alaric's armies."

One of the women looked at Bard and he caught the ironic flicker of her thought. *Another of the Kilghard Wolf? I should think one of him to be more than abundance!* He supposed she was a friend of Melisendra's. But they shrugged, quickly shielded again, and said, "Yes, my lord, if that is your wish."

He could sense their surprise, distaste, wonder; but they made no audible protest, making their preparations, setting seals on the room so that no alien presences could enter and no other *leroni* spy on them from elsewhere.

When all was prepared, Dom Rafael signaled to Bard to take his place before the screen, to remain silent and motionless. He obeyed, kneeling silently. He was so placed that he could not see his father, nor any of the three telepaths, but he sensed them near him. Bard did not think he had much *laran*, and what he did have had never been properly trained. He had always rather despised the art of sorcery, thinking it a skill or craft for women; he felt a little frightened as the almost tangible web of their thoughts tightened around him. He sensed that they were extending their thoughts *into* him, deep into brain and body, seeking out the very pattern of his being; he thought, fancifully, that they were seeking out his very soul, tying it up tight and imprisoning it in that glassy screen there.

He could not move a finger or a foot. He felt a moment of paralyzed panic . . . no. This was a perfectly ordinary piece of *laran* sorcery, with nothing to fear; his father would not let anything harm him.

He remained motionless, looking at his reflection in the glassy surface. Somehow he knew it was not only the reflected shadow on glass but *himself* there in that multilayered screen, reinforced at all levels with starstone crystals which resonated to the starstones of the *leroni* around him. He felt the combined web of their layered thoughts swing out over vast gulfs of empty space, extending, searching, searching to find something to fit that pattern, fit it *exactly* . . . something came near, close to touching . . . near to captive . . . no. I was not a duplicate, a resemblance, touching perhaps a

196

ninety out of a hundred, but not the exact duplicate which alone could be captured within the screen. He felt the *other* slide away, vanish, as the search swung out again.

(Far away in the Kilghard hills, a man named Gwynn, an outlaw and fatherless—although his mother had told him he had been fathered in the sack of Scathfell by Ansel, son of Ardrin the first of Asturias, thirty years ago—woke from an evil dream in which faces had swung around him, circling, swooping like hawks on their prey, and one of the faces was like his own as twin to twin. . . .)

Again the web swung out, this time over greater gulfs, starless night, a tremendous void beyond space and time, with swirling, nightmarish vortexes of terrible nothingness. Again a shadow formed behind Bard on the screen, shimmered, wavered, twitched, struggled as a sleeper struggles to wake from nightmare; somewhere a spark flared in Bard's brain; myself, or the *other?* He did not know, could not guess. It struggled for freedom but they held it, imprisoned in their web, moving from point to point of the pattern encased in the screen . . . searching to see that every atom, every trifle was congruent, identical. . . .

Now!

Bard saw in his mind before his eyes saw the flare of lightnings in the room, a searing shock as the *other* was torn loose from the shadow in his mind, the pattern doubled and breaking, splitting apart . . . terror flamed in him; was it his own fear, or the terror of the *other*, unimaginably hurled across that great gulf of space. . . . He caught a glimpse of a great yellow sun, hurling worlds, stars flaming across the dark void, galaxies spinning and drifting in shock. . . . Lightning crashed through his brain and he lost consciousness.

He stirred, conscious now of savage headaches, pain, confusion. Dom Rafael was lifting him, feeling his pulse. Then he let him go and went past, and Bard, sick and stunned with the lightning, followed with his eyes; and the *leroni,* behind him, watching, looked dazed too. He caught a wisp of thought from one of them, *I don't believe it. I did it, I was part of it but still I don't believe it. . . .*

Lying on the floor at the opposite pole of the great screen lay the naked body of a man. And Bard, though he had been prepared intellectually for this, felt a surge of gut-wrenching terror.

For the man lying on the floor was himself.

Not someone very much like him. Not an accidental or close family resemblance. *Himself.*

197

Broad-shouldered, and halfway between them, the blackish blotch of a birthmark which he had seen only in a mirror. The muscles bunching in his sword arm, the same dark-reddish patch of hair at the loins, the same crooked toe on the left foot.

Then he began to see differences. The hair was cut a little shorter, though at the crown of his head there was the same unruly whorl. There was no scar across the knee; the double had not been at the battle of Raven's Glen and did not have the sword-slash he had taken there. The other did not have the thick callous at the inside of the elbow where the shield strap rested. And these little differences somehow made it worse. The man was not simply a magical duplicate created somehow by the *laran* of the screen; he was a real human being, from *somewhere else,* who was, none the less, precisely and exactly Bard di Asturien.

He didn't like it. Still less did he like the confusion and fear which the *other* was feeling. Bard, without much *laran,* could still somehow *feel* all that emotion.

He couldn't stop himself. He got up and went across the room to the naked man lying there. He knelt beside him and put an arm under his head.

"How are you feeling?"

Only after he had spoken did he stop to wonder if the alien *other* could understand his language. That would be luck entirely too good, though he supposed that perhaps his kin somewhere in the Kilghard Hills had probably fathered this duplicate. Could any man be so like without being kin somehow? The strange man's skin looked darker, as if it had been burned brown by a fiercer sun. . . . No, that was folly, the sun was the sun . . . but still, the picture was in his mind of spinning galaxies, a world with a single cold white moon, and the frightening thing was that somehow all those images seemed to *belong* in Bard's mind!

The strange man spoke. He was not speaking Bard's language; somehow Bard knew that no one else in the room could understand him. But Bard knew what he had said, as if they were linked in the strongest *laran* bond.

"I feel like hell. How do you expect me to feel? What happened, a tornado? Hell—you're *me*! And that's not possible! You're not the devil by any chance?"

Bard shook his head. "I'm not any of the devils, not even nearly," he said.

"Who are you? What is this? What happened?"

"You'll find out later," Bard said, then, feeling him stir urgently, held him unmoving. "No, don't try to move yet. What's your name?"

"Paul," the man said weakly, "Paul Harrell." And then he fell back, unconscious. Bard moved, spontaneously, to raise him, support him. He shouted for help. The *laranzu* came and examined the unconscious man.

"He's all right, but the energy expended in that journey was frightful," he said.

Dom Rafael said, "Get old Gwynn to help you carry him; I'd trust him with my life, and more." Bard helped the old *coridom* carry the stranger to his own old rooms, laid him in his bed, locked the door of the suite—not that it was necessary; the *laranzu* assured them that he would not wake for a day and a night, or perhaps more.

He returned, to find that Dom Rafael had ushered the *leroni* into an adjacent chamber, where the old *coridom* had laid ready a hot supper, with plenty of wine. Bard, desperately curious about the stranger, reached for contact with his father, but for some strange reason his father was wholly shielded against him.

Why should his father barricade his mind so strongly?

"Food and drink is prepared for you, my friends. I have been a *laranzu*, I know the terrible hunger and thirst of such work. Come, eat and drink and refresh yourselves. Then I have had rooms made ready for you to sleep, and rest as long as you will."

The three *leroni* went quickly to the table and began to raise the wine glasses. Bard was thirsty too; he began to pick up a glass, but his father seized his arm in an iron grip, preventing him. At that moment one of the women screamed, a dreadful raw-throated scream, and slithered down lifeless to the floor. The *laranzu* gulped, spluttered in shock, but it was already too late.

Poisoned, Bard thought with a thrill of fear, thinking how close he had come to drinking of that same wine. The other *leronis* raised her face in blind appeal, and Bard felt her terror, the dread of certain death; she had swallowed almost none of the wine, and he saw her look around, hunting against hope for a way of escape.

Bard hesitated, for the woman was young, and not without attractiveness. Sensing her confusion, she came and flung herself at his feet. "Oh no! Oh, my lord, don't kill me, I swear I'll never say a word—"

"Drink," said Dom Rafael, and his face was like stone. "Bard. Make her drink."

Bard's confusion was gone. His father was right; none of them could let the *leronis* live to tell of this night's work. Old Gwynn could be trusted with their lives; but a *leronis* whose mind could be read with another's starstone—no, not possible. Essential to their plan was the knowledge that he should not be known to have a double. The woman was still clutching his knees, babbling in terror. Reluctantly, he bent to his work, but before he could touch her the woman dodged away, springing to her feet, and ran. He sighed, foreseeing a really nasty chase and the need for cutting her down at the end of it; but she ran around the table, caught up the goblet and drank deeply. Even before the third swallow she gave a small strange cough and fell lifeless across the table, upsetting a tray of bread, which fell with a *clunk* to the floor.

So this was why his father had not brought Melisendra!

Dom Rafael poured out the rest of the poisoned wine on the stone floor.

"There is a wholesome bottle here," he said. "I knew we would need it. Eat, Bard, the food is untouched, and we have work to do. Even with Gwynn's help, it will be a night's work to bury them all three."

BOOK THREE

The Dark Twin

Chapter One

If he is me, then who in hell am I?

Paul Harrell was not sure whether the thought so strong in the forefront of his mind was his own thought, or that of the man who stood before him. It was immensely confusing. At the same time, two emotions warred in him: *this man would understand me,* and *I hate him; how dare he be so much what I am?* It was not his first experience with ambivalence, but it was his most disturbing awareness of it.

The man who had introduced himself as Wolf said his name again. "Paul Harrell. No, that is not one of our names, although the Harryls are among my father's most loyal men. It would have been too much to ask that you should have been one of them."

Paul felt his head again, finding, rather to his surprise, that it was all in one piece. Then he thought of the perfect way to test whether this was, after all, a bizarre nightmare of the stasis box.

"Where's the head?"

He knew that the other man had understood even the slang phrase—how the *hell* did he do that thought-reading trick?—when he pointed. "Across the corridor."

Paul got up, naked, and went through the indicated door. No locks. He wasn't a prisoner, whatever they wanted with him, so it had to be an improvement. The corridor was stone, filled with an icy draft, and his feet felt freezing. The room was a reasonably well-appointed bathroom. The fixtures were somewhat strange in appearance, and he couldn't even imagine what they were made of, though it certainly wasn't porcelain, but it was easy enough to figure out the plumbing; he supposed there were only a few designs among humans. There was hot water—in fact, there was a large sunken tub filled with steaming hot water that looked somewhat like a Japanese bath-house fixture, and from the faint medicinal smell he supposed it came right up from a volcanic spring somewhere. Relieving himself, Paul supposed this was the ultimate reality testing. He caught up a fur-lined rug or blanket from a bench and wrapped it around himself.

Returning to the room, the other looked at Paul in his improvised blanket, and said, "I ought to have thought of that. There's a bedgown on the chair."

It looked like an old-fashioned bathrobe, but bulkier, lined with some silky fabric that felt like fur, and fastened tightly up at the neck to keep out draughts. It was very warm; in his own world it would have been good for a topcoat intended for traveling in Siberia. He sat down on the bed, drawing up his bare feet under the warm robe.

"That'll do for a start. Now, where am I, and what is this place, and what am I doing here? And, incidentally, who are you?"

Bard repeated his name and Paul tried it over on his tongue. "Bard di Asturien." It was not so outlandish, after all. He was trying to assimilate what Bard had told him about the Hundred Kingdoms. He wondered what the name of the sun was—if they were a pre-space culture, they probably called it The Sun—and he didn't know of any world within the Confederacy which had a sun as large as this, or as red. The really big red suns usually didn't have habitable planets. "Are there really a Hundred Kingdoms?"

He was thinking of a kind of United Confederacy where the kings all met together, as in the four-yearly Congress of the Confederacy of Worlds. Only there weren't a hundred inhabited planets. A hundred kings together would be quite an assembly, especially if they got along no better than the embassies of the Confederacy usually did! And there were only forty-two of them!

Bard took his question quite seriously.

"I am better at strategy than at geography," he said, "and I have not consulted a map maker recently; there may have been some new alliances, and the Hasturs have recently taken over a vacant throne or two. I think perhaps there are seventy-five or eighty, no more. But the Hundred Kingdoms is a good round number and sounds well beyond their borders."

"And how did you manage to bring me here?" Paul asked. "The last I heard, even with hyper-drive, to go much farther than the Alpha colony took an enormous amount of time, and I notice that my hair and nails haven't grown all that much."

Bard scowled and said, "I haven't the least idea what you

are talking about." *Does he have sorcery stronger than ours?* Paul heard the unspoken thought perfectly well.

"I take it, then, we're right outside the Confederacy of Worlds."

"Whatever they may be, we are," Bard said.

"And the Terran police have no jurisdiction here?"

"It, or they, certainly do not. The only law within this kingdom is that of my father, as regent for my brother Alaric. Why do you ask? Are you a fugitive from justice, or a criminal under sentence of death?"

"I spent enough time as a fugitive," Paul said. "I was remanded for rehabilitation twice before I was eighteen. At this time I am supposed to be in custody, and under sentence. . . ." It made no sense to speak of the stasis box. They evidently didn't have it here and there was no sense in giving them ideas.

"Your country imprisons, then, rather than giving death or exile?"

Paul nodded.

"And you were—imprisoned? Then, since I delivered you out of prison, you owe me service."

"That's a moot point," said Paul, "and we'll moot it later. How did you bring me here?"

But the explanation—*starstones, a circle of wizards*—made no more sense to him than, he suspected, the stasis box would have made to the Wolf. Come to think of it, it was as likely as anything else that could get him out of a stasis box. It had been tried, of course, but had never been managed before; or if it was, the government wasn't telling anybody.

"What about the people who brought me here?"

Bard's face was grim. "They're in no condition to go blabbing about it." Paul knew perfectly well what he meant. "In your own idiom, they are in earth, except for my father. He will meet you later; he is still sleeping. His night's work was—strenuous, for so old a man." Paul had a fragmentary picture: three graves, hastily dug by moonlight, and suddenly he turned cold. This was no place for frightened conformists. Well, that was the kind of place he had wanted all his life. The people in this place played by rules he could understand. He knew Bard was quite willing to frighten him, and he decided it was time to let this self-styled Wolf know that he didn't scare easy. *Who's afraid of the big bad wolf? Not me.*

Bringing him here this way must have been illegal; or else they wouldn't have killed off all the witnesses; so he had something already on Bard, and on his father.

"I don't suppose you brought me here out of pure-hearted love of knowledge," he said, "or you'd be shouting it from the housetops, instead of hiding me here and murdering anyone who knows about it."

Bard looked disconcerted. "Can you read my mind?"

"Some, yes." Not nearly as much as he wanted Bard to think he could. But he wanted to keep the Wolf a little off balance. He knew this was a man who played rough, played for keeps, and he needed every advantage he could get!

But Bard wouldn't have gone to all this trouble for nothing. He was probably safe until he knew what Bard wanted him for, and unless it was to impersonate the guest of honor at a public execution, it couldn't be worse than the stasis box.

"What do you want with me? I didn't get any good-conduct medals—any more than you did," he said, making a shrewd guess.

Bard grinned. "Right. I was outlawed at seventeen, and I've been a mercenary soldier ever since. This year I came back and helped my father claim the throne of Asturias for my brother."

"Not for yourself?"

"Hell, no. I've got better things to do with myself than sit in council with all the graybeards in the kingdom, making laws about keeping cattle in their pastures and mending roads and stocking travel shelters and whether the Sisterhoods of the Sword should share fire-watch with men!"

Put like that, Paul decided that the business of kingship sounded a bit dull after all. "You're a younger brother and your elder brother is the king?"

"No, the other way around. My younger brother is the legitimate son. I am *nedestro* . . . more than a bastard but not in line of succession."

"Born the wrong side of the blanket, huh?"

Bard looked briefly puzzled, then chuckled as he caught the image. "You could put it that way. I've no complaint about the old man; he reared me in his own house and supported me in my quarrel with the old king. And now my brother's put me in charge of his armies."

"So what do you want me for?" Paul demanded, "and what's in it for me?"

"At the very least," Bard said, "freedom. If you're as much like me on the inside as you are on the outside, that means a lot to you. Beyond that? I don't know. Women, if you want them, and again, if you're anything like me, you want them and you'll get them, too. Riches, if you're not too greedy. Adventure. Maybe a chance at the regency of a kingdom. Anyway, a better life than you led in your prison. Isn't that a good start?"

It sounded like one. He'd have to keep an eye on Bard, but at least he hadn't been brought here for any prisoner-of-Zenda complications where he sat and rotted in prison so his double could get out and do things.

He caught pictures in Bard's mind that already excited him. This, damn it, might be a world worth living in, not a tame one that relied on keeping everybody mushed down to a level of bland conformity, and lopping off the head of everyone who stood up above the pack!

Plenty of important personages, generals, rulers, had doubles; but somehow he thought it was going to be more than that. They could probably have found someone who resembled Bard pretty well, a relative or kinsman, without going nearly so far, and minor differences would have been covered by the convenience of having someone who knew their language and customs. Somebody like Paul, who couldn't even dress himself in this society without being shown how, and who had to communicate by thought-reading so far—and only with one person, at that—that would be a grave inconvenience, so that there simply had to be a good reason, an *overpowering* reason to put up with him. They needed someone who was like Bard, but not just on the outside. They needed someone who was like him on the inside as well.

This might be a real world, then. Not just an existence within circumscribed limits, a real world where he could be a real man, among real men, not bloodless androids and clerics!

Bard stood up.

"Hungry? I'll have them bring you something to eat. From what my father says, if it suits me, it ought to suit you. And I'll send you some clothes. You're about my size—" he remembered and broke into a mirthless laugh. "No, damn it, you *are* my size. We can't do anything until your hair grows out—I can't be seen without the warrior's braid. Which gives us some time to teach you the rudiments of civilized life here, I suppose you do know the rudiments of swordplay—no? Your world must be a stranger place than I can imagine! I'm no duelist, so you won't need to know the fancy stuff, but you have to know something of self-defense. And you have to learn the language. I won't always be around, and it's a nuisance to have to read each other's minds all the time. I'll see you later." He stood up unceremoniously and went out, leaving Paul to shake his hand and wonder, again, if this were only some bizarre dream inside the stasis box.

Well, if it was, he might as well enjoy it.

Chapter Two

But it was only ten days later that they set out for Castle Asturias. Dom Rafael had been unwilling to leave the government longer in the inexperienced hands of Alaric. And so the plan to wait until Paul could completely impersonate Bard had had to be abandoned too. On the contrary, they decided, it would be well to have them seen together, and a *slight* resemblance between them noted; thus, later, when Paul was *actually* impersonating him, no one would believe that the kinsman who resembled him somewhat, but not much, could be enough like him to do it. He didn't want the idea to get around that there was actually someone carefully hidden away who was enough like him to impersonate him. People, Bard reminded his father, usually saw what they expected to see, and if he was seen often with a (supposed) kinsman who resembled him somewhat, but not too much, people who liked to gossip about things which were none of their business would be quick to point out that the resemblance was really not so great after all.

So, for the time being, Paul's short hair, sun-bleached from a brighter sun than Bard's, was darkened with streaks of a dye that made it gingery red, and he cultivated a small ragged moustache. Differences in manner and carriage, they felt, would do the rest. For the time being, it was to be given out that he was a *nedestro* grandson of one of the brothers of Ardrin and Dom Rafael who had died before Ardrin came to the throne, and therefore Bard's cousin, discovered by him during his years of exile.

It would be given out that he had been living far north of the Kadarin, near to trailman country. This region was so remote that there was not the slightest chance of anyone who spoke that language, or observed those alien customs, coming to court; so that any mistakes Paul made would be put down to his rustic and uncouth fostering.

And it was good that Paul could be at court openly for a

little while and learn for himself the manners and the political situation. Bard was relieved to see that Paul rode well, though not quite as well as he did himself. The thought-reading had helped. Paul already spoke *casta* somewhat, and his odd accent could be explained by his supposed rural upbringing in the Hellers. Their first task, Bard thought, must be to get rid of the last traces of that accent.

For the audacious plan was no less than this: to divide the armies they could raise, and send them on two separate campaigns, one against the Serrais to the west, the other to confront Carolin's armies in the east; with each army believing that Bard himself was leading them; and at last to unify all the realm, and in the end, all the Hundred Kingdoms, under the overlordship of Alaric of Asturias. Then, with the Hasturs subjugated, the domains could be united, and there would be peace, without the tyrannical rule of Varzil's infamous Compact! Peace, without the pressure of small fratricidal wars coming to the boil at every season from spring thaw to harvest, or a new kingdom springing up every time some little group of men didn't like their lord and resolved to set up a new kingdom without him!

And then, Bard thought, such a Golden Age might return as had not been known since the Lord of Carthon made compact with the forest folk!

Central to this plan, though, was the military genius of Bard di Asturien and the particular charisma of the Kilghard Wolf. Paul, riding slowly behind Bard and Dom Rafael—as his assumed character of a poor relation demanded—could pick up a little of his thought, even now. *So I am to be Dog to his Wolf? We'll see about that!*

Paul thought about the theory that had brought him here; that he and Bard were, in essence, the same man. He was inclined to believe it. He had always known himself to be larger than his fellows, not in body alone—though that helped—but cut out, in mind, for a bigger and more heroic age than the one into which he'd been born.

The way he put it to himself was that most men had brains but no guts, or maybe vice versa; and of the rare men who had brains *and* guts, most had no imagination whatever. Paul knew himself to have all three; but they were wasted in the world he lived in. One of his early psychiatrists, back when they were still trying to reclaim him for the establishment, had told him frankly that he belonged on a frontier, that in a primitive society he would have been outstanding. Which hadn't helped at all. The psychiatrist had owned up, just as frankly, that in Paul's own society, unless he could resign himself to conform, his assets would all be liabilities.

Now he was putting both brains and imagination to work on Bard's world. The four colored moons had already told him that this was none of the known colonies of the Confederated Worlds. Yet the inhabitants were perfectly human, so far, which would have strained credibility beyond endurance if they were not of Terran stock; and although he was no linguist, he knew that the *casta*, with its admixture of Spanish words, could not possibly have descended from anything but a Terran culture. He could only hypothesize, tentatively, that they had been descended from one of the Lost Ships—sent out, in the old days before hyper-drive, for colonization in a universe they had already found to be all but unpopulated. One of these ships had formed the Alpha colony, others the early ones, but most of them had vanished without trace and been assumed lost, with all aboard. Paul knew that the Confederated Worlds were prepared to find one or two survivor colonies, isolated, some day. He hoped they wouldn't find this one in his lifetime. It would be a tragedy to see it beaten down to the same mediocrity as Terra, or Alpha, or any other known world!

Riding down toward Castle Asturias, a little before midday, Paul realized that it was a form of fortified building which had not been built on Earth for a few thousand years. It did not look much like the pictures of historic castles he had seen. The building materials were different, the life-style which dictated the architecture was different. But in the past few days he had been introduced to the theory of fortifications and strategies, and he set his mind to the problem of wondering how he would take this castle. It wouldn't be easy, he thought. But it could be done, and he was fairly sure that if it came to that, he could do it.

However, he reflected, it would be easiest with an accomplice inside. . . .

Dom Rafael went ceremoniously with his retainers to make his return known to Alaric and the councillors. Bard assigned Paul a couple of servants, a room or two in his own suite, and took himself off about unexplained business. Paul, left alone, went to explore the rooms he had been given.

He found a little stair which led down into a small enclosed courtyard, filled with late-summer flowers—though to Paul the climate still seemed cold for any kind of flowers. There were flagged walks everywhere, and the fragrance of herbs, and an old well. He sat down to enjoy the rare late-day sun, and think over the curious situation in which he found himself.

He heard a noise behind him and whirled—he had been a fugitive too long to ignore anyone or anything behind him—then relaxed, with a sense of foolish relief, to see that it was only a very small boy, bouncing a ball along the walks.

"Father!" the child cried. "They didn't tell me you were back—" Then he stopped his headlong rush toward Paul, blinked and said with a charming little dignity, "My apologies, sir. Now I see that you are not my father, though you are very like him. I ask pardon for disturbing you, sir—I suppose, I should say *kinsman*."

"That's all right," he said, deciding—it didn't take much thought to figure it out—that this must be Bard's son. Funny—he hadn't thought Bard would be the kind to have a wife and kids, to tie himself down that way, any more than he was himself. Come to think of it, Bard had said something about arranged marriages, they'd probably married him off to somebody without asking, though he couldn't imagine Bard tamely going along with that, either. Well, he supposed he'd learn.

"I've been told that there *is* a resemblance, after all, to your father."

The child reproved solemnly, "You should say 'the Lord General' when you speak of my father, sir, even if he is a kinsman. Even I am supposed to say 'the Lord General' except among the family, for Nurse says I will be sent to be fostered soon, and I must learn to speak of him with the proper courtesy. So, she says, I should always call him so except when we are alone. But King Alaric says 'my father' when he speaks of my grandsire, Dom Rafael, and *he* does not call my father 'Lord General' even when they are in the throne room. I don't think that's fair, do you, sir?"

Paul, hiding a smile, said that royalty had privileges. Well, he had wanted a society where people were not worn down to a tiresome egalitarianism, and now he had it. At that, he had probably gotten a higher place in it than he deserved at the start!

"I suppose, kinsman, that you are from beyond the Hellers. I can tell by the way you speak," said the child. "What is your name?"

"Paolo," Paul said.

"Why, that is not so strange a name after all! Do you have names like ours in the far lands beyond the Hellers?"

"That is the *casta* for my name, or so your father tells me. My own name would sound strange enough to you, probably."

"Nurse says it is rude to ask a stranger's name without giving one's own. My name is Erlend Bardson, kinsman."

Well, Paul had guessed that already. "How old are you, Erlend?"

"I shall be seven at midwinter."

Paul raised his eyebrows. He would have thought the boy was nine or ten, at least. Well, perhaps their year was a different length.

"Erlend," called a woman's voice. "You must not bother your father's guests or his sworn men!"

"Am I bothering you, sir?" Erlend asked.

Paul, amused by the child's dignified manner, said, "No, indeed."

"It's all right, my lady," said Erlend, as a woman came along the curving path. "He *says* I am not bothering him."

The woman laughed. She had a sweet laugh, very low and mirthful. She was young, her face round and freckled, and she had two long braids that hung almost to her waist, as red as the boy's. She was not shabby, but she was dressed plainly, without richness or any jewelry except a small and shabby locket with a blue stone around her neck. She was probably the boy's nurse, he thought; some poor relation or hanger-on. From what he knew of Bard, the Wolf would have dressed his mistress or fancy-woman in something more elaborate, and his wife would have been dressed according to her rank.

But how had Bard managed to overlook her? For to Paul it seemed that the rounded, womanly body, the low laugh and graceful hands and quick, mirthful smile, were the very embodiment of woman—yes, and of sex. He wanted her, suddenly, with such violence that it was all he could do to keep his hands off her! If the child had not been there. . . .

But no. He wasn't going to risk his position here, not right away, anyhow, by woman trouble. That, he knew grimly, was what had wrecked the plot and the reason he'd wound up in the stasis box. He hadn't had the brains and judgment to keep his hands off the wrong woman. He had guessed, from random conversation among the bodyguards and paxmen, that the Kilghard Wolf was quite a man for the women—he'd have expected that, if Bard was his own duplicate—and he wasn't going to quarrel with him on trivial grounds like that. There were plenty of women.

But this one. . . . He watched her with fascination, her

213

delicate hands, the movement of the ripe, womanly body in her plain, simple dress. Her cheek was dimpled, curving into a light laugh as she admonished the boy.

"But I have to know all their names, *domna*," said Erlend. "When I am old enough to be my father's paxman I will have to know all his men by name!"

She was wearing a rust-colored dress. Strange that he had never realized how that color set off red hair. The dress was the exact color of her freckles.

"But Erlend, you are not to be a soldier or paxman, but a *laranzu*," she said, "and in any case this is disobedience, for you were told to play quietly in the other court. I shall have to ask Nurse to watch you more carefully."

"I'm too big for a nurse," the boy grumbled, but went along obediently at the woman's side. Paul watched till she was out of sight. God, how he wanted that woman! It was all he could do to keep his hands off her. . . . He wondered if she were someone accessible to him. Well, a child's governess couldn't be very exalted in station, even if she was a relation—as he suspected from her faint resemblance to the boy. He wondered where Bard's wife was. Dead, perhaps. On primitive worlds, childbearing was a risky business and, he knew, the mortality rates were fairly high.

He thought, with a cynical grin, that he was reacting normally. Reprieved from death, recalled out of the stasis box, what better way to spend a few odd hours than with women? But just in case this was real, he wasn't going to make the same mistake that had got him into the box in the first place. If by some strange chance this was one of Bard's women, he'd adopt a strict hands-off policy! There were plenty of other women. . . .

But damn it, that was the one he wanted! Too bad the child had been there; he wasn't *quite* enough of a bastard to grab a woman with a youngster looking on. He had a feeling she wouldn't be coy. The ripeness of that bosom, the red mouth which looked well kissed, told him she was no innocent virgin! To do her justice, he couldn't say she'd given him any clear signals; she'd been modest enough, but he bet his life she wouldn't make any fuss once he got his hands on her!

Bard sent for him late that evening, and they sat before the fire over a stack of campaign maps which Bard had insisted Paul should understand thoroughly. It was not too early to start. They talked for a long time about tactics and campaigns, and although it was professional, strictly business, Paul had the sense that Bard welcomed this companionship

214

enjoyed teaching him this; that he seldom had anyone to share his interests.

He's like me, a man who doesn't often find anyone he can talk to as an equal. They call him Wolf, but I have a feeling that "Lone Wolf" would be more like it. He's been a loner all his life, I bet. Like me.

There just weren't that many people who could follow his mental processes. It wasn't at all an unmixed blessing—to be brighter than ninety per cent of the people you met. It made men seem like fools, and women like worse fools, and most people never had the slightest idea what he was talking about or thinking about.

Even when Paul led the rebellion that had brought him to disaster, he had already known that it was hopeless. Not because the rebellion was impossible—it could have been successful, if he'd had a couple of intelligent allies who knew what the hell he was really trying to do—but because, basically, the men he led weren't half so committed as he was himself. He'd been the only one who really *cared*, deep down, what they were fighting about. The other men didn't have that rage at the center of themselves; he had suspected, sooner or later, that most of them would climb down—as, in fact, they had done—and crawl to the powers that be for another chance; even if that chance meant having their whole selves carved up until there was nothing left of them. Well, there'd been nothing much to them in the first place, small loss! But it meant he had always been alone.

I can make myself necessary to the Wolf.

Because I'm his equal, his duplicate, the nearest to an equal he'll ever have. He looked at Bard for a minute with something very akin to love, thinking, *He'd understand. If I'd had just one follower like him, we could have put some steel into the spines of the men who followed me. We could have done it, together. Two like us could have changed the world!*

Rebellions, Paul knew, usually failed, because the brains and guts and imagination to lead them came along only once in a century or so. But this time there were two of them.

I couldn't change my world alone. But the two of us can change his, together!

Bard looked up sharply, and Paul felt sudden disquiet. Was he doing that thought-reading trick again? But the Wolf only stretched and yawned and said it was late.

"I'm for my bed. By the way, I forgot to ask, shall I have the steward send you a woman? There are enough useless females, heaven knows, and most of them just as eager for a

215

man in their bed as the men are for them. Have you, perhaps, seen one that's to your liking?"

"Only one," said Paul. "Your son's governess, I suppose;
long braids, bright red, freckled—curvy, not very tall. *That*
one—unless she's married, or something. I don't want
trouble."

Bard flung his head back and laughed.

"Melisendra! I wouldn't advise—she has a tongue like a
whip!"

"It was all I could do to keep my hands off her."

"I should have expected that," Bard said, still laughing. "If
we're the same man! That was how I reacted when I was seventeen, and she wasn't, I suppose, fourteen yet! She made a
great fuss, and my foster mother has never forgiven me for
it, but damn it, it was worth it! Erlend's her son. And mine."

"Oh, well, if she's yours——"

Bard laughed again. "Hell, no! I'm sick to death of her,
but my foster mother's shoved her off on me, and she's getting above herself! I'd enjoy teaching her a lesson, prove to
her she's no better than any of the other women around here
and that it's only by my good nature, not as a right, that she's
allowed to be my woman and stay here to raise my son! Let
me think—if I told her to go to you, she'd run whining to
Lady Jerana, and I haven't the heart for a quarrel with my
father's wife. But just the same——" He grinned with mischief.
"Well, you are supposed to be my duplicate! I wonder if she
would ever know the difference? Her room is there, and she'll
think it's me, and know better than to make a fuss!"

Something in Bard's tone bothered him, as Bard added
with a sarcastic grin, "After all, you *are* me; she can't complain that I've given her to someone else!"

Who the hell did Bard think he was, to fling him at Melisendra this way? But the thought of the red-haired woman's
lovely ripe body stopped any thought of resistance. No
woman had ever aroused him so, like that, at first glance!

His heart was pounding, as, later, he went toward the darkened room Bard had pointed out to him. And behind the excitement, the thought of the woman, was a note of cynical
caution.

Bard would find it hilarious, he sensed, to guide him, not
into Melisendra's room, but into the room of some withered
old hag, some ancient virgin who would rouse the house
screaming.

But even if Bard tried that, he'd find her; somehow he'd
hold Bard to his promise.

He's my size and he's been fighting all his life. And right now, after God knows how long in the stasis box, he's probably more fit than I am; but he's not any stronger. I bet I could take him. I doubt, for instance, if he knows much karate.

But he dropped the thought of their inevitable confrontation from his mind as he came into the room. Moonlight from an open window lay across the bed, and he could see the loosened waves of the copper hair, rich and thick, the freckled face he had seen before. Her eyes were closed and she slept. She was wearing a long nightgown, embroidered at neck and sleeves, but it could not conceal the round ripeness of her body. Carefully, he shut the door. In the darkness, how would she know he was not Bard? He wanted her, somehow, to *know*, to want him too! And yet, if this was the only way he could have her . . . what the hell was he delaying for? If she was the kind of woman who could be handed from man to man, would it matter? But she obviously was *not* that kind of woman, or Bard would simply have handed her over, without this ruse. . . .

Or perhaps not. He found that thinking of Bard's body, his own body, entangled with this woman, was curiously arousing. Somehow it gave him a charge to think of it. Did Bard have the same kink, that it would give him some kind of kick to think of *his* duplicate, making love to *his* woman?

He sat on the edge of the bed to take off his clothes. It was pitch dark, but he would not risk a light. She could have told the difference, perhaps, by the fact that he did not have the warrior's braid of hair. . . . He discovered, with an amused grimace, that he was actually shaking with anticipation, like a boy about to take his first woman.

What the hell?

And Bard had given Melisendra to him, not to please Paul but, he sensed, to humiliate Melisendra. Suddenly he was not sure he wanted to collaborate with Bard on humiliating this woman.

But she would probably never know the difference anyway; and if this was the only way he could have her, he wasn't going to give up that chance! He got into bed beside her, and lay a hand on her under the blankets.

She turned toward him with a little sigh, not of acceptance or welcome, but of resignation. Was Bard so inept a lover as all that, or did she simply dislike him? Surely there was no love lost between them now! Well, perhaps he could change

217

her tune; no woman who gave him half a chance had ever failed to welcome him as a lover.

She lay passive under his caresses, not refusing his touch, not accepting, simply acting as if he were not there at all. Damn the woman, he didn't want her that way, he would rather she'd scream and fight him than accept him as a loathsome duty! But even as he formulated the thought, she sighed again, and put up her arms around his neck, and he pulled her to him. He could feel her growing excitement, and felt her trembling against him as his own arousal grew greater and greater.

He let himself fall, spent and gasping, across her. He lay there, his hands still caressing her, covering her with kisses, unwilling to let her go even for a moment. She said quietly into the darkness, "Who are you?"

He drew breath in astonishment. And then he realized he should have known. He and Bard were physically doubles, yes, doubles even in personality perhaps. But sex was, of all activities, the most subject to total cultural conditioning. He could not possibly expect to make love in the way a Darkovan would do. The mechanics of the act were the same, but the whole psychological milieu was entirely different; he might have deceived her with a familiar face and body while he kept still, but every caress, every movement, betrayed a whole world of conditioning too deep to be altered. He could no more have made love to her in Bard's way—even if his duplicate had, unimaginably, told him the customary method—than he could have performed the sexual act in the manner of a Cro-Magnon man!

He said quietly, "Please don't cry out, Melisendra. He sent me here; I could not resist, I wanted you so."

Her voice was low and agitated. "He has played a cruel trick on us both; it is not his first. No, I will not cry out. Do you mind if I strike a light?"

He lay back while she lit a small lamp and held it where she could see him.

"Yes," she said, "the resemblance is—is demoniacal. I noticed it when I saw you with Erlend. But it is more than just resemblance, is it not? Somehow I could sense a tie between you. Even though you are—are very different," she said, and her breath came, ragged.

He reached out and took the lamp away from her, setting it down on the bedside table. "Don't hate me, Melisendra," he pleaded. Her mouth trembled, and he discovered that he wanted to kiss away whatever troubled her. That was not at all the usual reaction he had toward women! Damn it, usually when he'd had what he wanted of them he couldn't get away fast enough! But this one did something very strange to him.

She looked at him, shaken.

"I thought—for a moment, I thought, perhaps, something had changed in him. I—I—I have always wanted him to be this way with me—" She swallowed, hard, choking, and he sensed that she was trying very hard not to cry. "But I have only deceived myself, for he is rotten, rotten to the core, and I despise him. But I despised myself more, for—for wishing that he were such a man as I could—could come to love. For, since I must belong to him, since I have been given to him, I cannot help but wish he were—were a man I could love—"

He pulled her down to him, kissing the shaking mouth, the streaming tears beneath the pale lashes.

"I can't regret anything," he said. "Not when it brought me to you, Melisendra. I'm sorry for your grief, I'm sorry you were frightened; I wouldn't have hurt you or frightened you willingly—but I'm glad to have had you, once, when you wouldn't protest—"

She looked at him soberly, her eyes still wet.

"I am not sorry either," she said. "Believe me. Even though I suppose he was trying to humiliate me. I always refused when Lady Jerana would have given me to another, even when she offered to marry me honorably to one of Dom Rafael's paxmen. I feared it would be even worse. Bard has done his worst to me, I have no more to fear from him, and I thought, better the cruelty that I knew than new cruelty from a stranger. . . . But you have taught me otherwise." She smiled at him suddenly in the lamplight, a very faint smile, but he knew he would never be wholly content until she smiled at him as today she had smiled at the child, a wholehearted, mirthful smile of love.

"I think I am grateful to you. And I do not even know your name."

With one hand he put out the light and with the other he drew her down to him.

"Then are you willing to show your gratitude?"

He heard her surprised, grateful sigh in the moment before she turned and kissed him, with a surprised delight which shook him to the roots.

"I have never hated Bard before," she said, trembling, holding herself tight to him. "Now, because of you, I have learned how to hate him, and I shall never cease to be grateful to you."

"But I want more than gratitude," he heard himself say, to his own surprise. "I want your love, Melisendra."

She said in the dark, with a frightening intensity, "I am not sure I know how to love. But I think if I could learn to love anyone, I would love you, Paul."

He said no more, drawing her fiercely against his mouth. But even in the midst of his wonder and delight, a troubling thought nagged at him.

Now I can't turn back, now I am committed to this world, now there is someone here who means more to me than anyone and anything in the world I came from. What will happen now that I can't treat it all as a crazy dream?

Chapter Three

A tenday later, Paul Harrell rode to war for the first time beside Bard di Asturien.

"The men of Serrais have broken their oaths," Bard told him as they made their preparations. "We may not have to fight. But we do have to remind them of what they have sworn, and the best way to do that is with a show of force and a sight of our armies. You had better be ready to ride within the hour."

Paul's first thought was triumph, *so, there will be a chance to strike for power!* His second, displacing even that, was one of dismay; *Melisendra!* He did not want to be parted from her so swiftly. He had just begun to suspect, and for the first time in his life, that he did not want to be parted from her at all. Yet a moment's sober reflection told him that this parting was the best thing that could possibly have happened.

Sooner or later, he knew it soberly, he would quarrel with Bard over Melisendra. He wanted her, still, as he had never wanted any other woman. Ordinarily, a tenday's possession would have satiated him and he would be more than ready for anything that removed him from any woman's hold. But he still wanted Melisendra. He dreaded this parting, he wanted her—and he couldn't explain it—in a new way. He wanted her for all time, and with her own consent; he was dismayed to realize that her happiness had become more important to him than his own.

He had always thought that women were there for the taking, and that was that. Why, he wondered, should he feel differently about Melisendra?

I always swore I'd never let any woman lead me around by the balls. . . . I knew it in my heart that women wanted to be mastered, to have a real man they couldn't dominate. . . . Why is this one so different?

He knew he still wanted Melisendra; and he wanted her, undisputed, for the rest of their lives. But he also knew that

Bard, produced by a less sophisticated society, regarded Melisendra as his property, his prize, his possession. He might pass her on to Paul for a time, to humiliate her, but he was not likely to give her up entirely. She was, after all, the mother of his only son.

And at the moment there was nothing he could do about any of it. A time would come when they would quarrel over Melisendra, and when that happened, Paul knew he must be prepared.

For when that time comes, he thought grimly, *either he will kill me or I will have to kill him. And I don't intend to be killed.*

So he gathered his pack for riding, and told Bard, "I would like to say farewell to Melisendra."

"Why, as to that, there is no need," said Bard, "for she rides with the army."

Paul nodded, at first without much thought; he was accustomed to women soldiers, even to women generals. Then the shock hit him. Yes, in warfare which was a matter of button-pushing and guns, women would be as competent in combat as men—but in this world, where war meant close-order fighting with swords and knives?

"Oh, we have those too," said Bard, reading his mind. "The women of the Order of Renunciates, the Sisterhood of the Sword, ride into battle with men, and they fight like berserkers. But Melisendra is a real woman, not one of those; she is a *leronis,* a spell-caster who rides with the armies to fight off sorcery."

Paul thought perhaps that might be more dangerous still, but he did not say so. As they rode out an hour later, Bard said that this was just as well.

"There are those who would recognize my style of fighting," he said, "and while we are on this campaign—since you are supposed to be a *nedestro* kinsman of mine—it will not strike anyone as significant if I have you given lessons from my own arms-master."

Paul, riding unregarded with a small group of Bard's aides, noted for himself how the armies greeted their general: cries of "The Kilghard Wolf! The Wolf!" cheers and shouts of acclaim. His very presence seemed to encourage and inspire them with courage and enthusiasm for this war against the Serrais.

So Bard would someday trust him with that power—and believe that he would tamely render it back again when the time was past? Not likely. There was, Paul knew with a chil of certainty along the spine, only one explanation. Bard would use him on his climb to conquest—and then, rather than rewarding him and sending him away as he had pledged, it would be back to the stasis box, by the same sorcery that had brought him here. Or perhaps, more simply still, a knife in the ribs on some dark night, and a corpse to the *kyorebni* wheeling around the cliffs. Paul kept his face impassive, joining in with the men who cried out in Bard's acclaim. It would not be easy. For now, Bard had other things to think of than the duplicate being trained to be his double and his dupe; but at other times they could read one another's thoughts, and he had had no training in blocking them. Perhaps Melisendra could help him, if she was truly a sorceress; but Melisendra would not be all that eager, either, to kill the father of her son. She might say that she hated Bard, but Paul wasn't entirely sure of the depths of that hate.

Still, confronted with an accomplished fact, he could probably trust her to be silent about the substitution.

For now there was only one thing to do; and that was just what Bard wanted him to do—to ready himself, not only to impersonate, but to *become* Bard di Asturien, the Kilghard Wolf, general of all the armies of Asturias. And perhaps, one day, more.

To his own surprise—for he knew nothing of the Darkovan style of swordplay and war and had never held a sword—he took to it as if he had been born to it. A little thought told him why. He had been born with the identical reflexes and superb physical organization that made Bard an incomparable swordsman; and he had trained that physical mechanism to the utmost with martial arts and the skills of unarmed combat during the rebellion. Now it was just a case of adding another set of skills to the trained muscles and brain, as a trained dancer can learn variation of steps.

He found he enjoyed the campaign, riding lookout with the aides, making camp each night and sleeping beneath the four moons that waxed and waned again. He thought often that if he had been brought up to this life he would have been happier. Here there were few expectations of conformity, and those there were came naturally to him; there was plenty of outlet for aggression. In his first close-quarters battle he found that he had no fear and that he could kill, if he must, without fear and without malice, and, better, without squeamishness. A corpse hacked by spears and swords was neither more nor less dead than one riddled with bullets or blasted with fire.

Bard kept him close at hand and talked to him a good deal. Paul knew this was not out of good will; the Wolf simply had to know whether Paul had his gift for strategy as well. It seemed that he did; a talent for handling men, a sense for the strategy of battle or attack, as city after city fell, almost undefended, to the armies of Asturias, and the men of Serrais fled, or went down before them, to the very borders of the Serrais lands. In forty days they had conquered half as many towns, and the road lay open before them to the old lands of the Serrais people. And Paul discovered that he knew instinctively what was the best strategy to take each city, to strike down each fighting force spread against them.

"My father said once," Bard told him, "that with two like me we could conquer the Hundred Kingdoms. And damn it, he was right! I know now it's not only likeness skin deep; you and I are the same man, and when we can lead two armies at once, the whole of this land will lie open to us like a whore on the city wall!" He laughed and clapped Paul's shoulder. "We'll have to—one kingdom would never hold us both, but with a hundred, there ought to be room enough for us both!"

Paul wondered if Bard really thought he was as naïve as all that. Bard would certainly try to kill him. But not yet awhile, maybe not for years, because he would need him until all of the Hundred Kingdoms, or as many of them as he wanted, were in subjection.

And meanwhile, paradoxically, he enjoyed Bard's company. It was a new experience for Paul to have someone to talk to who could follow what he said and understand it intelligently. And he felt that Bard enjoyed his, too.

It would all have been quite perfect if he could have had Melisendra actually *with* him on this campaign; but Melisendra rode with the other *leroni*, men and women in gray robes sternly chaperoned by a gray-haired elderly man with a lame leg, so severely lame that he rode with a special device attached to his saddle to prop it up before him, and another to unfold and help him in dismounting. In all the first three tendays of the campaign he had no opportunity to exchange more than half a dozen words with Melisendra, and those were such as could be spoken in front of half the army.

The walls of Serrais were actually within sight when Paul, riding with Bard's aides, saw that Bard had dropped back from his usual leading place to ride with the *leroni*. After a moment, seeing that Paul was watching them, he beckoned and Paul rode back toward the cluster of gray-robed men and

224

women. Melisendra raised her eyes in greeting, with a secret smile beneath her gray hood, somehow as intimate as a kiss.

Paul asked, "Who is Master Gareth?"

"He is the chief among the *laranzu'in* of Asturias; also, he is my father," Melisendra said. "I wish that I might tell him—" she broke off, but Paul knew what she meant.

He said in a whisper, "I miss you," and she smiled again.

Bard beckoned imperatively to him and said, "Master Gareth MacAran, captain Paolo Harryl."

The gray-haired sorcerer gave Paul a formal bow.

"Master Gareth was lamed in my first campaign," Bard said, "but he seems to bear me no ill will, for all that."

The old wizard said genially, "You were not to blame, Master Bard—or must I call you Lord General now as the young guardsmen do? No one could better have led such a campaign. That I caught a poisoned dagger in the leg muscle was ill fortune, the fortunes of war, no more. Those of us who ride to war must accept such things."

"It seems long since that campaign," said Bard, and Paul, who was as always catching some spillage from his mind and feelings, realized that the tone was the bitterness of regret.

And in truth Bard was feeling the sharp sting of regret, a longing for days long past, of which the presence of Master Gareth was a sharp reminder, and the copper sheen of Melisendra's hair beneath the gray sorcerer's cloak more poignant still. Beltran had been at his side then, and still was his friend. And Melora. He found he could not resist the temptation to ask, "And your elder daughter, sir, how does she; where has she gone?"

"She is in Neskaya," Master Gareth said. "In the circle of Varzil, Keeper there."

Bard frowned, displeased, and said, "She serves, then, the enemies of Asturias?" And yet he felt it might be better to think of Melora as an enemy, since she had gone beyond his reach. She was the only woman alive who had ever come near to understanding him, yet he had never laid a hand upon her.

"Why, no," Master Gareth said. "The *leroni* at Neskaya have pledged to work with starstones and live only for the good of all mankind, and to give allegiance to no king or ruler whatsoever, but only to the gods, and to help or heal. So they are not the enemy, my lord Wolf."

"Do you really believe that?" Bard's voice was contemptuous.

"Sir, I know it; Melora does not lie, nor would she have

reason to lie to me, nor can one *laranzu* lie to another. Dom Varzil is exactly what he says he is, sworn to the Compact, to use no weapons, make no weapons, allow no weapons by *laran*. He is an honorable man and I admire his courage. It cannot be an easy thing to renounce your weapons knowing that others still carry them, and that others may refuse to believe you disarmed."

"If you admire him so much, then," Bard said peevishly, "must I look for you too to desert my armies and rally to the standard of this wondrous great man Varzil? He is a Ridenow of Serrais."

"Born so, sooth," Gareth said, "but now he is Varzil of Neskaya, with no loyalties other than that. And your question, Master Bard, is needless. I have sworn to King Ardrin an oath lifelong and I will not forsake it for Varzil or for any other. I would have held to the standard of Ardrin's son, had Lady Ariel not fled the country with him. I follow your father's banner because I believe truly that this is best for Asturias. But I am not the keeper of Melora's conscience. And indeed she left Ardrin's court in that same night that you were exiled, sir, long before there was cause to choose between Valentine's cause and Alaric's—in fact, Valentine was yet unborn. And she left with the king's leave."

"Still," said Bard, "if she has chosen not to fight against the enemies of Asturias, should I not rank her among them?"

"That's as you see it, sir. But you might also say that she has chosen not to fight alongside the enemies of Asturias, either. She could have done that easily enough; all of Varzil's circle did not swear the Compact, but left him and went to the Hastur supporters among that army. She stayed in Neskaya at Varzil's side, and that meant she's chosen to stay neutral, sir. And my granddaughter Mirella went to Hali Tower, which has also sworn to stay neutral alongside Neskaya. I'm an old man, and I'm loyal to my king while he needs me, but I pray the young people may find some way to end these damnable wars year after year while our countryside is laid waste!"

Bard did not answer that. He said, "I would not like to think of Melora as my enemy. If she is not my friend, I think it well that she is neutral."

Paul, riding between Bard and Melisendra, wondered why Melora could bring to Bard's face that note of anger and grief and misery. Master Gareth said, "Indeed, she'd never be your enemy, sir. She always spoke well of you."

Bard, sensing that both Melisendra and Paul could read his

emotions, made an angry effort to control them. What was that woman Melora to him anyhow? *That* part of his life was over. At the end of this campaign, he would put all his *leroni* to seeking out a way to attack the Island of Silence and bring Carlina home to him, and then he need never think of Melora again. Or—he thought, intercepting a look between Paul and Melisendra—of Melisendra. Paul could have her and welcome. It would, at least, keep Paul safely preoccupied for awhile.

For awhile. Until I am safely established, with Alaric king over all these lands. Then he will be too dangerous to me; an ambitious man, accustomed to wielding all that power. . . .

And then he felt an unexpected surge of pain. Was he never to have a friend, a brother, an equal, that he could trust? Was he to lose every friend and peer as he had lost Beltran and Geremy? Perhaps, after all, he could think of another way; perhaps Paul need not die.

I do not want to lose him as I lost Melora. . . . He stopped himself, furious. He would *not* think of Melora again!

Suddenly Melisendra jerked her horse to a violent stop; her face contorted, and at the same moment Master Gareth flung up his hands as if to ward off some invisible evil. One of the other *leroni* screamed; another choked aloud in terror, bending over his horse's saddle and clinging there by instinct, almost unable to sit. Bard looked at them in dismay and bewilderment. Paul moved swiftly to steady Melisendra, who sat swaying in her saddle, paler than the snow at the edges of the paths.

She paid no heed to him. "Oh—the death, the burning!" she cried, and her voice held terror beyond expressing. "Oh, the agony—death, death, falling from the sky—the fire—the screams—" Her voice died in her throat, and she sat with her eyeballs rolled up until only white showed, as if they stared at some inward horror.

Master Gareth choked, "Mirella! Dear gods, Mirella—she is there—"

This brought Melisendra back, but only for a moment. "We cannot be sure she has come there yet, dear Father, she—I have not heard her cry out, I am sure I should know if she were among them—but oh, the burning, the burning—" She screamed again, and Paul reached over from his own horse. She let her head fall against him, sobbing.

He whispered, "What is it, Melisendra, what is it—" but

she was beyond answering him. She could only cling to him, weeping helplessly. Master Gareth, too, looked as if he were about to fall from his saddle. Bard put out a hand to steady the old *laranzu* and at the touch the images flooded into him.

Flaring light. Searing pain, intolerable agony as flames rose and struck inward, consuming, tearing . . . mounting fire, walls crumbling and falling . . . voices raised in shrieks of agony, terror, wild lamentation . . . air-cars booming and fire, death raining down from the sky. . . .

Paul had been immune, but as Bard's mind opened to the images, he saw and felt them too, and felt himself go pale in horror. "Fire-bombing," he whispered. He had believed this world civilized, too civilized for such warfare, and war almost a game, a manly test of courage, of domination and challenge. But *this.* . . .

A woman's body flaring like a torch, the smell of burning hair, burning flesh, agony searing. . . .

Bard steadied the old man, as he would have with his own father. He was sick with the horror of the images flaring through his mind. But Master Gareth managed somehow to pull himself free from the horrors within. *"Enough!"* he said harshly, aloud. "We cannot help them by sharing their death agonies! Barricade yourselves, all of you! At once!" He spoke in command voice, and suddenly the air around them was free of smoke and the smell of death and burning, the intolerable screams of agony gone. Paul looked around, dazed, at the peaceful trail and the soft silent clouds overhead, the small sounds of an army on the march. A horse whinnied somewhere, supply wagons creaked and rumbled, a drover somewhere good-naturedly cursed his mules. Paul blinked with the suddenness of the falling quiet.

"What was it? What was *that,* Melisendra?" His arms were still around her; she straightened, a little abashed.

"Hali," she said, "the great Tower by the shores of the Lake; Lord Hastur had sworn that the Towers should be neutral, at least Hali and Neskaya—I do not know who struck them." Her face was still stunned with the horror she had shared. "Every *leronis* in the Hundred Kingdoms must have shared that death. . . . This is why the Lord Varzil has sworn neutrality. If this goes on, soon there will be no land to conquer. . . ."

They all looked sober; many of the *leroni* were weeping. Melisendra said, "Not one of us here but has a sister, a brother, a friend, a loved one at Hali. It is the largest of the Towers; there are thirty-six women and men there, three full

228

Circles, with *leroni* from every one of the kingdoms and *laran*-bearing families. . . ." Her voice died again.

"So much for the Compact," said Master Gareth fiercely. "Shall they sit quietly in Elhalyn and limit their warfare to sword and crossbow when fire is sent against them from the sky? But who would have dared to strike them? It is not the forces of Asturias, surely?"

Bard shook his head, numbed.

"Serrais, now, has no such strength, and why should the Lord Hastur strafe his own Tower who were loyal to him and had sworn to hold themselves neutral? Can it be that the Aillard or the Aldaran have joined in this war, and that all the Hundred Kingdoms are aflame?"

Paul listened, shaken. On the surface this world was so simple, so beautiful, and yet *this,* this hideous telepathic warfare lay hidden. . . .

"It can be worse than fire-bombing," Melisendra said, picking up his thoughts as she so often did. "At least they were borne by aircraft and the defending Tower could have knocked them out of the sky. I once struck down an air-car bent on such attack. But I have known a circle of *leroni* to put a spell on the ground beneath a castle under siege—" she pointed to a ruin atop a distant hill—"and the ground opened, and shook—and the castle fell in ruins and everyone was killed."

"And is there no defense against such weaponry?"

"Oh, yes," Melisendra said indifferently, "if the Lord of the Castle had had his own circle of wizards and they were stronger than the attackers. For generations, all of our family—and all the great families of Darkover—had *laran* ever stronger bred into them; that was while all this land lay under the rule of the Hastur kin, the descendants of Hastur and Cassilda. But there is a limit to what can be done with breeding; sooner or later there is too much inbreeding, and lethal recessives take over. My father—" she gestured to Master Gareth, who still looked pale and exhausted—"was married to his half-sister, and of fourteen children, only the three survived, all daughters. There are no MacArans in these hills now, only a few away to the north who were never taken into the breeding program . . . and few Dellerays, and the old line of Serrais died out; the Ridenow took the name when they married into that line. And my sister Kyria died in bearing a daughter, so that Melora and I brought up her child. . . . Mirella is a *leronis* too, one of those kept virgin for the Sight, and I pray she may stay so, for I know she fears to die the same way."

Paul was not really in rapport with Melisendra now, but he could sense the waves of old, half-conquered fear; he remembered Melisendra had borne a child, and felt sudden sympathy for the terrors she must have known. Always before this he had had but little sympathy for the special problems of women; now it struck him with remorse. In his own world, a woman would have known enough to make certain she was not at risk of pregnancy, but he had not bothered, here, to inquire, and it occurred to him, troubled, that Melisendra had not stopped to weigh the cost of their lovemaking.

"It has begun to be lethal in our family," she went on, almost absently—Paul wondered if she was talking to him, or trying to ease her own tensions and fears. "Erlend is healthy, the Goddess be praised, but already he has *laran*, and he is young for it. . . . Bard is only distantly related to us, of course, and Kyria married a cousin, so that may be why. . . . Melora and I must be careful to whom we bear children; even if we survive, the children may be stillborn. . . . I do not think Mirella should have children at all. And there are certain *laran* gifts which could combine with mine so that I would not survive forty days of such a pregnancy. Fortunately those are rare now, but I do not think their virulence is wholly lost in the line, and since records are not now kept, and the old art of monitoring cell-deep is not known now, the last of those who knew all of it died before she could teach what she knew. . . . None of us can know, when we bear a child, what may come of it. And some of these new weapons. . . ." She shuddered and resolutely changed the subject again, but not much. "I was fortunate that Bard was not carrying any of that heredity. It was perhaps the only fortunate thing about that whole affair."

It took another day of marching before they came up with the armies of Serrais, and that meant another night encamped on the road. Under ordinary conditions, Paul did not even see Melisendra when they were with the army; but near the camp was a little grove of trees with a well, and when he strolled that way, as the nightly drizzle began to fall (Bard told him this was normal for the season, except in the high summer—what a climate!) Melisendra, wrapped in the gray cloak of a *leronis*, beckoned to him. They stood embracing for some minutes, but when he whispered to her, moving his head suggestively toward the concealing trees, she shook her head.

"It would not be seemly. Not like this, with the army. Don't you think I want to, my beloved? But our time will come."

He was about to protest—how did he know they would have any time at all, after this campaign?—but the look in her eyes stopped him. He could not treat Melisendra like a camp follower. Quite soon, she went back to the other *leroni*—her father, she said, would have been angry at even this surreptitious embrace, would have thought that she was behaving badly—not that he minded whom she loved, but to do it furtively, like this, on campaign, when all others must leave their loved ones behind, was shameful. When she had gone he stood watching her reflectively, thinking that this was the first time he had ever listened to a woman's refusal. If any other woman had done this, he would have considered her a cheap, manipulative slut, trying to lead him around by the balls. . . . What was happening to him? Why was Melisendra different?

And, an unwelcome thought, was it possible that his own attitude, in those days, had left something to be desired? Paul was not given to questioning the rightness of his own motives and actions, and this was a new idea to him, one he put aside at once. Melisendra was different, that was all, and love was the art of making exceptions.

But it seemed to be his night for unwelcome thoughts. He lay awake, unable to sleep, and wondered what would happen when Bard knew that it was not a casual affair with Melisendra but that he wanted her for all time. And if he and Bard were the same man, with the same sexual tastes and desires, why was it that he had not tired of Melisendra at once, as Bard had done?

I have no consciousness of guilt toward her, and so Melisendra does not make me uncomfortable . . . and Paul almost laughed; Bard, feel guilty about anything? Bard was as free of the neurotic pattern of guilt as any man Paul had ever known, as free of it as Paul was himself. Guilt was a thing created by women and priests to keep men from doing what they wanted to do and had the strength to do, a tool of the weak to get their own way. . . . Still it was a long time before Paul could get to sleep. He wondered dismally what was happening to him on this world.

At least it was better than the stasis box. And with this thought he finally managed to sleep.

The next day was gray and dismal, with rain flooding down, and Paul was surprised that they tried to march; though a little thought told him that in this climate, if they let rain stop them, they'd never do anything. And indeed, he saw herdsmen, mounted on strange horned beasts, watching over flocks in the fields, flocks of what Bard told him were rabbithorns; and farmers, many of them women, shrouded in thick tartan cloaks and wrappings, digging in the fields. At least, he thought glumly, they didn't have to worry about watering their crops. He was glad he wasn't a farmer. From what little he knew of them, it was either too wet or too dry. They rode by a lake and saw small boats out in the rain, hauling in nets. He supposed fish-farming was a good trade to be carried on in the rain.

Around noon—the days were longer here, and Paul could never be sure of the time unless he could see the sun—they stopped to eat the cold trail rations served out by the quartermasters: bread, coarse, with raisins or some kind of dried fruit, and nuts baked into it, a kind of bland cheese, a handful of nuts in their shells and a pale, sourish wine which, nevertheless, had considerable body and was refreshing and warming. It was, he knew, the commonest home brew of the countryside, and he felt he could get to like it.

Halfway through the meal, Bard's aide came to summon Paul to him. As he rose to obey the summons, Paul was conscious of looks and comments; he should, perhaps, warn Bard that this supposed favoritism to one who was, after all, newcome to his armies, could get him into trouble. But when he mentioned it, Bard shrugged it off.

"I never do the expected thing; that's one of the reasons I got the name Wolf," he said. "It keeps them off balance." Then he told Paul that one of his runners had come in, bearing news that the Serrais army was not far away. As soon as the weather cleared, he would have to send out sentry birds to spot their exact position and formation. "But I have a young *laranzu* with the Sight," he said, "and it may be that we can take them by surprise in the rain. Ruyven," he said to another of his aides, "run and tell Rory Lanart, when he has finished his meal, to come to me at once."

When Rory came, Paul noted with dismay that the young *laranzu* was only about twelve years old. Did children fight battles of sorcery and wickedness in this world, too? It was bad enough to have women in the field, but children? Dismay struck more deeply as he thought of young Erlend, the starstone about his throat. Would Erlend grow up in a world like

232

this? He watched the child looking into the starstone, relaying the information they wanted in a quiet, faraway voice, and wondered what Melisendra thought of having her son brought up to this.

Bard, after all, is no more than a barbarian chief in a barbarian world. He and I are not the same man. He is the man I might have been in this barbarian society. There but for the grace of God, and all that.

He raised his head to find Bard watching him; but his double did not give any sign or hint as to whether or not he had read Paul's mind this time. He only said, "Finished your meal? Bring along what you want to—I always put some nuts in my pocket to eat as I ride—and tell the aides to get the men started again. Rory, ride at the head of the army with me, I'm going to need you, and someone should lead your horse if you're going to be using the Sight."

They had not ridden for more than an hour, as Paul judged it, past the time of the nooning break when they came to the top of a hill; and Bard pointed, silently. Spread out in the valley below them, an army lay, formed up and waiting, and Paul identified, even at this distance, the green and gold banner of the Ridenow of Serrais. Between them and the Serrais army below was a little wood, a sparse grove of trees and undergrowth. A sudden flight of birds racketed upward, disturbed at their feeding in the bushes. Paul could hear Bard thinking: *that's done it, that's the end of any idea that we might possibly take them by surprise. But their* leroni *would have better sense than that. And surely they have* leroni *with them.*

Aides were riding along the ranks of the men, forming them up in the battle plan Bard has discussed, briefly, with Paul—one of the things which the other aides resented, he knew, was that their leader spoke to Paul, outsider and newcomer, as an equal. They had, of course, no idea quite how much Paul was Bard's equal. But they sensed something and it made them angry. Some day, Paul knew, when there was time, he would have to deal with it. And he thought, with a trace of amusement, that when he and Bard were leading separate armies, each believing that it was led by the Kilghard Wolf himself, at least that source of friction would be gone; there would be no intrusive outsider to come between the Wolf and his loyal followers.

The signal was, as always, the drawing of Bard's sword. Paul watched, his hand on the hilt of his own sword, waiting for Bard to give the sign for the charge. The rain had drizzled itself out, and only stray drops were falling. Now, suddenly, through a great break in the clouds, the great red sun came out and blazed, spreading light into the valley. Paul looked at the sky, thinking offhand that it was better to fight without the rain, but aware that the turf underfoot was still wet and the horses would find it slippery in the charge. Master Gareth had drawn his little army of sorcerers, gray-cloaked, off to one side, to keep them out of the way of the charge. When Paul had first ridden into battle, he had been anxious about Melisendra. Now he knew that she was in no physical danger in a battle such as this. Even under the concealing gray cloak, he could tell Melisendra by her riding.

He saw Bard draw his sword—then heard him cry out, and saw him raise the sword to slash at empty air. *What, in God's name, does he see?* And all the men riding near him were behaving the same way—slashing at empty air, crying out, raising their arms to shield their eyes against some unseen menace; even the horses were rearing and whinnying in distress. Paul saw nothing, smelled nothing, even though one of the men cried out, "Fire! Look there—" and fell crashing from his horse, rolling away, screaming. And suddenly as he caught Bard's eyes, in contact with his twin, he saw what Bard saw: over their heads, wheeling and screeching, strange birds flew, diving viciously at the eyes, causing the horses to rear up as their foul breath pervaded everything; and the horror was that the birds had the faces of women, contorted with lewd grins. . . .

Paul saw this through Bard's eyes; and through his own eyes . . . the day lay quiet, sunlit below them, the armies of Serrais quickly moving to repel the charge. Paul rose in his stirrups, his own sword flashing out. He bellowed—in, he knew it, Bard's voice, "There's nothing there, men! It's illusion! What the hell are the *leroni* doing? Come on—*charge!*"

Bard's swift response to the words reassured him. He shouted, "Charge!" and led the charge, riding *through* the illusion—Paul saw through his eyes the evil harpy that dived at his eyes and felt Bard duck, even while he knew that it was illusion. He smelled the stench of the beast-woman, but the frozen horror had broken; Paul had snapped back to his own awareness and was thundering, sword in hand, toward the first rank of the oncoming Serrais army. A man cut upward at his horse and he slashed and saw the man fall. And then he was fighting hand to hand, without the least instant to spare for magic horrors, or for seeing them through Bard's eyes. At this moment he did not care what Bard might be

234

seeing, whether or not it was there to be seen or was the product of sorcery or *laran* science.

They had still caught the Serrais army, who had relied on their sorcerers to delay the charge, at least partly by surprise. The battle was not brief; but not as long as Paul, helping Bard to assess the forces mastered against them, had believed. Bard came through miraculously unwounded. Miraculously, Paul thought, for throughout the battle, wherever he looked, Bard was in the thick of the fighting. Paul himself took a slash in the leg, which did more harm to his trousers than anything else. When the Serrais army, demoralized, fled, and Dom Eiric himself surrendered—Bard hanged him out of hand as an oath-breaker—the sun was setting, and Paul, his leg freezing under the flapping remnants of the leather breeches, rode to help the aides set up headquarters in one of the houses in the nearby village, commandeered. The men were set to plunder and rape, then burn the village, but Bard stopped them.

"These are my brother's subjects; rebellious, it is true, but still our subjects, and while they may have been terrified into doing the will of the Serrais army, they shall have a chance to prove their loyalty or otherwise when they can act freely without an army at their throats. It will go hard with any man in this army who touches one of our subjects, loyal or disloyal. Pay for what you take, and lay no hand on any unwilling women."

Paul, listening as Bard gave the order, reflected that he had not known Bard had this kind of sense, or that he could hold back men set on plunder. But when he spoke of this to Bard, Bard smiled. He said, "Don't be a fool. I'm not being generous, though what I said is true, of course, and even more that the royal house of Asturias, and I, will get the credit for being generous with our subjects. But it's more than that, much more. There's simply not enough, of either plunder or women, to satisfy this army. And when they'd taken all there was to take, they'd fall to quarreling over it and cut each other to pieces—and I can't have that in my army." He grinned wickedly and said, "Anyhow, the officers have a little leniency—and you'd get first choice since you led the charge. We may not be so like after all—you're braver than I, to lead the charge right through that nest of harpies! Or did you simply begin to suspect, earlier than I did, that they were illusion?"

Paul shook his head. "Neither," he said. "I simply didn't see anything."

Bard stared. "You didn't—not at all?"

"Nothing. I began, after a little, to see them through *your* mind—but then, I was only seeing what *you* saw, and I knew it."

Bard pursed his lips and whistled. "That's very interesting," he said. "You picked up the burning of the Tower of Hali—gods above and below, that was a ghastly business! Wars should be fought with swords and strength, not with sorcery and fire-bombing! That hellish stuff they use is made by sorcery in the Towers; no normal process can manufacture it!"

"I couldn't agree more," Paul said, "but I picked it up, again, through Melisendra's mind. I didn't see it myself."

"Yes. Sex creates a bond. And I've often suspected that Melisendra's a catalyst telepath. In a Tower she'd be used to awaken latent *laran* in someone who for some reason can't use it. I suspect, without meaning to, she's awakened what little of it I have. God knows, she'd never think she owed me any favors! And there are times I suspect that it's no favor at all, though most people would think it so; there are times I wish I was immune to *laran*, or at least to illusion. If you hadn't led the charge this morning, we'd have lost the last bit of our advantage. As for being immune to *laran*—unless you pick it up directly from my mind, or Melisendra's, or from someone very close to you—well, that might be an advantage. We'll talk about that afterward, maybe. I can think of a service you could do me." His eyes narrowed and he looked sharply at Paul. "I'll have to think about it. Meanwhile, I have this rebel village to deal with. Stand back there and listen to what's happening; you might have to deal like this sometime."

Paul, admonished, listened as he gave the commands about the men who had actively assisted the Serrais army. They were to pay double taxes this year; anyone who could not pay the taxes to do forty days of free labor on the roads—Paul had already learned that the forty-day cycle, corresponding to that of the larger moon, served the social purpose of a month, making up four tendays. Women, too, followed the forty-day menstrual cycle of the largest moon. At the end they cheered his leniency.

One of Bard's fellow officers said, "With respect, Lord General, you should have burned them right out," but Bard shook his head.

"We're going to need good subjects to pay taxes. Dead men support no armies, and we need the work of their hands; and if we hanged them we'd somehow have to support their

236

wives and children. . . . Or are you suggesting we emulate the Dry-towners and sell the women and children off into brothels to earn their keep? How would people like that feel about King Alaric, to say nothing of his armies?"

Master Gareth said quietly behind him, "I am surprised. When he was a boy, no one ever suspected that Bard di Asturien, brave as he might be, would have grown up to have any political sense at all."

A pretty, red-haired, round-bodied girl came up to them, bending in a low curtsy. "My father's house is your headquarters, Lord General. May I serve you wine from his cellars?"

"Now that," Bard said, "we'll gladly accept. Serve it to my staff as well, if you will. And all the more for your serving it, my dear." He smiled at her, and she returned the smile.

Paul, remembering that the women of the *leroni* had all been quartered at the far end of the village, in a house set apart, and that four guardsmen had been told to protect their privacy, remembered tales among the soldiers that Bard had a hell of a reputation with the women.

But before the girl could return with the wine there was a knock on the door, and one of the Sisters of the Sword, her scarlet tunic slashed and still battle-stained, burst into the room.

"My lord!" she exclaimed, and fell on her knees before Bard, "I appeal to the justice of the Kilghard Wolf!"

"If you are one of those who fought for us in the battle, *mestra*," Bard said, "you shall have it. What troubles you? If any man with my army has laid a hand upon you—I personally do not think women should be soldiers, but if you fight in my army, you are entitled to my protection. And the man who has touched you against your will shall be gelded and then hanged."

"No," said the woman in the red tunic, laying a hand upon the dagger at her throat. "Such a one should have perished already by my hand or that of my sworn sister. But there were mercenaries of the Sisterhood in the army of Serrais, my lord. Most of them fled when that army fled, but one or two were wounded and some of them stayed by their sisters; and now that the battle is over the men of your army are not treating them with the courtesy which is allowed by custom to captured prisoners of war. One of them has already been raped, and when I appealed to the sergeants to stop it, they said that if a woman took the field in war she should be sure

237

not to lost her battle, or she should be treated not as a warrior but as a woman—" The woman soldier's mouth was trembling in outrage. Bard rose swiftly to his feet.

"I'll put a stop to that, certainly," he said, and gestured to Paul and one or two of his officers to follow him as he strode out of the tent.

They followed the woman in red through the village and through the hurly-burly outside that was the army making camp, but they had not far to go past the village when they knew what the woman had been talking about. They heard a screaming of women, and a group of men had gathered around one of the tents, making lewd noises of encouragement. At one side a fight was going on, where a group of women in red were fighting to get through. Into the noise and confusion came Bard's bellowing voice.

"What the hell is this all about? Stand back!"

"Lord General—" Murmurs, shocked noises of recognition. Bard thrust back the flap of the tent, and a minute later two men came staggering out under a savage kick. A woman was sobbing wildly inside. Bard paused to say something to the guard that Paul could not hear, then raised his voice again.

"Once and for all, I gave my orders: no civilian is to be touched, and no prisoner ill-used!" He jerked his head at the men he had kicked. They were sitting dazed on the ground, already drunk, their clothes undone, confused. "If these men have any friends here, take them back to their own quarters and sober them up."

There was muttering in the ranks, and one of the men called out, "We can take what the other army has, that's custom in war! Why do you refuse us what's customary, General Wolf?"

Bard turned toward the voice and said harshly, "You're allowed by custom to take their weapons, no more. Have any men in the opposing army been made your minions by force?"

There was a mutter of outrage at the notion.

"Then hands off these women, hear me? And while you're at it, let me repeat what I told the soldier here." He gestured toward the woman of the Sisterhood. "Any man who lays hand on one of the Sisterhood who has fought beside us for the honor and strength of Asturias and the reign of King Alaric, shall be first gelded and then hanged, if I have to do it myself! Understand that, once and for all."

But the woman in red flung herself at Bard's feet.

"Won't you punish the men who have outraged my sisters?"

Bard shook his head. "I've put a stop to it; but my men acted in ignorance, and I won't punish them. No one else will touch a prisoner; but what's done is done and I won't give the women who fought against me the same kind of protection I give my own armies—or what's the good of being in my armies at all? If the mercenaries in your Sisterhood want to swear allegiance to Asturias and fight alongside my armies, I'll give them that protection; otherwise not. Although," he added loudly, glancing around at the assembled men, "if anyone touches a prisoner except as custom allows, I'll have him whipped and his pay stopped, is that clear?" The woman was about to say more, but he stopped her. "Enough, I said. No more fighting. Come on, men, break it up. Get about your business! Any more fighting and there'll be whippings and broken heads tomorrow!"

Back in the commandeered house, the staff had finished their wine and were going to make their own arrangements. The red-haired girl, who reminded Paul elusively of Melisendra, put a cup into his hand and smiled.

"Here, my lord, finish your wine before you go."

He raised his face to her and drank, sliding his arm about her waist. Her flirtatious smile made him understand; this was not an unwelcome advance, and he pulled her close. A hand fell on his shoulder, and Bard's voice boomed out, "Let her be, Paul. She's mine."

Mentally Paul cursed, knowing he should have expected this. Already, on campaign, he had discovered that he and Bard had the same taste in women. Naturally enough, if they were the same man, they'd want the same thing in women, and it wasn't the first time their eyes had fallen on the same camp follower or woman of pleasure in a fallen city. But it was the first time it had come to a direct confrontation. Paul thought, he owes me something for leading the charge, and his arm stayed stubbornly around the girl's waist. This time, damn it, he would *not* give in!

"Oh, hell," Bard said.

Paul realized that he was already drunk; also that the rest of the staff had gone, leaving them alone with the girl. He put a hand under the girl's chin and asked, "Which of us do you want, wench?"

Her smile turned from one to the other. She had been drinking too. He could smell the sweet fruitiness of wine on her breath, and either the drink had heightened her percep-

239

tions or she had a trace of *laran,* for she said, "How can I choose between you when you are so much alike? Are you twin brothers, then? What is a poor girl to do when if she chooses one she'll have to give up the other?"

"No need for that," Paul said, as he swallowed the wine, realizing it was much stronger than what he had had before, and was consolidating his drunkenness. "There's no need to prove one of us the better man this time, is there, brother?" He had never voiced this knowledge of their unconscious rivalry before this. And if Bard were somehow a hidden half of himself, was this not a way to come to terms with it?

The girl looked from one to the other of them, laughing, and turned to lead the way. "In here."

Paul was just drunk enough to retain a merciless clarity. Bard made some show of flipping a coin. Paul wasn't surprised—that kind of chance-choice was common in some very unlike cultures—but he stepped back, watching the clouded and elegant dance of bodies, Bard and the girl, *his* body and hers, as Bard sank down, pulling the girl atop him. Paul felt a momentary flicker of surprise—*he* would have pinned her down beneath his own body—but the thought was remote, dreamlike. He sank down beside them, his hands straying along her curving back, through the silken hair. She turned a little and her lips fastened on his even while she drew in a gasp of excitement as Bard entered her. She found a moment and a free hand to tease his manhood with her fingertips. Paul, embracing her, found that he had them both in his arms, but it didn't seem to matter; it was dreamlike, nothing now seemed forbidden, and he knew their three bodies, enlaced, became a shifting dance. The woman's softness seemed somehow only an excuse to savor *himself,* knowing Bard's excitement and sharing it. It was dreamily perverse; he knew that when he took her, Bard, in full rapport now, shared the pleasure even as he had shared his twin's. He never knew, never wanted to know, how long it lasted, or at what point, the girl forgotten, he found himself in Bard's hard clasp, all softness gone now, a struggle almost to the death, locked together in what he could not isolate as either passion or hatred; and in a final sardonic flicker of apartness he wondered if this could be called, if they were actually the same man, sex or the ultimate masturbation, and then it did not matter whether the violent explosion was orgasm or death.

He woke alone, his head thundering. The girl was gone.

nor did he ever set eyes on her again. She had meant nothing, she had only been the excuse for that violent confrontation with his dark twin, his other half, his half-known unknown other. He sluiced his face with the icy water in the bucket, and was still gasping with the shock of it when Bard came in.

"My orderly brought me a pitcher of hot *jaco*. If your head's doing what mine is, you could use half of it," he said. The stuff smelled like bitter chocolate, but the effect was about the same as extra-strong black coffee, and Paul was glad to get it. Bard poured himself another mug.

"I want to talk to you, Paolo. You know you saved the day yesterday. That damned harpy illusion is a new one, and the *leroni* weren't prepared for it. It was so real! And you didn't see it at all?"

"Only through your mind, as I told you."

"So you're immune to that kind of illusion," Bard said. "I wish I dared confide in Master Gareth! He might be able to explain it. And among other things, it gives you an edge if you should have to lead the army some day. And the men will follow you; but you'll have to be careful about the *leroni*, they'll sense something strange about you." He barked short laughter. "One good thing about Varzil's God-forgotten Compact—we can fight without having those wretched corps of wizards along with us, if they ever decide to put the Compact into effect!"

"I thought you and Master Gareth were friends—that you depended on him!"

"True," Bard said. "He's known me since we were boys, my foster brothers and I. But I'd still be glad to dispense with his services and send him to spend a nice peaceful old age in a Tower! When this land is at peace again, perhaps Alaric will swear to the Compact after all. I don't like my future subjects being bombed out of their homes, and down where they spread bonewater dust last year I hear the midwives report children being born without arms or legs or eyes, cleft palates, backbone sticking through the skin at their butts, things you don't see twice in a year and there are *dozens* of them—got to be some connection! And men and women dying of thinned blood—and the worst of it is, it's *still* dangerous to ride there. I suspect the land will be blasted for years, maybe a generation or two! There's too much sorcery about!"

How, Paul wondered, had they managed, by mind-power, to make radioactive dust? For what Bard had described was certainly some kind of radiation product. Well, if *laran* could do the other things he knew it could do, it should be no very

241

great trick to break down molecules into their component atoms, or to combine them into heavy radioactive elements.

He said wryly, "And to *that* kind of *laran* I should certainly not be immune!"

"No, I shouldn't think so. Your mind may be immune, but your body's no different from anyone else's. But there are kinds of *laran* to which you would be immune and I'm not; and so I have a task for you. Serrais's main strength is broken. I heard today that the Aillards, after the bombing of Hali, have sworn to the Compact, which means that all those lands down south on the plains of Valeron, twelve or thirteen kingdoms in all, will be ready for the taking. And so I have a task for you." He frowned, staring at the floor. "I want you to go to the Lake of Silence and bring back Carlina. It is guarded by sorcery, but you won't mind that. You can get through their defenses and ignore their illusions, and kidnap her, and bring her here."

Paul asked, "Who is Carlina?" But he knew the answer before Bard spoke it.

"My wife."

Chapter Four

Dawn was breaking over the Lake of Silence, and on the Holy Isle a long procession of women, each robed in black, each with a dark mantle covering her head and the sickle-shaped knife of the priestess hanging from her girdle, wound slowly down along the shore, from the beehive-shaped temple toward the houses where they dwelt.

The priestess Liriel, who had, in the world, been known as Carlina, daughter of King Ardrin, walked silently among them, a part of her mind still hearing the morning prayer;

"Thy night, Mother Avarra, gives way unto dawn and brightness of day. But unto thy darkness, O Mother, all things must one day return. As we do thy works of mercy in the light let us never forget that all light must vanish and only thy darkness remain at last. . . ."

But as they turned into the large wattle-and-daub building which was the dining hall of the priestesses, Carlina's mind turned to other things; for it was her turn to help in the hall. She hung her heavy dark mantle on a hook in the hallway and went into the big dark kitchen, where she wrapped herself in a big white pinafore apron, covering her black skirt and tunic, tied up her head in a white towel and fell to dishing up the porridge which had simmered all night in a big kettle over the fire. When all the porridge had been ladled into wooden bowls, she sliced long loaves of bread and set them out on a wooden tray, filled the small crocks with butter and honey which were placed at intervals along the breakfast table, and as the benches filled with black-clad forms, passed among them, pouring from pitchers of cold milk or hot bark tea. At breakfast talking was permitted, though the other meals were taken in the silence of meditation. The tables were loud with chattering and cheerful laughter, a daily respite from the solemnity imposed at most times upon the priestesses. They giggled and gossiped as any group of

243

women might do anywhere in the kingdoms. Carlina finally finished serving and took her appointed place.

"—But there is a new king in Marenji now," said one of the sisters at her left, speaking to a third, "—and it is not enough that they have to pay tribute to the king, but they have summoned every able-bodied man who can bear arms to fight against the Hasturs in the Lord General's army. King Alaric is only a boy, they say, but the commander of his armies was once a famous bandit they called the Kilghard Wolf, and now he's the Lord General. They say he's a terror; he's conquered Hammerfell and Sain Scarp, and the woman who came to bring leather for shoe soles, *she* told me that Serrais has fallen to him too. And now that he's marching on the plains of Valeron, he'll have all the Hundred Kingdoms raised against the Hasturs—"

"That seems to me impiety," said Mother Luciella, who was—they said—old enough to remember the reign of the old Hastur kings. "Who is this Lord General? Is he not of the Hastur kindred at all?"

"No. They say he's sworn to take the kingdom right out of Hastur hands," said the first speaker, "and all the Hundred Kingdoms. He's the king's half-brother, and he's the real ruler, whoever sits on the throne! Sister Liriel," appealed the priestess, "didn't you come from the court of Asturias? Do you know who this man could be, the one they call the Kilghard Wolf?"

Carlina was surprised into an unwary "yes," before she recalled herself and said severely, "You know better than that, Sister Anya. Whatever I was before this, now I am only Sister Liriel, priestess of the Dark Mother."

"Don't be that way," sulked Anya. "I thought you would be interested in news of your homeland, that perhaps you knew this general!"

It must be Bard, Carlina thought. *There is no one else it could be.* Aloud she said fiercely, "I have now no homeland but the Holy Isle," and dug her spoon fiercely into her porridge.

. . . No. She had now no interest in what went on in the world beyond the Lake of Silence. She was no more, now, than priestess of Avarra, content to remain so for life.

"You may say so," said Sister Anya, "but when those armed men came against the island half a year ago, it was for you they asked, and by your old name. Do you think Mother Ellinen did not know that once you were called Car lina?"

244

The sound of the name rubbed raw on already lacerated nerves. Carlina, Sister Liriel, rose angrily. "You know well that it is forbidden to speak the worldly name of anyone who has sought refuge here and been accepted under the mantle of the Mother! You have broken a rule of the temple. Now, as your senior, I command you to do appropriate penance!"

Anya stared at her, round-eyed. Before Carlina's anger she dropped her head, then got out of her seat, kneeling on the cobblestone floor. "I humbly ask your pardon before us all, my sister. And I sentence myself to a half-day digging out the grass around the stones on the temple pathway, with no noon meal but bread and water. Will this suffice?"

Carlina knelt beside her. She said, "It is too harsh. Eat your proper food, little sister, and I will myself help you in digging the stones when I have done with my duties in the House of the Sick, for I was guilty, too, of losing my temper. But in the name of the Goddess, dear sister, I implore you, let the past be hidden under her mantle, and speak that name never again."

"Be it so," said Anya, rising, and she gathered up her porridge bowl and cup, carrying them to the kitchen.

Carlina, following with her own, tried self-consciously to smooth away the frown she could feel between her brows. The sound of the name she had laid aside—forever, she had hoped—had disturbed her more than she wanted to say, aroused emotions long since put aside. She had found peace here, companionship, useful work. Here she was happy. She had not, really, been troubled or frightened when Bard had come here with armed men; she had trusted in Avarra to protect her, and she was confident that the protection would hold true as it had done then. Her sisters would protect her; and the spells they had laid on the waters of the lake.

No, she had not been afraid. Let Bard seize all Asturias, all the Hundred Kingdoms, it was nothing to her, he was gone from her mind and from any meaning he might ever have had for her. She had been a young girl then; now she was a woman, a priestess of Avarra, and she was safe within the walls of her chosen place.

Sister Anya had gone to do the hard work on the stones of the path, which must be done but which could not be assigned to anyone and must wait until such time as someone saw fit to volunteer as penance for a broken rule or some real or fancied imperfection of conduct. Or, occasionally, as an outlet for superfluous energies. Carlina knew that she would welcome the hard physical work of pulling out the tightly knotted grass which was shifting the stones of the path, losing her anxieties in the strenuous and sweaty task of lifting and changing the stones and clearing the grass and thorns. But she was not yet free to seek that mind-soothing monotony; it was her day to tend the sick. She took off the pinafore and towel, laid her crockery for the young novices to wash, and went to her allotted work.

In the years since she had come to the Island of Silence, she had learned much of healing, and now was ranked as one of the most skillful healer-priestesses of the second rank. One day, she knew, she would be among the best, those entrusted with the training of others. It was only her youth which kept her, now, from that post. This was not vanity, it was merely a realistic awareness of the skills she had learned since she had come here, skills of which she had had no idea at home in Asturias, for no one at the court had ever troubled to coax them forth and teach their use.

First there was the minor routine of every day. A novice had burned her hand on the porridge kettle. Carlina dressed the burn with oil and gauze and gave her a little lecture about being mindful of what she was doing when she handled hot things. "Meditation is all very well," she said severely, "but when you are handling hot vessels over the fire, that is not the time for prayerful contemplation. Your body belongs to the Goddess; it is your business to care for it as her property. Do you understand, Lori?" She brewed tea for one of the Mothers who suffered from headache and a young novice who was suffering from cramps, went to pay a visit to one of the very old priestesses who was slipping away mindlessly into a calm, painless death—she could do little for her except to stroke her hand, for the old woman could no longer see or recognize her—and gave some liniment to a priestess who worked in the dairy and had been stepped on by the clumsy foot of a dairy animal.

"Rub it with this, sister, and in future remember, the beast is too foolish to keep from stepping on your foot, so you must be sensible enough to keep your feet out of her way. And do not go to the dairy again for a day or two. Mother Allida will probably die today; you may sit by her and hold her hand and speak to her if she seems restless. She may grow lucid if the end is near. If she should, send at once for Mother Ellinen."

Then she went to the Stranger's House, where, twice in a tenday, she had been given the task of first seeing the sick who came to ask help of the priestesses of Avarra, usually after the village healer-women had failed to help them.

Three women sat silently on a bench. She beckoned the first into a small inner room.

"In the name of the Mother Avarra, how may I help you, my sister?"

"In the name of Avarra," said the woman—she was a small, pretty, rather faded-looking woman—"I have been married for seven years and have never once conceived a child. My husband loves me, and he would have accepted this as the will of the gods, but his mother and father—we live on their land—have threatened to make him divorce me and take a fertile wife. I—I—" she broke down, stammering. "I have offered to foster and adopt any child he might father by another woman, but his family want him married to a woman who will give him many children. And I—I love him," she said, and was silent.

Carlina asked quietly, "Do you truly want children? Or do you look on them as your duty to your husband, a way to keep his love and attention?"

"Both," said the woman, furtively wiping her eyes on the edge of her veil. Carlina, her *laran* awareness tuned high enough to hear the overtones in the answer, could *feel* the woman's sincerity as she said, weeping, "I told him that I would foster his sons by any other woman he chose. We have his sister's baby to foster, and I have found that I love little children. . . . I see the other women with their children at their breasts and I want my own, oh, I want my own. You who are vowed to chastity, you can't know what it is like to see other women with their babies and know you will never have one of your own—I have my fosterling to love, but I want to bear one too, and I want to stay with Mikhail. . . ."

Carlina considered for a moment, then said, "I will see what I can do to help you." She made the woman lie on a long table. The woman looked at her apprehensively, and Carlina, still attuned to her, was aware that she had suffered the painful ministrations of midwives who had tried to help her.

"I will not hurt you," Carlina said, "nor even touch you; but you must be very quiet and calm or I can do nothing." Taking her starstone from about her neck, she let the awareness sink deep into the body, finding after a time the blockage which had prevented conception; and she let herself descend, in that consciousness, into nerves, tissues, almost cell by cell unblocking the damage.

Then she gestured to the woman to sit up.

"I can promise nothing," she said, "but there is now no reason you should *not* bear a child. You say your husband has fathered children for others? Then, within a year, you should have conceived yours." The woman began to pour out thanks, but Carlina stopped her.

"Give no thanks to me, but to the Mother Avarra," she said, "and when you are an old woman, never speak cruel words to a barren woman, or punish her for her barrenness. It may not be her fault."

She was glad, as she saw the woman go away, that she had actually found a physical blockage. When there was nothing to be found she must assume either that the woman did not really want a child and, with *laran* she was not aware she had, was blocking conception—or that the woman's husband was sterile. Few women—and fewer men—could believe that a virile man could be sterile. A few generations ago, when marriage had been a group affair and women as a matter of course bore children to different men, it had been simple; a matter of simply encouraging a shy or timid woman to lie with two or three other than her own husband, perhaps at Festival, so that the woman could sincerely believe that the child was fathered by the one she had chosen. But now, when inheritance of property rested so firmly on literal fatherhood, she had the unpalatable choice of counseling a woman to accept her barrenness, or take a lover and risk her husband's anger. The old way, she thought, had made more sense.

The second woman, also, was concerned with fertility—which did not surprise Carlina, for it was to the Goddess that women usually came for this.

"We have three daughters, but all our sons died except the last," the woman said, "and my husband is angry with me, for I have had no children for five years, and he calls me worthless. . . ."

The old story, Carlina thought, and asked her, "Tell me, do you really want another child?"

"If my husband were content, I would be content too," said the woman, shakily, "for I have borne eight children, and four still live, and our son is healthy and well and already six years old. And our eldest daughter is already old enough to marry. But I cannot bear his anger. . . ."

Carlina said sternly, "You must say to him that it is the will of Avarra; and he must thank her mercy that a single son was spared to you. He must rejoice in the children he has, for it is not you who denies him children, but the

248